AS LONG AS YOU LOVE ME

#

**Also available from
Ann Aguirre
and Harlequin HQN**

I Want It That Way

Coming soon

The Shape of My Heart

AS LONG AS YOU LOVE ME

#

ANN AGUIRRE

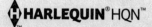 HARLEQUIN® HQN™

Recycling programs
for this product may
not exist in your area.

ISBN-13: 978-0-373-77984-0

As Long As You Love Me

www.Harlequin.com

Printed in U.S.A.

For Viv, who really is all the good.

CHAPTER ONE

It would be hard to argue with anyone who called me a failure.

By twenty-one, I'd lost my college scholarship, passed up a great guy and moved back in with my mom. Who was glad to see me, but it wasn't the glorious homecoming I'd dreamed of when I packed my bags three years ago. Still, even flavored with regret, I couldn't deny a certain happiness about being home. Sharon, Nebraska, wasn't much, just a tiny dot on the map. The downtown had all of six stores, and there were no shopping centers at all, at least not without driving forty miles, unless you counted the Walmart. We had McDonald's and Pizza Hut, a roadhouse, two bars and a place called Patty's Pancakes. Not surprisingly, they specialized in pancakes. The Grove was the only fancy place, a restored historic site; none of my dates had ever taken me there. But the smallness of the town meant everybody knew you, and there was some comfort in the familiarity and the gossip.

At the moment, my life was kind of a mess—but as I unpacked the last box, I sighed in relief. No more classes, no more faking interest in my alleged future when I talked to my best friend and roommate, Nadia. It used to be hard as hell, pretending everything was okay when my life was imploding. Yet even though I couldn't share what I'd been going through, I'd miss Nadia; she was still in Michigan while I'd returned to Sharon to start over.

My mom tapped on the open door. "I didn't really change anything. We can paint if you want or I could make new curtains."

"That sounds fun." I wasn't being sarcastic. This room hadn't been redecorated since I was thirteen, and the lavender was a little much. Not to mention the full-on princess theme going on here, between the white and gold furniture, the fluffy purple rug, all of my stuffed animals and a bookshelf overflowing with fantasy novels featuring knights and orphaned heiresses. The floral print bedspread and curtains made me want to crawl under the ruffled bed skirt and stay there.

"What did you have in mind?" Mom asked.

She looked great; the transformation I'd noticed when I'd last seen her at Thanksgiving had continued. It was now February and she'd lost that final twenty pounds, so if anything, she was slimmer than me. That should probably agitate me, but it was so good to see her rebounding. After my dad left, I thought she was wrecked permanently.

"White on the walls, red plaid curtains?"

"Could be cute. Bedspread?"

"To match the curtains, if you can make one. Or would that be too much?"

She cocked her head, thinking about it. "Probably not, as long as you don't do patterns on the pillows as well."

"I didn't plan to."

"I'm so happy you're here. Even if it means things didn't work out at Mount Albion." She was careful not to state it aloud—that I flunked out of school, came home in disgrace, or at least, that was the talk around town. The worst of the church ladies whispered that I was pregnant, too.

"Thanks." I gave Mom a quick hug. "Can I borrow the car?" *So weird to be asking that.* "I need a few things."

"Not a problem. Can you pick up milk and eggs?" Her eyes sparkled as they met mine, conveying her awareness of how many times we'd enacted this same scene when I was in high school.

"It's the least I can do." I paused a beat, as she expected, then added, "Wait, no, that would be nothing. But then I don't get the car keys."

"Right again." She led the way downstairs and dropped them into my open palm. "Don't do anything I wouldn't do."

I grinned, gesturing at my messy up-do and grungy gray sweats. "It's tough when you look like this, but I'll try not to break any hearts."

Mom smirked. "See you later, Lauren."

It was half past three on Saturday afternoon as I skipped down the front steps. The house, a two-bedroom shotgun style, looked better than it had in years. Though my mom hadn't admitted it yet, I suspected she had a guy coming around for upkeep and repairs, maybe more. She might think it would be awkward to tell me she was dating again, but in my view, it was past time. My dad had been gone for ten years, and the divorce had been final for eight. By no means could this be considered a sudden development.

I got into the old Plymouth and started it up. It made sense for me to buy my own car, but I couldn't afford it at the moment. Ten minutes later, I pulled into the Safeway parking lot. Since I needed lotion and deodorant, I'd get milk and eggs at the same time. No reason to drive farther for more choices. As kids, we used to do crazy shit in the parking lot, mostly because there was nothing else to do. I remembered drinking behind the store and Nadia pushing me around in a shopping cart until management came out to yell at us.

The nostalgia that swept over me was deep and rich; no matter where I went, this would always be home. To a lot of people, Sharon seemed stifling, I guessed, a complete dearth of opportunities, but I hoped to get into computer science and land a job where I could telecommute. I'd always been more into fiddling with programs and apps than anyone else I knew, but I also had causes. So I tried the latter first and discovered I hated it enough to start over, even if it meant losing momentum on the academic track. Nobody knew this—and I'd never admit it—but the reason I flunked out was because I stopped trying. People always seemed to think I must be dumb, possibly because I'm blond and curvy. And that pissed me off.

Six cars in the lot—I counted them as I went inside. No need for a cart. I picked a wheeled basket instead and got the groceries before heading to the small cosmetics section. There, I found Nadia's brother. As ever, my pulse went into overdrive and my knees went soft. I'd always had this reaction to him; too bad he treated me like an honorary sibling.

Belatedly I noticed he was deliberating the merits of two body sprays. They were both that terrible, smelly stuff that commercials claimed would make guys irresistible to the ladies but really reeked like chemical muskrat death. I mustered some normal and stopped peering around the shelf at him.

"Neither," I said, stepping into sight. "Please? Have mercy, seriously."

Rob glanced up in surprise. "Not good, huh?"

"Your sweat smells better, I promise."

"That's a weird thing to say, Lauren." His expression was unreadable, but that was no surprise. Nadia always compared her brother to a tree stump.

I suspected he was more like one of those giant sequoias. There might be all kinds of things going on, but you'd never climb high enough to see it. The worst thing about Robert Conrad? In eighth grade, I had a killer crush on him. He was a senior in high school at the time, lettered in both football and basketball, while I was a chubby little grease spot with braces and a terminal case of the stutters anytime he spoke to me. We'd both moved on from those awkward days, but any time I ran into him, I felt thirteen again, nerves jangling like a car alarm.

In some cases, time was unkind to high school athletes. They lost their hair and muscle tone. But the opposite was true of Rob. He worked construction alongside his dad, and at twenty-five, his shoulders were so broad that I wanted to climb him. Not with the giggly uncertainty of junior high, either. He was all solid muscle, great guns, ripped abs and incredibly defined deltoids. When you added chiseled features, strong jaw, blue-gray eyes and dark hair, it was hard not to drool. But it was *so* wrong to think that way about my best friend's brother. I had no idea if he'd noticed my crush back in the day, but if so, he was kind enough to ignore it and not tease me. I'd slept with other guys since then, enjoyed sex just fine, but I still tingled whenever he was nearby.

Yeah, I'm taking that secret to my grave.

"You're staring."

Shit. I was.

"Sorry, I was considering some better options for you, cologne-wise, but I don't think you'll find anything here."

He sighed and put the two sprays back. "Avery should buy it then. Because I have no idea what she's talking about."

"What did she say?"

My fist balled up, a knee-jerk reaction to hearing about his girlfriend. They'd started dating back in the fall and were still together, apparently. At Thanksgiving, I'd gone home with Nadia, who'd invited my mom and me over to Casa Conrad to eat. Watching Rob with Avery, it had been all I could do not to yank her hair out. She was so beautiful—model thin, with natural red hair, green eyes and the sort of face I'd call ethereal; she could dress up as Titania, the fairy queen, and totally pull it off. That day, he'd taken such great care of her, filling her plate, making sure she had a drink and was never just sitting, lonely. Seeing that made me ache.

"She wants me to be more upscale."

"What are you, a trendy eatery?"

In my opinion, Rob didn't need improving. He was rocking those Levi's, along with a blue plaid flannel shirt and navy down vest. No, he wasn't a *GQ* guy, but why the hell would any woman want that from him? Also, I kind of wanted to hug him, if he thought he could buy "upscale" at Safeway.

He laughed. "Not hardly."

It might not be any of my business, but… "Don't change for her, okay? You're great the way you are."

His eyes widened. Not for the first time, I noted that his irises were a swirl of charcoal and mist with specks of blue, fringed by ridiculously thick black lashes. In a face without such a strong nose and firm chin, those eyes would make him too pretty. When I had sleepovers at Nadia's, back in high school, I imagined him cornering me and shoving me against the wall, overcome by his unspoken longings. That was pretty much my favorite fantasy when I was sixteen, but Rob never gave any sign he suffered from ungovernable passion.

Too bad.

"That's not true," he said quietly.

A little flicker in his eyes, a twist of his mouth, and I got the impression that he was incredibly sad. He didn't have an expressive face, and truthfully, his at-rest look suggested he didn't have much going on in his brain box. Behind his back, people had been calling him the quintessential dumb jock for as long as I could remember. The girl he went out with in high school dished about his body, but she never mentioned any other traits. In my rich fantasy life, I'd never wondered about his thoughts or feelings, either, and staring up at him now, a pang of remorse went through me.

"I disagree. But don't take my word for it," I said breezily. "I'm just the idiot who flunked out of Mount Albion."

"Bullshit. You were always on the honor roll along with Nadia. You're only here because you want to be."

I was astonished into silence for a few seconds, then I rallied. "That's a bold statement. What about the love child I'm having?"

His gaze swept down my body, quietly intense. "Nope."

I wished I was wearing anything but sweats and that my hair wasn't a bird's nest. But he'd known me since I was seven, and he'd never seen me as a potential anything, so that was pointless regret. A dress or a hairstyle wouldn't change a lifetime of indifference.

"I should get going," I said. "My mom's waiting for the milk and eggs."

Clearly, I should win a prize for clever comments. But Rob nodded like I didn't sound like a sixteen-year-old dipshit with a specialization in being weird around boys. Which was so messed up; at school, the *one* damn thing I excelled at was witty banter, making guys laugh. I was fucking popular at Mount Albion.

"You doing anything tonight?" he asked.

Huh? Somehow I managed not to let my jaw drop open. "Not really. I just got unpacked and most of my friends from high school are gone."

"Avery's visiting her cousin in Omaha this weekend, so

I thought maybe you want to split a pizza. I don't feel like cooking."

Wow. This is definitely *not a date.*

"Sounds good," I said. "What time?"

"Five-thirty?"

"Sure. You remember where I live?" He'd driven me home a few times when Nadia called him to rescue us from out-of-control parties, but I didn't imagine those occasions made much impression on him.

To my surprise, he nodded. "Out on Dover Road still, right?"

"Yep, that's the place." With a friendly wave, I pulled my basket past him and went to the checkout lane.

I kept the excitement in check until I got into my car, then I full-out screamed. My favorite high school memory involved Rob pulling up at a farmhouse, drunken teenagers all over the yard. I'd stumbled outside with a guy who was wasted enough that he wouldn't take no for an answer. The dude pushed me against the garage, his mouth loose and wet on my neck, while I shuddered and shoved at him. In the next instant, he wasn't touching me anymore. Rob yanked him off and took him out with one punch. Then he put a gentle hand on my shoulder and helped me to the car. He'd always protected me like a little sister, but I responded to it differently than Nadia. She was impatient over his protective streak, sharp and annoyed, while I wanted to make out with him instead of the high school boys on offer. I'd spied on him kissing his girlfriend, and it fueled my fantasies for, like, two years.

Telling myself not to be stupid, I drove home and put away the groceries. My mom was getting ready for a date, which proved I was right about Mr. Handyman. I propped myself in the doorway to the bathroom and watched her put on lipstick.

"So when do I get to meet him?"

She flushed. "You don't mind?"

"Of course not. It's good to see you happy."

"There's leftovers in the fridge—"

"Don't worry about it. Rob's picking me up in an hour."

"Nadia's brother?" Her brows shot up. "Isn't he dating that awful Jacobs girl?"

Sharon didn't have much of an upper class, but Avery Jacobs definitely belonged to it; she wore nothing but name brands and had a driver who made sure she never rode the bus. In school, her nose had been so far in the air, it was a wonder she didn't drown during a rainstorm. Nadia had been friends with her when we were younger, but I never was, and I liked Avery less when she ditched Nadia as soon as the cliques formed in junior high.

"She's out of town, and it's just pizza. He probably feels sorry for me, what with my mom having a better social life and all." I grinned to show I was teasing.

She threw a cotton ball at me. "That's not funny. If you knew how long I waffled over telling you about Stuart…"

"So that's his name."

"He sells insurance," Mom said. "You'd think that makes him boring, but he's very sweet."

"No need to convince me. I need a shower, though, if you're almost done in there."

"No problem. I can finish my makeup in the kitchen."

Damn. She's pulling out all the stops.

Though it wasn't a date, I did the same. An hour later, I had on my best jeans, a blue sweater that framed my boobs perfectly, plus my favorite leather jacket. I also did my eyes to full bam, straightened my hair and put on awesome knee boots. Rob pulled into the driveway right on time, so I yelled *bye* to my mom and bounded down the steps. He drove a newish red pickup, though I wasn't into vehicles enough to be sure of the make or model.

He was still in blue flannel, but I'd expected no less. As he had when I was a drunken senior, he went around to open my door. There were no running boards, and I was short, almost a full foot smaller than him; before I could clamber up, he set his hands on my waist and lifted, setting me on the passenger seat with the sort of casual strength that stole my breath.

"Wait, sorry, I should've asked before manhandling you." He seemed dead serious, worried that he'd offended.

"It's fine." Or it would be if these shivers would stop. I could still feel the imprint of his hands at my waist.

"You're not as touchy as Avery," he said as he climbed in. "I haven't done a single thing right for her in the last month."

Maybe she's not the right person for you. But if I said that, it would definitely come from an ulterior motive, because I'd be hard-pressed not to follow with, *Maybe you should get naked with me instead.* Then I'd die from the startled, awkward silence that followed. At worst, this was pity pizza; at best, it might be better-than-eating-alone pizza.

"Is something bothering her?" I asked, more curious than I cared to admit.

He paused, his expression clouding. "Seems like it, but I can't get her to tell me."

Since I wasn't the confiding type, I understood her reticence. Which sort of pissed me off. I didn't want to empathize with Avery. "Maybe she's afraid you'll think less of her if she whines to you about her problems?"

"I need to tell her that's not true." He let out a slow breath, obviously relieved at hearing there might be a simple solution.

"Anyway, there's nothing to be tetchy about," I said. "I'm vertically challenged, you helped me out. It's all good."

That won me a smile that simultaneously brightened his

eyes and crinkled them at the corners. He jogged around the truck and climbed in, stretching his arm across the back of the seats to back out of my driveway. There was essentially no traffic, so we zoomed straight to Pizza Hut. The restaurant was nearly full, mostly families and a few high school students; we were lucky to snag a two-person booth tucked in the corner back near the bathrooms. When I was in high school, it was a huge deal when they installed the tiny salad bar here.

"So what do you like?" he asked, not bothering to open the menu.

You would've been the obvious answer, but I hadn't come back to Sharon to let my first crush swell back into unmanageable proportions. So I replied, "Lots of meat."

That was apparently the best news he'd had all day. Rob gazed at me as if I'd said he was the sexiest man on earth. "Meat lovers it is. Should we get salad, too?"

I grinned. "Should and will are wildly different. I'm living dangerously tonight."

"The training wheels are coming off, huh?" He was smiling; the faint sorrow I'd noted at the supermarket seemed to have dissipated.

For a few seconds, I forgot who he was and answered with a flirty glance and a half smile. "Oh, they've been off. You have *no* idea how well I ride these days."

Shock made him drop his straw as I fought the urge to bang my head on the table. Then he surprised me by laughing softly. "You had me going. Well played, Lauren."

That's me, a laugh riot. Send in the clowns. Oh, wait, I'm already here.

CHAPTER TWO

In the end, we were complete maniacs and got both the meat lovers pizza and a pitcher of root beer. I'd never eaten alone with Rob before, but as long as I remembered he had zero awareness of me, everything would be fine. I had two pieces and one glass of soda while he finished everything else. His metabolism must be awesome.

"So what's next?" I asked, as we split the bill. Or rather, Rob consented to letting me pay a quarter of it since he ate and drank more than I did.

It was more of a general question than a demand he justify his life plan, but he straightened with a hint of tension. "What do you mean?"

"Are you taking me home, or are we headed to the road-house to cause some trouble?" That was highly improbable, but when he relaxed and shook his head, I was glad I went to the silly end of the spectrum.

"I was gonna drop you off, then work on my dining room," he answered.

"Well, obviously. I think I'll go home and do the same. I

could totally get it to be more formal if it just focused a little and stopped watching so much daytime TV."

That startled a quiet chuckle out of him, and I realized that until earlier today, I'd never really heard Rob laugh. The deep rumble of sound sent a pleasurable shiver through me, and I immediately wanted to make it happen again. At this point, I didn't even care if that involved dressing up in an actual clown suit, complete with red nose and humungous shoes. In the past, I'd seen him smile, but he was so careful, guarded and tentative in his expressions—for reasons not entirely clear to me.

"I bought a house in December. When you were home before, I was still living with my parents. It's a fixer-upper, and once I get done, I plan to flip it."

"That's when you restore a place, make it awesome, then sell for a profit, right?" I'd watched a few home makeover shows.

"I hope so. Dunno if Sharon is the right place for it, though."

"Yeah, I imagine the market's a bit sluggish here."

"If I can't sell it, I'll have a nice place to live. So it's not a loss." He sounded faintly defensive, as if he'd explained this before, and with less success.

"Sounds like a good move. Plus you have the satisfaction of remodeling your house exactly the way you want it."

He nodded, excitement sparking his expression. "I've already taken out a wall downstairs, opening up the layout from kitchen to dining room."

"How much work have you done?"

That question acted on Rob like a key turning in a lock. He opened up with a click, telling me everything he'd done so far and what projects were yet to come. I was impressed by the time he finished his recitation because he'd obviously put a lot of thought and planning into this. Moreover, he didn't intend to stop until he finished the house properly.

"It's a little complicated to live there sometimes," he said with a sigh. "With power tools and dust everywhere, I can't get Avery to set foot inside. She says she'll judge the results once I'm finished."

"I bet it's not that bad." I mostly said that for the silent satisfaction of disagreeing with his girlfriend.

"You want to see it?" His invitation came as a surprising bonus.

"Sure. I'll be able to visualize what you were saying better."

"Sweet." Rob studied the bill with a faint frown, likely trying to figure out the tip. So I plucked it from his fingers, skimmed the total and dropped four singles.

"You paid way more for dinner," I said, as if that were why.

"Thanks." Fortunately he let it drop.

Rob waited for me to precede him, a polite gesture that only made me like him more. Which I definitely didn't need— I was already hauling around the weight of an old crush. If he insisted on being sweet and considerate, I didn't know how I'd deal. As before, he settled me in his truck before he got into the driver's seat, then instead of heading to Dover Road, he drove across town to the west side.

His house was on the outskirts of Sharon, off the highway instead of in a neighborhood like mine. The driveway was a quarter of a mile long, and the house was nestled in a small clearing with snowy trees framing it on either side. Everything was too wintry for me to judge the landscaping, but I liked what I saw of the side-gabled bungalow, from the deep eaves to the tall, stately chimney, and especially the front porch with its slender columns. It wasn't huge, but definitely big enough for a porch swing.

"Watch your step," he said as he got me out of the truck.

I could seriously get used to Rob touching me. My pulse fluttered as his hands lingered long enough to make sure I wouldn't pitch face-first into the pile of dirty snow he'd shoveled to the sides of his driveway. It was impossible to restrain a smile, though, and he answered it with an unguarded friendliness I'd rarely seen. When he was goofing around with his teammates, he unlocked like this, but seldom with anyone else.

He went ahead to open the door, then he stepped back so I could come in. A flick of his wrist turned the overhead light on, and I saw what Avery might complain about. Everything was coated in a fine layer of dust, and there were tools everywhere, along with plastic sheeting. Raw beams showed through the wall he'd knocked down, and his kitchen had only a subfloor, while the hardwoods in the living and dining room needed refinishing. But I saw potential in the chaos; I spun in a slow circle. He'd already done a lot, considering it had only been a few months since he bought the place.

"It's a mess," he said, seeming slightly crestfallen, as if he'd expected there to be more tangible progress.

"No, I can envision how it'll eventually look. What's next in the dining room?"

He studied me for a few seconds, likely checking that I wasn't feigning interest. Then he started a monologue on moldings, sparkling with enthusiasm for the project. He told me all about eighty versus a hundred grit sandpaper, that you could use a putty knife to work in tight corners, and how important it was to start with paper that fit the wood. I had zero experience with home repair, but he made it seem appealing. Of course, that could be his general hotness talking.

When he finally lost steam, he wore a chagrined look. "But you probably didn't want to hear all of that. Sorry for boring you."

"I did or I wouldn't have asked."

"You're a strange girl." He shook his head, smiling.

"I pride myself on it." Moving a few paces toward the

kitchen, I grinned at Rob. "So basically, when you said you didn't feel like cooking, you meant heating soup on that hot plate."

His kitchen was wrecked—no stove, ancient refrigerator, subflooring and all of the cabinets had been torn off. I'd be surprised if he had running water in there. Plastic draped the cupboards, giving the room a serial-killer vibe. But before my dad left, we'd had enough contractors in the house for me to understand this was par for the course.

"Pretty much. Though don't underestimate the hot plate. You can do a lot in a wok."

Smiling up at him, I teased, "Tell me more."

"You're making fun of me." The warmth drained from his expression, and I didn't understand until that moment how it felt to have Rob shine for me until the light went out.

"I am *not*. I'm seriously impressed you can cook anything on a hot plate."

"It's not that big a deal." He was tentative, and I wondered if he'd always been this unsure of himself.

To the best of my recollection, Rob had never been a talker. He didn't lead when he hung out with his sports buddies, and he didn't say much when they joked around. That left me with little to go on, no sense of his ordinary self. Maybe he was always like this?

"Stop trying to decide what amazes me." I poked him in the side. "I also gasp in awe over monkeys riding bicycles and parrots cussing in Portuguese."

"Who doesn't?" But his eyes had lightened, a faint smile playing at the corners of his truly kissable mouth, perfectly shaped in a manly bow.

If I didn't say something, fast, the next words out of his mouth would be, *I'll run you home.* "If you want, I can help with the sanding. That's low-skill work, right?"

Rob stared at me. "It's Saturday night. I'm sure you have better things to do."

I wasn't dressed for manual labor, but I didn't want to leave. This had all the earmarks of a scenario I'd dreamt up multiple times in high school. Silently, I chided myself, *He has a girlfriend. Be cool. You can be friends with Rob. It's not a huge thing.*

"Debatable. My mom's out, so I'd just be watching cable."

"If you say so." He sounded skeptical, but he got the sandpaper and showed me how to use it like a pro.

I shrugged out of my jacket and glanced down at my sweater. "Do you have anything I could put over this?"

Though I hadn't meant to draw attention to my boobs, he followed my gaze, and if I weren't crazy, his gaze lingered for a beat too long, then a flush colored his cheeks, creeping toward his ears. Relatively few guys *my* age could be embarrassed by that; the vast majority were shameless. I loved that Rob wasn't. There was a solid goodness about him that reminded me of Nadia, though not in a *Single White Female* sort of way.

"Sure, let me get you a work shirt."

Once I had plaid flannel, his favorite thing, apparently, I went into the kitchen to swap shirts. Rob didn't expect that, so when I came around the corner rolling up the sleeves, his eyes widened. "You could wear that as a dress," he blurted.

"I suspect I'd be cold."

"Do you want me to turn on some music?"

"Good idea."

"What do you like?" That was the second time he'd asked me that tonight, more than any guy I'd ever dated, truth be told.

"Surprise me."

He clicked his iPod into a dock safely stashed on a high shelf. The dining room had a hutch built into the wall, and I could picture how it would look once he refinished it, gleaming with age and care. It was the perfect place for a woman to display her fancy dishes. Not that I had any, but I admired beautiful craftsmanship. Rob fiddled with his music player, then Blue October popped from the speakers. I'd heard "Hate Me" before, but it wasn't the kind of song I associated with Rob. If anyone had asked, I would've guessed uncomplicated country, maybe Garth Brooks or Shania Twain.

"I like this," I said. "Sad, though. Do you have 'Sound of Pulling Heaven Down'?"

He nodded. "It's next in the playlist."

I looked forward to learning what Rob listened to, left to his own devices. *And he said Avery's never been here, so you're learning something about him she doesn't know.* After pulling off my boots, I got to work, sanding as Rob had showed me. It was hard on my back and knees, but there was an odd satisfaction in smoothing away the damage from years of neglect.

After working for a while in silence, I said, "There are deeper scratches here and they're not coming off."

Rob stopped what he was doing and knelt beside me to examine the baseboard. "Normally you sand with the grain, but you can go across at a forty-five-degree angle to work those down. We'll go over the whole thing with a finer grit paper later anyway."

We? Mentally I questioned the pronoun but I wasn't silly enough to do it out loud. That would only make him tighten up again and if he let me, I'd definitely help out another time. Though I could build a website from the ground up in my sleep, I was unclear on what he meant—a ninety-degree angle was a full corner, so…

"Like this?"

"Almost." He put his hands over mine and adjusted my strokes. His palms were big and rough, completely covering my fingers. Until just then, I didn't realize how much

I liked big guys; in Michigan, I'd mostly dated lean, pretty ones, though that was a kind interpretation of my social life. I specialized in partying and in hookups, not relationships. My mom's misery biased me early on against the wisdom of letting a guy matter deep down.

"Okay, I've got it." My arms actually hurt from the pressure, however. Bonus, helping Rob might tone my biceps. "Thanks."

"Not a problem." He retreated to his corner to work, and the iPod cycled through five more songs, an eclectic mix of David Gray, Josh Ritter, a band I'd never heard of—Good Old War—along with Snow Patrol, and most surprising of all, Enya. When she came on, singing about the evening star, my head jerked up and I stared at Rob. Never in a thousand years would I have credited this; I wondered if his football buddies knew.

He met my look with a sheepish shrug. "Her voice is haunting."

I didn't disagree, even if my tastes ranged more toward top forty. "I'm not a music snob, dude. In fact, I've lost all credit with most of my friends because, if it comes on the radio, nine times out of ten, I like it, even if critics say it's terrible."

"Miley Cyrus?" he challenged.

"Hey, 'Wrecking Ball' rocks. And I've been known to scrub my bathtub to 'Party in the U.S.A.'" I wasn't ashamed of liking popular tunes, so his grin didn't bother me.

"Ke$ha?"

"Not my fave, but I don't hate her. The duet with Pitbull is catchy, even if it doesn't make any sense."

As we sanded, he asked about random artists until I disclosed that there were only three pop songs I'd shut off: "Blurred Lines" by Robin Thicke, "Barbra Streisand" by Duck Sauce and "Loca People" by Sak Noel. Otherwise, I didn't have elevated tastes or think some bands were cooler or more important than others.

"For some reason, I thought you'd be more like Nadia. She's into stuff that hasn't been discovered yet."

"Are you calling her a hipster?"

Rob lifted a shoulder in a half shrug. "If the chunky ankle boot fits…"

Given my best friend's penchant for indie music and microbrewed beer, he wasn't wrong. Still, I didn't let him get off scot-free. "Like you should talk. I never heard of Good Old War until you played that song."

"'Looking for Shelter'? It's a good one. And actually, Nadia was listening to them before she left for college. So—"

"You disclaim any credit for finding them. Suspicious." I pretended to narrow my eyes, studying him in mock assessment. "I bet you could dig up indie bands if you tried."

"Luckily I don't have to. Nadia sends me emails with playlists she's made, stuff she thinks I'll like. She gets it right half the time."

"I didn't know that."

He tilted his head. "Why would you?"

Once he asked, I felt like a dipshit. "You make a valid point."

At that point, silence seemed like the best option, so I worked my way to the corner. The molding looked a lot better just from what I'd already done; Rob had finished two walls to my one. When I sat back on my knees, he straightened and came over to give me a hand up. With an easy tug, he hauled me upright. The motion brought me a little too close; I thumped against his chest and for a confused moment, I breathed in the clean scent of him, an incredible mix of wood shavings and wintry air.

"Sorry about that. We should take a break or you'll get cramps. Want a beer?"

"Not really. Water's fine."

Rob opened a bottle and got me a glass of ice water, then he beckoned from the stairs. Curious, I followed him up; the hall was dark and cold, but then he opened a door, and I discovered the one room he'd completed. It was a good size, divided into living and sleeping, which made sense. I suspected this was where Rob spent his time if he wasn't working. On the opposite wall, beside the window, he had a full-sized bed with a nightstand beside it, and he was using a bookshelf at the foot to divide the space. A couple of chairs sat centered on the other side, facing a small entertainment center to the left of the door.

None of the furniture in here was prefab; everything was real wood, polished to a high gloss. The floor gleamed around the edges of the area rug, and I dug my toes into the green plush. He'd painted the walls caramel, though he'd call it light brown, and there were blinds on the windows, unlike the rest of the house. An electric fireplace hung on one wall, providing light and warmth. I walked across the room to run my hand over the table, admiring the smooth finish.

"You like it?" he asked.

"Definitely, it's great." There were no drawers, only a lower shelf, but Rob didn't have much clutter. The bookshelf held only a few magazines, along with a handful of change, receipts, bits and bobs he must've pulled out of his pockets.

His smile twisted me up. "That was the first thing I ever made. The bed's mine, too. I put it together from salvage."

Startled, I took a closer look; it was a slatted headboard, stained dark, attached to an impressive platform bed. But on closer inspection, I could see how he'd taken two railroad ties and covered them with plywood. Ingenious, really.

"Wow, you could seriously design furniture."

"That's the dream." But he didn't sound like he believed anyone would pay him for it. I totally would, though. It was solid and beautiful, just like Rob.

"How much to build me a bed like yours?"

I'd surprised him in the middle of a swig of beer. "Seriously?"

"Yeah, how much? My mom and I were just talking about redecorating my room." We hadn't mentioned a new bed, but it was *my* money.

"Twin or full?"

"Twin." A pang of chagrin went through me because that was a kid's bed, but I couldn't afford a bigger one and a new mattress. At this rate he'd always see me as a little girl.

"A hundred bucks."

I frowned at him. "That sounds low."

Which he met with a melting smile. "You're getting the friends-and-family discount...and hey, you're giving me the satisfaction of serving my first customer."

Somehow I didn't flirt, didn't say any of the cute things trembling on the tip my tongue. *He has a girlfriend. That means he's off-limits.*

Rob building my bed was likely the closest I'd ever come to having him in it.

CHAPTER THREE

Monday, I saddled up the wild interwebs and sent my résumé to a dozen places.

I didn't have high hopes for a day job, given my car situation, but it would drive me nuts to sit around waiting for summer session to start. I'd already decided against typical college enrollment. I hated sitting through lectures for many reasons, so University of Nebraska online fit the bill. I planned to apply for their information assurance program, transferring my general studies credits, so I needed the concentration courses... and maybe a few electives, depending on how things shook out. Their site promised that I could transfer up to sixty-four hours from Mount Albion, which was more than half of the 120-hour degree. Going part-time, it would take me three years or so to finish up, but it would be worth it, especially if I landed a job that let me stay in Sharon.

That took all of an hour. This chilly morning, my mom was at work, and I had no car. Buying one was a pipe dream, at least until I could afford gas and insurance. When Nadia was around, I never worried about it; in high school, I called her whenever I needed a ride, and it was the same in Michigan. My heart twisted when I thought about how sad she had been to learn I hated college, but the longer we went to Mount Albion, the clearer it became to me that it was her dream, not mine, and I was going through the motions. The more my grades dropped and dropped, the more I drank and partied, trying to hide my unhappiness.

Until I couldn't anymore.

I had just over five hundred bucks in my checking account because I'd just deposited my last paycheck, but I owed half to my former roommate, Angus, in return for buying my plane ticket home. In a burst of financial genius, I'd promised another hundred to Rob to build me a bed. That left me relatively little to survive on until I found a job. The humiliation would kill me if my mom tried to give me an allowance. Though I was happy to be back in Sharon, sometimes it was hard to shrug off the stares and speculation.

With a faint sigh, I wrote out a check to Angus Starr. I'd often teased him that he totally had a porn star name. *I miss you, dude.* I wondered how my three former roomies were doing; they were all I missed about Michigan. I smooched the stamp when I stuck it on the envelope, then I wrote a card to go along with repayment. While Angus had a fat enough bank account not to miss a couple hundred bucks, I didn't enjoy mooching off my friends. Sadly, walking out to the mailbox and raising the flag took care of my to-do list for the day.

I huddled deeper in my down jacket, turning back toward the house. Except a red truck slowed, then pulled into our gravel drive. I recognized Rob right away; I just had no idea what he was doing here at two on a Monday. The sky sputtered snow that drifted down in light, delicate flakes. If the ground wasn't already frozen, this wouldn't stick.

"I brought some stain samples," he said in lieu of greeting.

Ah, so this was about the bed. "You should probably bring them inside. It's really cold."

"Thanks." He followed me into the house while I tried to figure out how bad I looked on a scale of one to ten. Definitely better than when we ran in to each other at the Safeway, nowhere near as good as Saturday night.

Then I dismissed the question as absurd. "Do you want some coffee?"

"Sure, if it wouldn't be too much trouble."

"Not at all."

After dumping the old stuff my mom made this morning, I brewed a fresh pot, then poured him a cup. He laid some small boards on the table, touching and naming each in turn. "Oak, pine, mahogany, maple, red chestnut, cherry, walnut."

"The red chestnut is beautiful."

"Okay." Rob put away the samples and took a sip of his coffee, relaxing into his chair with a pleased expression.

"We might have some cake, too, if you want."

"Like I'd say no to cake."

I took that as an invitation to rummage in the fridge and I came out with a couple of slices of German chocolate, which was my absolute favorite. My mom made it a few days ago in honor of me moving back in. I should probably be ashamed that there were only two pieces left. Mentally I shrugged and served him on the good plates.

"How come you aren't at work? I know why I'm not." I pointed at myself and whispered, "Unemployed," like it was a curse word.

"I don't do a lot in the winter," he said, seeming surprised. "Spring and summer are better for construction, and I have to make my money last the whole year. I'm…not awesome at it."

Hmm. Rob wasn't the first person I'd known to struggle

with that, but most of my friends were like, *Whee, there goes my textbook money,* while ordering another round of shots.

"You just need to divide your total income by twelve and work out how much you can spend monthly. It helps if you track expenditures and figure out where your disposable income goes. I could put together a spreadsheet."

"That sounds complicated."

Not to a computer girl. In my secret nerdy heart, I loved spreadsheets, pie charts, line graphs and all kinds of numbers. Once I made up a sex flow chart of everyone I'd slept with, and their partners that I knew of but that started to get weird, so I deleted the file. I'd be taking that secret to my grave.

"I don't mind helping," I said, mostly because I didn't want to admit it would be easy, at least not with Rob looking like I'd confessed to speaking ancient Greek.

"What would you need?"

"Bank statements, basically. And you'd have to help me classify your expenses."

"If you do that, I can't let you pay for the bed."

Oh, look, an excuse to spend hours with Rob. High School Me shouted in elation, but she also bitched about what a stupid reason it was to hang out with him. There was nothing sexy about formulating a monthly budget.

"Then a trade definitely benefits me."

He nodded, finishing his cake. "Avery won't be back from Omaha until next month, so this is a good time to figure things out."

"I thought you said she was visiting her cousin for the weekend."

A sigh escaped him. "Yeah, well, I got it wrong. She left early to spend time with her cousin. Then today, she started a management training seminar. She'll be back in March. I think." But he didn't sound sure. "I have to *really* piss her off to get that tone."

"Which one?"

"'Jesus, do you even listen to a word I say'?" He captured her icy snap so well, a shudder went through me.

I can't believe she talks to him like that.

Before I could decide how to respond, he went on, "It's a good thing I'm hot, right?" Under most circumstances, that would qualify as a cocky remark—one that was supposed to make me laugh—but the underlying sadness I'd glimpsed in him before rebounded, lending him a stark, shadowed air.

I weighed my response before saying, "That's not *all* you are, Rob."

He got up and took his plate to the sink. "You don't know me well enough to say that."

Shock reverberated through me. I'd said the same thing in Michigan when I rejected a guy who wanted to date me. Luckily Rob's back was to me, so he didn't notice my reaction. I schooled my expression, so by the time he turned around, I was clearing the table.

"I've known you longer than Avery." While they'd been dating since October, I had been wandering around his house since second grade.

"That's true."

In a tone I'd use for an oral report, I said, "When I was in fourth grade, you carried my science fair project to the gym for me, even though you had to walk six blocks to the junior high afterward, and you got detention. That same year, you got into a fight with Ellis Whitcomb over Melissa Fredericks. She would later become your first high school girlfriend, though not the last. That honor went to Katie Everett, who you dated right up until she left for college."

And then she left without a second look. Maybe I should change this up.

"When I was a junior, you punched Kent Walker for me, and my senior year, you took me to see my dad for the first time in seven years."

My mom still didn't know about that, and at the time, I was so mad at her, sure it was her fault—that she'd driven him away somehow. I blamed them in stages, back and forth, like the clicking balls in a Newton's cradle. Back then, Rob drove a different truck, an old green one passed down from his granddad, nicknamed Tessa Green-tea for reasons known only to Rob. I'd cornered him in the garage while he was working on the engine. Nadia had been upstairs doing homework, and she thought I'd gone to the kitchen for a snack. Instead, I'd slipped outside and shuffled around until Rob straightened and faced me.

At twenty-one, he'd been leaner, with less muscle built over years of summer construction jobs. "Need something?"

"I was wondering if you'd do me a favor."

"Depends on what it is."

My breath came out in a shaky rush. "I need to see my dad. I have to talk to him."

I'd had a horrendous fight with my mom. Her apathy and apparent lack of self-respect—the way she could barely manage to go through the motions—had made me scream at her, *Just look at yourself. I so get why he left you.* I'd planned to race to my dad's side and tell him I understood everything now and *please, can't I be part of your awesome new life?* A fresh start away from the rumors about my mother's sanity had sounded perfect, what I wanted most.

Rob had wiped his hands on a rag, then said, "What did your mom say?"

"She doesn't know. Will you take me? I can give you

gas money." At the time, Nadia had her license and a car. I could've asked her to drive me but I was afraid she'd punk out and blab to my mom about the plan. Why I had no such fear with him, to this day, I didn't understand.

"Why don't you call him?"

"I just need to see him. Please, Rob?" What I didn't tell him was that I didn't plan on coming home. I'd live with my dad from then on; my mom could ship my clothes, presuming she could manage it. Whatever, I'd buy more. I just wanted out. Her depression had only made my issues worse, and it had been all I could do to sit through a school day. It would be different with my dad; everything would be fine.

In the end, Rob had sighed and agreed.

With his help, I found my dad, unemployed, living in a shitty apartment with some woman I'd never heard of, apparently raising a couple of her kids. One might've been his—I was too upset to get the facts straight. But the worst part was, he didn't even look happy to see me. To him, I was a nuisance. He invited us in, but we didn't stay longer than half an hour, after coming all that way. Out in the parking lot, I burst into tears and Rob just hugged me. He didn't say anything at all, probably because he knew no words could make it better. So there was no way I'd let him disparage himself now when he'd been proving his worth my entire life.

"I remember that," he said finally.

"Me, too."

The silence between us was odd and fraught, laced with old memories. I wondered if he had any idea that I used to crouch beneath the banisters and watch him with Katie Everett. In my head, he was still the gold standard for kissing, just endless tenderness without rushing straight for boobs or butt. Though four of the eight guys I'd slept with were good in bed, none had that quintessential Rob patience, and if he'd been that way in high school, his control as a man must be awe-inspiring.

Lucky Avery.

I siphoned the bitterness out of the thought as he studied my face. I'd never noticed him doing that before, but I felt each shift and slip of his gaze, as if his eyes were zoom lenses. My heart thumped so hard in my chest that I was afraid he'd hear it. Really, I should be over this.

"Do you mind if I take some measurements in your bedroom?"

Do anything you want in there.

"Go ahead. I do that all the time for fun. I'm like, 'I wonder if this wall is ten or eleven feet long. Let's find out!'" My voice came out manic-perky.

Rob cut me a strange look as he brushed by and headed for the stairs. He was efficient with the tape measuring, checking the spot my new bed would occupy. But having him up here made me want to die because it reinforced every preconception he must have about my maturity. I sat on a stuffed unicorn and hated my life.

But then he surprised me by saying, "I can see why you're redecorating. It's been a long time, huh?"

Grateful, I beamed up at him. "Yeah."

Smiling back, he tapped the tip of my nose. "So when do you want to work on my spreadsheet?"

I shrugged. "It's not like I have a job. And I meant to tell you, if I was remotely helpful the other day, I'm glad to pitch in again, anytime you need me."

"If you're serious, we could get a lot done while Avery's gone." His expression suggested this was a prison furlough. Or maybe that was wishful thinking on my part.

I quelled the urge to snap at him to break up with her already. When a guy like Rob committed to a relationship, only C-4 could shake him loose…and questioning his choice might make him determined to dig in.

"Absolutely." Though I hated myself for wondering, I had to know. "Do you miss her?"

He nodded. "We don't make sense on paper, but she needs me. That…doesn't happen a lot. She calls me some nights before bed, says she can't sleep unless she hears my voice. She's really funny, too."

In a mean way, I guessed silently. But these insights actively wounded me, picturing their conversations while Rob lay in bed. Her voice was the last thing he heard, too.

I kept my tone level as I changed the subject. "How about this? We work on remodeling until we're tired. Then we rest and tackle your budget. When you get sick of that, we resume sanding or whatever."

"I can't take up all your time," he protested.

"What's a month? I need to keep busy or I'll doubt my decision to come home."

"It's a deal. I'll have your bed done by next week."

"Do you deliver?"

"If you need me to."

So many things I could say. But I forced myself not to be flirty. That was mostly a front anyway, manufactured to keep guys from figuring out how weird and awkward I could be. Left to my own devices, I'd rather watch llama gifs than go to a club. Ironic, since I'd learned all kinds of moves from music videos on the internet. Nadia thought I'd suddenly blossomed in tenth grade, but everything I knew about hair and makeup, I'd learned from YouTube tutorials. I could fake being a regular girl, but really, I was still besties with my laptop and PlayStation, which helped me perfect mad dance skills through gaming.

I grinned. "Considering I'd have to carry it home from your place, yeah."

"Okay. When do you want to start with this trade-off?"

"Tomorrow?" I suggested.

"Is nine too early?"

With résumés turned in, I had nothing else to do. "Nope. Do you mind picking me up?"

"Not at all." Rob headed for the door because our business was done, but he paused, wearing a faint frown. "Don't wear anything cute."

"Because…we hate cuteness? It—and not money—is the root of all evil?"

To my everlasting delight, he played along. "Truly. In fact, we'd better set off on a world-saving mission instead. You and me, destroying cuteness wherever we find it."

"We'll have to burn all the Build-A-Bears. The children will never understand."

"But that's why we have to succeed, Lauren. For the children." His mock-earnest look was so perfect and adorable that if he were *my* boyfriend, I'd shove him onto my unicorn-strewn purple comforter and do dirty things to him.

I met his gaze and nodded with resigned stoicism. "I'm in."

For the second time, I made Rob laugh. He pocketed his tape measure and strode toward me, tipping my face up as he would if he meant to kiss me. My heart went nuts, but he pecked my forehead, as I'd seen him do to Nadia a thousand times, usually when she was being a goofball. In that moment I must've looked like a deflating balloon.

"Seriously, I just meant—wear something you won't ruin working on the house."

I nodded. "See you tomorrow."

This partnership was probably a terrible idea, but since the universe kept handing me excuses to hang around with Rob,

I couldn't say no. Deep down, I suspected I'd been skating toward my first broken heart since I was thirteen years old, and there was nothing for it now but to make good. I flopped onto my bed with a heavy sigh.

Well then, world. Bring it on.

CHAPTER FOUR

The first week of working with Rob, I got two blisters and we finished his budget.

Though he wasn't well-off, if he ate at home more and bought dinner for Avery less, it should be simple enough to make his money stretch until construction picked up again in mid-April. If he stuck to the plan, he could sock some away in savings, too. I hadn't brought it up yet, but I had some ideas on how he could make his money work smarter, better than leaving it in a low-interest bearing savings account anyway.

None of my remodeling tasks was difficult or specialized, but some of them were messy and exhausting. At the end of the day, I was often filthy and on the verge of collapse. At least I'd acquired the knack of being around him without going tongue-tied or blurting the first thing that crossed my mind. However, I liked hanging out with him too much for my own peace of mind while he treated me like a kid sister and had a girlfriend who called every night from Omaha.

The first night, the phone rang at half past six. Rob switched off the power sander and took the call in a rush that would've made me superhappy, had I been on the other end of the line. At first, he was smiling, glad to hear from her, but soon his responses shortened to monosyllabic and his shoulders hunched. By the time they were done, fifteen minutes later, all of the light and pleasure had left him.

After that, I asked to leave before six.

"You're spending a lot of time with Rob," my mom said, cutting into my thoughts.

I focused on my Salisbury steak and made a noncommittal noise.

She persisted, "Is that wise? You had the biggest crush—"

"I remember," I interrupted, just a shade sharp.

Her eyes widened. "Sorry. I didn't mean to butt in, especially when you've been so understanding about Stuart."

I shot her a quizzical look. "About what, exactly? That you're not ready to introduce us or because you're dating at all?"

Either way, it didn't bother me. If her boyfriend would rather not get entangled with the whole faux-family scenario, it was fine by me. I definitely wasn't looking for a father figure.

"Both. But you just got home, so it feels too soon to bring the two of you together. Once you settle in, I'll—"

And I tuned her out. If it got serious, I'd look for somewhere else to live. My mom was fine, but I had no interest in cohabitating with her middle-aged boyfriend. But I smiled and nodded because it wasn't like I resented Mom getting her life together and deciding she didn't hate all men because of my dad, a healthier attitude by far.

"Did you know Krista Montgomery's back?" That question snagged my attention.

"No, that's awesome. For how long?" Krista had been my second closest friend in high school, and our junior year, she'd moved to California with her dad when her parents split.

"Janet didn't say. But from context, I suspect she'll be here a while."

"Context?"

"She's pregnant."

"Oh, wow. How far along is she?" That wasn't what I wanted to know; my curiosity ranged more along the lines of, *Is she keeping the kid? What's the deal with the baby daddy? Why'd she come back to Nebraska?* But I hated gossiping about people I liked, so I'd call and talk to Krista, see how she was doing, instead of grilling my mom for secondhand details.

"Six months, according to Janet."

"Is the landline still the same?" I had the number memorized when I was sixteen, and if I'd forgotten, it should be in my old address book. That was the last thing my dad bought for me before he left, and I'd taken a dorky pride in writing down all my friends' contact info.

"As far as I know. I only use Janet's cell these days."

"I'll call Krista later."

"I'm sure she'll appreciate that."

It was an unspoken agreement that I'd take over the bulk of the housework since I wasn't contributing anything for groceries or rent, so I cleaned up the kitchen and then picked up the phone. I dialed from memory, and the call went through. Krista answered on the fourth ring, sounding slightly out of breath.

"Moshi moshi." She'd always been into all things Japanese, from guys to anime.

"Hey, it's me." I'd lost count of the times in junior high that we'd done this, before we got cell phones.

"Oh, my God, my mom told me you were back. How awesome is this? How come you didn't text me?"

"I wasn't sure if your California phone was still working."

"Good point, it's not. I got a new number here, and I meant

to message you with it but it's been nuts getting settled and I *just* found out you're back, too." The last sentence came out in a girlish squeal. She sounded excited and happy, actually, not like a single mother in crisis. "I can't wait to see you."

Unlike Nadia's family, Krista's mom lived close enough for me to walk. Her house was on the other side of the subdivision, half a mile or so away. As kids, that meant we could hang out without adult facilitation. Proximity contributed to our friendship in the early days but by high school, we genuinely liked each other, and it hurt when she moved.

"I can come over tonight, if you're not busy."

"That would be *awesome*."

"See you in fifteen minutes."

Fortunately I'd already showered, rinsing all the remodeling dust off, so I just had to bundle up and grab my purse. "Going to Krista's," I called to my mom, who was watching TV in the living room.

"It's like we've gone back in time," she mumbled.

There were no sidewalks, so I kept to the slushy edges of the road. Minimal traffic meant I wasn't completely soaked when I rang her bell. She answered the door with a broad smile. Unsurprisingly, she'd cut her hair since I saw her last, but she pulled off the tapered bob. Krista was small, shorter than me by two inches, and she'd always been slim, though the baby had changed her silhouette. Friendly hazel eyes sparkled as she pounced, pulling me into a tight hug.

"Mom, Lauren's here! We're going to my room."

"Is she hungry?" her mom shouted back.

I pitched my voice to carry. "Nope, I just ate."

"Okay, have fun!"

Bemused, I saw my mom's point about the time-warp thing. Krista dragged me upstairs, where the familiarity ended. At some point, her mom had erased all traces of her adolescence, maybe because Krista had chosen to go with her dad instead of staying here. I hadn't been offered that option. Whatever the reason, this was a guest bedroom more than Krista's space, but it was private when she shut the door behind us.

I perched on the bed, cocking my head at her. "Okay, tell me everything."

"Wait, you must have a story, too?"

"I bet mine is shorter and significantly less interesting than yours. I flunked out of Mount Albion on purpose so I could come home."

She wore a puzzled look. "Why didn't you just admit you hated it and transfer? No need for the flunking."

"Because I was in denial. I didn't realize that was *why* I was doing it until after the ink was dry on my test results."

Krista plopped on the other end of the bed, resting against the headboard. "You're right, that's a superboring story."

"Then tell a better one."

"It's not as racy as people seem to think. My boyfriend's in the army on deployment in Afghanistan. I didn't realize I was pregnant before he left, or I'm sure he would've proposed. Not that I'd say yes just because of the baby."

"Does he know?"

"Yeah, I emailed him, and we Skype when he can get a stable connection." From her expression, that wasn't as often as she'd like.

"Boy or girl?"

"Girl."

"And her dad?"

"Private first class, Kenji Nakamura. I met him in San Francisco. Do you want to see a picture?" Her eager expression prompted me to nod.

Krista dug into her purse, got out her cell phone and showed me a veritable slide show, pose after pose of her absent boyfriend. He was a handsome Japanese-American guy who looked even better in uniform. I could see why she'd fallen for him. The uncertainty would probably drive me crazy, though.

"So why the army?" I asked.

"To help with college costs later. His tour will be up next year." I could tell she was eager for him to leave the service.

"So he enlisted right out of high school?"

"Yep. We've been doing the long-distance thing forever, and I'm so sick of it."

Wow. I didn't know if I was concerned or impressed that they'd kept the relationship going for so long through such difficult circumstances. For him, it probably wasn't as much of a sacrifice because he likely didn't face much temptation in Afghanistan, and it had to help, knowing somebody who loved him was waiting back home.

"Well, he obviously gets leave time now and then." I smirked.

Krista ducked her head, but she grinned back. "We tend to make the most of it."

"How does your dad feel?"

Her face fell. "He's furious. When he found out, he called the baby a blight on my future. He says I can do much better than Kenji."

That explained why she wasn't in California anymore. Since I hadn't met the guy, I couldn't say if he were the best person for Krista, but she seemed to love him. On the other hand... "How long have you been together?"

"Since my senior year."

Wow. So she's been dating this guy since high school, and he's been gone since graduation. I understood her dad's reservations, though it wouldn't be supportive to say so. Part of me wondered if she'd checked out the alternatives. At this point, Krista had less experience than me, which wasn't a good thing.

But hey, it's her life.

"I know what you're thinking," she said then.

"You do?"

"That we should've broken up. I should see other people. Two years ago, we took a break, and…I did. But nobody makes me happy like he does. So we got back together."

"Gotcha. Well, I bet your dad's just being protective. That's his job. Hopefully he'll get over it by the time the baby gets here. Have you thought about names?"

"So far, we can't agree on one. My mom was bothering me about delivering on my own, so I finally agreed to move back." She let out a quiet sigh. "Honestly, she didn't push much. I was so scared, thinking about doing this by myself."

"You know I'll do anything I can to help, right?"

I was thinking more of a baby shower, but Krista perked up. "Really? Mom offered to be in the delivery room, but I can't handle the thought of her seeing that. I will never understand people who film it. Would *you* stay with me?"

While your kid's being born? Shit.

But I'd already offered. So I answered, "Sure. I don't promise not to freak out, but I'll hold your hand and feed you ice chips, the whole nine, okay? Are you doing natural childbirth?" I thought there were classes or something, so I was probably too late to be her partner in that.

"Depends on how much it hurts. The idea of a needle in my spine…"

"Right? Welcome to modern medicine." Though I hadn't thought much about how I'd handle reproduction down the line, I wasn't a fan of pain. "So when are you due?"

"Late May."

"I'll be there," I promised.

After that, we went downstairs and joined her mom. We watched TV and made popcorn; Krista put real butter on it, and it was so good that I probably gained five pounds just from the taste. My cell phone complained that I was down to ten percent battery, so I shut it off. It was late when I walked home, but this was Nebraska, and it was only six blocks, so I wasn't worried. Still, we'd watched horror movies, so I was twitchy by the time I got in the door.

Mom was asleep, so I checked my email. I had the usual spam, plus notes from all my former roomies, which made me happy. I missed all of them, even Max, though things were unspeakably awkward between us at the end. I opened Nadia's first:

LB! You know I miss you like crazy, right? Courtney's in your bed right now, and she has completely alphabetized my books. I'm pretty sure there will be a lending library program implemented the next time I get home from work. So how's Nebraska? Did you find a job yet? Have you started applying to any schools? I have like ten more questions but you'll get grumpy if I dump them on you all at once. Hug and kiss my family for me, okay? Write back soon or I'm sending my brother to track you down.

She didn't mention the hot single dad she'd broken up with right before I left. Mr. Hot Ginger had dumped Nadia for her own good, which would drive her quietly crazy. I'd felt horrible about the timing, but there was little I could do about it. I hadn't gotten to know him well before I left, but Ty seemed like a good guy. He was only a few years older than us, but already had a four-year-old. That was the crux of the conflict.

Writing back, I didn't quite nail the tone, talking about Rob too much and inventing interesting anecdotes because there was so little going on. I could've mentioned Krista, but Nadia had never been as close to her, and there was some tension by the time she'd moved. Mostly I didn't want Nadia to worry; things would be fine once I got a job and had less time to fret about whether I'd made the right decision.

I opened Angus's email next:

Hey, you. Got your check. It appears not to be rubber, but I said you didn't have to pay me back. I hate you for leaving. Come back right now. I'll wait. This is me, waiting. It's been at least five minutes. You're shattering my faith in humanity, Lauren. Take responsibility for it! Not sure what you've heard from Nadia, but she's such a hot mess. I can't believe you abandoned us. All the light has left my life. All of it! Okay, enough drama. I'm working on getting over Josh. Classes suck but I will survive. (You're singing it now, aren't you?)

"Damn you, Angus Starr. You know me too well." I got up on my bed with a hairbrush and sang two verses before reading on.

In all seriousness, there is a Lauren-sized hole in my life. Please don't lose touch. Write soon. Love and hugs, Angus.

It was simpler writing back to Angus; our friendship was sweet and uncomplicated. Briefly I considered deleting Max's email without opening it, but that seemed like an asshole move. In the end, I read it, two lines only:

I'm sorry about everything. Take care of yourself.

Max had nothing to apologize for; if anything, I should be saying that to him. But I couldn't. So I just closed the email without replying.

Belatedly, I remembered to plug my phone in and when it

powered up, I saw I had a message waiting. I dialed into voice mail and listened. *Could I come in to interview for the receptionist position?* I'd applied for, like, ten jobs, but only the car dealership had called. The months I worked in the fine arts department at Mount Albion must factor into this request. They were likely looking for someone inexperienced so they could offer the lowest possible salary.

It was too late for me to do anything tonight, so I went to bed and checked first thing in the morning. The woman I spoke to asked if I could make it at one-thirty on Thursday, and I said yes, though I was less sure how I'd get there. My mom had a forty-five-minute commute and she needed her car. I obviously had to sort my transportation situation as soon as possible, but my resources wouldn't stretch to running a vehicle, to say nothing of gas and insurance. The chicken-and-egg problem made me cranky—to get a job, I needed a car, to get a car, I needed a job.

So I was in a mood when Rob picked me up. I didn't smile at him as I usually did, and I must've been distracted, because by the time we parked at his house, he was frowning.

"Are you okay, Lauren?"

My head jerked up. His arm was across the back of the seat, and he'd shifted to face me, one knee crooked away from the steering wheel. It would be so easy to fall into his arms like I did when I was seventeen, but he wasn't *my* big brother, so that meant I needed to solve my own problems. I mustered a weak smile.

"Oh, just life, y'know. Shit happens. What excitement do we have in store today?" I reached for the door handle, and to my astonishment, he clicked the lock button.

"Nope."

"Excuse me?"

"I don't accept that answer. Something's wrong. You should tell me."

"Why?" I'd never snapped at Rob, but I hadn't slept well the night before, twisted up about Krista, childbirth and the potential job interview.

"Because we're friends."

"Nadia's my friend. And *you're* not my brother."

His quiet, patient expression made this moment even worse. Bitching at Rob made me feel like Avery, and I'd rather be a sponge or a sea urchin. If I could've gotten out of the truck, I'd have run for it.

"I know that." He was just too calm, and it irked me. Did anything ever rile him up?

"You want to know about my problems? Fine. I have an interview on Thursday, but I don't have a ride. And if they make an offer, I don't have a way to get there because this is Sharon, there's no public transportation and I have *no idea* why I wanted to come back here."

"Because it's home," he said quietly. "And I'll take you to the interview. You know I don't mind…and it's not the farthest I've driven you by a long shot. If you get the job, you can borrow my old truck. It looks like crap but I keep it running."

I stared at him. "You have *two* trucks."

"You remember the green one? It's handy when I have the other one serviced."

"I can't just take your truck." Avery would shit her pants. Plus, there should be a law against anyone being as nice as Rob. People probably took advantage of his good nature.

"I'm not *giving* it to you. When you can afford wheels of your own, it'll go back in storage. Not a big deal."

Once more I tried to get out of the truck, but he didn't let me. I sighed. "We'll freeze to death if I don't agree, huh?"

"Nope. I've got a full tank of gas, a working heater and all day."

"You win," I muttered.

He smiled and brushed a hand against the top of my head. If only he didn't look so amused and indulgent, whereas I wanted to rub against him until I purred. It had never stung so much to be Nadia's best friend. There didn't seem to be any way I could make him realize that I was twenty-one, not eleven, and Rob was focused on Avery like a laser beam.

He climbed out of the truck and led the way to his front door. "To answer you, I thought I'd let you try the power sander. I moved everything out of the dining room."

"It sounds like you expect things to go horribly wrong."

"Nah," he said with the smile that wrecked my heart. "I'm just careful."

How well I know it.

CHAPTER FIVE

After I ran the power sander like a boss, finishing the dining-room floor, Rob fixed one-pot macaroni and cheese for lunch. He started it while I was sweeping up the dust. I didn't even know it was possible, but he boiled the pasta in butter and milk, so by the time it was soft, he just added cheese and bacon crumbles. It was pretty close to the best thing I ever tasted. On a *hot plate*. In a real kitchen, he had to be amazing.

We took our bowls up to his room, and he turned on the TV. I made incoherent this-is-so-delicious noises as we ate. I probably would've licked the bowl, if I hadn't noticed him staring. "What, this is really good. Tell me what else you can cook, preferably with pictures."

He smiled at me, an easy warmth in his expression. "Sorry, no food porn for you, or I'll never get you back to work. But I'll brag a little. Should I start with breakfast?"

"I'll allow it."

"Oatmeal, omelets, sausage scramble, French toast, pancakes."

"How the hell do you make all of that on a hot plate?"

"The key is preparation. I have cooked bacon and sausage in the fridge at all times."

I nodded sagely. "In case of a meat emergency."

"You never know," he said.

Suddenly I wasn't in a bad mood anymore. I hadn't set out to let Rob solve my problems, but I'd be an asshole to blame him for caring, just because his affection didn't take the shape I preferred. Surreptitiously I licked my spoon.

"Lunch," I prompted.

"That's usually a sandwich. I'm showing off because you're here."

That made me happy. "And dinner?"

"Stir-fry, various soups, quesadillas, country-fried steak. I can't make anything that requires more than one burner and a microwave. If I get in the mood for something else, I go to my mom and dad's."

Or you take Avery out for dinner. His receipts had told me that much.

"It sounds like you enjoy cooking."

"In a better kitchen, I do."

"Yours will be beautiful when it's finished."

"I hope so. Once we finish the dining room, it's next on my to-do list."

"Most people would've done the kitchen first." I didn't mean to criticize; it was just an example of how Rob's thought processes differed from the rest of the world.

His pleasure dimmed. "Yeah. But I'm already taking my food up, and even if I finished the kitchen, there's no room to eat it in. So I wanted to have somewhere to go first."

"You mean when you christen your new stove and cook something complicated, there should be more ceremony than just carting it up the stairs." Put that way, it made sense to finish the dining room first, even if it *seemed* backward and lengthened inconvenient meal preparation. It also established the fact that such milestones mattered to Rob; he was sentimental.

He seemed relieved, flashing me another bright smile. "Yeah, exactly."

"You should invite me over. After all this effort, I'd like to be part of the inauguration." After I said it, I realized my mistake. He'd be cooking for Avery, not me, when the kitchen was pretty and polished, the dining room ready to receive guests. My next breath actually hurt.

"Maybe." He didn't mention her, much to my relief. "We should get back to work."

"Don't remind me."

Rob did, in fact, have running water, but he washed up in a basin. I went back to the dining room and got the right grit sandpaper to complete the final pass on the floor. If I'd processed everything he told me correctly, the next step would be staining. After that, we'd wash the walls and paint them, along with the baseboards. It was possible I'd never see the finished product, of course. Once I had a job, there would be no excuse to hang around.

I was on my hands and knees when he came in; I didn't look up. He stood over me long enough for me to feel weird, so I finally sat back on my heels. "What?"

"Let's do something else."

"But we're almost done with the floor." The perfectionist in me was going to be annoyed if he decided the built-in hutch was more important.

"Not in here. Out there." He gestured at the world beyond the windows.

"Like what?"

"I'm wondering if you know how to drive stick."

Shit. Now that he mentioned it… "The green truck's a manual, isn't it?"

"Yep."

Sighing, I shook my head. "My mom never taught me. I don't think she's ever owned anything but automatics."

"You need to learn." His tone was no-nonsense, as he plucked the keys out of a basket by the door. There were so few on the ring that I knew this was his spare set.

"Right now?"

"I'm feeling cooped up," he admitted.

"Then by all means, let's uncoop you, chicken-man."

Rob laughed and slung an arm around my shoulders. When I leaned against him, my eyes closed. This was the first time he'd hugged me since I was seventeen. Interesting that making him laugh had the same effect as my tears. I didn't know what I'd do with that information, but it fascinated me. I expected him to shove me away or to hear the impatient jingle of keys, but his other arm came around me, closing the circuit.

Surprised, I tipped my head up, waiting for the punch line. "Are we having a moment?"

His eyes were warm and soft, roiling deep like a thunderhead, and he wore a half smile that melted me down to the bone. "I'm glad you came back."

Then he ruined it by messing up my hair and shoving me out the door ahead of him. I could *absolutely* envision him treating Nadia this way, and I ground my teeth against the certainty that he didn't see a pretty face or nice rack, cute butt, none of my feminine attributes. I could honestly say that Rob loved me like a sister, and that was a deep hole to climb out of. I mean, he'd been looking after me and keeping me out of trouble for, like, fourteen years.

Glumly, I followed him to the garage, shivering while he hauled the doors open. The green truck looked a bit better than I remembered, which meant Rob had been working on restoring it, too. That fit with what I knew of his personality; he didn't discard things or give up on them. It was in his nature to tinker and repair, even if it took forever and other people would've given up long ago. Not for the first time, I thought, *Lucky Avery*.

"You should be wearing hat, scarf and gloves," he said as we climbed in.

In the dim garage, I could only make out the strongest angles of his face: slope of nose and curve of jaw. My breath misted before me, and I rubbed my palms together, afraid to touch the steering wheel. "How old are you again? Forty-six? Besides, I thought I'd be working in your nice, warm house all day, no need for winter bundling. So you should really apologize for springing surprise stick lessons on me. I'm coping like a champ, right?"

He grinned and reached over to stick the key in the ignition. Ridiculous as it was, when his arm brushed close to me and the metal clicked in, my stomach fluttered. I was too flustered to listen when he explained how to start the car, so he had to repeat himself, and then I felt like such a dipshit that my cheeks burned like twin emergency flares. *So much for learning to relax around him.* Somehow I managed to pump the gas while doing whatever with the clutch well enough to start the motor. The truck *sounded* like it was in good shape.

"Let it run for a few minutes, get the engine good and hot." Seriously, did he have to say stuff like that? In anyone else, I'd be sure it was a double entendre, but that wasn't how he operated, and *certainly* not with me. He proved it by continuing, "It'll take a while for the heater to kick in, too."

Nodding, I rubbed my hands together, trying and failing to warm them. Rob took over, pressing my fingers between his palms. My toes curled. "You know, the ancient Norse had a long tradition of warming their hands on each other's bellies."

I didn't expect that to work, but Rob rewarded me with another smile. I'd say all kinds of crazy shit to keep him looking at me like that…while *holding my hands*. The next moment proved definitively that I didn't have mind-control powers, though, because the frantic refrain of *kiss me kiss me kiss me* running through my head didn't stop him from letting go.

"Good thing I'm not Norse," he said, checking the vents for hot-air flow.

You're better, like Thor's hotter, sweeter cousin. But I didn't say it out loud. He didn't enjoy being praised for his looks; in fact, it made him feel bad, probably because nobody but me could find any other good points to mention. *I* could've written a dissertation on *The Ways Robert Clayton Conrad Is Completely Awesome,* but for some reason, no graduate program was offering credit for this expertise.

"Explain the gears to me one more time?" The imprint of what gears were located where had faded somewhat over the years. Rob doubtless knew it by touch, but I was a manual novice. Any other guy would be making all the penis jokes in the world, but he only repeated the information with imperturbable calm.

"Got it?" he asked.

I huffed out a breath. "I'm freaking out. I'll ruin your truck. You shouldn't trust me to do this—there's snow on the ground."

"But not on the roads," he said patiently. "Put it in Reverse, give it some gas. You can do it, Lauren. You're smart and it's *not* that hard. If I can learn, anyone can."

Only the fact that I was doing things with both feet *and* backing out of his garage while trying not to hyperventilate kept me from yelling at him. Even though I grew up multitasking, I could only do so many things at once. Swear to God, I was seeing stars by the time I cleared the doors, and my hands were shaking on the wheel.

"You weren't kidding," he said, brows furrowing. Then his hands were on my shoulders and he brought my face really close, to the point I could feel the warmth of his breath and see the dark stubble on his chin. I'd never been this close to Rob's mouth, his amazing, perfectly shaped mouth. But he maintained eye contact, intent on calming me down. "It's okay. You've got this. You can do it. Breathe for me. Okay? In. Out."

He probably didn't mean for me to think about sex when he said that, but I couldn't help where my mind went. Ironically, it took care of my nerves and made me squirmy, suddenly aware of the powerful engine rumbling the seat of the old truck. I'd much rather climb on top of Rob than learn how to drive stick, but he registered that I was no longer a vibrating anxiety ball and let go of me.

"Better? I don't want to force you."

This wasn't even a full-on panic attack. Imagine how he'd react if he ever saw one. Because I couldn't stand for him to think of me as broken, I nodded. "Let's do it."

Then the lesson commenced for real. I stalled out the first time I switched out of Reverse and it took me forever to turn the truck around. But I did not launch the vehicle through the wall of his house and I eventually made it down his driveway. I had another mini-panic attack about getting out on the open road, but once I made the turn, upshifting wasn't such a problem. He explained how I'd likely have the most trouble at stop signs and traffic lights—that downshifting was trickier, unless I was going up a mountain.

At that point, I laughed and shook my head. "I have *no*

plans to take your truck any farther than work and home. I'm afraid I'll ruin it."

"Don't be nervous," he said. "You're already better than I was my first time. My granddad predicted I'd strip the gears, the way I was going, and the transmission would fall out." He paused. "That didn't happen, either. In time, you'll be so good at this, you'll wonder why you were ever scared. Turn here."

Here was the Walmart parking lot. I managed to stop the truck and shut it off without anything catastrophic happening. "Thanks." At the inquiring tilt of his head, I added, "That wisdom applies to every new thing I'll ever try in my life."

He shot me a surprised look. "Seriously?"

"Well, yeah."

"Nobody's ever said that to me…when they weren't fucking around."

"It's good advice." Hesitating, I wondered if I should admit this, but he'd said that we were friends. "I'm not very adventurous. It stresses me out to change my routine. In some respects I'm close to obsessive about doing things the same way."

That was part of why I was so unhappy in Michigan— because I was fighting my instinctive tendencies, playing a role and thinking if I just tried hard enough, I could just feel like other people did, and I could act like the stress of seeing hundreds of people daily didn't bother me. Nadia was fine with it, but she was closer to normal. She didn't spend an hour bracing for social contact and when we went out, she was more or less herself whereas *I* was always playing a part—the role of extrovert Lauren.

For a few seconds, he didn't reply, and I wished I hadn't opened up. Swallowing hard, I dredged up a cheerful expression. "Too much, huh? So did you want to get something or—"

"I count things," he said.

"Huh?"

"I don't like odd numbers, either."

Astonished, I studied him, trying to decide if he was screwing with me. But the slightly anxious pleat between his brows promised sincerity.

"I'm not crippled by it or anything, but when I take nails out of a package, I always get two, and I decided *not* to buy the first house I liked because the address ended in three." He stared at his hands like he expected me to condemn him for being weird, when I'd just confessed to being overly attached to my little rituals.

Learning this made Rob feel more like a real friend, less the guy who solved my problems and who I'd never get to be with for oh-so-many reasons. It helped to discover he had quirks, too, in addition to the insecurity over the looks-versus-brains dichotomy I already knew about.

I leaned over and bumped my shoulder against his. "Your secret is safe with me."

Rob's gaze was steady on mine. For a few seconds, I felt like he actually saw me—not as Nadia's friend or his surrogate sister, but as a person—and that moment was electric. His fingers flexed against his knees, then he cleared his throat.

"I don't need anything from in there. I just thought you could practice driving around the parking lot. It's empty over there."

"Got it, boss." Without prompting, I started the truck, and the engine only sputtered a little when I backed out, swapping from Reverse.

We had been looping for half an hour while I practiced going from first to second when a blue Honda Civic pulled into the lot. I didn't recognize the girl driving it, but Rob clearly did. From what I could see through her window, she was in her early twenties, shoulder-length dark hair, round face and turned up nose. I'd call her plain, but that might be a result of the scowl. After a few seconds, I placed her as someone who'd hung out with Avery in high school, though she'd put on some weight since graduation, judging by the fullness of her cheeks.

Staring at Rob, she nearly hit us, and he shifted all the way around, clearly torn on how to handle things. Since it was a near miss, not a collision, I didn't have to stop or give insurance information, but he signaled for me to park near the other vehicle. The girl glared until Rob hopped out, hands in his pockets, and he went to the driver's side. He didn't ask me to come, so I stayed where I was, but a nosy impulse made me crack my window to eavesdrop.

"This is what you're doing when Avery's out of town?" she was snapping.

"What?" He glanced over his shoulder at me with a puzzled look.

"I can't believe you're hooking up with some skank behind her back."

Hey. This is not *a skanky outfit. At most, these sweats are hoochie.* They didn't even claim that my ass was "Juicy."

Sadly, there was nobody to appreciate the genius of my silent retort. Besides, Rob had more class than to cruise the Walmart parking lot with his side piece, but this girl didn't know him at all. If she did, she wouldn't be spitting accusations like that. I half wanted to get out of the car and pull her hair, then shout at her that he'd never cheat on Avery, especially with me, but that would likely make things worse and escalate the situation to reality TV levels of awful.

Shock must've paralyzed him for a few seconds. Then he said, "Lauren is my sister's best friend. And I'm giving her driving lessons."

"Let me guess," the girl purred. "You're teaching her all about how to handle stick?"

Rob's jaw tightened, but he didn't answer. She screeched off, nearly running over his feet in the process. He was pale when he came up to the window, anger written all over his face. *No good deed goes unpunished.* When Avery found out he was loaning me Tessa Green-tea, her head would explode. She couldn't understand what kind of guy Rob was, or that he was thoughtful without expecting sex in return. Or maybe I was just being judgmental; for the sake of his relationship, I should probably hope I was wrong.

"Sorry," he said, "for getting you involved in that. It never occurred to me that anyone would take this the wrong way."

I found it pretty surprising, too. Avery's friend had leaped to that conclusion so fast, I had to wonder what kinds of reports she had been getting. Were there problems I didn't know about? Rob didn't talk that much about his girlfriend with me…not that I wanted him to. It was painful hearing about her and then imagining them together.

"Is there anything I can do?"

He shook his head. "Looks like we're cutting this short today. I have to call Avery before Jillian does."

I understood why he wouldn't want to with me sitting here, listening in. "It's okay. I'm sorry for messing things up for you."

"You didn't. It's a misunderstanding. I'll fix it."

A tiny, horrible part of me hoped that he couldn't.

CHAPTER SIX

The next morning, Rob delivered my bed. I was expecting him to pick me up to work on his house, not for my furniture to arrive, but I stepped back so he could bring the pieces inside. He was quiet as he disassembled my old bed frame, then he asked, "Where do you want it?"

I could tell he was upset, but if he wanted to talk, he'd invite me into his business. So I answered, "Let's store it in the attic for now."

We had one of those doors that pulled down from the ceiling. With easy physical prowess, he stowed the components and then put the new bed together. Like Rob's, it was made of salvaged wood, platform base attached to railroad ties and a slatted headboard that gave it an intricately woven aspect. The red chestnut stain was beautiful, too. My mom was still working on the red plaid cover and curtains, so my lavender stuff looked even girlier against the rugged wood, but the bed gave the room some much-needed character. Once we repainted, it would look like a different space altogether.

"This looks fantastic." Inwardly I was giddy as a schoolgirl over having a bed that matched Rob's. There was no way I wouldn't fantasize about *that*.

As he finished up, he said without looking at me, "I broke up with Avery."

My immediate reaction was, *Yes!* But I knew better than to say it out loud.

"What happened?" I had some idea, but it would do him good to get it out. And selfishly, I wanted to hear it.

"She said some unforgivable things." He set the mattress in place, and with his help, I made up the bed.

Then I sat down on it, inviting a longer conversation. It was a little weird to have Rob in my room, given how many of my fantasies he'd starred in over the years, but right now, he needed a friend. "Like what?"

With a faint sigh, he plonked onto the foot. "She didn't believe me when I explained that you're helping me with the house. Or why you needed driving lessons."

"Didn't she know about the house already?" The lessons had been an unexpected development, and it would be weird to call your girlfriend at work for permission.

Rob blinked at me. "It didn't seem like a big deal. I've known you forever."

Mentally I sighed. While he might see me as a sexless foster sister, Avery probably didn't view our hanging out in the same light. I hated empathizing with her. Again. But this didn't seem like the time to tell Rob he'd screwed up. Clearly he already felt bad enough.

He continued, "It sucks that she thought I'd cheat, but—"

"With me of all people?" His incredulity stung, reinforcing how he absolutely did *not* see me as a woman. "Yeah, right."

"No, that's not what I mean. You'd never hook up with someone else's boyfriend. And it pisses me off that she said you did. Especially when I'm him."

"Wait…so you broke up because of what she said about *me*?"

His mouth tightened. "She crossed the line. I can fix a lot of things, but I can't change a person with that kind of mind. And if she doesn't trust me now, it's unlikely to get better."

Since I didn't want him dating Avery in the first place, I could hardly argue, but it seemed odd that he was more bothered by what she said about me than by her condemnation of his own behavior. "You're mad about what she said about you, too, right?"

Rob shrugged. "I've heard it before."

"What?"

"That I'm too dumb to notice when somebody's hitting on me. Mind you, I don't enjoy being accused of shit I didn't do." But he seemed more resigned than angry; his outrage was reserved for me, apparently.

"And wouldn't. You're positive I'd never go after a guy who's taken, but I know you, Rob. You'd never cheat on your girlfriend, either." I paused, wondering if it was too soon to ask. *But what the hell.* If they got back together, at least I'd know the answer. "What did you like most about her?" It couldn't be as simple as her looks.

He sighed softly. "She said I had potential."

"Excuse me?"

"Avery was always saying I could make something of myself if I tried. Nobody else *ever* thought that, not even when I was a kid. My parents talked about Nadia going to college from the time she was eight years old, but with me, it was always, 'Rob's got a good heart. Rob gets along so well with people.' My aunt's always mumbling, 'At least he's handsome,' like I don't know what that means."

Wow. I normally liked Rob and Nadia's family, but right then I wanted to punch them.

He went on, "There was a state school that offered me an

athletic scholarship. Football. But my dad goes, 'Some people are meant to work with their hands, and there's no shame in it. I got you through high school but I can't carry you to a four-year degree. So unless you can make it on your own, I think you have to pass.'"

"Why didn't you try?"

"Because he was right," he said quietly. "I'd have needed tutors to get through pretty much every class and I'm not so great at football that the university would've paid for that, definitely not good enough to go pro. Even if I did squeak out a degree, I can't think of any job that would suit me better than what I'm doing. So what would've been the point?"

I had no answer for that. Though I had all kinds of quirks, my brain was sharp enough to do pretty much anything I wanted it to. Rob's pain was tangible, built up over years of people dismissing him as a sweet, good-natured lummox without the acuity to register the offense of it. And that just wasn't true. I reached over and took his hands; they were big and rough, a testament to years of building. He cupped his fingers around mine, apparently taking comfort in the connection. For me, it wasn't enough. But he didn't let down his walls often enough for me to pull back.

"So then Avery came along. She was smart, pretty and ambitious. When we started dating, she said she saw the potential for greatness in me—between the two of us, we could go places. With her help, I could run my own business. That's why she was so critical…she was trying to make me better."

I didn't think that was why at all, but now I understood why Rob let her get away with it—because of what she represented. She was clever, no question, and if it took her questioning my morals to make him break free, then I wouldn't argue that point. But I couldn't let the other assumption stand.

"That's predicated on the bullshit opinion that you need

fixing," I snapped. "You don't need to be molded into somebody else. Right now, without Avery's help, you can run a business. Outsource the bookkeeping. A lot of business owners do it to free up time for more important stuff. And you can do it *without* listening to somebody catalogue your faults."

He stared at me with a guarded expression. "You think I can make a go of the furniture design thing we talked about?"

"Absolutely. That, or house flipping. You're kind of amazing. I mean, you're a great cook, you bought a house already and you're renovating it top to bottom. I've already learned a lot from working with you. Bottom line, I believe in you, Rob, and not because I'm sleeping with you. I don't want to change anything about who you are. I *also* don't expect you to make a ton of money and buy me things." I stared at him, hard, willing him to make the connection.

Comprehension dawned slowly, but there it was. "I had a lucky escape, huh? If I'd married her, the divorce would've wiped me out."

There was no benefit to being anything but brutally honest. "Knowing you, if there were kids involved, you would've stuck it out, no matter what she did or said."

"Probably," he admitted.

I grinned. "Then you should thank me for being such an irresistible home wrecker."

"Thanks, Lauren." He tugged gently on our joined hands and I tumbled into his arms.

He smelled of minty soap and snowy air, a freshness that made me breathe him in. I was in no hurry to get free, so I tucked my face against his neck and shivered each time he exhaled into my hair. Maybe he thought it was weird that I didn't just thump him on the back a few times, but the last time he held me this way, I was sobbing too hard to enjoy it. This time I registered the strength of his chest and arms, his fierce, protective heat. Once Rob came down on your side, he never wavered. His hands were gentle as he stroked my back; each pass lit me up with more tingles.

I never saw him touch his sister like this.

Though I'd be happy to do this all day, we had work to do. So I sat back and curved my hand against his cheek, not something I'd have done before this talk, but we were closer now. "You okay?"

"Yeah," Rob said in apparent surprise. Then he pulled my palm down so it was open, facing up, and with one fingertip, he traced a curve. "You…" Then he repeated the motion on the other side, joining the invisible lines. "Are good for me."

As he released me, and I curled my fingers instinctively, I realized he'd drawn a heart on my hand. Flustered, I tried to downplay my role in this conversation. "Avery wasn't right for you. Anyone who cares would say the same."

"Not everyone sees me like you do," he answered.

Tiny shivers washed over me as I replayed how good it felt in his arms. "Their loss."

Our eyes met for a long moment. I fell into the deep blue, briefly veiled by the thick fringe of his lashes when he blinked. His jaw was lightly stubbled, his mouth soft with the hint of a smile. I wished for some kind of secret message hidden in this silence, but it was enough that Rob seemed to be in a better mood; I considered cheering him up for a job well done.

"Thanks," he said, clearing his throat. "Ready to get to work?"

When we got to Rob's place, the dining-room floor was ready to be stained. He must've been up half the night, completing preparations, but he didn't reveal any hint of how exhausted he must be. That was when I realized fully how much he'd mastered the calm facade—to protect his privacy and keep the world at bay. People made the mistake of thinking he didn't feel much, but it wasn't that way at all. Everything was just hidden like a deep, deep well, and then sealed shut with an iron lid. Wistfully, I wondered what it would be like if he let me in. In retrospect, my crush seemed embarrassingly juvenile, based mostly on, *OMG, he's so hot.* But there was so much more to him. Because after getting to know him better, I was falling hard. I couldn't write it off as infatuation; these feelings were real.

He seemed oblivious to my inner turmoil. More cheerful now, he showed me the proper way to apply the stain. I was surprised when he damped the wood with meticulous care. At my puzzled look, he clarified, "It's the best way to make sure the stain soaks in. I'm glad you're here, this is actually a two-person job. I'll apply the stain, then you go behind me and wipe it off."

That seemed counterintuitive, but he was the pro, and it wasn't like I minded working so close. At some point, I needed to back off, invent a reason why I couldn't see him every day, but I wasn't heartless enough to do it the day after he broke up with his girlfriend. With luck, I'd get the receptionist job, solving this dilemma without any need for complicated machinations.

By the time we finished the first coat, I was incredibly sticky. No euphemisms, I just wasn't as tidy as Rob. Fortunately, he'd foreseen that we needed an exit strategy, and we finished on the side by the living room, not the far wall.

He laughed when he saw I'd managed to smear it on my shirt. "That probably won't come out."

"It's well worth the sacrifice." The floor looked fantastic, a smooth shade of golden oak that brightened the space. "Does it need another coat?"

"I don't want it darker, so I'll probably do a satin finish seal next."

I nodded, like I completely understood what he was talk-ing about. "What color for the dining room?"

"White ceiling and baseboards. I haven't decided on the walls yet."

"Lemon-yellow would be pretty." But that might be too girly.

"Come with me to pick out the paint…I'm not much of a color guy. You could probably guess that from the tan bed-room."

Maybe I was reading too much into this, but it seemed too personal to help him decorate, like imprinting myself perma-nently on his house. "Are you sure?"

"Yep. I trust you."

Nothing he could've said would have made me happier. "Then I'm in."

Before we ate lunch, he sent me upstairs with special solvent to clean up. It was no wonder he'd snickered; I was a mess. I yelled down the stairs, "Do you mind if I shower?"

"Go ahead," he called back.

I'd used the bathroom before. Like his bedroom, it was finished, remodeled in blue and white tile. The space didn't have much character, but the workmanship was sound. He needed some fluffy bath mats and pictures on the walls, maybe some candles and good-smelling soap. But he'd said decorat-ing wasn't really his thing. His house would be simple when he finished, waiting for some woman to add the finishing touches. A pang went through me, so sharp I couldn't meet my own eyes in the mirror.

I used the chemicals on my hands to remove the stain, then I soaped them, rinsing the stuff off my skin. Afterward, I hopped in the bath to wash up quickly. It gave me a silly, illicit thrill to use Rob's soap and shampoo, but I shut those feelings down fast. Rob needed time to get over Avery, and in his eyes I was still just a supportive friend.

Fifteen minutes later, I came out with wet hair; not my hottest look, but I felt much better. This wasn't the normal way to attract a guy—I knew that—but Rob wasn't the type to be drawn by cleavage shirts, fancy hair or makeup. It seemed like only honesty could pull him.

Rob had BLTs and potato salad waiting down the hall in his room. Taking the plate, I settled in the chair beside him with a happy sigh. "I eat better here than I do at home."

"My mom made the salad. She thinks I'm living on ramen."

"The woman doesn't give you enough credit," I said absently. "Nobody does."

He shot me a shy, pleased smile, and his response came out soft, hesitant. "I…like hearing that."

"It's the truth," I said around a bite of sandwich, before I could think better of it.

Sexy. Talk with your mouth full, Lauren.

But he wasn't even looking at me. Rob tilted his head back, staring up at the ceiling with an inscrutable look. "Until we started hanging out, I didn't even know how bad I felt. Like, it was normal." He curled a fist and set it against his chest. "To have a knot here constantly. But the more I talk to you, the looser it gets. Until I can't feel it anymore, and it's like I'm taking my first deep breath in a long time. Did you ever have that?"

"You mean not realizing something hurt until it stopped?"

"Yeah."

"Leaving school was like that. I didn't want to admit I was different. You know how many mornings I freaked out silently about going to class?"

"Because you hate being around people?"

It was impressive he knew that. Even Nadia had bought it

when I reinvented myself in high school, changing my personality, my habits, everything. She never questioned that I'd turned into a social butterfly when, in fact, I was just a caterpillar with a pretty parachute. But ultimately, living a lie made me miserable. With my personality, there was no way I could work as a lobbyist without a constant barrage of anxiety attacks.

I nodded. "And you know, maybe I should be strong, get over it and be normal. But that feels like shaving my edges to fit in the wrong slot."

"There's nothing wrong with you," Rob said. "It's not like you're afraid to leave the house or can't buy milk from the Stop & Go. So what if you don't like people?"

That much was true. My social anxiety didn't prevent me from accomplishing routine tasks. It was more that I'd realized that being a lobbyist would require constant interaction on a level that horrified me. As for college, I hated the parties that other people seemed to view as the Holy Grail, and the only way I could cope was to become someone else. Also, I drank a lot, more than I'd liked to admit. Though I wasn't a full-on lush when I left, I could've easily turned into one of those people never spotted without a glass of wine.

"I was just in denial," I said.

"About what?"

"The fact that I'm computer dork and always will be. I'm more comfortable behind a screen than joking around at a party. Only booze makes the latter possible. And drinking led me to some questionable life choices."

"Like what?" I could tell from Rob's expression that he didn't expect me to say anything truly shocking.

How cute, Lauren thinks she has a dark past.

It wasn't like I'd killed anybody, but I did feel bad about

hurting Max, my former housemate. I hadn't realized he really liked me until it was too late.

A contrary impulse made me mutter, "Fucking my roommate, for example."

"Why was that dumb?" From the slight widening of his eyes, he hadn't expected me to bring up sex; he radiated a sort of reluctant curiosity.

"For so many reasons. But that wasn't the stupidest thing I ever did."

"Maybe I shouldn't ask." Finally, Rob was looking at me as if he understood this wasn't a joke, and I wasn't playing around.

I shrugged. "So don't."

"But now I'm curious."

"Well?" I prompted. "Are you asking?"

"I guess I am." He shifted to face me, eyes steady on mine.

Was I really telling him this? Nadia didn't even know. But the scare convinced me I had to rethink everything, coming on the heels of another blunder. I couldn't tell him about that one.

"Drunk Lauren got caught—by a cop—while giving a BJ in a moving vehicle. That's a misdemeanor, by the way. Indecent exposure and reckless driving."

"Did you get arrested?" That wasn't what I expected him to ask.

"The cop gave us both a Breathalyzer test. Luckily, the guy I was with passed. I didn't. The officer decided my judgment was impaired and let me off with a warning." I couldn't face Rob, so I stared at my hands, preparing for the brotherly lecture about my abysmal behavior that was sure to follow.

"I can't talk about this with you," he said huskily.

I raised my head, puzzled. "Why not?"

His eyes were storm-dark, not angry. Something else. An

emotion I'd never seen in Rob. "I'm human, Lauren. Damn. Like you said before, I'm not your brother, and that mental picture? It's…distracting."

CHAPTER SEVEN

"Oh." Since I'd almost resigned myself to the idea that Rob would *never* see me the way I viewed him, I had no idea what else to say.

His cheeks reddened. "Great. Now you think I'm a perv."

"Are you kidding? No. But I didn't tell you that story to… entice you or whatever." Though if I'd thought of it and had known it would work, I probably would have.

"You have more sense."

"I do?" I raised a brow.

"Definitely."

"I'm not even sure what we're talking about here."

Rob sighed, setting his plate on the bookshelf behind us. "I'm saying I understand that you'd never go for me, that's all."

I couldn't read his tone; it bothered me, but there was a complex assortment of emotions striving for supremacy, too many to be easily sorted. So I studied his face, hoping for a clue, but his features were impassive, except for the fact that he couldn't hold my gaze. His lashes swept down, effectively severing eye contact.

"You don't know that." Maybe it wasn't good for my pride, but they said the truth shall set you free, right? Maybe partial honesty could earn me a day or two of liberty. "I had a real thing for you when I was thirteen."

A fleeting smile curved his mouth. "I know. You were pretty obvious about it. The year I was seventeen, you didn't say a single word to me without stuttering and turning red."

"Well, there you go, then. At any moment, I could leap on the opportunity to make my adolescent fantasies come true."

He shook his head. "Funny, but no. Girls don't want me once they grow up. Or after they get to know me."

"Are you crazy?" I demanded.

"It's the truth, Lauren. I'm not a guy women dream of settling down with…. They don't go out with me once, then start planning our futures. I'm the one they sleep with *before* they meet Mr. Right. Anyone who ends up with me, she'll just be settling."

I'd noticed that Rob didn't have a lot of confidence, but this was the first time I realized how deep the fissure in his psyche ran. "That's absolute bullshit."

"You think I haven't seen it often enough to work out the pattern? I'm the fling, the rebound guy. Sometimes they use me to make someone else jealous because I make good arm candy. But I never get the girl at the end."

"Maybe you're reading the wrong stories," I said softly, then swallowed, battling a rabble of butterflies. Confessing this didn't mean I was asking him to date me; it just seemed like his ego needed a boost. "If *I* was writing the book, you'd definitely be the main love interest. You're sweet, funny, considerate, protective—"

"All of those qualities could apply to a German shepherd."

"Not considerate. Big dogs get fur and mud all over the place without a second thought. Probably, they'd tip over the garbage, too." I didn't mention his hotness. Rob had heard enough about his appearance to last a lifetime. "You're also ingenious and hardworking, plus you have this extraordinary ability to see things other people miss."

"I know you're just trying to cheer me up, but…it's working." His smile did ridiculous things to me. Really, his mouth should come with a warning label.

"Yeah? Good. Now I don't want to hear any more crap from you, Robert Clayton Conrad. I happen to think you're wonderful, and my opinions are always right."

"Is that so?"

"Ask anyone. Nadia will back me up."

He laughed. "That's no fair. You guys have been teaming up against me for years."

But he seemed much more upbeat when we went back to work. When he dropped me off at home several hours later, he confirmed, "Interview tomorrow?"

"Yeah. I'll be ready."

"I'll be here at half past."

My mom was home when I came in. She had dinner on the table and there was a strange man adding the silverware. His back was to me so I only saw that he had narrow shoulders. Since I knew about Stuart, I wasn't shocked exactly, but I did stop short.

Damn, some warning would've been nice.

"I need to wash up before I'm presentable," I called, heading straight up the stairs.

"Okay, the rolls need ten more minutes anyway."

Wow, if she was baking fresh bread, it meant she really wanted the meal to go well. In my mom's mind, fresh-baked goods equaled fancy. I didn't necessarily disagree with her. So I took a quick, second shower to rinse off the remodeling sweat and blow-dried my hair just enough so I didn't look like

I just got back from the gym. Then I put on a decent pair of jeans and a nice sweater.

They were drinking wine in the living room when I came down. Stuart stood up as soon as he saw me, a sign of impeccable manners. He was in his late thirties, I guessed, which meant he was somewhat younger than my mom, but not enough of an age gap for it to seem like she was in the market for a boy toy. Plus, he wasn't the type, physically: medium height, thinning dark hair, average features with a bony build. He also wore glasses and he seemed really anxious about his tie. By the look of him, I guessed he had Chinese heritage.

"Nice to meet you." I offered a hand for him to shake.

"Likewise." His palms were sweaty, which meant he was nervous. "I'm Stuart Lee."

I extrapolated that he cared about making a good impression. Since my mom liked him, it was enough for me to give him a fair shot. She hovered until I caught her eye and smiled; she relaxed visibly and hustled us both into the kitchen, where she had chicken stew simmering on low. I helped her dish it up and then she rescued the bread. As we were using the fine dishes, I was glad I'd swiped on some makeup.

We ate a few bites in awkward silence before Stuart waded in with his game face on. "Miriam tells me you're starting at a new college this summer."

"Yeah." Through the main course, I explained my plans, trying to sound friendly and welcoming, even when the answers to his questions were obvious.

"I hear computer science is a great field to get into," he said. "Lots of growth."

"So I hear. How's the insurance game?"

"Steady. Auto insurance is required by law, and the older people get, the more they worry about death benefits."

Depressing dinner conversation, but his words had the ring of truth. "I can imagine."

"When you add in home owners, renters and those who need flood insurance, I have a pretty steady stream of customers." He was trying to sound jovial. "And I get a lot of referrals, too. Once you build a rapport with people, they tell their friends about you."

My mom wore a frozen, slightly desperate look, as if she'd noticed that the conversation was a beached and dying whale but she didn't know how to shove the unwieldy thing back into the ocean. "But there's more to life than work, am I right? My favorite thing about Stuart is his incredible Frank Sinatra voice."

That was interesting. "You sing?"

He blushed a little, and I saw what drew my mom to him; there was the sweetness she'd mentioned. "Not professionally."

Mom put in, "We met at karaoke. Stuart was on stage when I came in, and I just kind of…forgot to sit down."

He smiled at her, softness in his eyes. "I thought she was giving me a standing ovation, so I went over to talk to her."

She put her hand briefly over Stuart's and said, "Well, I was, indirectly. I never heard a more beautiful rendition of 'I've Got You Under My Skin.'" Turning to me, she added, "He sang three more times that night, and he'd just quietly walk on stage, perch on a stool and then just *own* the room. Everyone shuts up the minute Stuart opens his mouth."

He laughed. "That doesn't necessarily sound like a good thing, Miri."

So cute. I like them together.

"It is, you know it is. Lauren, you have to come with us some night. I'm terrible, but we can sing the Spice Girls or Destiny's Child together."

"Who?" I teased, like I hadn't heard her blasting them before. My mom and I shared a mutual penchant for popular music. Hers was just…older than mine. "Let me know what night you want to go. Wait, since when does Sharon have a karaoke bar?" I considered the nightlife options around here and drew a blank.

"We don't. I drove over to Edison."

I smiled at Stuart. "Seems like it was a good move. Is that where you're from?"

"Not originally. I grew up in Peoria."

"Did you go to college in Illinois?"

The question opened up a barrel of interesting conversation. Apparently Stuart graduated from Illinois State University in Normal, and then got his first job offer. He worked in Illinois until they transferred him to the office in Edison. I had to suppress a smile when he earnestly assured me he'd held the same job for seventeen years, he was thirty-nine and he owned his own home. In addition, he enjoyed classic movies, big band music, going to antique shops with my mom and, of course, karaoke. Thankfully, these revelations carried us through the chocolate cake she'd made for dessert and I avoided having more questions aimed my way. It wasn't that I minded chatting with him, more that most people would judge my life a mess at the moment and I didn't want advice from a guy I hardly knew.

As I stood up to clear the table, I patted him lightly on the shoulder. "You can relax now. I approve and support you two."

He pretended to blot his brow with a napkin. "Whew. Miri said if I didn't pass muster tonight, I'd be kicked to the curb."

"I never did," she protested.

"Why don't you guys go watch a movie? I'll wash up."

"Are you sure?" But it was obvious Mom wanted some Stuart time, so I made shooing motion and tidied up the kitchen. Then I tiptoed behind the couch and up the stairs. There was no question he was better for her than my dad, but their happiness made me feel a little melancholy. I mean, I didn't begrudge her some companionship, but before, it was Mom and me, against the world. Now it was Miriam and Stuart. After I closed my door, I could still hear the rumble of their voices, so I stuck in my earbuds and curled up on the bed. Weirdly, I'd much rather be at Rob's house, even though his kitchen was jacked up, and he only had one room that wasn't a work in progress.

Maybe that was because *I* was a work in progress.

With a wistful sigh, I opened my computer to check email. No surprise, there was nothing new from Max since I hadn't answered him. Both Nadia and Angus had written. Nadia sounded down, though she was obviously trying to hide it. The breakup must still be bothering her; she had been absolutely nuts about Mr. Hot Ginger. I'd never known a guy to make her skip work or blow off obligations. I'd answered her questions from before, so that meant she took it as clearance to ask new ones.

So you're applying to University of Nebraska? It'd be pretty awesome not to have to get up for classes. You can join lectures in your pajamas. Unless, will there be video? That could be awkward. Things here are suckish without you but there has been drunkenness. That's the college deal, right? Work isn't bad lately, but the practicum sucks. Do you miss us at all? Update me on the job situation! And oh, my God, you must be so bored if you're hanging out with my brother. Don't tell him he's a crappy substitute for me! It would break his widdle heart.

I laughed, then said out loud, "Oh, dude. I love you, Nadia, but no. Just…no."

Angus's email was deliciously gossipy with details about some ongoing scandal related to Courtney, my replacement housemate, who apparently had both a druggie roommate in the dorms and a crazy ex. I replied to that, feeling like I was missing an awesome soap opera. Okay, maybe I did miss some things about Michigan. Sometimes I wanted to curl up with Angus and watch *Project Runway* so bad that my stomach hurt.

The next day, Rob showed up right on time, as promised. I had changed my outfit four times before settling on a black pencil skirt, white blouse and red jacket. With my hair up, I looked like I should be giving tours of the UN, but Rob actually stared. His eyes dropped, traveling slowly up my body like he'd never seen me before.

"I wouldn't hire you looking like that," he said.

"What? Why not?"

"None of the guys in the office would get anything done for checking you out."

I grinned as he scooped me up to put me in the truck, just like he always did, but this time his hands lingered at my waist, and he didn't step back immediately. A crackle of heat went through me as I opened my knees an inch wider, as much as the pencil skirt allowed, so the rough denim of his jeans brushed my legs, sexy even through my tights.

"You realize that's discrimination."

Gently, he tucked a strand of hair behind my ear. A shiver ran through me when I registered the rough pads of his fingertips against the tender skin of my neck. My lips parted; I'd never been so close to him in quite this way before. I wanted to curl my fingers into his belt loops and pull him all the way in, delve under his jacket and find out if his abs were as nice as I suspected. Rob, shirtless and sweaty, had fueled a lot of my private time over the years.

"I was trying to boost your confidence. Apparently I'm not very good at it."

"No, it was great. I'll take 'too hot to hire' over 'sadly unqualified' as the reason I don't get the job."

"But you will," he said. "They'd be crazy not to want someone so smart and capable handling their front desk."

"Thanks." Before I could think better of it, I put my hand to his unshaven jaw and leaned in to kiss his cheek.

Rob surprised me by taking the kiss on the mouth. So warm, sweetly chapped and rough against mine, and it took *all* of my self-restraint not to nip his lower lip, begging for more. In the end, it only amounted to a peck, but my heart raced like I'd run half a mile and my cheeks felt hot.

He was smiling when he pulled back, his breath misting against my skin. "For luck."

Oh. My. God.

My imagination went nuts, and I spent the drive envisioning what a real kiss from Rob would be like. Just the little touches were driving me crazy, teases that I never expected to bear fruit. My knees were still jellied when we arrived at the car dealership fifteen minutes later.

Rob aimed a stern look my way. "Don't move." He ran around the truck and lifted me down. "Those shoes are sexy as fuck, but you'll turn your ankle getting out."

They were chunky-heeled retro-pinup shoes, similar to Fluevog, but less expensive. As he wrapped his arms around me to lift me down, he was definitely checking them out, along with the curves of my calves. Unless it was wishful thinking, he was more physical than he had been before breaking up with Avery. I had no idea what was going on, but...*hells, yeah. More, please.* Breathing him in, I fought the urge to press closer. It would be a wonder if I could answer any questions inside.

"Don't worry, Lauren. You've got this."

"Thanks. See you soon."

Picking a careful path across the car lot, I stepped into the glass-fronted space and wiped my feet on the mat. The showroom was enormous with a couple of brand-new cars inside. A woman smiled at me from the front desk, and I headed her way.

"May I help you?"

"I have an interview with Mick Davies." Checking the time, I added, "In ten minutes. I'm a bit early."

"He'll appreciate that. I think he's in a meeting with the sales team at the moment. You can sit over there if you like." *There* was a round table with magazines on it, probably used by the salesmen when chatting with prospective customers. "Would you like some coffee? Water?"

"Water, please."

She brought me a paper cup and I sat down with it, pretending I wasn't supernervous. In my life, I'd had two jobs—one as a cashier at Teriyaki King and the other as a receptionist in the fine arts department. I worked at TK for two years, more like three months in reception, so in this market, they probably had people a lot more qualified sending résumés. Sipping my water, I paged through a car magazine and tried not to sweat.

At promptly one o'clock, the salesmen returned to the floor and a supertan guy came out behind them. He looked like the proverbial used-car salesman, down to the shiny suit and poor quality hair plugs. His white teeth probably glowed purple in UV lighting, and his skin made my spray tan look natural. I kept my smile in place. Dealing with the public was easy; though I hated people socially, professionally, it was easier to pretend. Because y'know, money. Not that I saw myself doing this forever. Once I got my computer science degree, I'd be done with retail-type employment forever.

"Miss Barrett? Thanks for coming."

When Mr. Davies elevator-eyed me, it was fairly horrible. I pretended I didn't notice.

"My pleasure. I'm looking forward to hearing more about the job." I almost said *position,* but pervdar hinted he was the kind of guy who would leap on even a mild double entendre.

Yeah, somebody more qualified probably wouldn't take this job.

"Excellent. Let's go to my office and talk. Shelly, hold my calls."

"Of course." I caught an eye-roll from Shelly on the way past. *Uh-oh.* In a burst of foreboding, I wondered why she'd given notice. Hopefully not because of Davies.

Let it be a better job offer.

The manager's office was a shrine to lost youth, a combination of old sports trophies, sales plaques and pictures of hot women. I suspected he wasn't dating any of them currently, as they were obviously old photos. But they still lined his walls in a testament to what he valued, and that was apparently T&A.

"The dealership is open from ten to eight, Monday through Saturday, and twelve to five on Sunday. We're looking to replace Shelly, though Lord knows it'll be tough. The girl's a peach."

Girl. Since Shelly was thirty if she was a day, I was offended on her behalf. But I didn't show it. "I understand. What hours would the successful candidate be working?"

"Nine-thirty to five, Monday through Friday. My niece fills in for nights and weekends."

"That would be fantastic."

"I saw on your résumé that you've completed some college. Will you be going back?"

"Not in a way you have to worry about. I plan to take online classes and I can do that at night and on the weekends."

He smiled at me. "Sounds like we're made for each other."

Oh, God, no.

Somehow I managed not to show my distaste. "This job could work out very well. What are the primary responsibilities?"

Davies ran through the list of requirements, mostly first-customer contact, heavy phone work, support the sales team as needed, light clerical work, some scheduling. It didn't sound like anything I couldn't handle, so I relaxed a little. He asked me the usual questions and I gave my best answers. The pay was nine bucks an hour—not amazing, but decent for a town like Sharon. Cost of living wasn't bad here, and I'd be at my mom's house as long as she didn't get sick of me and demand I move out.

In the end, he shook my hand, then escorted me back to the front desk. "We have a few more applicants to interview. I plan to call the lucky girl next week."

Not the "successful applicant," I noted. His tone pretty much guaranteed that if a guy applied, he was out of luck.

"Thanks, I'll be looking forward to it." *Too much?* From his grin, apparently not.

Exhaling a long breath, I hurried out to the parking lot, where Rob was waiting. He hopped out and installed me on the passenger side, then ran back around.

"How did it go?"

"Well. I think. I won't know for sure until the phone rings."

"It will."

"How can you be so sure?"

"Because I can't imagine any guy *not* calling you when he has the chance."

A flood of warmth washed through me because I was 90 percent sure he wasn't just talking about the job. If I wasn't crazy, this was subtle, low-key Rob flirting. "And why's that?"

He paused for a long moment, his gaze steady on mine, and

he seemed to weigh his words before coming to some con-clusion that made him smile wryly. "Because *I* think about it all the time."

CHAPTER EIGHT

"Calling me?" I felt like it was wise to confirm.

Rob started the truck and pulled out of the parking lot before answering. "Yeah. The urge usually kicks in late at night."

"I'm not sure if you know this about me, but I definitely have an impulse control problem. What's your number?"

"I don't remember," he confessed, gesturing toward the dash. "It's on my phone somewhere."

Taking that as an invitation, I picked it up and was amused to see it had no password protection. I'd bet anything Avery used to scroll through this, making sure he had no dirty secrets. I went to the information screen and memorized the number, then added him as a contact in my list. Afterward, I sent a quick text.

There, now you can call me.

"Problem solved," I said. "I hope you drunk–dial me. I can only imagine how much fun that would be."

He slid me a smile lightly spiced with wickedness. "That's not my style."

"What is?" Any more, and I might literally hyperventilate. This pencil skirt was going straight to the top of my favorite outfit list.

"I guess you have to wait and see."

"Now that's just cruel," I mumbled. "I thought you were a nice guy, Rob."

"Nobody's good all the way to the bone. You know that." He angled the truck back through Sharon, but instead of heading for my place, he turned toward the small downtown.

"Where are we going?"

"You look too pretty for us to go straight home." His voice was matter-of-fact, and that made me appreciate the compliment even more. "I thought I'd buy you lunch, unless that's not okay for some reason?"

Come to think of it, I'd been too nervous about the interview for breakfast, and it was past two. "No plans, except for helping this guy fix up his house later."

"Does that loser ever take you anywhere nice? Or is it work, work, work, all the time?"

"We'll see," I said with what I hoped was a mysterious smile. "And he's not a loser."

To my astonishment, he parked at the Grove, the swankiest place in town. The restaurant was situated at the back of a wooded drive, hence the name. Like twenty years ago, the owners bought an old Victorian and restored it completely. Downstairs, it was gorgeous—I knew girls who went there before prom—and upstairs, there were six bedrooms available for romantic weekends. Apparently the place did fairly well, despite the obscure location.

As usual, Rob was in jeans and flannel, but I doubted they'd say anything during lunch. If they did, I didn't want to eat here anyway. The hostess proved me right with a broad smile, leading us to a corner table nestled in front of the windows, where we had a beautiful view of the wintry garden—very postcard picturesque with the trees iced over and snow piled up.

"Have you been here before?" Rob asked.

I shook my head. "To be honest, I didn't date much before I went away to school."

Realization spilled over me like hot coffee. *Shit. Now he thinks I think this is a date. Is this a date? Should it be, so soon after his breakup?* Sweat broke out between my shoulder blades, and I feared taking off my jacket. Between the white blouse and the job interview, I was probably a puddle of perspiration swaddled in librarian clothes.

It occurred to me that being his rebound girl might not be the best idea, but I couldn't bring myself to object. *There are exceptions to every rule, right?* And part of me felt like it would be better to get a few weeks with Rob than nothing at all.

No reason to freak out. It's just lunch.

"Too picky for the local talent?" he guessed.

I laughed. "Sure, let's say that."

Before he could ask, the waiter came over to fill our water glasses and deliver menus. There was no possible way I could've been more relieved. I took refuge behind my menu, trying to decide what to order. The Grove did food like mushroom risotto, grilled salmon, fried quail, beef tartare, chicken confit and potato gnocchi. To start, they had cheese-and-fruit plates, ceviche and chickpea hummus, along with various soups and salads. There were no prices listed, which made me nervous, especially since I'd just helped Rob make a budget. Yet my eyes still went straight to the dessert menu, where I proceeded to salivate over butterscotch caramel pudding, salted dark chocolate fudge and honey pistachio cake.

"Do you know what you're having?"

"I think so. You?"

He nodded, lifting a hand for the waiter with a confidence that was both surprising and hot. "We're ready to order. The lady first, please."

"The squash soup to start, followed by the shrimp and grits."

"Anything to drink?"

"Just water, thanks." While Rob wouldn't thank me for thinking of his wallet, I figured this should deduct three or four bucks from the bill.

"And for you, sir?"

"I'll have the warm vegetable salad and the smoked pork tenderloin. Water for me, too."

The waiter used an iPad to tap in our food choices. "I'm sending this to the kitchen right now. While you wait, I'll bring you some homemade bread and herbed butter."

"That sounds incredible. Am I drooling?" I wiped the corner of my mouth, only half pretending. "I was too uptight to eat anything this morning."

"Is that normal?" He didn't sound like he was judging me, only curious.

"Before I meet new people or go into some new situation? Unfortunately, yeah. Before I learned better coping mechanisms, I used to throw up a lot. Not eating is preferable."

"I'd say so."

"Once I survive the ordeal, I eat everything in sight. I call this relief feasting. I also suspect the skipping of meals and then eating like a Roman senator is why I can't shake the extra weight." Not that I was trying, honestly. Fiddling with my laptop, eating whatever was easiest and avoiding workouts didn't exactly qualify as healthy. That said, the renovations at Rob's house were definitely making me stronger.

"Huh?"

Oh, crap. Now he probably thinks I'm fishing for a compliment. There was no way this would sound anything but clumsy. "I need to lose about twenty pounds."

Okay, thirty, if you listen to certain stupid weight charts.

"In what world?" He scowled openly, dark brows drawn together. "You'd lose all the oomph and most of your bam."

A giggle slipped out before I could stop it. I hadn't made that noise since I was thirteen and Rob offered me a ride home. "Tell me, is the oomph up front or is that the bam?"

He grinned, the broadest smile I'd ever seen from him. *Oh, my God, he has a dimple.* "It's your body. By now, you should know all about your oomph and bam. I shouldn't have to explain these things to you."

Green light means go. Time to flirt like I mean it.

"Then I guess I'll have to go home and practice in the mirror until I work it out."

His eyes blazed like there was light shining behind him, but the waiter came back with a bread basket and tiny crocks of butter. Too bad, I wanted to hear how he'd have replied. He had himself under control by the time the guy walked away, but there was a new focus to his gaze, and the intensity of it sent a shiver through me.

For a few seconds, the table was silent except for his drumming fingers, muffled by the fine linen. "I have to ask...are you winding me up? Because I'm here, you need an ego boost, you're lonely or—"

"No," I cut in. "I wouldn't do that to anyone, but definitely never to you."

"You say that like I'm special."

I have to tell him. The thought nearly sent me straight into a panic attack.

When I was eleven, Nadia and I went to the Y to swim. That first time, she was fearless, immediately running toward the high dive despite the clearly posted No Running sign. I followed slower, weighed down by my ruffled floral bathing suit, earplugs, nose plugs, goggles, both our towels and a book, in case I wanted to take a break. She went up the ladder like a shot and just launched into space. The summer was nearly over before I got the courage to climb, and I was never a good swimmer. Too much uncertainty, bobbing bodies, unbreathable water.

I still remembered the terror screaming through my veins while everyone shouted for me to jump. On the way down, I nearly peed myself, and I didn't dive so much as fall. The water stung like a bitch as I went under, and Nadia had to drag me out of the deep end. I cried in a snotty ball for ten minutes afterward.

Until now, that was the worst fear I ever knew. My throat tried to swell shut, but I spoke through it, and my voice came out weird. "To me, you always have been."

"Don't get mad at me, okay? But I have to ask."

"What?" Now I was really worried.

"Is it possible you're kind of…fixated on me? Because of your dad, and what happened when we went to see him? Transference, whatever. This might not be healthy."

The rage surprised me. If I'd had a glass of wine, I'd have thrown it at him, old-school-movie style. Water just didn't have the same impact, plus he was my ride home. While grinding my teeth, I counted to a hundred. I was whispering fifty when Rob realized how upset I was.

"Lauren—"

The starters arrived. I stared at my soup until I could speak without freaking out. "Nadia says I have daddy issues, yeah. And I'm sure she thinks that's funny. It's not so funny to me because she still has her dad. He's always been around. Always. He'd never let either one of you guys down." Tears prickled in my eyes, but I refused to give in. "How many of your games did he miss when you were playing?"

"None," he said quietly. "Not ever."

"Exactly. Yeah, you saw me during a weak moment, but I don't equate you with my father. You're *four* years older than me, not twenty. I suspect you just don't think much of yourself, so you can't figure out what I'd see in you. And I'm kind of done saying that you're awesome because it pisses me off when you don't believe me. So let me make one thing super-clear…. I have never, never—not once—thought of you as an older brother. In my head, you're the dream guy who'd never look twice at me, even if I was dancing naked on the table."

His blue eyes smoldered like the heart of a flame, as if he was picturing it. When he spoke, his voice was rough and deep. "Three things. First, if you're ever dancing naked on a table, I better be the only other person in the room. Second, please don't stop being sweet to me. I'm just starting to think maybe some of it might be true, and I'm not ready to lose that. Third, and this is the important bit, so listen up—if I'd known your crush survived getting to know me, I'd have broken up with Avery weeks ago. See…I've wanted you since you were eighteen and I probably shouldn't have been checking you out."

"Wait. W-wait. What?" Incoherent, yep. He'd given me absolutely *no sign*. Emotionally, sexually, he had been like the Mojave. "When?"

"Eat your soup before it gets cold. I'll tell you more later."

"Are you kidding? No. You can't drop that on me and then—"

"Sure I can. Otherwise I'll take you home after lunch and we won't talk again until tomorrow." He smirked.

"That's blackmail. I'm starting to think you're kind of evil."

"I can live with that."

With a frustrated snarl, I ate my soup. Then the bastard made me chew through a delicious plate of shrimp and grits while we talked innocently about stuff we planned to do later in terms of home renovation, like I wasn't seething. Rob appeared to be enjoying it, too. I'd never known he could be such a sadist. Did this mean he'd want to tie me up and paddle me?

Hope not. Given his worries about my daddy issues, that might get weird.

I was eating salted dark chocolate fudge with a tiny fork when he said, "So you want to hear the story?"

"Most definitely."

"Let me set the stage. You were just turning eighteen, still in high school. Which makes me a perv, I'm aware."

I shook my head. "It doesn't count since you didn't hit on me."

"I try not to be creepy, it's one of my life goals."

"So far, you're succeeding. Fudge?"

He took the bite from my fork, and I couldn't help but recall all of the manga I'd read, where girls went crazy over the indirect kiss. Deliberately I licked the fork when I brought it back to my mouth, and he seemed to forget to speak. It took a full minute of him watching me eat before he resumed the narrative.

"You and Nadia were in her room, getting ready for some party. I could hear you upstairs, laughing, but back then, we never hung out."

"Yeah, Nadia was very much 'your world, my world, let's not cross dimensions.'"

Rob nodded. "I was watching TV with my dad when you came down wearing a red dress and suddenly, you were all oomph and bam."

"I remember that dress. Still have it, I think."

"That night, I couldn't take my eyes off you. It sucked when I realized you were headed out to hook up with some high school assholes."

"There was no joy in Mudville for me that night. Nadia got drunk and locked herself in the bathroom because her dipshit boyfriend was making out with somebody else in the garage."

"If I'd known, I'd have beat the shit out of him."

I smiled to take the sting out of my reply. "That's why we didn't confide in you more."

"Anyway, that's it, not much of a story, huh? Before, you were the sweet kid who hung around the house and stared at me a lot."

"And after?"

"Honestly?"

"Please." Fixing my gaze on his face, I watched the sheepish smile widen.

"I wondered what you looked like naked. A lot. Felt like a deviant, too. Because there's a certain kind of guy who's attracted to high school girls in his twenties, and I definitely didn't want to be one of those. But I'd still think about asking you out and then remember you were my sister's friend, and how awkward would that be, plus you were still in school, and I knew you wouldn't be sticking around past graduation." He hesitated, as if I might yell at him again for what came next. "And I knew you were too smart to be drawn in by physical stuff or the fact that I played football, so I figured—"

"It was best not to make a move."

Rob nodded. "At the time, it was the only play I could make."

"Or not make," I murmured. "You never let on at all. I never guessed."

"Yeah, well. I learned early on not to show people how

they're making me feel. Otherwise I'd always be the dumb kid crying in a corner."

"You're not like that with me anymore," I realized aloud.

"I trust you," he said softly.

I melted around a mouthful of fudge. At his gesture, I fed him another bite of the shared dessert, imagined what it would taste like on his lips. Hot, sweet, slightly bitter, sharp with salt, rich as sin. *In the not-too-distant future, I might be kissing Robert Clayton Conrad*. Back in the day, I wrote his full name on my notebooks a lot, always on the inside, where Nadia wouldn't find it and tease me.

This should make him laugh, plus it would show I trusted him, too. "You know, I always thought you had a kingly name. I have a folder on my computer devoted to your fantasy adventures, like three hundred thousand words, all terrible."

Finally, I'd succeeded in startling the ever imperturbable Rob. "What?"

"You heard me. In the world of Nebaskalan, your evil uncle stole your throne and left you for dead. But with the help of your talking horse, you swashed a lot of buckles, slew dragons, restored your kingdom to prosperity and won your lady love."

"Did I now? Was her name Lauren by any chance?"

God, I'd let him *read* those god-awful fanfics if they'd make him smile like this. "Please. Laurenara, that's completely different. She's a gorgeous, irresistible sorceress with red hair and purple eyes who can turn people into mist, superhandy for breaking into castles occupied by villainous relations."

"Seriously, I can't rest until you've shown these to me. Do the stories have titles?"

"Book one is *The Fallen Crown*, book two is *The Weeping Throne* and book three is *The Undying King*."

Grinning, I had no idea why he was looking at me like that, until he stood, rounded the table, drew me up out of my chair and kissed me. Sensation careened through me: the hardness of his chest pressed against mine and the roughness of his hand tangled in my hair. I tasted salt and chocolate, heat as promised, more in the hard demand of his mouth and the fleeting sweep of his tongue. I could've kissed him forever, except that the waiter almost knocked into us with a tray of plates.

"Maybe this isn't the place," I whispered, breathless. "What now?"

"You'll see."

CHAPTER NINE

The gravel parking lot was rough, and when I stumbled, Rob swept me into a princess carry. Startled, I wrapped my arms around his neck. "Are you serious? You're completely showing off right now, aren't you?"

"Maybe a little." But he didn't put me down until I was safely ensconced in the truck.

"Admit it, you do *not* lift everyone in and out. Your ride's not even that tall." I could get in unaided; it just wouldn't be graceful.

"Just you," he said, starting the engine and adjusting the heater.

"Why?"

"Because I needed an excuse to touch you. I didn't think you'd suspect me of being anything but overprotective."

He was right. In my wildest fantasies, I'd never daydreamed about Rob liking me back. For different reasons, we both had confidence issues. Buckling in, I indulged in a happy silent squee as Rob put the truck in Reverse and made a perfect three-point turn to get us facing the right direction. He didn't say much on the drive to my house, which surprised me a little. Maybe he was already regretting the impulsive kiss?

"So—" I began, as he parked in my driveway.

"Was it okay?" he cut in.

"What?"

"Me kissing you. I guess I should've asked first, but you were just being so cute. You didn't make up the whole thing about the stories, did you?"

Oh. Now I get it.

"Come in."

This time, I didn't wait for him to get me down; I just opened the door and hopped out. He followed me to the front door, waiting patiently while I shivered and fumbled with the key. A few seconds later, we stepped inside. Since it was late afternoon, my mom would be home in an hour or so, but for now, the house was empty. The front door led into the living room, cozily decorated with my mother's various arts-and-crafts projects. She'd always enjoyed finding things at antique stories, kitschy character pieces that added color to the room. Consequently, our house was more shabby than chic since she didn't have the knack of bringing old things back to life. If I spent enough time with Rob, though, I might change that.

"My room's upstairs." A prickle of excitement crept through me, ridiculous as it might be. I had no plans to sleep with him right then yet it was enticing to lead him to my bedroom.

"I remember."

He's been here before. He delivered and set up your bed.

But the kiss changed everything.

"Give me a minute."

"No problem." There was something off in his demeanor, a change I couldn't put my finger on. I was better at reading him, but he didn't come with a translation guide or a manual.

Sighing, I went into my small walk-in closet and changed

into yoga pants and a sweatshirt. Thick socks completed my ensemble—not sexy, but perfect for working on the house. *Assuming he still wants me there.* I stepped out to find him perched at the edge of my bed, looking at a ballerina figurine my mom bought me when I was ten.

"All right, before I break out any volumes of Rob-homage, tell me what's going on."

"What makes you think anything is?"

"We had a fantastic time at lunch. Then you kissed me. After that, you shut down like Sharon at ten p.m. on a Tuesday night."

"I'm not sure if I like you having the keys to the kingdom, so to speak." But he was smiling a little, proof he didn't mind *too* much. "I just...I timed it wrong, that's all. It should've been special, and instead, we almost got hot soup dumped on our heads."

Oh. "I can't speak for other women, but I prefer being kissed because you want to so bad you can't help it. All the orchestration and polish in the world can't compensate for lack of passion. I'd be bummed if you could've stopped yourself. That'd mean you don't want me as..." I trailed off, deciding not to reveal that much.

"What?" There was a soft, vulnerable look in his eyes. He was never this open, even around his own family.

I mustered the nerve to say, "As much as I want you."

"So you don't mind that I fumbled our first kiss?"

"That wasn't a fumble. I'm calling a moratorium on you doubting yourself, Rob."

His gaze went flat. "Yeah, I don't know what that means."

Shit, I hadn't meant to make him feel stupid. "It's like a suspension, I'm saying enough. Anyway, it seems like you're freaking out and looking for reasons to pick a fight. Maybe *you* wish you didn't—"

"No. I'm just…worried," he said quietly.

"About what?"

"Whether this is a good idea."

Since I'd suspected it might not be, I couldn't blame him. But I no longer wanted to ride the brake, now that I knew I wasn't stuck in an unrequited attraction. It was time to chase after what I wanted, the guy I'd longed for as long as I could remember.

"Nobody ever knows that before they start dating someone." I was making a leap, assuming he wanted to steer me toward girlfriend territory.

For all I knew, maybe he just wanted to sleep with me while I was helping with the house. I probably wouldn't say no; it wouldn't be the first time I'd banged a guy as a discovery exercise. There had even been a couple that I considered as relationship material, but in all honesty, Rob was always there in the back of my head. If it didn't work out between us, maybe sex would get him out of my system.

"That's true."

"But look, if you're uncomfortable or unsure, we can pretend it didn't happen." That offer nearly choked me on the way out. But I meant it. "You just broke up with someone. Maybe that's why you're backing off."

"I'm afraid you'll get bored." He spoke the words while turning the ballerina statuette over in his hands, carefully not looking at me.

"You didn't worry about that with Avery?"

"Not really. I would've needed to care more. With her, it was about trying to improve myself. I didn't feel much of anything, but then, she never noticed."

Wow.

"I can't tell you what to do, but I won't push you into anything." Turning away, I headed back into my closet, hoping it didn't show how crushed I was. Like, I could curl into a ball and cry. *One lunch, one kiss and he's done?* It wasn't even a *long* kiss.

Two minutes of rummaging later, and I produced the epic works of genius, as promised. Sure, I had the files on my computer, but that wasn't enough for a true fan. My stories were all printed and collected in three-ring binders. God, the hours I collated paper and slaved with a hole punch to make Rob's fantasy adventures look more official.

"Wow, you were serious," he said as I handed him the stack.

"I don't joke about fanfic."

Smiling, he paged through the first volume, fast enough that I didn't think he was reading. "Nobody's ever cast me as regal before."

"I was thirteen and reading a lot of sword-and-sorcery books."

"Tell me I get to use a magic sword."

"Obviously." After flipping pages, I pointed to a particular scene. "This is where you defeat an evil wizard and liberate all of his stolen artifacts. You return most of them, but with a few items, the original owners are dead. Which is how you end up wielding Daystar."

"See, this is why I kissed you. Your cuteness is fucking irresistible right now, Lauren."

I smiled at him. "Yet here you are, resisting. Cut it out, Superman."

"I'm starting to think it's one of my dumber ideas." He leaned in, threading his hand in my hair, and cupped the back of my head.

I closed my eyes.

This time, he felt different, more measured and deliberate, as if he'd considered the implications. Heat spilled through me from the delicate play of his lips across mine. For the first few seconds, his mouth was all candied curiosity, and then I wrapped my arms around him. Rob made a muffled sound and hauled me onto his lap, his other arm coming around me in a possessive movement, and the tenor of the kiss changed.

Hot and rough, sparks of sweetness interspersed with nips of teeth, and the thrust of his tongue. Breaking contact with a gasp, Rob fell back on my bed, intentionally, I thought, and when I followed, he rolled me beneath him. My whole body quivered. His weight pressed me into the mattress, but I only shifted to perfect our fit, and then I drew him down again.

He didn't stop at my lips. His mouth traveled along my jaw, my ears, down my throat and back up for the most scorching kisses yet. He was molten in my arms, all hard muscle and barely leashed sex. Rob shifted once, twice, until I opened my legs a little. A quiet moan escaped me. If this was a mere preview, the sex would be amazing. He exhaled into my mouth and I breathed it in, tasted him in turn, until he was shaking, and each kiss felt deeper, hungrier, with an edge of wildness to every brush of his hands.

"God, you feel good," he whispered.

"Mhm." I dug my fingers into his deltoids, urging him on.

With a groan, he rolled off me. "If we don't stop now, I won't be able to."

"Is that a bad thing?"

"I just don't want you to feel like we rushed into anything."

"You *do* understand that women suffer from sexual frustration tóo, right?" If he insisted, I could take care of it myself, but that seemed like a waste. But talking was never a bad thing, especially if it resulted in better understanding.

"I know that. Damn. I just…" He cursed, jaw clenching. "Jesus, I want you so bad."

"It's sweet of you to be concerned, but I'm not the kind of person who regrets sex." I wondered what he'd think if I told him that I was drunk when I slept with my roommate, and I'd done it mostly to prove a point. Yet that didn't make me bad or stupid. Even if I did it for depressing reasons, the sex was good, and we were careful. "Basically, I don't think pleasure between two consenting adults is ever shameful."

He grinned at me. "You're such a hippie. I suspect you're trying to seduce me, but it won't work."

"Why not?" Yeah, I totally sounded disappointed.

"Because I'm not exactly prepared to finish this right now."

"Oh, protection." How cute, Rob was the kind of guy who used euphemisms. I guessed that meant he wasn't a dirty talker. Hopefully he didn't have hang-ups about what good girls did or didn't do in bed. Though going without a condom wouldn't be impossible since I was on birth control, we didn't have time to fuck properly. "There are other things we could do."

A zing of lightning went straight through me at the way his gaze sharpened. "You are…incredible. Shouldn't you make sure I intend to date you before we go down this road?"

I shook my head. "My self-respect isn't tied to that, Rob. So you either want to fool around or you don't. No strings."

The smile he offered me was…radiant, no other word for it. You'd think no woman had ever messed around without tying it to other expectations. And hell, maybe that was the case. I didn't care if this was a politic move, mostly because I didn't see relationships in that light; sex shouldn't be a leash to keep a guy in line or a choke chain that made him obey.

"Hell, yes," he said huskily.

Beaming, I got up to close the door and lock it, then fetched a washcloth. By my calculations, we had just under an hour before my mom got home. Lots of interesting things could happen before then. As soon as I got within grabbing distance, Rob pulled me down on top of him. He seemed to want me in charge, so I straddled his hips and unbuttoned his shirt. His chest was fantastic, firm and muscled with an etched six-pack, but he wasn't manscaped, just the right amount of chest hair. I ran my palms across his skin and flexed my fingers into his pecs. He moved under me, circling his hips so I could feel how hard he was, even through his jeans.

"I feel so dirty with you touching me like this."

"Good or bad?" I asked.

His throat worked. "Good."

"We don't have time for everything I want," I said. "So… is this okay?"

I put my hand on the fly of his jeans, and he arched off the bed. "Yeah, definitely. Christ, yes," he growled as I unzipped him. "More, Lauren. Please."

God, he looked sexy as he shifted back against my pillows, getting into a better position. His jeans were open to reveal a taut abdomen and boxer briefs, while his shirt bared his gorgeous chest. I wanted to lick him all over, but there was no time, if I was getting a turn, too, and I wasn't selfless enough to forego his fingers in my panties. Shivering at the thought, I drew him out of his underwear and adjusted his clothes so it would be comfortable. I stared for a few seconds, riveted by the hard length of him jutting from my curled fingers. His skin was fever-hot and so smooth, but I'd never really pictured this part of Rob. My sex dreams of him tended to be soft R, but this was full-on triple-X and he was flipping luscious.

"This good?" Maybe I was admiring him too much while I stroked, but from the way his eyes went glassy and the high flush on his cheeks, he liked it.

"Yeah."

As I put my face closer, exhaling warmly, he actually quivered, and a dot of pearly fluid appeared on the tip. That reminded me of what I needed to make this good for him, given the time allotted, so I grabbed the bottle of lotion on my night table and warmed some in my palms until they were slippery. Rob reacted to the lubrication, a soft jerk upward before I even touched him. When I curled my hand around him, he made the most delicious noise.

Moving my hand, I whispered, "I need you to tell me how you like it."

If Rob wasn't a talker now, he would be by the time I finished with him. There was no better way to please him than to make him ask for he wanted, plus hearing it turned me on. I was soft and slick, aching, when he turned his face toward me, lips slightly parted, like he'd forgotten how to speak, just because of what I was doing to him.

"Like that, only more." He swallowed. "Harder."

"Show me."

He didn't resist. Relaxing, he covered my fingers with his and refined my strokes, each movement longer and rougher than mine. *So Rob doesn't want gentle. Noted.* Once I had the rhythm, his hand fell away, but he gave his whole body to the motion, lifting his hips to push into my hand until it felt like he was fucking my fist, and I could *so* imagine how that would feel for real. I ached for him, echoing each throb with one of my own. Watching his face as the pleasure blazed higher— that was the sexiest thing I'd ever seen.

"You said you used to think about me naked. What else?"

"Now?" he gasped.

"Definitely now. And not the most innocent fantasy. I want your dirtiest secret."

"I can't." But he didn't stop moving. If anything, his hips worked faster.

"Tell me, or I stop." I wouldn't, but he didn't know that.

"At this point, I'd finish on my own."

"But it wouldn't be as good." My fingers loosened, teasing him. I wanted so badly to find out what kind of sex Rob fantasized about.

He groaned, thighs tensing. "You were in high school... that was dirty enough."

"Tell me."

"You come out to the garage like you did that one time. Only not to ask for a ride."

"Are you sure?" I worked harder, prompting a moan.

"Not in my truck. You have on that red dress and you're not wearing any panties. I know, because you just...show me, without saying anything." His voice sounded hoarse, but also eager, as if speaking the first words unlocked some secret door inside him.

"What happens next?"

"You climb up on the hood on my truck and...touch yourself. I'm just watching at first."

"Not for long?"

"Eventually I can't stand it and I have to join you. Taste you. I go down on you right there." As he whispered the last, his body locked and he came, panting my name.

I caught the fluid in the washcloth, minimizing the mess, and then I snuggled up against him, stroking his chest gently. For long moments, his arms were unsteady as he held me but eventually, he captured my chin in warm fingers and gazed at me sternly. "I can't believe you made me tell you that."

As dirty fantasies went, it wasn't so shocking. I might make it come true someday; I still had the red dress. "Pfft, you need to do me now. Or would you rather I just use you?"

"I'm interested."

"Lay back, jeans off."

I didn't have the patience for him to figure out my sex buttons right then anyway. For a quick orgasm, it was better this way. Rob shucked his jeans off and tucked his penis back into the briefs. "I'm yours to command."

In answer, I rose up on my knees, peeled out of my yoga pants and settled myself on his thigh. Leaning forward slightly, I circled my hips while keeping my eyes on his. He licked his lips and set his hands on my waist, not trying to control my movements but steadying me. I was grateful he didn't do anything but watch; in fact, that got me hotter. I was already so turned on that the rubbing felt incredible; if his hard thigh was this good—*oh, shit. Yeah.* His hands moved to my ass, pressing me forward even more. This angle was even better. Rob tensed and relaxed his muscles in conjunction with the grinding, adding another layer, until I just couldn't hold on. I came in my panties, just from riding his leg.

I was flushed and gasping when he rolled me into his arms. "There's a problem with your strategy," he said. "You should've gone first."

"Why?" I asked dreamily.

"Because now I'm turned on again."

CHAPTER TEN

By the time my mom got home, we were on our way out. She smiled when she saw Rob and hugged him. "How are you, hon?"

"Good. Work going okay?"

They seemed really comfortable with each other, which surprised me. My mom had been kind of a hermit after Dad left, and Rob had that whole Iron Man thing going with people he didn't know well. Yet they seemed friendly. I was instantly suspicious.

"Yep. I might be in line for a promotion. Fingers crossed."

"Hope you get it. Ready, Lauren?"

"Sure. Just let me get my coat."

"I'll go warm up the truck." That was sweet of him and typical of Rob.

I'd counted on his consideration because I needed an excuse to linger to ask, "Okay, what was that all about?"

"What?"

"*That.*"

She gave in with a teasing smile. "After you went away to

school, Rob came by to shovel the drive, fix anything that needed it. I thought his dad put him up to it, but when I mentioned it, Ned didn't know anything about it."

"Then I'll have to thank Rob for helping you out."

After studying my face for a few seconds, her eyes widened. "What about Avery?"

"They broke up."

Her brows shot up. "When? His mom didn't say anything to me about it."

"Night before last," I admitted with a pang of guilt. *Hey, nobody cheated. You just...moved in fast.*

"In that case, be careful. Keep it PG-13."

Smirking, I said, "Like that'll happen. I'll film it for you."

"Get out. You're not my daughter at all, are you?"

"Changeling," I mumbled. "You said something about karaoke when Stuart was here. When did you want to go? And would you mind if I invited Krista and Rob?"

"You really think they'd want to?"

"We won't know until we ask."

"Of course they're welcome. I'll talk to Stuart and get back to you." She seemed bemused that I'd want to hang out as a group, but this was part of giving her new man a fair shake, and it would help to have other people around, cutting some of the tension. Plus, I was dying to hear his awesome Frank Sinatra croon.

"Sounds good." I got my coat out of the hall closet, shrugged into it and paused by the front door. "I don't know for sure if I'll be home tonight."

"Don't do anything I wouldn't do." At my look, she tried, "Be safe. Make good choices."

Grinning, I swept out and down the drive. This time I caught Rob off guard and vaulted into the truck before he managed to open the door. "What're you reading?"

"*The Fallen Throne,* obviously." With a sly grin, he held up the binder he'd somehow smuggled out of my room.

"Are you kidding?" I smacked his arm.

But I didn't try to take it away from him. As he backed out of the drive, he added, "This is riveting. I really feared for my/Robert's life in the first few pages."

"Because the story is punishment enough, I'm letting you keep that."

"I'd fight you for it," he said.

"Hey, don't discount me. I'm scrappy." Then it occurred to me to loop him in on the nascent plans. "So…my mom has a boyfriend, and he's apparently the karaoke king. Would you be interested in going along? I plan on inviting Krista, too. Remember her?"

He thought for a few seconds, then shook his head. "Sorry. Unless they played sports, I didn't know many underclassmen when I graduated, basically just you and Nadia."

"Irrelevant. Karaoke, yes or no?"

"I don't promise to sing, but I'll go."

It occurred to me that we'd spent a lot of time together, and he never mentioned hanging out with the guys. "What do you usually do for fun anyway?"

"Sports bar. Every few weeks I meet up with some old teammates who're still in Sharon. My best friend, Russ, works a couple hours away, but we get together when he visits his parents." Thoughtful, he added, "I have a few gym buddies, but we don't do more than grunt and nod while we work out."

"Deep and meaningful."

"That's not really what I'm known for," he said. "Anyway, I had plenty of male bonding in football, basketball, baseball—"

"Okay, I get the idea. Now you're a lone wolf who does lone things. Alone."

He slanted me a look through his lashes, so I could only

glimpse a sliver of blue. "It doesn't have to be that way. There comes a point where a guy's kind of tired of fucking around with other dudes, and he just wants one woman instead."

"Is that right, Spartacus?"

He flushed when he realized how that sounded. "No. I mean—*no*. Not that there's anything *wrong* with—if that's what you're into, but that guy wouldn't ever want a woman, oh, unless he's—"

"It's okay, I know what you mean." I resolved never to tease him like that again. His knuckles showed white from gripping the wheel too hard, likely frustrated at his words for coming out clumsy, making him sound dumb. "It's fun to go out drinking but after a while, you get the urge to settle down."

"Basically." Quiet tone.

"I'm sorry, that was rude."

"You're funny, Lauren. I knew that. Very sharp and witty." But his look said I'd made him feel bad by pouncing on the connotation rather than accepting his words as intended.

"Yeah, but humor only succeeds if you make the people you care about laugh. If you hurt them, then it's mean-spirited. Therefore, I'm an asshole."

He smiled, though it didn't quite reach his eyes. "This is when my dad would call me a wuss. I love the guy but he doesn't always make it easy." Then he seemed to recall my paternal situation. "Damn. I shouldn't be complaining about how I have it when you—"

"It's not a contest. Me having a sucky dad doesn't mean nobody else can talk about theirs without me playing the abandonment card. So are we okay?"

"Yeah. Was that our first fight?"

"Only if we start yelling and one of us flounces off afterward."

That night, Rob was quiet when we worked on the house,

not unusual, but after the exchange in the car it had me worried. We ate dinner together, worked some more, and around ten, he said, "I'll take you home."

"Oh."

It wasn't like I'd assumed he'd invite me to sleep over, though I had been confident enough to give my mom a heads-up. Was this the opposite of the walk of shame? The walk of no-game? I lacked the courage to ask him why; I mean, we'd already fooled around once today. Maybe he just wanted to sleep, or he was tired from the renovations. Possibly he thought that would be rushing the main event or he was just sick of me.

"I won't be around tomorrow," he said, pulling into my driveway. "Or the next few days, for that matter."

If things weren't a little...weird, I'd have asked why not. But with the silent tension in the air—and I didn't know how to fix it, other than apologize, which I'd already done—it felt like overstepping. So I just nodded.

"Okay. Have a good weekend." I jumped out of the car, not wanting to learn the hard way if he'd come around to get me.

Wow. One day. This went pear-shaped fast.

I was unlocking the front door by quarter past ten, much to my mother's surprise. "No dice, huh?"

"There's something going on with him."

With an inviting smile, she patted the other end of the sofa. "I have cookies."

"See, this is why I eat my feelings. I'm following your example."

"So talk about your problems instead. I will fall on this cookie-grenade for you." Mom crammed a whole chocolate chip cookie in her mouth and mumbled, "Sehowmuckiwubu?"

It was impossible to brood when I had my cheerful, fun-loving mother back. After my dad left, it was literally years before I saw her smile again. At the moment, I could hug

Stuart if he were responsible for this transformation. But no, Nadia's mom had said the change started a while back, longer than they'd been together. So he was a happy side effect, not the cause.

In the end, I ate two cookies and watched a few episodes of *Storage Wars*. Though I felt like a dipshit, I kept an eye on my phone, but it never buzzed. That weekend I hung out with Krista, as promised. Feeling like a loser, I borrowed my mom's car since she was with Stuart and drove to the nearest theater, half an hour away. Krista talked the whole time about the travails of pregnancy, which didn't increase my desire to reproduce.

"Pull over," she yelled, twenty minutes into the trip.

Worried, I did as she ordered and she opened the door in time to upchuck all over the gravel shoulder. I looked away, but the smell was horrific. "Should I take you home?"

"It's fine. It'll pass. For some reason, driving makes the morning sickness worse."

"It's almost four in the afternoon," I pointed out.

"Yeah, it'd be awesome if the problem cut off at 11:59 a.m. sharp." With shaky hands, she opened her purse and fished out some kind of hard candy. "Ginger. It helps."

"Tell me when you feel better." I was a little bit worried about watching a movie with her, but she ought to know her limitations better than me.

Five minutes later, she was okay to continue. Luckily there were no more issues and we managed to get tickets for a comedy starting in fifteen minutes. The film wasn't awesome, but spending time with Krista was. Afterward, we had dinner at a chain restaurant nearby.

"Have you heard from your dad?" I asked.

"Actually, yeah." She beamed.

"I told you he'd come around."

But mine never did.

That made me kind of sad, though I didn't show it. Midnight had come and gone when I dropped Krista off and headed home. My mom wasn't back yet. A twist of melancholy tightened my insides as I headed upstairs alone. Everyone in Michigan was probably having fun with Courtney instead of me. *I'm sure Angus and Nadia miss you, at least.* After what happened with Max, I suspected he was glad I wasn't around to remind him.

I didn't hear from Rob all weekend. *He's busy,* I told myself. But it was hard not to wonder if I'd given him the wrong signals by fooling around so fast. Yet if he was the kind of guy who'd hold that against me, he could fuck off. That burst of anger carried me through Wednesday when the manager from the car lot called to offer me the job.

"Can you start a week from Monday?" Davies asked.

"Sure, that's not a problem."

"Bring your ID and social security card. I look forward to working with you, Lauren." God, until this moment, I'd always liked my name, but he said it in this trying-to-be sexy tone.

"Me, too. Thanks for the opportunity."

That night, I celebrated with Mom and Stuart; he took us out for Chinese in Edison, a long drive just to eat, but the food was worth it. Overall I had a good time. And I still didn't hear from Rob. Anger gave way to hurt. Yeah, I was kind of a dick in the truck, but if he gave Avery the silent treatment over every little thing, no wonder she thought he was cheating on her. Guys didn't do that when they were emotionally invested. *I guess, in the end, it was easy for him to walk away.*

On another note, I had no idea how I'd be getting to work since I couldn't exactly demand a truck from somebody who wasn't talking to me. Because I had no solutions to this problem, I followed the path of all true warriors—and got on the internet to play video games. That coping strategy lasted for two days, and I didn't shower. My mom eventually made me by threatening to withhold dinner.

The woman knows how to motivate.

Friday night, my phone vibrated, but I didn't look at it right away; I killed ten more fluffy bunnies with pointy monster teeth before pausing my game. 1 message. When I swiped the screen and tapped it, the text read:

Rob: im not ok, can you come over?

Omw, I sent back.

My first thought was that he was sick—and that it might be serious. Otherwise, what would keep him on radio silence for so long? Maybe I'd worried for bullshit, self-involved reasons, asking all the wrong questions. I jammed my feet in the first shoes I found and ran down the stairs. My mom was out with Stuart, so her car was parked in the drive. After scrawling a note for her, I snatched my coat and keys.

The trip lasted at least a thousand hours, though the clock insisted it was more like fourteen minutes. I raced to the steps and knocked with more impatience than care. Rob must've been watching for me because he opened the door right away. His face was…indescribable, eyes gleaming with tears and mouth compressed into a white line, probably to hold in the pain.

"What's wrong? What happened?"

Without speaking, he drew me into his arms and put his face in my hair. His arms were so tight, it almost hurt, but I wrapped my own around his waist, holding him just as fiercely. I could barely breathe against his chest, but that didn't matter, either, given how he was shaking.

We stood like that for countless minutes before he calmed enough to take my hand and lead me upstairs. I understood we were going to talk, and it seemed better to let him tell me in his own time, though fear was silently chewing through my stomach lining and starting on my spleen. Rob settled in one of the chairs and pulled me onto his lap; it was like he couldn't deal unless he was touching me. I threaded my hand through his hair, stroking lightly.

"Just tell me. We'll figure it out, okay? I promise."

"Okay, so…for the last two weeks, I've been going with my dad t-to the doctor. I didn't know, but…he was diagnosed with Parkinson's last year. My mom couldn't get the time off work to drive him this time, so they had to tell me." From his bleak, taut expression, that stung, like he was a last resort.

I suspected they'd done it not to upset him or to spare him pain, but for Rob, it had to feel like a vote of no confidence. "Oh, God, I'm sorry."

Shit. Oh, shit. I wonder if Nadia knows. I hope she's okay.

"He's been trying different treatments to control it. But it looks like he probably won't be on the job too much longer. The worst part is, I saw him every day at work this summer. And I never noticed anything was wrong. A better son, a smarter one, would have. And my mom wouldn't be so fuck-ing scared and exhausted if she could rely on me."

"They did come to you." I kissed his forehead, realizing nothing I said would get through right now.

"Only when there was no other choice. I'm surprised they didn't fucking call Nadia and ask her to transfer."

"If your dad loses his job, they won't be able to afford her tuition."

"Trust me, I know. And if I earned more money, I could help her. Help *them*. But in the last ten days, it's been made painfully clear how little they expect of me."

"Is that what's bothering you?"

"Everything is. I think about how long my dad will suffer.

From what I've been able to figure out, there's no telling how bad it will get, and there are so many potential problems. I'm *fucking terrified* of losing him, even if I hate him sometimes for thinking I'm a stupid, worthless jackass, no good at anything that matters. And I can't stand that I was just whining to you about him, like a sack of shit, when he and my mom w-were…" He put his face in my throat, so I couldn't see when he broke down, but I felt the tears hot and damp against my skin.

The words clotted in the back of my throat. Really, what the hell could I say? And maybe it was more important to listen. He shook in my arms for over half an hour, according to the changing programs on the flickering TV. I held him and stroked his back until his breathing steadied. This was deep, uncharted territory; I'd never been the person a guy called when he was drowning and desperately needed someone to pull him back to shore. Rob's vulnerability made me feel stronger, like I *could* tread water as long as he needed me to, because there was no way I'd let him go under.

I'm the jackass. I should've known there was a reason he didn't call. It wasn't sex. It wasn't the dumb joke I made. It was serious.

Though I'd tried to have faith in him, my dad did screw me up. In the back of my mind, I knew this about men—*when shit gets tough, they bail.* Most of me fought that conditioning, and I honestly wanted to give Rob a chance. He might not be perfect, but from what I'd seen, he was honest and he didn't run.

I hope.

"Why didn't you tell me before?" I asked eventually. "Before you disappeared."

He raised his face to meet my gaze, a touch of regret lingering there. His lashes were tangled and wet, eyes bruised from sleepless nights. This was the face of someone who wanted to save his family but didn't know how. "My parents asked me not to mention it. They're afraid if word gets back to the company, my dad will be fired as a safety risk."

"It's a reasonable concern," I admitted.

My tone must've revealed my ambivalence because he added, "I'm so sorry. But I couldn't see you without you realizing something was really wrong."

"Would that've been so bad? I'd never repeat anything if you asked me not to."

"Not even to Nadia?"

Tough call. I hesitated, torn between my loyalty to her and the desperate appeal in his eyes. She'd been my best friend since we were seven…but in the end, I said, "Fine. The news should come from your mom and dad anyway, not me. That would just hurt her more. When *are* they planning to tell her?"

"Closer to the end of the semester," Rob answered. "Dad was hoping he'd be able to work longer, but he's not even driving these days."

"Maybe he could train for some other kind of work."

"My mom said that, but he's pretty pissed off at the world right now. I would be, too."

Damn. Rob losing coordination, tremors, physical weakness…it would be devastating because he felt like he didn't have anything else to compensate. I clutched a handful of his hair, silently corralling my dread. If I let it, my messed-up brain would chase demons down a rabbit hole and fixate on Rob ending up with the same diagnosis, years from now.

"So you got their permission to explain things?"

Rob shook his head. "I just… I couldn't carry it alone anymore."

"You don't have to. You know that, right? I won't let on to your folks that you spilled."

"I know. God, I missed you." He pressed a tender kiss to

my forehead, then he put his head down on my shoulder with an exhausted sigh.

A tiny corner of me wondered if he'd known about the impending doctor visits. Maybe that was preying on his mind when he'd dropped me off? But this wasn't the time to grill him about my doubts and bruised feelings. In this situation, there was only one thing to do.

"I hope it's okay if I stay over," I said. "Because I'm not leaving you tonight."

CHAPTER ELEVEN

"I was hoping you'd say that." Rob eased me to the floor and stood up. "There's a spare toothbrush in the bathroom, and you can use it first if you want to get ready...or whatever."

Though I wasn't completely sure what he meant, I hoped he was talking about bed and not fooling around because that seemed like a bad idea, given everything he'd just unloaded on me. People made reckless decisions when they were upset, and I didn't want to be a mistake that made Rob cringe down the line. I brushed by him to use the bathroom and when I got back, he gave me a shirt to sleep in, one of his, obviously, so that was one teen fantasy fulfilled.

I crawled into bed and clicked the remote until I found an old movie. When Rob got back, I was propped up on his pillows, scowling at Goldie Hawn and Kurt Russell. This movie was my crack; I disapproved of so many things about it yet anytime it came on, I had to watch it.

"Overboard?" he asked.

"It's so wrong that I can't help but love it."

"Yeah, it's all wrong plus wrong equals true love."

"You've seen it?"

"More than once," he admitted.

I patted the bed. "Then hop in. He's about to convince her that she's his wife."

Rob seemed better than he had when I first got there, less on the edge. As he got under the covers, he said, "Thanks for coming over. I'm surprised, though. I figured you'd be an anger ball, after what happened between us at your place and then silence."

"I was. Then I was hurt. But none of that mattered as much as the fact that you needed me. It's kind of nice that somebody does."

Without replying, he wrapped his arms around me and settled me against his chest. I had never been a big snuggler, but maybe the wrong guys had been holding me. Up until this point, I didn't care to stick around after sex; I was always the one making an excuse and tiptoeing out before the sweat dried. Yet here I was in Rob's bed without the promise of an orgasm to keep me here. *How about that.*

Though it wasn't that late, he fell asleep before the movie ended, freeing me to gaze at his face close up. His beauty was really remarkable, enough that it was startling when you compared him to the rest of his family. Nadia, my best friend, was striking, but not gorgeous, and his parents were both average. I ran my fingers down the line of his nose, traced his mouth lightly and then brushed the hair away from his forehead. He let out a little sigh and pulled me closer. There was no way I could sleep with my face smashed into his chest, though, so I wriggled until he let me roll. Spooning would be better, or at least I presumed so. I'd never slept with anyone before.

I stayed up late enough for Goldie and Kurt to unlock their happy ending and then I turned the TV off and tried to sleep, but I was wired, both from comforting Rob *and* being in the same bed with him. At home, I'd masturbate to relax, but that seemed dirty and wrong. Obviously, the fact that it was forbidden only made me want it more. His body was big and warm behind me; his arms felt heavy and possessive. That turned me on, too.

If I'm quiet, he'll never know. Challenge accepted.

Feeling like a perv, I eased my fingers into my panties. *Yeah, already wet.* Around Rob, it didn't take much to light me up, and it had been that way since before I was old enough to understand what I was feeling. It was important not to moan, no matter how good it felt. I couldn't breathe loud or move around too much. Hell, I might not even be able to come under these conditions, but I had to try, or I'd lay here all night.

Tensing my thighs, I strummed my clit, working the juices around until it was so hard not to react. But the need for silence made it even hotter. *Can't believe I'm doing this.* The fact that Rob was holding me added another layer of delicious tension. I rubbed harder, all but riding my hand, though the sideways angle hampered me somewhat. Not insurmountable, as the rising pleasure proved. *So good.* As I came in silent gasps, his arms tightened.

"You okay?" Sleepy voice.

"Mhm." My muscles went lax, and sleep rushed in like the ocean at high tide.

In the morning, I woke to the sound of someone pounding on the door. Rob jolted up beside me, and I scrambled into my pants, then followed him down the stairs. He was wearing only a pair of boxer shorts, so I stopped him. "Get dressed. I'll stall whoever it is."

Fearing it was his parents with more bad news, I opened the door with some trepidation. Instead, my mom was waiting on the porch, wearing a sheepish look. "I need the car. Stuart stayed over last night, but he needs to get back to Edison, so…"

Though I wasn't ordinarily the blushing type, heat washed my cheeks over the awkwardness of this moment. There was no telling what my mom suspected I'd been doing last night, and she was looking everywhere but at me. I rubbed a rueful hand against my cheek, but I didn't clarify. I'd promised Rob I would keep his dad's secret.

"Shit, sorry. What time is it?" I asked.

"Just past nine."

Summoning some composure, I said, "Let me get the keys."

"Rob can bring you home later?"

He appeared behind me in time to hear the question. "Definitely, it's not a problem. I hope you weren't worried?"

"No, she left a note." Her half smile said she thought the evening had gone much different than it had, but clearing up her misconceptions wasn't a big priority. "See you later, Lauren."

I handed over the keys and waved at Stuart, who was parked in the drive. He lifted a hand, then blew a kiss to my mom, who hurried down the front steps to claim a real one before letting him back out. Then she took off with a wave for Rob and me. My breath showed in puffs of white, so I was shivering by the time I shut the door.

He wrapped his arms around me, anchoring me against his chest to warm me up. "That wasn't as bad as it could've been."

"She likes you. I admit, it's hard not to. So what's on the agenda today?"

"I'm working on the house for a while, then I have dinner with my mom and dad." His expression said he wasn't looking forward to it.

"Am I allowed to tag along?" The offer burst out before I could stop it.

"Do you want to?"

I pinned on a look of faux good cheer. "I can't think of anything I'd like more."

Rob laughed. "Too far. But if you could stand coming, it would take some of the pressure off me. That way, they can't talk about certain things."

"Because they think I don't know."

"Exactly."

"So let's do it. Do you mind swinging by my mom's so I can change before we head to Casa Conrad? What I wore over here is crumpled from being on your floor all night."

"Are you *trying* to be distracting?" he demanded.

"That depends. Is it working?"

"Only always. I woke up last night wanting you, and I still do. Since you came back, I've been hard so much that I'm thinking about seeing a doctor."

"No need. It's normal for a guy your age to have certain... urges."

"All the damn time?" he grumbled, but there was a playful light in his eyes.

"I'm willing to take you on," I answered. "It'll be exhausting, but I can train up."

"It's too early for you to be this cute." Rob kissed my forehead and went into the kitchen to make breakfast while I headed up to shower.

No clean underwear, so I went without. I considered mentioning this over breakfast in his room, but that would mean that nothing got done on the house. Yet maybe I should give him the choice. As we ate, I said, "So the way I see it, we can be good worker ants today. Or...we can go back to bed since you don't have anywhere to be until tonight."

His fork paused partway to his mouth. "What?"

"It's just a question of priorities," I teased. "Are you a hedonist or a pragmatist?"

"Explain."

I realized I'd used a couple of words he didn't know and not given enough context for him to figure it out. "A hedonist lives for pleasure. A pragmatist puts work first."

"Hmm." His expression didn't reveal the shame I'd noticed before, however. Such a relief; it would kill me if I hurt his feelings all the time.

"So which is it?"

"Would you think it's weird if I want to work on the house?"

I shook my head. "Though I'm wondering why."

Rob chewed his lip for a few seconds before admitting, "I'm enjoying the anticipation. Once we have sex, all the questions will be answered, but right now, we can imagine anything. Everything. While waiting is making me nuts, I...like it, too." His gaze captured mine, so darkly, beautifully blue, like a building storm.

We'd definitely have blue-eyed babies.

"Then I'm curious why you let me—"

"Jerk me off? I needed that, Lauren. You have no idea how much. But I want to take my time with the rest."

I'll make it good for you. I'll just put it in a little. Come on, you know you want it. Lines I'd heard from other guys flashed into my head, and my cheeks heated as I imagined using them on Rob. How odd, fighting the impulse to pressure a guy for sex.

"Okay, remodeling it is."

He hesitated, obviously concerned. "Are you disappointed?"

"Of course not. You're not a stud horse. If we fuck, you should be ready emotionally and want it every bit as much as I do."

"When," Rob said softly. "Not if. But I need to get my

head on straight first. I did just break up with Avery, and I was with her for all the wrong reasons. Now there's this shit with my family, and I don't want to use you as an escape hatch."

I shivered a little as his knuckles grazed my cheek. "What if I'm okay with being used?"

"You shouldn't be."

Dammit, he was right, and it was so sweet, I couldn't stand it. "Then let's make some progress on the house."

We worked for six hours, then Rob dropped me off at home to get ready for dinner. "I'll be back in an hour. Is that long enough?"

I grinned. "If it's not, you'll have to wait."

"Deal."

My mom came home while I was in the shower. She yelled something up at me but I couldn't catch it, so I shouted back, "Give me ten minutes."

It was more like half an hour, but I eventually came down in my robe, only to find Stuart and a couple of elderly people sitting in our living room. The woman was in a pretty floral dress while the men had on suits, and my mother looked beautiful with a new strand of pearls around her neck. Stuart's eyes widened slightly while the woman blinked and the older man shifted his face away as if he was distressed by my dishevelment. Glancing down, I saw my robe had gaped open and I hauled it shut quickly, my hands shaking. They didn't speak for several beats, leaving me with a sick hole opening in my stomach. "Uh, hi."

My mom wore the frozen look of a woman bound for purgatory. "Lauren, these are Stuart's parents. We're all going out to dinner at the Grove."

Humiliation nearly choked me, but fortunately, social, Party Lauren surged to the fore. There was nothing for it but to play the scene without proper costuming. "So nice to meet you. I hope you have a wonderful time. The food is fantastic there. But if you'll excuse me, I have to finish getting ready now. I'm so sorry for coming down like this. I didn't realize we had company." I flashed the smile I'd been told was pert and charming and then retreated.

For a full five minutes, I sat in a ball in front of my closed door, as my stomach roiled. I didn't budge until I heard them leave. I fought the urge to bang my head on the wall, but no time for that—Rob would be here in twenty minutes, and I was spending the evening with his parents, a task that seemed fucking impossible. I tried, God, I *tried* to pull myself together before he got there, but I was still in my robe and on the verge of tears when the bell rang.

I tiptoed downstairs, knees shaking. *If they haven't left yet…* But there was nobody around, freeing me to let Rob in. When I opened the door, he asked, "Are you okay?"

His gaze was fixed on my face, so it couldn't be the robe giving him the impression I was a mess. In a breathless rush, I told him about making an ass out of myself in front of Stuart's parents. This was the kind of thing normal people wrote off. They shrugged and went on, but if I let it, it would become another brick of anxiety in the wall that made me terrified of going places, talking to people. Each humiliating moment stuck to me like glue, a lifetime of fuckups that was driving me crazy, until I became someone else. But I couldn't stand that life, either.

By the time I finished, I was just about crying. Rob didn't try to shush me. He didn't tell me to calm down, either. He just picked me up and carried me to the couch, then settled me against his chest and stroked my back in long, slow sweeps. His touch calmed me faster than anything besides meds ever had. Normally I'd just go to bed and stay there for a day or two. He also didn't mock how much I was overreacting to a small embarrassment, but the thing was, it wasn't like I didn't *know* that intellectually—some things just felt so horrible, I couldn't do anything else.

"Is there any way I can make it better?" he asked eventually.

I exhaled. "You already are."

"You don't have to go tonight, it's okay. I don't—"

"No, I want to. Unless you can't give me fifteen minutes?" Pushing to my feet, I aimed a questioning look his way, a little worried that he didn't want me around, now that he'd seen my Achilles' heel. I mean, I'd talked about it, but just hearing secondhand wasn't the same as walking into a meltdown.

"I'd give you fifteen years," he said quietly.

Please stop saying things like that. You're making it so hard for teen-me. She already thought you were perfect, and it's really hard to disagree.

"Okay, then. I'll be right down."

I rushed in getting ready, doing the minimum hair and makeup and pulling on the first decent outfit I found: jeans, red sweater, puffy jacket. By the time I added a pair of fur-lined boots, my time was almost up, and I ran down the stairs to find Rob watching TV calmly. He didn't seem to have stirred, but my agitated subconscious had been sure he'd dodge out as soon as he had the chance. *That's what men do, they leave.*

But maybe not all of them. Not Rob.

When he noticed me, he pushed to his feet. "You look beautiful. Ready?"

"Are your parents expecting me?" The worst of the shaking had stopped, and though I normally wouldn't go out after freaking, it was good to push through it when possible.

"Yeah, I called to tell my mom and to let her know I'd be a little late."

He helped me into my jacket and escorted me to the truck, but as far as I could tell, his manner hadn't changed much;

Rob wasn't more protective or less, failing to make eye contact or staring at me too much. That was kind of…amazing.

"You don't think I'm an idiot?" I managed to ask, once we pulled out of the driveway.

"You're human. Would you make fun of me if you found out I was scared of spiders?"

"Are you?" I wondered aloud.

"Kind of. When I was a kid, I woke up with one crawling on my face, and I screamed the house down. My dad's never let me forget it to this day."

"Well, I'm not afraid, so if we run into any, I'll handle them for you. I'm not a killer, though, so I'll just put them outside."

"Where they'll freeze to death," he joked.

"Probably. But I just don't have it in me to crush things."

"That's part of what I…" He trailed off, suddenly absorbed in navigation, though he could likely find his parents' house in his sleep.

"What?"

"Like about you." But he didn't look at me as he said it, and I had the feeling that was a substitution. But Rob didn't *love* me. He couldn't.

It's too soon.

Though that was the wrong word also, since we'd known each other so long. Whatever this was had been years in the making. Deliberately I turned up the radio, giving him space. He relaxed visibly, and things were normal between us when we pulled up at Casa Conrad. His mom was already in the door, waving, like it had been months since she'd seen him. She was sweet and affectionate that way.

"So good to see you. What a surprise. How's Nadia doing?"

I didn't have the heart to admit that I talked to Rob a lot more these days. I missed Nadia so much. Like she'd said, we had been together, inseparable, for years, so the separation sucked. Lately I woke up wanting to whisper to her like we used to, but instead I had an empty room. Sometimes I got up to reread her emails. The distance between us had started because I couldn't admit my real problems to her, and I had no idea how to fix things, how to get back to where we were.

So I said, "Last I knew, she's insanely busy with school, work and the practicum. I don't know how she does it." Nadia was already working with special needs students a few days a week, and it sounded taxing.

Mrs. Conrad beamed. "I know. We're so proud of her."

At my back, Rob stiffened, and I had to wonder how often he'd heard that. Time to change the subject. "What's for dinner? Something smells wonderful."

"Homemade potpies—do you like them?" she asked, ushering me into the house.

"It would be impossible not to. It's so cool of you to feed me. My mom's quite the social butterfly these days."

"So I hear. You'll have to tell me all about Stuart. She's too busy to gossip like we used to. Oh, dang, I need to..." Mrs. Conrad hurried to the kitchen with a mumbled request for us to take a seat.

There, that wasn't so bad. My anxiety receded. For him, I could do this, even tonight.

Rob pressed a hand between my shoulder blades to draw my attention and when I glanced up, he smiled. I glimpsed an ocean of gratitude in his blue eyes.

CHAPTER TWELVE

A week and a half later, I'd survived both dinner with Rob's parents and my first few days on the job. As expected, my new boss was kind of a pervert, but the woman I was replacing explained some tricks for keeping him in check, like never being alone with him behind closed doors and helping the sales and garage crew as much as possible.

"Why?" I asked.

Shelly paused in packing up her desk. This was the last day she'd be working with me. After today, I was on my own. "If the salesmen and the mechanics like you, they'll step in if they see Davies bothering you."

"Step in, how?"

"Ask you for a file or to make a call, maybe a cup of coffee."

"Ah, so I have an excuse to leave."

She nodded. "It's not like you're the manager's personal assistant. You're expected to support the dealership as needed."

"Are you leaving because you can't put up with it anymore?"

"Nope. I'm moving to Omaha. My fiancé and I got transferred."

"Well, good luck."

Before Shelly left, they threw a farewell party for her with sparkling cider and cupcakes—and the guys from the service center seemed really bummed, which told me I had big shoes to fill. But all told, it wasn't that much different from working in the fine arts building. As the days passed, the work didn't offer any challenges I couldn't handle, and I was making progress with the stick shift.

It was Tuesday night, and I was on my way home from a successful day at the dealership. All things considered, I was in a good mood, though I missed hanging out with Rob. He'd texted earlier to tell me that he'd finished the dining room completely. Though it was March, it was still cold enough to snow, as proved by the whiteness spluttering down. My phone buzzed.

Get milk, my mom ordered.

"Yes, ma'am." I pulled into the Stop & Go parking lot, along with four other cars. In another two minutes, I would've passed the store.

After the deepening dusk outside, the lights were so bright that I stood for a few seconds blinking as I wiped my feet. A red-haired woman had her back to me, browsing the snack shelves. From behind, she was slender and graceful, even bundled for cold weather. *I have a bad feeling about this.* As if she sensed me looking at her, she turned—and across the racks of pastries and engine oil, I locked eyes with Avery Jacobs.

Seeing her with Rob last Thanksgiving had driven me crazy. I'd gone out of my way to avoid her; we hadn't exchanged more than ten words. But seeing her now that she was Rob's ex wasn't any better, especially when I compared us. There was no question she was beautiful: tall and slim, natural red hair, stunning features and cool green eyes. Girls had whispered they must be contacts, but if you peered close enough, there was no telltale ring. Her hair was a little shorter, a few more layers, and if anything, she was even thinner than she had been in November.

Shit. Well, this will be awkward. I swung my gaze away and headed for the freezer at the back of the store. Gallon of milk, coming up. But before I could open it, someone grabbed my arm. I didn't need to turn around to know who it was.

Pulling free, I said, "Hey, Avery. I didn't know you were back in town."

"How can you stand yourself?" she demanded.

"Excuse me?" There was an old man trying to get past me to the beer, so I sidestepped, coming up against the hot dog-and-nacho counter.

"You crashed and burned in Michigan, and then, it wasn't enough to ruin *your* life, you had to take a run at mine, too."

"Look, whatever your friend told you, I have nothing to do with any problems you had with Rob." It seemed best to get it out in the open.

"Bullshit. My cousin saw him kissing you at the Grove."

Fucking small town. No question, this looked bad, but I refused to accept the home-wrecker tiara. Whatever my feelings for Rob, I'd indulged none of them while he was taken. "*After* you broke up, because you accused him of cheating."

"So *I* gave him the idea? Rob's slow, but he's not clueless. In other words, fuck you."

I sighed. My feet hurt, and my mom was waiting for the damn milk. "How, exactly, do you see this conversation ending?"

"With you admitting that you're a bitch and a blight on womankind."

With some effort, I swallowed a scorching retort, mostly because we were attracting an audience. "Agree to disagree. If you'll excuse me—" She wrenched on my arm, whirling me around, and it fucking *hurt*. "Get your hands off me."

"Don't walk away. I'm not done talking."

"Well, I am."

"Don't you think you owe me something after stealing my boyfriend? Everyone knows you're desperate, a college drop-out." Her gaze dropped to my stomach. "Oh, I see. You're hoping to trick poor Rob into thinking the kid's his."

"Nice. And *I'm* the bitch in this situation?" I spoke the *b*-word deliberately, and she reacted by slapping me so hard I saw stars.

Lifting a palm, I touched my cheek incredulously. "Did you seriously just hit me?"

She opened her mouth to reply, but before she could, I smacked her back. No turning the other cheek. I tried to be fucking reasonable; I tried to leave, but no. She was furious and wanted to kick my ass. *So fine, bring it.* Avery grabbed my hair and pulled, so I yanked on her earrings. She landed a kick on my shins, which was so third-grade that I rolled my eyes. I stumbled back and laid hands on a cold tray of abandoned nachos. When she came at me, I flung it at her and burst out laughing at her murderous expression as the goopy orange cheese slid down her pretty blue jacket.

"That's enough out of you crazy bitches," the cashier shouted. "Keep it up and I call the cops. How'd you like that?"

Avery's eyes narrowed. She glanced between me and the redneck behind the register. "What did you say to me?"

"I'm wondering if you want to repeat it, too." I picked up a jar from the aisle next to me. "Because if I heard you right, I'm about to get crazy with the Cheez Whiz."

Other customers were backing out of the store, and when Avery grabbed a withered old hot dog off the rack like it was a lethal weapon, the clerk actually cowered. What he thought she could do to him with that, I feared to ask. Tonight, I would not be buying milk, obviously. Weighing the situation, I took a few breaths, wondering what Avery would do. She was still glaring at the cashier. I picked up a handful of napkins and wiped the crap off her coat while everyone watched. In my opinion, we'd created enough of a scene.

"Let's get out of here," I said.

"No shit."

Outside, Avery stood, breathing hard, with one fist still clenched around that desiccated wiener. I was surprised when she didn't immediately tackle me and shove me face-first into the dirty snow. Instead, she hurled it into a distant bank and impressed me, reluctantly, when it sank in to make it look like a phallic Jabba the Hut. Then she let out a bloodcurdling yell. When she spun toward me, I braced for round two, but she didn't rush me. She only stared.

"*What?*" I demanded. "You want to trash me some more?"

"Why did you have to ruin everything?" Her plaintive tone made me feel horrible.

I could handle her fury, but the idea that she might be hurting bothered me. Though it was technically true I didn't cheat with Rob, I'd wanted him while they were together and I'd bonded with him emotionally while she was gone. I couldn't feel 100 percent good about the situation. Maybe I could explain, set the record straight.

No peace of mind until I try.

"We didn't finish up in there. You want to go to Patty's for coffee? I'm buying."

She looked like she thought this was a trick, but then she did a double-take, staring over at my ride. "Is that…Rob's old truck?"

"Yeah. You can take your car."

Then she made a quick decision. "Okay. See you there."

At this hour, people were crowded into the lobby because Patty made awesome pancakes and sometimes the only thing right in life was eating breakfast for dinner. Luckily, I got there in time to snag the last two-person booth and Avery hurried in a few minutes later. She shucked off her stained jacket with a grimace. I felt bad.

"Sorry about that."

"I lost my shit. It could be argued that I had it coming."

Before we could say more, the waitress came to take our order. I got the pancake special and coffee, figuring it had been that kind of day. Avery was more carb-conscious and went for salad and hot tea. No wonder she was a sylph.

"Okay, let's try this again. Without slapping, hair pulling or projectile food."

She nodded. "But if you tell me nothing's going on with you and Rob, I'm leaving. Because it's not really about him anyway. It's…"

"What?"

"You just don't *do* that, you know?" By *that,* I guessed she meant screw somebody else's boyfriend. "What I had with him wasn't perfect, but he was mine."

So she was sad that Rob had broken up with her; her ego was bruised more than her heart, but I understood her feelings. In her situation, I'd be upset, too.

Reality could be so hard to explain. "Let me lay it out for you. Have I been half in love with Rob for most of my life? Fuck, yeah. In fact, it's kind of embarrassing. But that kiss your cousin saw? It was the first time he touched me like that. After you broke up. You don't have any reason to believe me, but hey, I have no reason to lie. We're *not* friends, so if I wanted to hurt you, I'd say we did it like monkeys the whole time your back was turned. I'm honestly trying to clear the air, swear to God."

"So…I just hurt him by assuming the worst? I mean, when Jillian saw you together before, that was seriously just driving lessons?"

I nodded. "Before that happened, he never talked about breaking up. He was yours, not mine. And I was jealous, but I wouldn't do that. To anyone."

She tilted her head. "Why not? I'm the town bitch, remember? Nobody likes me because I think I'm better than everyone else."

It didn't surprise me that she knew what people said about her. Avery had an unpleasant personality, and she was never shy about expressing dissatisfaction. I suspected her attitude might be a front, though I had no idea what it was covering.

"That doesn't mean you don't deserve to be happy."

For a few seconds, she just stared at me. "Are you for real?"

"Most of the time. Except for Wednesdays, when I'm imaginary."

The laugh started in her eyes, popped out of her mouth in an actual giggle. When she unwound, Avery wasn't bad. Didn't mean I wanted her dating Rob, but maybe she wasn't as awful as everyone claimed. Just then, our food arrived, curtailing the conversation for a moment. I dug into my pancakes, as it seemed like a long time since lunch.

She played with her salad for a few minutes. "I'm sorry I hit you."

"Sorry I hit you back. And about the nachos."

A smirk curved her mouth. "Actually, the whole thing was kind of fun. I've never been in a fight before. My parents would die."

"Not very ladylike," I admonished. "Think of your dignity, Avery."

"I will cram my dignity down the throat of the next person who mentions it."

"Ouch. But I get the feeling you're not this angry about Rob—that it's more of a symptom. You want to tell me what's going on?"

Startled, she cocked her head. "Ten minutes ago, you said we're not friends."

"No, but we could be. If you want." The impulsive words surprised me as much as her, but she had such a lonely look there for a minute that I couldn't help it.

Hesitating, she murmured, "I'm not sure how it works. I stopped making new friends years ago."

"No offense, but that's kind of sad." *And that's coming from someone who finds it a chore to go to a party with new people.*

"I know."

"So explain your deal. Why are you stuck in Sharon and why are you so mad about it?"

She was the kind of girl everyone expected to blast out of town at the speed of light, head to an Ivy League school and never come back unless somebody died. Maybe not even then. Instead, she'd gotten a job at the bank straight out of high school, and she was living at home. From what I re-membered, something had happened our senior year, but her family hushed it up and nobody ever knew exactly why she missed two weeks of school.

"It's my own fault," she said quietly. "Everything is."

That was the last thing I expected to hear. "What?"

"Never mind. This was a bad idea." She stood up, leaving most of her salad untouched.

"Avery?"

"If you seriously want to be my friend, the first thing you'll learn is not to ask certain questions because I won't answer."

"It sounds like you have no friends at all," I said gently. "Because even I can tell something's eating at you."

"I thought Rob might get me out of here, that's all. Thanks for dinner."

"Did it ever occur to you that you don't need a guy for that? You're more than smart enough to go on your own."

"Spoken like someone who has *no* idea."

"Did Rob?" I asked.

She shook her head, already turning for the door. "Are you kidding? No. It was always easier to focus on his faults than mine. Tell him I'm sorry, by the way. And…I hope you guys can make it work." With that, she was gone.

Confused as hell, I ate my pancakes in silence. A few minutes later, the waitress brought the check, wearing a conspiratorial look. "Dinner with Avery Jacobs? Did you lose a bet?"

Huh. God, if people talked about me that way all over town, I'd probably turn into exactly what they expected of me—a giant, snarling bitch. My brows went down. "Do you talk about *all* of your customers like this?"

She flushed. "Sorry. Let me get your change."

After she brought it, I hurried out to the truck, where I remembered I had no milk. Belatedly I texted my mom back: sorry, something came up.

Rob?

Wow. Where the hell did she find *that* emoticon? I tilted my head, both revolted and impressed.

We are not having this conversation.

It took some finesse to start the truck in this weather, but I got it running, then I called Rob. "Do you mind if I come by tonight?"

"Please. I miss you." The simple words took the sting out of the rest of the day, long and confusing as it had been.

We needed to talk about so many things, but right now, Avery seemed the most pressing. I drove carefully from the pancake house out to his place. The trees overhead made it extracreepy, and I heaved a long sigh when I parked outside his house. Before I could get out, the garage opened, and Rob waved me in. Since the space was clean, I didn't hit anything.

God, he was sweet. He gathered me close as soon as I hopped out. I could've stood in his arms forever, but the cold air made me shiver.

"You know you don't need to call, right? You can come over anytime you want."

"Yeah?"

Ignoring the rhetorical question, he shrugged out of his jacket and wrapped it over the top of my head, then led us toward the front door. "Go inside. I'll close up out here."

As ever, the house was warm and inviting. First off, I noticed how gorgeous the dining room looked. He'd painted the walls according to sample cards I'd picked out, a sunny hue that complemented the natural wood. Now he had a table in place, and I recognized his handiwork in the craftsmanship. If I knew him at all, his home would end up like a showroom full of samples that people could admire and covet, just as I had with his bed.

You're smarter than anyone gives you credit for. Even you.

"Beautiful," I said as he closed the door behind me.

"I was just thinking that." Only I could tell he wasn't talking about the room.

I fought a blush. When I turned, getting my first good look at him, I stumbled in shock. "What happened?"

"Oh, this?" Sheepish, he touched a hand to his split and

swollen lip. "Avery came by earlier. I thought she wanted to talk, but she popped me in the mouth and stomped off."

"Wow. Well, I don't think you'll have any problems with her in the future."

Alarmed amusement flickered in his expression. "You didn't kill her, did you?"

Quietly I summed up the encounter, and he touched my cheek gently, tilting my face toward the light. "God, I'm sorry she went off. Our breakup wasn't your fault."

"I wasn't sorry about it, and I didn't exactly wait the usual cooling-off period before I was making out with you in public."

"You're exaggerating that kiss," he chided.

"I'm not. You don't even know how long I waited for it."

"Since I just finished *The Fallen Throne,* I think I do."

Oh, God. "You kept reading that?"

"Every word. It's my favorite book now."

The quip nearly popped out—*how many books have you read*? Meant as self-deprecation, but that wasn't how Rob would take it. So I swallowed the urge to take refuge in humor as a defense mechanism. With him, it was worth some discomfort to meet my emotions head-on.

"I am awash in humiliation," I said honestly. "But…I'm happy, too, because you actually liked my adolescent ramblings."

"It helps that I'm the star." He brushed his lips tenderly against my temple.

A shiver ran through me, and I rose up on tiptoes to give the kiss back. I placed it on the sharp curve of his jaw. *God, he has a gorgeous profile.* Objectively speaking, I wasn't hot enough for people to understand why he'd want me. I still couldn't believe he did.

"You missed a spot." He pointed to the other side of his face, and I nuzzled him.

His lashes drifted down, giving him a sleepy, sexy look. Then he pulled me closer, leaving no doubt as to how he felt. I pressed against him with a little whimper. *Impossible to believe this is Rob and me.* His hands drifted to my hips.

"You're making it really hard to take things slow."

I grinned. "I could say the same."

Rob cleared his throat and stepped back. "So…" That reminded me of why I was here. Not for sex.

Please, sex? No, I'm being patient. Dammit.

"Right. I really came by to ask…do you mind if I make friends with Avery? Would that be weird for you?" In the name of honesty, I had to add, "Even if it is, I'll probably do it anyway. But it'll be over your noted objections."

"I guess I'm wondering why, more than anything. She can be…difficult." That was such a Rob way to put it.

"She seems really alone. And I don't know—I guess it feels like Jillian wins if her making shit up results in Avery hating me forever. I want something good to come out of that badness. Does that make any sense?"

"Yeah. I hope you can get through to her. God knows I never did." He struggled to find the words, but not in a way that seemed to trouble him. "With us, it seemed like she was always playing a role, performing even when we were alone."

"I know all about that," I muttered.

High school had been a nightmare. The first two years, I was sick so much, I nearly got held back. But it wasn't an illness a doctor could cure, though therapists tried. Only my mom yelling about emotional trauma in her housecoat convinced the principal to let me do summer school instead. After my sophomore year, I decided, *no more. No more of this. I hate Lauren Barrett, I hate everything about her.* So I changed her clothes, her attitude, her hair, her *fear,* pulled myself into a different shape and lived in that skin for five long years. I rarely wrote fan fiction, stopped playing on the computer for hours. The worst thing about that? Nobody questioned it. Nobody—not even Nadia—said, *Wow, what's wrong? You're not yourself.* It was more like everyone heaved a collective sigh of relief and thought, *Thank God, she's finally normal.*

"You don't do it, though. Not with me."

"That's because you're my safe place, Rob. You always have been."

He sucked in a sharp breath, his eyes kindling to an electric-blue that curled my toes. "That's the best thing anyone's ever said to me."

CHAPTER THIRTEEN

"It's the truth," I said.

"I know." He reached for me then, and I settled against his chest; it felt like coming home after a long journey. "And in case it wasn't clear, I don't mind about Avery."

Since she'd just punched him in the mouth over something he didn't do, that comment spoke volumes about the type of guy Rob was. I slipped my arms around his waist and hugged him, inhaling his rich, layered scent. Other guys might smell of expensive cologne, but he was all wood dust and the faint chemical scent of the product he used to seal the floors. There was also a touch of mint from his soap each time he moved his hands on my back, making me think he'd just washed them.

"Thanks. I was wondering…would you be open to an idea I've been kicking around?"

"Depends on what it is." He ran a gentle hand through my hair, covering me in shivers from head to toe.

Focus. He's not trying to get you hot. It just happens. Or maybe he *was*. Teasing me. He was turned on before, and now that I was holding him again, it was evident he still hadn't calmed down. His desire to take his time was both flattering and frustrating when I contemplated all the delicious, dirty things we could do together instead.

"Now who's a distraction?" I accused.

He actually grinned. "Then my plan's working?"

"If you're trying to drive me crazy, I'm halfway there." As I drew away, I ran my fingers down his chest.

A visible tremor went through him as his hands clenched into fists, showing off the veins and tendons, along with the sexy swell of his biceps. I fought the urge to bite him. Rob's gaze met mine and I forgot to breathe.

He cleared his throat.

"What...what did you want to ask me?"

"You know how you want to design and build furniture? We can get going without a lot of start-up capital."

The question seemed to divert him from the sexual tension, at least. To most people, his expression wouldn't give anything away, but I noticed the sharpening of his focus, a minute tilt of the head, the narrowing of his eyes. "I'm listening."

With effort, I quashed the desire to get him naked immediately and explained my plan to build him a website with a simple merchant system. "You can post pictures of what you've built, then customers can request a similar item. I was also thinking it makes sense for you to start a YouTube channel for cross-promotion of the business. We'll need a catchy name for your 'show'...you can talk about furniture, woodworking, renovations on your house—"

Setting two fingers against my mouth to silence me, he cut in, "Wait, slow down. Why would anyone care?"

It was beyond me to resist the urge to kiss his fingertips. Smiling, Rob let go.

He might not like hearing this, but... "Don't underestimate the interest in hot people on the internet."

"Seriously? You think my face will make people care what I have to say? It hasn't at any point in the last twenty-five years."

"*I* care," I said quietly. "Besides, these are strangers with no preconceptions. They'll start watching because, hello, look at you, but it's your message that will make them come back."

For a few moments, he paced, wearing a thoughtful, conflicted expression. I could tell he thought I was wrong about the potential demand for his skills. But Rob had *no* ability to gauge his own self-worth. Hardly breathing, I waited for his response.

With a sigh, he finally nodded. "If you think it could sell furniture, let's try it."

I understood how big of a leap that was for him. He hated the idea of using his looks to get anywhere, but people wouldn't order a table just because he was gorgeous. They might watch his video channel for that reason…and if he got enough hits, they could be monetized. But we'd talk about secondary revenue streams another time. This was enough for today.

"Awesome. I'll head home and start building the site. I can come back tomorrow to record the vlog, if you don't have plans?"

He shook his head. "I'll be working on the kitchen."

I remembered what he'd said about wanting the dining room done before he finished. "What are you planning to do?"

Fierce enthusiasm fired his words, and as I listened, I realized this was exactly what we needed for his first vlog. I could already imagine it, and if I came back early enough, I could film him working, too. A hot guy with a hammer, ripping cabinets out of the wall would get a ton of hits from a certain demographic. I was less sure if they'd actually order furniture, but even a few sales would boost his confidence.

I hadn't slept over since the night he told me about his dad, mostly because the temptation of sleeping next to Rob was way more than I could handle. I'd already perved out on him once, and I didn't intend to rush him into sex. When we took this to the next level, it had to be his choice, all-in. The timing was already weird because of his breakup with Avery, so if he needed space, I could give it to him.

"Okay, see you in the morning." I stretched up on tiptoe to brush my lips against his cheek, mostly because I'd gotten my fill of being seduced by centimeters. But Rob had other ideas; he circled my waist with his arms and lifted me onto the dining-room table.

"Not so fast, beautiful." He kissed me in a way that left me no doubt as to how much he wanted me, as if the point hadn't been made already several times tonight.

You're killing me.

His bruised mouth seared mine with heat and longing, and he tasted me so thoroughly that I forgot all my plans. His split lip flavored the kiss faintly of copper, and I traced my tongue over the swelling, butterfly-gentle. Sinking my hands into his hair, I kissed him back and wrapped my legs around his hips. He skimmed his palms down my sides, up and down, until I thought I'd die if I didn't take my coat off. As if he'd read my mind, Rob unzipped it and slid warm hands under my sweater. The contrast of his rough palms against my skin sent a shiver through me. For a few seconds, he only touched my sides, my stomach, and I was sixteen again, squirming with the need for a guy to round second base. My nipples peaked with each scrape of his fingertips, teasing higher as he nuzzled the side of my neck.

"Please," I whispered.

My sweater was retro, buttons down the front, and he gazed at my face for a few seconds before he undid them, one by one. I was shivering by the time he bared my bra, a nice one, thank God: black satin, front-fastening. Somehow, it was incredibly hot to be perched on his dining-room table, jacket still on, skirt, tights, shoes…yet undone, as well. This felt…naughty.

"Want me to?"

Wordless, I nodded.

He unhooked my bra, baring my breasts. My jacket and sweater framed them, and I felt—for once in my life—beautiful enough to be photographed, an erotic display. And it was all for him. His eyes flared as if he shared the thought. A dark flush swept his cheekbones as he lowered his head, bringing my nipple to his mouth. The first lick made me cry out, and when he used his teeth, I tangled my hands in his hair.

"Rob," I breathed.

"Be still. Let me taste you."

"Mhm."

I couldn't have argued if my life had depended on it. He sucked and licked, bit gently, back and forth, until both throbbed with equal need. Longing shivered through me, so sharp it sank its teeth in like pain, but I couldn't stand for him to stop. Then, unbelievably, he did, with a final kiss to each of my nipples.

While I trembled, he fastened up my clothes. "There, now you can go."

"Seriously? You want me to leave? *Now?*" God, I sounded so breathless.

"Not at all," he whispered. "But anticipation, remember? By the time we fuck, Lauren, you'll want me more than anyone who's ever been in your bed."

My only consolation was that he was shaking, too, and he clenched his right hand into a fist so tight, his knuckles burned white, like the bone beneath. Trying to tempt him, I blathered something incoherent about that already being true, but he only kissed my forehead and escorted me to the truck. Rob started it, and we sat in the dark cab, waiting for it to warm up.

His sweetness combined with this teasing… Damn, it might be the end of me. I'd never been one for delayed gratification.

It took all my willpower not to beg for sex, so this game he was playing—it was definitely working. My only consolation was that when I leaned over to kiss Rob goodbye, his shoulders were as tense as two slabs of granite. *At least I'm not suffering alone.* That assurance let me drive off, cautiously, into the snowy evening. Twenty minutes later, I pulled into my driveway. My mom's car was there, but the lights were out. I guessed she must be with Stuart.

I changed out of my work clothes, then sat down at my laptop. Over the years, I'd built enough websites that I could do this in my sleep. With stock photos and Photoshop, I pulled together some graphics, then started coding. I hated Flash sites, so I worked in CSS, putting together a basic template in earth tones…*drop-down menu, there we go.* Finally, I added rugged photos of lumber and men at work to set the tone. When I had the chance, I'd take some pictures of Rob to spice things up.

A couple of hours later, I finished the basic template. Products needed to be added to get the storefront working and Rob had to create the content—I figured I'd help. If he liked what I'd done on the free hosting that came with my mom's internet, then I'd register a domain and pay for permanent hosting. Stretching, I stood up from the computer.

After showering, I got in bed to watch TV. I was nearly asleep when the text came in. Thinking of you.

I hoped that was as dirty as my imagination painted it. So I sent back, Me too. And it's SO good. See you in the morning.

The next day, I was eating breakfast when my mom got in, but she wasn't in the same outfit. *So she's got clothes at Stuart's place. Wonder if he has some here.* But it wasn't my business, and I wasn't the kind of person who would freak out about my mom finally having a life. Yet I couldn't resist teasing her a little.

"I hope you were careful. You could ruin your life with an unplanned pregnancy."

She grinned. "Do you really want me to answer that? I will."

"Never mind." God, it was so weird to have my mom responding when I joked around like this. But it was good, too, like seeing a statue come to life. That didn't mean I wanted any more information on this topic, though. So I hurriedly dumped my bowl in the sink and washed it out. "I'm going to Rob's. See you later."

"How are things going?" she asked.

"Good, I guess. He doesn't want to rush."

I let her make of that what she would, but my mom apparently had lines she wouldn't cross, either. "Well, I think it's sweet he's taking things slow."

Aside from the sexual frustration, I didn't really mind. Rob didn't make me feel like his interest would wane as soon as he got into my pants. So in that sense, his approach was working. I already believed he wanted more than my body.

"It's…endearing," I admitted.

"Does tomorrow night work for you?" my mom asked, changing the subject.

I cocked my head, trying to follow the sudden skip. "For what?"

"Karaoke."

Oh. "Rob said yes. I still have to ask everyone else. But for us, sure. Looking forward to it."

"Me, too," Mom said.

Waving to her, I got all my tech gear, bundled up and drove to Rob's place. Though it was early for a Saturday—before ten—he was already watching for me. I parked in the garage as the doors opened, and he helped me unload.

"What is all this?"

"My laptop and a decent camera, plus various cables. I hope you like the site. Oh, and we need to talk about the name. I was thinking 'Rob the Builder' might be cute, but it's also really close to that kid show—"

He cut me off with a kiss. "Good morning."

"Heh, sorry. Morning. I'm just excited."

"You're adorable."

He carried my bag into the house, where I set up my computer so I could walk him through the website features. "It's really customizable, so if there's anything you don't like, it'll be easy for me to change it. Obviously we need to add pictures, content, products, but...what do you think?" I slid the laptop to him so he could explore.

After a few minutes of clicking around, he turned to me with an astonished expression. "This is so impressive. This would've cost thousands of dollars, wouldn't it?"

"Maybe. Hundreds more likely, because I started with a free template, so a lot of the heavy lifting was done. I just—"

"I can tell you worked really hard. I love it. And thank you."

"Awesome. Now I have an idea how we can both get what we want today. While you're working in the kitchen, I want to film you. If possible, unless it'll be too distracting, explain what you're doing as you go. Would that be okay?"

"I don't know why anybody would want to watch that, but sure."

"Trust me," I said.

"I do, more than anyone." The gentleness of his tone made my heart hitch. Somehow, though we'd only slept together in the most literal sense, Rob had burrowed so deep inside me that it was terrifying.

Don't panic, I told myself. *You can rely on him. He's not the leaving kind.*

"After that, we can have lunch and work on fleshing out

the website. My goal is to launch by Monday. I have some ideas on how to promote it. So be ready to take some orders."

"Yes, ma'am."

In a tool belt, Rob was every bit as irresistible as I'd imagined. While he banged away in the kitchen, muscles flexing, he explained to the viewer what he was doing and why. His manner was easy, relaxed, and the camera *loved* him. So did I.

Shit, what…? But it was too late to put that insight back in Pandora's box. This wasn't a crush. It was Lurve. Capital *L. Fuck,* why? My first instinct was to run. My heartbeat went into overdrive and my intestines twisted up in knots. I couldn't even see, let alone inhale, and I almost dropped the camera. *Breathe, breathe.* My palms started sweating.

"Lauren?" Rob had paused, frowning, hammer in hand, and he was coming toward me.

"I'm fine. I'm okay, I'm…awesome."

Oh, God, don't touch me. Not now. I might ravish you.

He cocked a brow, but he was smiling. "I agree."

Then he went back to work. Somehow I silently talked myself into calming down. And because I'd promised him a certain outcome, I finished shooting.

A while later, the mini panic attack dealt with, I checked footage in the window on the back of the camera. "This looks fantastic. Did you come up with a name yet?"

"Unless you think it's stupid, I like Rob the Builder."

"No, it's fine. I don't think there are any copyright issues. But I think that should be limited to your website. Your vlog segment needs a different title."

"'At Home with Rob'?" he suggested.

"Sounds great." I went to work creating the video channel.

"Okay, then. I'll make some lunch."

"Do you mind if I take a few pictures of the furniture you've made?" He had the bed, the dining-room tables, chairs, a few pieces up in his room. "Finished pieces will show better."

"Go for it."

While he browned ground beef, I adjusted the lighting and shot some photos—not professional quality, but hopefully good enough to interest customers who were drawn to unique, handcrafted goods. After I connected the camera to my laptop, I questioned Rob about his goals, which I then typed up on the welcome page. Next I fleshed out the product page with the pictures and brief item descriptions. Now I just needed to write something in the "about" section. Over lunch, Rob helped me with that. His construction résumé was really impressive; he'd worked on a number of huge projects. But people would be more interested in the progress he'd made on the house.

"Do you have any 'before' pictures?"

"Huh?"

"Of the dining room and your bedroom?"

"Oh. Actually, yeah. Let me get my phone."

I uploaded them to my laptop and spiced up the site further with before-and-after shots of the work he'd done. "There we go. That went a lot faster than I expected. Once I edit your vlog, upload it, link your site to the channel, then we'll launch."

"Today?" he asked.

"If I push, yes."

"You're amazing. Do you think anyone will even *see* all your hard work?"

"In time. I've learned a few things online. There are forums, places I can advertise you. It'll take a little money, but it's worth it. Have you been sticking to your budget?"

He frowned at me. "Yes. You're saying I should spend my savings on *this?*"

"Not all, but some. It's worth investing in your dreams, Rob. I believe in you, and you should, too." If he refused, I'd use part of my paycheck and buy the ads myself.

"Okay. Just tell me what to do."

Excited, I leaped up from the table and hugged him. "Just wait, you won't be sorry. If things go like I hope, you'll eventually be able to live on what you earn building furniture. You can set your own hours, be your own boss."

"That would be incredible." My enthusiasm fired his, and he swung me around in his arms, then buried his face in my neck. "I have never, ever been this happy."

His words went to my head like expensive champagne. My throat closed, so I couldn't speak. I just held him as hard as I could.

Rob went on in a whisper, "You're making it *really* hard to wait."

"Good," I said.

I shouldn't be the only one who's sexually frustrated.

"But why *are* you still waiting?" There had to be a reason other than anticipation, and maybe his answer would help me cool off.

His lips moved over my neck, then he bit down gently. The smooth stroke of his palms up and down my spine almost made me forget I'd said anything. But then Rob cleared his throat, drawing back enough that I could see the heat blazing in his blue eyes.

"Because I want to be sure the timing's right and that neither of us has any doubts. I don't want us to regret anything, Lauren. Plus, I need to show Avery some respect. I feel guilty about that public kiss, so soon after the split, but I couldn't *help* it. You were so damn cute and sexy—" He broke off, regrouping before he continued. "I couldn't control myself then, so I have to now. For a little longer anyway. Until it feels…decent."

Rob wasn't always the best at articulating his thoughts and motivations, so I wasn't 100 percent sure what to make of this. "Do you still have…feelings for Avery? Is that why you're worried about her?" If he said yes, I might hyperventilate.

He shook his head immediately. "No. It's about doing this the right way and me not feeling like an asshole over being with you."

"Okay," I said. "I won't push."

"I appreciate it. If you think this is easy, then you have *no* idea how much I want you or how long it's been that way."

"You could tell me."

In response, he pulled me onto his lap, the hard length of him like hot metal beneath me. I resisted the urge to straddle him, sensing that wasn't what he had in mind. *Not yet, anyway.* He cradled me against his chest, rubbing his cheek against my hair. I listened to him breathe, just waiting for him to speak.

"This is another story, I guess. Like the one when you were going out in the red dress."

"I'm all ears."

He traced the curve of the right one, fingers drifting lower to cup my cheek. Instinctively I lifted my face for a kiss, but he only ran this thumb against my jaw, closer, closer to my lips. I parted them, hardly able to breathe. My pulse went crazy.

"Seeing you at Thanksgiving…" He let out a slow breath. "It was like we came full circle. I remembered how you used to follow me around, but in November, you didn't even look at me, like I was a nonperson in your eyes."

It hurt to say this out loud. "That's because you were with Avery."

"One of the reasons I was with Avery was because I didn't think I'd ever have *you*. And that's not a good reason, you know? So I tried my hardest for her because my heart wasn't in it."

"You feel guilty about that, too," I realized aloud.

He nodded. "For you and me, this has been years in the making. It's not too much to ask for us to wait a little more, just to make sure Avery's okay, right?" Now that I understood everything, I could give him all the time he needed.

"Sure." For five minutes or so, he just held me, though his erection didn't subside in the slightest. Part of me felt bad about what seemed like incredible temptation, but if Rob could handle it, I could, too. At last he let go and set me on the floor, the banked smolder in his eyes like dry lightning on a hot summer night. I could almost forget there was snow on the ground outside.

Rob exhaled slowly, as if clinging by a thread to his self-control. Then he changed the subject and put some physical distance between us. "Any word on karaoke?"

It took me a minute to catch up. "Oh, tomorrow night. Can you make it?"

"Absolutely. I said I would, didn't I?" Rob kissed the tip of my nose. From anyone else, the move probably would've irritated me. I didn't do cute with the guys I dated. But then, Rob and I weren't officially there yet.

"Let me call Krista and Avery while I'm thinking about it."

"You're inviting Avery?" Rob tilted his head, grinning. "This should be...interesting."

Relief bubbled up. Though I'd told him I would befriend her even if he objected, it helped that he was such a good guy. A weaker man would let the regret keep him from facing her.

Getting out my phone, I dialed and got Krista on the second ring. The convo was short and sweet. "Yeah, I'd love to come. Pick me up?"

"Around six."

After hanging up, Rob programmed Avery's contact info

into my phone. Hopefully she wouldn't be too pissed at him for giving it to me or over the invitation in general.

As expected, she was a tougher sell than Krista. "Who is this? How did you get my number?"

I girded my loins for battle, nudging Rob away from my shoulder. If he kissed me, Avery would hear it in my voice. "It's Lauren. A bunch of us are going to karaoke tomorrow night, and I wondered if you want to join us."

The pause stretched out so long, I thought maybe she'd hung up. Finally, she asked, "Why?"

"Because it'll be fun. Maybe." Generally speaking, I enjoyed karaoke, though the company made *all* the difference. In that moment I missed Nadia more than ever. Maybe I hadn't been fair. I mean, I was secretly mad at her for not sensing things about me—she was supposed to be my best friend, after all—but she wasn't a mind reader. I shouldn't be so conflicted when I was the one who'd shut her out.

"Who's 'us'?" Avery sounded suspicious, like this might be a trick.

"My mom, her boyfriend, Krista, Rob, me—"

"You seriously expect me to go out with my ex?" Her tone was a mixture of disbelief and amusement.

"No, he'll just be there. Look, what better way to prove to people that you're fine? Come on, we'll have a blast. Don't be stubborn." She hesitated, so I added, "If you hang up, I'm calling back. I'll bother you until you say yes."

Finally, she sighed. "Fine. When?"

"Tomorrow at six-fifteen. We'll pick you up. See you then." I ended the convo before she could argue with me.

"You just got Avery to agree to karaoke? Wow. What's your next miracle?"

Making the rest of the world see you like I do.

CHAPTER FOURTEEN

That night, I edited the video and posted to the channel "At Home with Rob," then I uploaded it. A few finishing touches, then presto. I published. I had credits with a few services, so I used them to get some views on his videos, and then I went to bed. In the morning, I did a little more promo and sent in my college application. The cool part was that I could use Rob's website as part of my portfolio. Though I wasn't going into design, it wouldn't hurt my chances.

By half past five, I was ready when Rob picked me up. My mom and Stuart had already left, planning to meet us there. Though I doubted Stuart's concern about getting a big enough table would be a problem in Edison on a Sunday night, it was sweet of him to care. I bounded out the door, and Rob grabbed me like it had been more than twelve hours. Even through our coats, I admired the strength of him as he lifted me for a kiss. I'd never dated a guy so unabashedly physical. If we had time, he'd probably put me on the hood of his truck and make it last ten minutes. The urge flickered in his eyes, but it passed, and he let me climb into the cab on my own.

"Are you almost done teasing me? Death by sexual frustration will be superembarrassing on the coroner's report."

"I don't think I can hold out much longer," he admitted.

I grinned. "Best news I've had all day. Here, check this out."

He took my phone with a curious look, then his eyes widened. "Holy shit. I've got almost a thousand views."

"And forty comments." Most of which said how fucking hot he was, but that was beside the point. I knew the internet would love Rob.

"That's insane. You posted everything last night?"

"Yeah. I still need to set up the email to forward to your inbox. Or you can just tell me what password you want, and I'll text you the log-in to webmail for your site."

"I have no idea. Do whatever's easiest."

"Gotcha."

It didn't take long for us to get to Krista's house. She was already waiting on her front porch, bundled up against the cold in a cute red knit hat and matching scarf. Rob got out to help her in back. His truck had a double cab or I would've given her the front seat—no making pregnant ladies clamber behind the seat.

"You're Nadia's brother, right?"

"Yeah, nice to meet you."

Krista smiled. "Definitely. You were kind of a big deal when I was in junior high."

"He still is," I said, before he could reply.

"Oh, so it's like that? I thought you were dating Avery Jacobs."

I felt a pang of guilt over not updating her on our status. Between a full-time job, keeping in touch with the roomies and talking to Rob on the phone at night, plus video games and extracurricular coding projects, I wasn't holding up my end of our friendship. Silently promising to do better, I kept quiet and let him answer.

"Not anymore," he said. "Though we're picking her up next."

"Really? It's so cool you stayed friends. I don't think I could do that if I ever broke up with Kenji."

"Her fiancé's in Afghanistan," I explained.

Rob had questions, fortunately, so that carried us to Avery's house. I half expected I'd need to drag her out of the house, but she answered as soon as I rang the bell, wearing a cute leather jacket and designer jeans. Her house gave off a fairly foreboding vibe, with so many windows; it was a brick historical place with tons of character, but I also sensed dark history. But maybe that was just because I'd watched *Flowers in the Attic* recently.

"Ready to sing your hearts out?" I asked.

"I intend to watch and make fun of everyone," Avery answered.

"No way. I'm getting you drunk, then you're singing the Spice Girls with my mom and me. Or maybe TLC. We could rock 'Unpretty.'"

"Agreed," Krista said. "Since I'm not allowed to drink, *I'll* be taking the blackmail pics."

Avery offered a lip curl. "Your mom's going to be there. How much fun could this possibly be?"

As it turned out, the answer was—*OMG, a lot.* Stuart was on stage when we walked in, and my mother was right. I actually stopped moving, so Rob bumped into me. Perched on a stool with the spotlight on him, he was singing his heart out to my mom, an absolutely soul-melting cover of "It Had to Be You." I'd thought she must be biased, but nope. The guy had an absolutely amazing voice; there was no chatter whatsoever, and there had to be forty people in the bar. Everyone was completely focused on Stuart.

How unexpectedly awesome.

The pause gave me a minute to take a breath, resign myself to being around people. In settings like this, it wasn't so bad. I did best one-on-one or in small groups. At an event where I was expected to mingle and schmooze, the only way I could cope was to become Party Lauren and bury the real me under five shots of something strong. We waited until Stuart finished the song, then the wild applause commenced, led by me. He took a bashful bow, then jogged down the stairs to the table where my mom was waiting. Bending, he kissed her gently, then sat down beside her. If he kept treating my mom so sweet, I'd soon be Stuart Lee's biggest fan.

"We're here," I called, following Rob through the maze of other tables.

"Oh, great, you made it." My mom stood up and took care of introductions.

For the first few minutes, we were busy ordering drinks and appetizers while a few more people sang, none of whom were nearly as good as Stuart. Then the DJ called out, "Dee, your turn," and a statuesque African-American woman took the stage, dressed in baggy jeans and a gray sweatshirt. Stuart perked up, so I took this to mean she was worth hearing, and by the time she finished, I was *in tears* from her version of "Fancy." I'd never heard the song before, but the story it told was absolutely heartbreaking, and in her husky, gorgeous voice, *wow*. I had no idea anybody so talented even lived in Nebraska. Which was probably horrible of me.

"Excuse me," I said.

My admiration was such that it outweighed my fear of strangers and making an ass of myself. Mustering my nerve, I got up and went over to the bar, where the woman was rejoining her friends. "Not to be weird, but you have the most beautiful voice I've ever heard. If you had a CD, I'd buy it."

She ducked her head, pleased and shy. "Thanks."

I hurried back to my table before I said something stupid. My heart was pounding like crazy, my hands trembling, so I clenched them. For someone else, that exchange would be nothing at all, but I felt like I'd just run five blocks. All the noise in the room went weird and full of reverb; Rob quietly wrapped his fingers around mine and held on until the tightness in my chest passed. Nobody else seemed to notice, thank God. While the others were looking toward the stage, he opened my fingers like the petals of a flower and pressed a kiss to my palm. I trembled from the heat of his mouth, and his eyes were shockingly dark with desire. Rob didn't let go of my hand.

I noticed Avery looking at him now and then, but they didn't talk to each other. She always cut her eyes away before he caught her, and I understood his caution even more. About an hour in, she went to the restroom. Rob waited two minutes and then headed after her. I didn't want to be like this, but I *had* to know what he was going to say.

So I tried to be casual as I mumbled, "Bathroom."

Krista gave me a weird look but since she'd just gone fifteen minutes ago, she didn't offer to go with me. I skirted the room and moved quietly toward the hall under the unmistakable sign. There was no way I could go all the way down or they'd see me. So I waited just around the corner, straining my ears. I heard the doors open and close and a couple of clicks as if from Avery's heels.

Rob's voice was pitched low, barely audible at this distance between the guy crooning on stage and the karaoke track. "Are you okay?"

"I'm not the one who got punched in the mouth."

"You know what I mean."

By the sound on the wood floor, she moved a few steps, then stopped. "Jesus. What do you *want?*"

He won't let her leave. I pictured his big hand curled around her shoulder, her face tipped toward him. Eavesdropping was stupid and childish; I should go. But my feet were frozen.

"I'm sure you've already heard that there's something between Lauren and me. But I'll wait as long as you say. I don't want people talking about you."

"You want my blessing?" She sounded incredulous.

"Yeah."

"And you'll never do anything with her if I say no?"

"Not never," he said. "But I'll wait a lot longer than this."

"To salvage my pride?"

No verbal response. I imagined him nodding. Since this concerned me, I willed her to be generous. *Come on, give us the green light.* The silence seemed interminable.

Finally, she answered, "Fine. For what it's worth, you have it. I don't care what the idiots in this town think. But…it's nice that you checked with me."

I could only agree. *He's too good to be true.*

Before they caught me listening, I hurried back to the table. Avery and Rob joined us a few minutes later. A warm glow suffused me at the sight of him; it was impossible to think I'd ever meet anyone sweeter or more amazing. Stuart sang twice more before I drank enough to make me brave enough to put my name on a card, along with my mom, Avery and Krista. Rob took it to the DJ for us, wearing an adorable grin. I cocked a brow at him.

"Something funny?"

"I can't wait to see this."

"I will kill anyone who takes pictures," Avery warned.

Krista nudged her. "Don't look at me, I've been roped into singing, too."

Listening to everyone else was surprisingly fun. A white guy got up and rapped terribly, but he had so much personality that he got the rest of us to chime in on the chorus, helping him out. When the DJ finally called us up, most of my nerves had gone to sleep. I made Avery hold the mic we were sharing while Krista partnered up with my mom, then we sang the *hell* out of the Spice Girls. Or not. Because like half the club got up to smoke. I had a terrible voice, but I was a good dancer, so I worked shoulders, boobs and booty for Rob. He didn't even blink the whole time I was onstage; his intense, purposeful stare sent shivers through me.

When we finished, Stuart and Rob yelled for us, along with a couple of drunk guys at the bar, one of whom seemed to be trying to get Avery's phone number. She pointed two fingers at him, then shook her head in a no-way signal. He clamped his hands to his heart and pretended to fall off his stool.

Krista was laughing so hard that Stuart had to help her sit down. "Oh, God, this isn't good. I'm going to pee my pants."

Avery slid her a look and then quietly moved her chair two inches closer to mine. While Krista pretended to pout, the rest of us dissolved in muted snickers. Rob ordered another round, though I'd noticed he wasn't drinking. Likewise, Stuart stuck to soda and lime, which looked like gin and tonic. After a couple more beers, I had the urge to hug him, but I contented myself with messing up his hair.

"You're a great guy, you know that?"

"Uh. Thanks?" he said, slightly worried-looking.

"Okay, that's enough for you," my mom said, and I grinned.

We sang one more group number just before ten, and then it was time to head our separate ways. Most of us had work in the morning, plus it was almost an hour back to Sharon.

Outside in the frosty parking lot, I did hug Stuart, much to his combined pleasure and discomfort. He patted me awkwardly in return.

"There's room for my mom in the truck," I said. "No point in you driving there and back, unless you're staying over."

"Lauren!" I got a thump on the arm from Mom for my troubles.

"You're so weird," Avery mumbled.

"If you're sure?" Stuart glanced at my mom to be sure she was okay with the plan.

"It makes sense. I'll walk you to your car."

I took that to mean they were going to kiss, so I urged the rest of our group toward Rob's truck. He was already warming it up for us, and Avery sighed a little as she climbed in back. This must've been a little odd for her, but I thought she had fun. Krista definitely did, even if she couldn't drink.

Eventually, my mom hurried across the lot and got in the back. "Ready."

The drive was companionable, though we sang along with the radio instead of talking. An hour later, Rob dropped Krista off. "Thanks, this was really fun. We should do it again. Call me, okay, Lauren?"

Avery was less effusive but she sounded sincere when she got out next. "I had a good time. Surprisingly." The bite of the last word was mild, considering her reputation. "See you."

"Take care," Rob said.

She turned to study him through the truck window, and I recalled their private conversation near the bathroom. It was like she was mentally drawing a line between them. Then she jerked a nod. "You, too."

"That was surprisingly civil," Mom said as we pulled onto the road.

"We need to cut her some slack. You know how people talk around here," I pointed out.

She nodded. "According to them, I have a drug habit and you're pregnant."

"Huh?" I swiveled my head. "I knew about my unborn love child, but since when are you into the crack? On the horse? What're the cool kids calling it these days?"

She laughed softly. "Since I've lost weight, honey."

"I would happily beat the shit out of anyone who talks like that about you two." Rob's tone was so conversational, that at first, I thought he was kidding. But I met his gaze in the passing headlights of another car. And nope.

"That's sweet," Mom said, apparently not realizing how serious he was.

Wow. Rob's got a secret caveman side. Love that.

Too soon, he pulled into our driveway. It was just past eleven, and if I were a good girl, I would kiss him, then take a shower and get ready for bed. My mom thanked him for the ride and climbed out, evidently granting us privacy. It was bizarre having to worry about this sort of thing.

"So this is where you peck me on the cheek?" I touched his lower lip gently. "Because I won't let you wind me up like you did yesterday."

"No. This is where I ask you to pack a bag and drive to my place."

"Huh?" My eloquence knew no bounds.

"I'm not sure how much you know about mechanical stuff—"

"Nothing. That'd be nothing." Not polite to interrupt, but I desperately wanted him to cut to the chase.

"Well, a spring can only hold so much tension before it snaps."

Wow. I let out a long, slow breath. "So tonight…?"

You got the all-clear from Avery. Now we're good to go. Exhilaration warred with insidious tenderness that made me want to hold him every bit as much as I'd love to lick him all over.

"If you'll come."

Pressing my mouth together didn't quite muffle the absurd sound I made, something between a giddy shriek and girlish laughter. "Give me fifteen minutes."

"I'll be waiting."

The hour trip from Edison had left me fine to take the wheel, so I jumped out of the truck and raced to my room. *Think, what do you need for work. Skirt, sweater, tights. Makeup kit. Underwear. Bra. Hair dryer.* I could use Rob's soap and shampoo, whatever he had, for one night. My whole body felt like it was on fire with a crazy blend of excitement and anxiety.

What if we waited too long? What if it's not good? Shut up, stop thinking. We're doing the sex.

"Going somewhere?" Mom asked.

"Rob's place."

"I *see*."

"You can tease me later," I yelled, grabbing my keys.

"Count on it."

In record time, I was parking in Rob's garage. Not a euphemism, but the symbolism made me laugh. He'd left it open for me, so I clicked the button and ducked out before the door closed on me. A controlled sprint landed me on his front porch. *Dear God. I'm sleeping with Nadia's brother.* At some point, I *had* to call her. Or Skype. This wasn't the kind of news you broke in an email or a text. But part of me suspected she wouldn't get it because (a) he was her brother and (b) she thought he was an idiot. And I didn't want to fight with her about Rob.

But that was a problem for another time.

I raced through the front door before I realized maybe I

should've knocked or that possibly, I might come across as overeager. How many fucks did I give about the latter? After all this time? Not many. Every part of me trembled with anticipation, but uncertainty gnawed at me, too. How many girls got to hook up with the guy they'd been fantasizing about for years? The answer was probably the same as the first question I'd asked mentally.

Not many.

Rob pounced on me as soon as I hit the dining room. In one motion, he scooped me into his arms and carried me toward the stairs. If I wasn't completely infatuated with his hand-eye coordination, I lost the battle when he kissed me as he climbed. I was dizzy and breathless when we hit the bedroom. My backpack dropped off my arm with a thunk.

Dammit. He made me wait too long. If we'd done this sooner, Party Lauren would've been in charge of the sex, as she always had been. But now, there was only overwhelming need crashing over me, like a rough tide against sharp rocks. I had no idea what to do when it wasn't light, when it wasn't just for fun. I'd never been with anyone I loved.

I took one deep breath, then another, hoping he wouldn't notice. This was *no* time for my brain to get overinvolved in my libido—bad enough it ruined so many other aspects of my life.

"You okay?" Rob set me onto my feet, lines forming between his beautiful brows. No joke, even his eyebrows were gorgeous. Not too bushy, not too thin, dark slashes that loomed over his so-blue eyes. And here he was, ready for me at last.

What is wrong *with you?*

"Yeah," I managed. "I just can't believe I'm here with you like this. It's like a dream come true, and I guess that scares me a little."

"Because dreams can turn weird so fast or because it's hard for reality to match them?"

"More the last. There's nothing wrong about being with you. In fact, you're all the good in my life right now." I meant it as a compliment, not that my life was such a train wreck. Hopefully he got that.

By his smile, he did. "Back at you, beautiful. You make me feel…everything, really. Stuff I didn't even realize I could. Relationships before always left me feeling like…I have a piece missing or something."

"There is *nothing* wrong with you," I snapped.

Talking to him was helping. The knots unkinked. Odd how Rob's voice could do that. Fear went away, replaced by yearning that coiled inside like the spring he'd mentioned before. Standing up, I yanked off my jacket and pulled my shirt over my head. In a few seconds, I was naked. Rob's gaze swept over me, and it was a hot lash that tightened my nipples. I resisted the urge to cover up. If Rob was my safe place, I had to prove it by being brave in my own skin—with all the emotions and none of the pretense.

"Good start," he said roughly. "Now I can say what I've wanted to for years. Lauren Barrett…get in my fucking bed."

CHAPTER FIFTEEN

I did.

Then I watched Rob strip; each movement revealed more of him, and it was foreplay. He had a gorgeous body, tautly muscled, a tan that stayed golden even in the winter. Strong shoulders, broad chest, a six-pack that didn't quit and arms that could probably lift the weight of the world from my shoulders. That didn't even begin to describe the raw, masculine beauty of his face, a flush across his cheekbones and eyes slumberous with barely leashed longing.

When Rob clicked the lamp off, I noticed he'd lit candles, less obvious with the lights on, but gorgeous now, flickering like fireflies at the corners of the room. "Romantic."

"I'm trying," he murmured.

"You know you don't have to, right?"

"I disagree. You deserve it."

"Ooh." He tilted my head and kissed the side of my neck, distracting me.

Based on what he'd said about being fully sprung, I didn't expect the easy, tender approach. But he blazed a trail down my throat to my shoulder, sending shivers down my spine. I was breathing fast by the time he kissed me, one big hand on my cheek. I wound my arms around him and pressed close, unable to stifle a sound of shocked pleasure at the heat of his bare chest. Digging my fingers into his muscled back spurred a groan from Rob, but I swallowed it and we kept kissing, deep and hungry, yet there was nothing fast or furtive about it. Incredible pleasure swelled, married to my complete certainty that he'd kiss me *all night.*

His patience could kill me.

"More," I whispered against his lips.

Pulling back, I caught his smile in the flickering light as he drifted lower, nuzzling down to my breasts. I shifted, widening the gap between my thighs to make room for him. His hands felt rough against my skin, but beautifully so, a sexy contrast to the softness of my skin. One thing about Rob, he was great with his hands, but when he added lips and teeth, I lost my breath. His gaze met mine as he licked a circle around my nipple. From the hot flush on his cheeks, he liked this a lot, and I wanted so many things all at once that the mental images scrambled my brain.

"So...boobs do it for you?" I managed to ask. "Not legs or ass?"

"With you? Everything. I'll get there. In time." Rob's voice sounded deep, gravelly even. I'd never heard that tone from him before, and a thrill shivered through me, realizing how thin his control ran.

What would it take to snap it? In my muzzy head, I only knew I wanted him to stop being...strategic and just do me. So I sat up, surprising him, and rolled on top of him, perched on his abdomen so he could feel how much I wanted him. His cock jerked against my ass, but I didn't move, only held his gaze for countless seconds.

"Time's up," I whispered. "My turn."

"Jesus."

I expected him to argue, but his lashes fluttered against his cheeks as if in surrender. His chest heaved, deep, steadying breaths, I guessed. If this worked, they wouldn't do him any good. Bending down, I teased him as he had me, running my lips down his neck to his shoulders, interspersing licks and bites. The sounds he made, little rumbling groans and gasps, only got me hotter. I ran my hands over his chest, marveling at his strength. He hissed when I curved my nails into his muscles but he didn't stop me. In fact, his hips came up, and his nipples tightened, so we were a matched set. I worked my ass against him for a few seconds while I traced a featherlight fingertip across his chest.

"You have to tell me what you want next."

"Your mouth."

"Where?" I eased closer, my lips hovering above his nipple.

"There. Anywhere." His hands fisted on either side on the covers, as if he thought he shouldn't touch me. Or maybe he was fighting the urge to throw me on my back and fuck me.

Stop resisting, Rob. We've had weeks of foreplay.

If he didn't do it soon, *I* would. The ache inside me escalated to tremors in my thighs, and it was all I could do not to just lift up, curl my hand around him, bear down and start grinding. But I needed him to lose control first. Too bad I was one kiss away from forgetting my name.

"Like this?" I licked his nipple lightly, knowing it wasn't enough.

With a muttered curse, he let go of the sheets and pressed my head down harder, and I bit him. He lifted us both off the bed with the force of his reaction. Melting all over him, I explored this revelation. *Rob likes teeth, a little pain.* So I gave it to him, commingled with tender suction and gentle kisses—

his chest, his nipples, back up to his shoulders and throat, and down again. The longer I tormented him, the more he moved, helpless motions against my ass.

"You're so hot," he whispered. "Killing me."

When he snapped, he shoved me off him and onto my back. But then he kissed a blind, desperate path downward. His hands shook as he lifted my legs onto his shoulders and settled in. I arched, bewildered, as he licked and bit my inner thighs, tasting the juices. With rough need, he parted my lips with his thumbs and worked in a maddening circle, just a whisper away from my clit. Aching, I needed his fingers, his cock, inside me, but I got his tongue, and that was... I moaned.

His fingers strummed my clit as he thrust, tasting me so deep that I lifted my ass, unable to breathe, only knowing I had to have more. Heat built, the sweet, soft friction, and he was whispering to me, *into* me, but I couldn't make out the words. Maddened, I fucked his face, desperate to get off. I'd never been able to come from oral, but the way the tension was climbing, *maybe this time, maybe, oh, fuck, yes.*

With shaking hands, I adjusted his touch on my clit, a little rougher, longer strokes, less of the tapping, and the orgasm roared through me. My body tightened on his tongue, and I came in a silent rush. I wanted to yell his name, but my throat clenched just like the rest of me, until it was all I could do to breathe. In. Out. Rob lightened the touches perfectly, not pushing me past what felt good. I had no idea when he moved because everything was dim and spinning, starlight in the room, no, candlelight, and his big body wrapped around me. His cock was hard as a railroad spike against my ass, and he was grinding against me slowly when I regained some sense of perspective.

"You are incredible," I whispered.

"You're delicious." The husky growl in my ear hardened

my nipples; I *should* be satisfied, but I wouldn't be until he was inside me.

I spun in his arms and threw a leg across his hip. That changed the angle completely. His breath caught, but he didn't—couldn't—stop the relentless pump of his hips. Each little movement opened me up a little more, teasing closer, and he shuddered, his head falling back as his cock slid between my labia. Moving with him, I watched his face, the pleasure opening his expression to me completely. *This* Rob was emotionally naked, vulnerable, and the intensity of his longing brought tears to my eyes.

"I'm safe," I whispered. "And I'm on the pill. Do you trust me?"

Before Rob, I'd always used condoms, but I'd wanted him for so long that I hated the thought of stopping for latex. *Want you inside me, nothing between us.* The thought alone, along with his hardness pressing deeper, almost made me come again.

"Yes, Lauren. *Yes.* I never…" He lost the thread, lips parting on a groan as I shifted. "Never…went bare. Baby, I need you."

"Then have me."

Rob shoved me onto my back, all gentleness and finesse forgotten. He claimed me in a single, powerful thrust, and I clamped my legs around his hips, breathless, dizzy with excitement. For a few seconds, he just froze, locked and holding inside me. I tightened instinctively, wanting him to feel good.

"Fuck, *fuck,* that's good. You won't be able to walk for a week when I'm done with you."

"Don't be done," I begged, moving under him.

"Jesus, Lauren. Do that again. Again—" His voice broke. Breath coming in ragged gulps, he moved in long, fast strokes, clearly focused on getting off.

But his selfishness only turned me on more, especially after the way he made me come with his mouth. I loved knowing

I'd driven him to this point. Rob—sweet, considerate Rob— wanted me so bad, he couldn't stop, couldn't think. I sank my nails into his back and raked downward, sparking a snarl of pleasure. His thrusts came harder and faster, wild and erratic, like he couldn't get deep enough, and I tilted my hips, pushing back as the tension coiled in my belly, bringing me closer to the edge with every furious push.

He broke before I did, and long shivering waves rocked through him. Rob lay down on me and gathered me close. The last of his pulses edged me into a light fluttery orgasm, not nearly as strong as the first one, but enough to soothe the heat. I held him as he jerked in my arms, reacting like each brush of my fingertips scraped across an exposed nerve.

Eventually his breathing steadied, and he rolled to the side, taking me with him. It even felt good when he slipped out of me. We were a sticky, delicious mess, but I didn't have the energy to suggest a shower. "You okay?"

"Brilliant," he breathed, kissing my shoulder. "It's been a while."

"Huh? What about Avery?" She was the last person I wanted to talk about while we were both naked, but the question was already out.

Dammit.

"We never got that far."

"But…you guys dated for, like, six months," I protested. It was beyond me how any woman could date Rob for that long and not demand to see him naked. But secret relief crashed through me, even stronger than the disbelief. I loved that she never got him this way.

"She wasn't into it. Anytime I hinted it might be time for us to move past kissing, she shut me down. Never told me why, though. Maybe she's religious, promise ring from Dad, saving herself for marriage?"

The idea of my father taking an interest in my sex life freaked me out. "Creepy. And I have no idea. Her family has money...otherwise, I don't know much about them."

"They're...formal. I met them twice in total. Her uncle *hated* me."

I kissed him. "Well, you don't have to worry about them anymore. On my side, there's basically just my mom and... maybe Stuart. But I'm pretty sure you can take him."

"Probably."

"You know, that's probably why Avery thought the worst of you so quick, though."

"Hmm?" He sounded so relaxed, it was adorable.

"The not-very-flattering consensus among women is—if he's not getting it from you, he must be getting some elsewhere. Which doesn't take into account guys like you."

"That's *so* offensive," Rob said. "Women really believe that?"

"Some of them do."

"You're not one of them?"

"Depends on the guy. You? No way."

"I'll take it."

"Be back in a minute."

After kissing him, I crawled out of bed and went to the bathroom with my bag. Then I cleaned up the sex mess. For a few seconds, I stared in the mirror, trying to decide if I should wash off my makeup. It was better for my skin, but that meant he'd see me in my unpainted glory in the morning, along with bad breath, gunk in my eyes and crazy hair. I'd never slept over after sex before, so I had no protocol in place. Turning the bottle of skin cleanser over in my hands, I recognized the budding flutters of a panic attack. God, what a stupid thing to freak out over. Apparently I took so long that Rob came looking for me.

A tap sounded on the bathroom door. "Everything all right?"

"No, you ruptured me with your monstrous penis."

"Lauren, that is *not* funny."

I exhaled. "Two minutes, I swear. My vagina is fine."

This is Rob. None of that matters.

Mustering my courage, I took my makeup off and returned to bed. He was still awake, propped up on the pillows, looking both concerned and delicious. You'd think I would panic more about trotting around naked, but my head was a messed-up place, and apparently lack of makeup was more terrifying. Rob pulled me into his arms.

"Talk to me."

Feeling like a dipshit, I mumbled my concerns, light years more than I'd ever achieved with anyone else. In the intimacy games, Rob and I were well into first place. He stroked my hair with gentle hands, listening to all my crazy with a miraculous sort of infinite patience.

"This isn't the kind of shit I worry about," he admitted. "But I promise I'll think you're beautiful—with or without makeup, first thing in the morning, whenever. Part of that's how you look, but the rest comes from how I feel when I'm with you. Lauren, you're the only person in the world who doesn't make me feel like half a ham sandwich."

Since he was being so sincere, I shouldn't have laughed. "What?"

He stirred against me, self-conscious. "You know. Like there should be more. That what's here isn't enough."

Oh. "Robert Clayton Conrad, you are *absolutely* the whole sandwich. In fact, you're one of those party subs that I shouldn't eat by myself, but I'm sure going to try. Because I'm just that greedy about you."

He tapped my nose in a stern mock-warning. "If you keep being this sweet to me, things could happen."

"Sex things?"

I walked a hand down his chest. He captured it and brought it to his lips with a tenderness that did a number on my heart. If I let myself, I could panic over this. Over Rob. There were no walls between us, none of my usual bullshit.

"Stop trying to seduce me, woman. You have to be up in six hours."

"Sleep is overrated," I tried.

"There's no need to cram everything into one night," Rob whispered into my hair. "I'm here. I'm not going anywhere."

"*Need* is one verb. *Want* is a better one." I brought his fingers to my mouth in turn and nibbled one, then licked another. Mostly I was playing, but I wouldn't say no to round two if he couldn't resist the urge.

"Are you trying to turn me on so much that I can't sleep?" he asked, kissing the corner of my mouth.

"Maybe."

In answer, he put my palm over the hard line of his cock, obvious even through the softness of the comforter. "You don't even have to touch me, baby. Before I broke up with Avery, you had me ready pretty much every single day."

"Wow. Really? How?"

"It's the things you say."

"Like…?"

"You want examples, so you can drive me even crazier?"

I grinned and kissed his chest. "If possible."

"The first time it happened, we were in Safeway."

"Seriously?" I thought back and couldn't imagine what I might've said that would turn him on.

"I was looking at cologne…at Avery's request. You told me,

'Don't change for her, okay? You're great the way you are.' It was so good to hear that I—"

"Reacted."

"Yeah. Told myself it was just because things were a little slow in that department, but the more time we spent together, the harder it got."

"Pun intended?"

He smacked me gently on the ass. "No. Eventually, it got so I thought about you constantly, but I didn't know what to do about Avery, because it wasn't her fault things weren't working out. I didn't want to hurt her, and it seemed shitty to break up over the phone."

"So you were waiting for her to come home to do it in person?"

Rob nodded. "By then, I didn't even care when she got back because all I could think about was seeing *you* again."

"I guess I do need to take some responsibility in your breakup then. If not for me, you'd still be together."

He tipped my face up for a slow, languid kiss. "Before you came back, I figured a bad relationship was better than none, and I already told you, I've never gotten it right with *anyone*."

"You're spot on, as far as I'm concerned. Though you could've put out sooner."

"But I want you to respect me," he said with admirable conviction.

"I do. So much. It's beyond me how you can put up with my crap."

Seeming to consider that a question, he thought for a moment. "It's part of you who you are. So the person who makes me feel so good sometimes needs me back. Big deal. The night I found out about my dad, I was a mess. Do you think less of me because of it?"

"Never."

Until then, my hand simply rested on his erection, where he'd set it. Now I burrowed under the covers to touch him. He lifted his hips, contradicting his sensible suggestion about going to bed early. It was sexy to explore his cock so tactilely, learning its shape under the covers and discovering what made him respond most. I watched his face as I stroked around the tip in leisurely motions. To my gratification, a trickle of fluid lubricated my hand, proving how much he liked it. Teasing, I jacked him for a few strokes, then took my hand away. Rob stared as I carried my fingers to my lips and tasted them.

"Mmm. Salty."

His eyes flickered shut, breath coming fast. "There's only one solution to this problem."

"What's that?" God, I hoped I already knew the answer.

He pulled me on top of him. "You got me so wound up, now you have to fix it."

CHAPTER SIXTEEN

To nobody's surprise, I got less than four hours of sleep.

I was a zombie when I took a shower, using Rob's toiletries—silly how much I enjoyed that. I shut the bathroom door afterward, hoping I wouldn't wake him while I blow-dried my hair. *So far, so good.* Getting ready for work at Rob's place, damn. I never thought we'd be here. Not that he'd called me his girlfriend or anything.

He didn't stir when I got the rest of my stuff, so I tiptoed out and crept down the stairs. A bowl of cereal was as much breakfast as I ever had at my mom's place, so I ate the same here. According to my phone, which I'd forgotten to charge, I had twenty minutes to get to work. Fortunately, that wouldn't be a problem in Sharon.

Since it was ice-cold, the truck gave me five minutes worth of trouble, so I barely dodged in on time. My boss, Mick Davies, shot finger guns at me as I hurried to my desk. Based on the coat over his jacket, he'd only just arrived, too.

But he gave me a creepy smile anyway. "Two minutes later, Lauren, and we'd have a discipline issue." The faint stress on the second-to-last word told me he had in mind a spanking more than a warning for my file.

Gross.

"But I'm on time," I said, pretending I didn't speak fluent pervert.

"So you are." He faked a hearty laugh. "Bring me a cup of coffee, will you? By now, you know how I like it."

A salesman caught me pretending to vomit into the trash can beside my desk, and he shot me a sympathetic glance. "I guess the boss is already here?"

"That's why you get the big bucks."

As I put on a pot of coffee, I thought, *Maybe I should've left a note.* I mean, Rob knew I had to work in the morning, but… *better to be sure.* So I texted, Thanks for last night. No reply, but he was probably still asleep. I put away my phone and took the chief butthead his morning jolt. Even though I hadn't been at the dealership very long, some days I was tempted to spit in it. I reminded myself that jobs were hard to find around here, and that the hours worked perfectly for my summer school plans.

Everything was fine until just past lunch when Davies yelled for me from his office. I was chatting with an elderly couple whom I'd already ID'd as perpetual window-shoppers. With a frozen smile, I invited them to look around the showroom. Then I hurried to the manager's office, bracing myself.

"What is it?" I asked, pausing in the open doorway.

"Come on in. Shut the door."

Crap. I remembered Shelly's warning and resisted. "Did I do something wrong?"

"Of course not, I just need to talk to you."

My skin felt like it was creeping off my bones. I stared over my shoulder at the front desk. "Should I leave the phones unattended?"

"I'll pick up, don't worry."

"Okay." This situation should definitely be avoided. But I had no idea what to do about it. Nobody on the showroom floor took any notice of my predicament.

I sighed and did as the boss ordered.

Once I shut the door, I skirted his desk, staying well out of reach, then I took a seat on the other side, being careful not to cross my legs so he could see anything.

Davies admired me for a long moment anyway, making me feel dirty. "There you go. How do you like it here so far, Lauren?"

"The work's fine, hours are great. The sales team has been friendly." *Actually, everything's awesome but you.*

Since his family owned the dealership, there was no chance of getting rid of Mick Davies. And there wasn't even a proper human resources department where I could report a complaint. In a business this size, if I said anything, I'd just get fired for "unrelated" reasons. While that might be actionable, I couldn't afford a court battle. Well, not and go to college like I planned. Some things sucked, but there was no fixing them.

"That's fantastic," he said, smiling. "How would you feel about some overtime? I need a personal assistant after hours for a *very* special project."

"Dear God, no." The words burst out of me before I could stop them. "That wouldn't be good for the baby at all. Working the hours I do, plus college classes—that's all I can handle, along with nurturing this miraculous new life." I patted my gut protectively.

What the hell did you just say? *Crap.*

Maybe I could whisper to the accounting girls about a miscarriage in a few weeks, and hope word got back to him. Otherwise, I'd have to gain thirty pounds around the middle or buy one of those prosthetic bellies, which was just too weird and comedy caperish. Maybe this came from watching too many *I Love Lucy* reruns on TV with my mom, during her I-hate-the-whole-world phase. Back then, we were too poor for cable, and network TV loved Lucille Ball. But this stupid story was the only thing I could think of that might keep him from moving forward with what he was about to suggest.

Davies was *not* amused. His overtanned brow folded into a scary frown, making him look even more like a wallet. "You said nothing about this in your interview."

"I didn't know," I babbled. "I *just* found out. My boyfriend and I couldn't be happier, though. Maybe you know him? He used to play football for the Cardinals. I mean, if—"

"That's enough, Miss Barrett. You're not a good fit for the project after all."

Ha-ha, I bet, you bastard.

I practically ran out of his office, beyond relieved to reach the sanctity of the front desk. Though I hated to ask, it might even be good to get Rob to come in, provided he was willing to play the role of baby daddy. *Jesus, FML.* It pissed me off, however, that I needed to trot a burly guy in to register myself as off-limits with Davies. Assholes like him had all the power.

Somehow I got through the rest of the afternoon without any problems. My mom wasn't back from work when I got home, so I changed clothes and started dinner. It seemed like the least I could do since we hadn't hung out as much, between Stuart and Rob. I had meat loaf burgers done by the time she walked in the door.

"Wow, something smells great."

"You're late tonight. Work stuff?"

"Yeah, there was a problem in the budget—" Whenever my mom talked about her job, the words pretty much all blended into white noise.

After we ate and cleared the table, she asked, "Do you want to watch some TV?"

I'd missed this, and since I didn't know how long it would last, I nodded. "Sure, whatever you want."

She picked a movie I'd already watched with Nadia, but I didn't say anything. It was good the second time with my mom arguing with the characters, as if they could hear her. I remembered all of those days when I'd come from school, and she was too sad to get out of bed...how I'd leave food outside her bedroom, and there would be a dirty plate outside the door in the morning. Since I was a kid, I gave her stuff like peanut butter and jelly with a side of cookies, so she just got fatter and sadder. Some days, she didn't come out at all, and I lived on whatever I could scrounge. Which could've been worse; I was eleven, not five. That shit went on for years. Nobody knew—not even Nadia—how bad my mom's depression was. I tried to hide it, like it was a shameful secret, much as I did my own anxiety.

Mom caught me looking at her instead of the movie. "Something wrong?"

"No, I'm just happy, that's all."

"About what? Rob?"

"That we're both okay," I said quietly.

Her gaze dropped. "Me, too. I know it was rough around here, and I'm sorry I let you down. It's a wonder you came out so well. No thanks to me."

"You did your best at the time. It's all anyone can do."

"I really didn't. I should've gotten help sooner, but...we couldn't afford it."

Nodding, I remembered how we'd done the shopping late at night, right before Safeway closed, so nobody would see her using vouchers instead of cash. Before my dad bailed, we'd sold the old house, leaving enough cash to buy this place outright. Otherwise, God knew what would've become of us. Things got better when they hired her as a bookkeeper six years ago, and now she was in charge of accounts payable or something. She was in a much better place when I left, but the real change, along with the weight loss, didn't happen for another year.

"We survived. That which doesn't kill us, et cetera."

"For what it's worth, I'm glad you're home."

"Me, too."

Once the movie ended, I hugged her and went up to my room. It was close to nine, and I realized my phone must've died at some point, so I plugged it in and got ready for bed. I had two messages waiting, one from Rob, and the other, surprisingly, from Avery.

Rob: Call me. That was time-stamped four hours ago. His messages were always sparse, and I didn't picture him ever sexting me. *Probably for the best.*

Avery: Had fun last night, my turn to host. You and me, Krista and Jillian. Friday night. Can you make it?

I wasn't sure it was a good idea to hang out with the girl who thought driving lessons equaled sex, but since Avery was a good sport about karaoke and she'd given Rob her blessing, I sent back, Yeah, what time?

Avery: 7:30, I'll drive.

Me: Is there a dress code?

Silence from her, so I took that as a no. After brushing my teeth, I climbed in bed with my laptop, but before logging in to a game server, I called Rob. His text was so terse that I had no idea if it was important, or if he just wanted to hear my voice. The romantic junior high geek inside me fervently hoped this was the case, and maybe he'd also read me some poetry.

He picked up on the second ring, slightly out of breath. "Lauren."

God bless caller ID for making me feel shiny. "You got me. What's up?"

"Did you see my thingie?"

I smirked. "Several times."

"No, on the web. The video channel."

"Let me look." Once I got on the site, I flipped through. "Wow, nice. Those are some excellent views, and you're up to two hundred subscribers already."

"What does that even mean?"

"It means you need to post another video, soon. I'll come over tomorrow to work on it, if you want. How would you feel about taking your shirt off in this one?"

"Lauren." His flat tone told me he wasn't amused.

"Fine, we'll save that for the membership drive later on." I was only half-kidding. If he was doing this well already, given time, his furniture business should see some traffic. "Have you gotten any orders?"

"Not yet."

"That's not a bad sign. It's easy to watch things on the internet—takes a little more to convince people to part with their money. We'll get there."

"I got two emails, though," he told me in a bemused tone. "Well, *lines,* I guess. One said, 'you're so hot,' and the other said, 'I'll pay you to build a bookcase in my bedroom.'"

"I think not," I said.

"People on the internet are so weird."

"Truer words." *Shit.* While I had him on the phone, I had to tell him about our love child. "So...you have to promise not to get mad at me."

"I don't like conversations that start that way. But okay."

As fast as I could, I summarized my encounter with Davies, along with my spontaneous, problem-solving lie. Rob didn't say a word. The silence started to make me nervous, so I filled it with babble. "Anyway, most of the town thinks I'm knocked up anyway, so no big deal, right? I know you can't be thrilled about being dragged into this, but—"

"Has he touched you?" Pure steel, no give.

"No. Just innuendos and slimy looks. I said all that stuff to put him off. So I was hoping you'd stop by tomorrow, if you have time. You don't have to do anything. Well, maybe pretend to look at cars, and shake his hand too hard—"

"I'll be there first thing. He won't bother you again." His tone alarmed me.

"Rob, I need this job. You know that, right?"

"Don't worry about it."

"Well, I am. You sound like you might pull his arm off and beat him to death with it."

"'Night, Lauren. See you tomorrow."

With that hanging between us, it was a wonder I slept, but the short night with Rob, plus work, left me exhausted. I was awake by six, though, a rarity, so I went down and got on my mom's elliptical. It had been a while since I'd worked out, but I needed to occupy myself, and this was better than killing things online before work. Also, if I started gaming first thing, I knew myself, and I'd likely end up calling in sick. Not the best move when your not-boyfriend might be planning to bludgeon your boss to death.

Today, once I showered, I dressed in the pencil skirt I'd worn on the interview. I paired it with a pink sweater and I spent half an hour on hair and makeup. My mom got up late by contrast, racing out without drinking the cup of coffee I offered. The worst thing about driving Tessa Green-tea was climbing in and out in heels, plus she was cranky first thing in the morning.

I delivered the butthead's coffee without being asked, but he was curt. No smarmy smile for me today. How sad. Apparently he couldn't objectify me if I was breeding. I was grinning when I went back to my desk.

We had been open for no more than half an hour when Rob pulled into the parking lot. Unquestionably, I was biased, but he looked even better than usual in a red plaid shirt and an expensive-looking leather jacket lined with sheepskin. The scruff on his jaw said he didn't shave this morning, and his mouth was set in a firm line.

He beelined toward me, ignoring the attention he was attracting on a slow morning. "Where's your boss?"

"I don't think this is such a good idea."

"You asked me to come, Lauren. Well, I'm here. Do you trust me?" That was so unfair since I'd asked him that before, and from him, the answer was always yes.

Swallowing hard, I nodded.

His eyes lightened, though he still looked grim. He no longer radiated murderous intent, just enough menace that one of the sales guys dodged out of his path as he strode toward the manager's office. I wished I could be a fly on the wall for this conversation, but to my frustration, Davies shut the door when Rob stepped in, so I had no idea what was going on. I craned my neck, watching through the gaps in the blinds. Rob stood across the desk, arms folded, speaking quietly to Davies. Whatever he said made the older man tug at his tie and back up a step. Rob tilted his head, said something else. Davies nodded emphatically.

Then the conversation was over. Rob strolled back to me, completely at ease. "Problem solved. I made him understand my point of view."

"Which is?" I whispered.

"I think you know."

"That if he messes with me, you break his kneecaps?"

"Not exactly. But close enough."

I sighed. "I wish we lived in a world without guys like that. If life was fair, I wouldn't need you to threaten perverts for me."

"It wasn't a threat," he said softly. "If he makes you uncomfortable, it'll go bad for him. I'll make him sorry."

"Then you'll go to jail. Not sure I agree with the merits of this plan."

Weirdly, uncomfortably, two conflicting emotions wrestled around inside me: pleasure and dismay, the former because he'd *hurt* somebody for me, and the latter that I couldn't do it myself. Rob was the kind of guy who solved problems with the tools to hand; he wasn't a thinker. With him, you got a hammer-and-nail guy. And I didn't really want to change him.

"I don't have to do anything." Rob winked. "He just has to believe I will. There are plenty of girls who *don't* have psychotic boyfriends, and that bastard goes after low-hanging fruit. The minute it looks like it might be tough, he's out."

"So you made me seem like more trouble than I'm worth." For a guy who didn't think much of his own brain, this was a solid plan, better than my having-a-baby gambit.

"Yeah. I think the twitch when I said your name was a nice touch."

I laughed. "You're amazing."

"Just so you know, I'm about to kiss you, just to make sure you don't have trouble with anyone else."

"Marking your territory with an inappropriate PDA?" I teased.

"Unless you tell me no." The softness in his eyes told me he'd listen.

"I doubt I'll ever be able to say that to you."

With Davies and the sales team looking on, Rob kissed

the crap out of me. If he hadn't let me go, I'd probably have banged him on the reception desk. He touched the tip of my nose and said loudly, "See you tonight."

CHAPTER SEVENTEEN

Work was better the next day.

After my shift, I had dinner at Rob's, then we shot another vlog. In this one, he was hanging cabinets. While I worked, he'd finished the formerly broken wall, so the archway was professionally framed, no longer a mess of broken plaster, bare wires and exposed posts. I asked a few leading questions to get him started, and once Rob was comfortable, he gave a great performance. He explained the progress he'd made since the last video and included the viewer in the project through body language and expression.

"That looks fantastic," I said.

He smiled, though he didn't stop until he finished with the installation. "This is actually kind of fun. Sorry to make you wait, but—"

"No, it's fine. The kitchen will be done soon, won't it?"

"Another week or two, depending on how hard I work."

I surveyed the progress. The subflooring was gone, replaced by a gorgeous wood grain. Kneeling to touch it, I realized it wasn't hardwood, though it was close enough to the dining room in shade that I doubted anyone would notice the difference.

"Vinyl?" I asked.

"Yeah. It's more durable and easier to clean, better for in here."

"Have you decided on countertops?" There were no counters or lower cabinets at all. He'd built the upper ones from scratch, then finished them with a lovely, mellow stain. Rob used half of the garage as his workshop, but really, he should have a separate building. If he started getting orders from our venture, like I hoped, then I'd suggest it.

"Do you want to see?" He was adorably eager to show me.

"Definitely."

He got his phone and flipped through to a picture he must've taken in a showroom somewhere. The pattern was earth tones, varying brown, caramel and dark chocolate. "Looks like granite, but easier to care for and more durable."

"I like it. I bet it'll be beautiful."

"I'm holding off on buying it until I get the cabinets finished. You want to stay for dinner? I just need to shower and sweep up the dust."

"You shower, I'll take care of it."

"I can't let you clean my kitchen." By his expression, you'd think I had suggested something truly scandalous.

"You can if you expect me to eat here."

"Fine." Rob drew me close in a tender gesture.

I breathed in his warm, delicious scent: cut wood, touch of clean sweat, along with the freshness of his soap. My eyes drifted closed. It wasn't in him to hurry this, and I stretched up to savor the heat of his mouth. His restrained longing flavored it with a sort of tempered urgency, his lips firm and knowing as he deepened the kiss. Already, he knew I liked it when he nibbled my lower lip, when he teased with his tongue and cupped my ass to pull me up against him. My pulse trebled, and it took all my composure not to grab him when he eased back and rested his cheek against the top of my head.

"Wow," I whispered.

"There will be more of that after dinner. You know, it gets a little harder to let go of you every time I have to do it."

"You're just showering, not moving to China," I teased.

He raised his head, taking hold of my shoulders with a wicked gleam in his blue eyes. "Any chance you're feeling dirty?"

"Only always."

I giggled as he pounced and princess-carried me up the stairs. "Wait, I'm supposed to be sweeping the kitchen."

"Yeah, that's a hard choice—naked girl in the shower with me or fully dressed downstairs. Sometimes I wonder about your life choices."

"If you get me naked, I might not care about dinner," I warned.

"I already don't."

Rob started the water, and I stripped out of my clothes, then I got to watch him get naked. Working construction year after year, along with his side projects, gave him a body that made me drool. It was even hotter that his muscles came from actual work, not gym equipment, along with the rough hands that felt so good when he touched me. From broad shoulders to chest to abs, he was mouth-watering. Maybe I should be ashamed of objectifying him, but from his expression, he was doing the same thing to me.

"You are so gorgeous," he murmured.

His shower wasn't necessarily designed for two people, but we made it work. Washing up definitely qualified as foreplay, as I melted thoroughly, running soapy hands all over his body.

What started out playful turned serious pretty fast. Rob didn't even let me wash my hair before he turned off the water.

"Are we done?"

"In here, we are."

"I suspect you of having nefarious intentions."

"I intend to make love to you."

"Cosigned."

We kissed down the hall, still shower-wet, dripping on the floors. The air was cold on my back, but with Rob plastered to my front, I didn't care. His hands were everywhere. More kissing, endless shivers of it, his mouth, my tongue, his teeth, his hands on my ass, hauling me closer, so his cock burned against my belly.

Rob tumbled me to the bed, tangling our legs together. With a wicked grin, he rolled me beneath him. "So many things I could do to you…"

"Make a list," I suggested, breathless.

I expected him to get down to it, but he went back to kissing, caressing my sides in long, lazy strokes. There was a new dimension to his touch, an intimacy I'd never known with anyone else. Fear prickled to life, white noise interrupting the pleasure. Before long, Rob noticed, and he rolled to the side, a frown knitting his brows together.

"You're not into it?"

This was going to sound so stupid. "No, well, yes, but—"

"What?"

"It felt different."

"Not as good?" I groaned, covering my face with both hands. He pulled them away and pressed a kiss to each palm. "Talk to me."

There was no way I could explain the difference between fucking and making love out loud, but I knew when I felt it. Yet if I brought up the *L* word, he might feel pressured to say it, and I wasn't ready to say it back. My breath came in a nervous shudder as a shiver went through me, not the good kind, the about-to-melt-down-for-no-reason kind. Sometimes I hated my brain and would happily trade it for a beard of bees.

"I can't," I managed.

"Did I do something wrong? Hurt you? *Has* someone… hurt you?" By the clench of Rob's jaw, if the answer was yes, he'd put on pants and go kill that somebody.

"No, no and no." I scooted toward him and put my face in his chest, willing myself to calm down before this escalated.

"Come here, beautiful." The gentleness of his voice, paired with his strong arms, nearly unraveled me. "Just tell me what you want. If the answer is this, that's fine. We can lay here."

For a few minutes, I matched my breathing to his, and the worry scaled back. The fact that Rob cared enough about me to change how he touched me? That was a good thing. We didn't have to be in a hurry to define this or slap a label on it. Rob was silent and patient, just running his hands through my hair like that was all he wanted in the world.

"Okay, I'm better now. But seriously, how does this not piss you off?"

Like most of my questions, he took this one seriously. Most guys would be like, *It does, I still want to bang you.* Rob eventually said in a thoughtful tone, "I don't understand why you freeze up, but…that's not new. I'm used to not getting things. So you just have to tell me what to do, and if you can't, then I'll wait until you can."

Right then, I almost blurted out how much I loved him. But I was afraid he wouldn't believe me, so soon on the heels of my freak-out. He might take it for gratitude, and though it wasn't, I had to save the confession for the right time, preferably not when we were both naked. Sex also contributed to people blathering stuff they didn't mean.

When we made love, it was tender and slow, so gentle that I almost cried when I came. And that had *never* happened before. He wrapped his arms all the way around me, coming in for a kiss as he worked faster and faster, thrusting to a hot, trembling finish. I tasted his orgasm in the gasping breaths against my lips. Unlike the last time, Rob didn't roll away immediately. He was big enough that when he shifted his weight off his arms and onto me, I sank into the mattress. The heat and weight of him didn't make me feel trapped, though. I loved holding him, stroking him through the afterglow.

We skipped dinner entirely that night.

The rest of the week went fast. On Thursday, I got word from admissions that I'd gotten into the computer science online program. Rob and I celebrated with dinner at the roadhouse, and then I spent the night at his place. He convinced me to start leaving a few things to make it easier to get ready for work. Truthfully, I didn't require much persuading.

Friday night, Avery picked me up on time. Krista and Jillian were already in the car. Since Avery drove a cute, powder-blue Beetle, that left Jillian and me in the backseat. I climbed in after Krista flipped the seat forward for me.

I hadn't gotten a great look at Jillian that day at Walmart, but up close in Avery's car, I recognized her from high school. Jillian Martinez was a chubby girl with brown hair and dark eyes. Her dad was from Mexico; God only knew why he'd decided Nebraska was the best place to settle. Maybe he really loved snow and agriculture programs. From her frown, Jillian hadn't forgiven me for stealing Rob. Which seemed weird since he was Avery's boyfriend, and if *she* was over it…

Jillian fixed a hard stare on me as I settled beside her. "So I hear you're having Rob's love child," she said.

My mouth dropped open. "Holy shit. Already? Doesn't anyone in this town have a life?"

"You grew up in Sharon," Avery said. "So there's your answer."

"Is it true?" Krista peered over her shoulder at me.

"Lord, no. I made it up to discourage my pervert boss, who was about to offer me the lucrative position of chief knob polisher."

Avery made a sound in her throat, almost a growl. "Men like that should be castrated."

"How many baby daddies is that now, Lauren?" Jillian aimed a sugary smile at me.

"That's enough. I already told you, we talked and it's cool." That was Avery, shutting down the bitchiness before it got started.

But I figured, *Why not answer?* "Two since I've been home. If the rumors keep spreading, I'll end up with a litter, each from a different sperm donor. I could sell them for fifty K a pop, Rent-a-Womb, Inc. What do you think, awesome get-rich-quick scheme, yes or yes?"

"Speaking as someone who's currently the size of a tuba, I can only say, *ouch*." But Krista was laughing as she said it.

Avery snickered, and Jillian unwound enough to grin at me. We drove through town and out to the highway; the scenery was pretty much all snowy fields, shadowed by the dark sky overhead. We cracked jokes all the way to Whitney, twenty minutes past Edison.

When I realized where we were, I said, "Jillian. Now you have to tell me what we're doing."

She answered, "Just Jill is fine. And have you heard of the Thunder From Down Under?" At my nod, she added, "Well, it's like that, only low-rent."

"We're going to a strip club? Why didn't anyone tell me?

I don't have any singles!" I half thought they were screwing with me until Avery pulled into a gravel parking lot, just off the interstate. There was a whole lot of nothing around this place, but the neon lights that read JOKERS WILD told a fairly compelling story.

"It's usually women, but once a month, they bring in some dudes," Avery told me.

"I'd watch the girls," Jill said.

"I *have* watched them." A few times, I'd gone out with guy friends in Michigan, and on those weird nights, we ended up in a strip club while they salivated and I drank. But drinking had gotten me into a lot of trouble, so I'd be careful tonight.

"Okay, the only rule of girls' night," Krista put in, "is that we don't talk about guys, other than to admire the ones shaking it on stage. No boyfriend talk, no relationship advice, got me?"

Avery nodded. "I like that plan."

Jill and I agreed to the terms as we hurried across the parking lot, shoulders hunched against the bitter air. Inside, it was warmer, and like a show club straight out of some 80s music video. I stifled a laugh when I realized there were five people in here, not counting us and the staff. Three women and two men. The guys seemed to be together, which couldn't be easy around here. Mentally I saluted them and wondered how Angus was doing back in Michigan; he wasn't just my roommate, but also one of my best friends.

I should call him.

"Let's grab a table near the stage." Krista led the way, giving the impression it wasn't her first time. The music was just cuing up as we sat down and ordered.

Sadly for the man-candy, the guys willing to take their clothes off around these parts weren't much to admire. The first stripper was incredibly thin—to the point that I wanted to bake him some cookies and knit him a scarf. He could dance, though, so that was something, and he did some interesting things with a fire extinguisher. But the point was to joke around with each other, not stare at hot dudes, and we did until Krista bolted for the bathroom.

When she came back, she shook a finger at Jill. "You have to stop it. I don't have any panty liners left."

That only made the rest of us laugh harder. I only had a couple of beers and Krista didn't drink at all. Avery and Jill, on the other hand, slammed back shots until I was impressed they weren't falling out of their chairs. Jill leaned over and put her hand on my arm, waving me closer with the other one. Smirking, I tilted my head for whatever drunken confidence she was about to impart.

"Sorry I misjudged you."

Wow. I didn't expect an apology.

Oblivious to my surprise, she went on, "Avery told me you guys talked. I'm sorry I was a bitch at Walmart, it's just…she hasn't really ever been with anyone…and, well, I thought maybe Rob… Fuck it, I'm not supposed to talk about dudes, never mind."

Damn. That was just starting to get good. But rules were rules.

So I said, "Don't worry about it. We're good now, right? I could use some people to hang with in Sharon."

"Yep. If Avery believes you, that's okay by me. Oh, my God, look at *that* guy."

When the tear-away pants came off, the first thing I noticed was gold lamé underpants. It looked like he was smuggling a salami down there. He was extremely tanned and fit, so my gaze lingered on his chest and thighs. I gradually worked my way upward, only to jolt in my chair when I realized the face I was looking at belonged to a guy old enough to be my granddad.

He caught my eye and winked. Pretty much everyone in the club was on their feet, howling in support. I chucked a five-dollar bill onto the stage. His number was campy as hell, the most original choreography we'd seen all night. I screamed when he did a little twirl, just like the guy in the song, who was also too sexy for his shirt. Jill held on to my shoulder, staring up in what could've been drunken adulation.

"God, I hope I'm that much fun when I get old," I said to the table.

"Amen, sister." Krista winced and put a hand on her belly.

"Crap. Too much excitement? Should we go?" It wasn't that late, but I'd die if we ended up delivering a baby in a strip club. Try explaining *that* to the paramedics.

"No, it's false labor. I'm told it's normal in the last few months or so."

"Wow, so you're about to pop," Jill marveled.

Krista scowled. "I'm not a balloon."

"Could've fooled me," Avery mumbled.

I snickered.

"Screw you guys, especially you, Lauren. You're supposed to be my sister in solidarity."

"Because of my faux gestations? I wonder if I could work up a hysterical pregnancy like dogs do." I widened my eyes at Krista. "Would that make you feel better?"

"Only if you actually get fat and milk shoots out your nipples."

"That would be superawkward to explain at work."

"But think of the credence it would add to the story you told your boss," Avery pointed out. "What are you doing about that anyway?"

"Hell if I know. I guess I'll lose the baby in a few weeks, and I feel *horrible* saying that when women are going through it for real."

"It's not your fault," Jill said, surprising me. "If you didn't work for such a complete creeper, you wouldn't even be in this situation."

"True," Krista said. "Somebody should teach that asshole a lesson."

On stage, Gold Lamé Grandpa took an impressively limber bow. The guys at the next table whistled as he walked off stage. Avery propped her chin in her hands, an odd and disturbing darkness in her green eyes. With one fingertip she ringed the top of her glass.

"It's true," she said quietly. "He should definitely pay."

CHAPTER EIGHTEEN

In early April Rob finished the kitchen and cooked dinner for us, which we ate in the gorgeous dining room. It was amazing how much progress he'd made on the house—and how much I'd actually helped, if less so in the past month since I started at the dealership. Though I missed lending a hand, it was good to have money coming in.

But we made sure to record weekly vlogs, and his views just kept increasing. At last count, he had an incredible number of subscribers. Rob didn't seem to realize how much promotion I was doing at night after I went home. He also didn't know about the ads I'd purchased for him, promoting his business. He was adorably excited when the furniture orders starting coming in. Not a ton, one or two a week, but it was more than he'd expected.

Maybe one day, he can make a living at this.

That night, I mentioned buying a car, but Rob shook his head. "That makes no sense. Just drive the truck, it's not like I'm using it. Save your money for tuition."

I started to argue, then I decided it was smarter to keep

quiet and do as I pleased. Since I'd never owned my own car, I wanted one, end of story. But I couldn't think of a way to explain it that didn't end with us arguing and me yelling, *You're not the boss of me.*

The week after, he went back to working construction full-time. The weather had warmed enough to make that possible, and I paid for my first round of classes. With no other living expenses, I didn't give up on the idea of my own wheels, however, no matter what Rob said. So six weeks after I started at the car lot, I got one of the salesmen to make me a deal on a trade-in. My credit was nonexistent, so he took $500 down, subsequent payments to be deducted from my paycheck for the next eighteen months, after which point I'd own my car outright. So working for Davies had some perks after all.

After work, I drove home to meet my mom. Rob had a longer drive since he worked outside of Sharon, and I'd felt a bit sneaky enlisting my mom to help me return his truck on the sly. But she approved of untangling our affairs because "it's a bad idea to be dependent on someone you're dating." Based on what I'd seen when her life disintegrated, she wasn't wrong.

"Are you sure this is a good idea?" she asked, parking behind me in Rob's driveway.

"He might yell at me. I'll get over it." Truthfully I couldn't picture it. I already felt like a bitch, as if I was chucking his kindness back in his face.

"If you say so."

The back door of his garage wasn't 100 percent secure if you knew how to jiggle it. I let myself in and hit the button on the garage, then put Tessa Green-tea safely away. Pondering for a moment, I tucked the keys inside the visor. *Should be safe enough.* After checking to make sure the place was secure, I pushed the panel and ducked out the front to my mom's waiting car. It wasn't cold, so she had the windows down, and the air smelled damp and green, the trees all around just starting to bud.

"He's really got some gorgeous property. The house needs some work, though."

From the outside, I agreed. He'd been focused on the inside, making it beautiful and livable, so the paint was chipped and peeling, the gutters needed to be cleaned after the long winter and the roof would probably need to be replaced in the next year or so.

"Let's get out of here before he catches us."

Laughing, my mom drove us to the dealership, and we didn't see Rob's red truck along the way. I was beyond excited when we got there. The final paperwork was ready, so I signed off, took the documentation and the keys and practically sprinted out to claim my beautiful, pre-owned Honda Civic, nicely nondescript in charcoal-gray. But the garage guys promised me it was reliable, and if it turned out they were lying, well, I knew where to find them.

My mom circled around the car once and gave an approving nod. "This is a really sensible purchase."

"Dammit. Now I have buyer's remorse. I knew I should've bought that old DeLorean on eBay instead."

"If you want, I can ask Stuart about car insurance for you."

"That would be great, thanks."

"Not a problem. Don't make any plans for next weekend, all right? Stuart and I are hosting a…thing. It would mean a lot to me if you came."

My gaze flew immediately to her left hand, which was ringless. I raised a brow. "Oh, yeah? Something you'd like to tell me?"

"There might be an interesting announcement." She glowed at me.

I couldn't remember ever seeing her look that way, even

before my dad went broke. "I'll be there. Just tell me where and when."

"Thanks, honey. It's next Saturday at eight. We rented a private room at the Grove. Are you coming home or…?"

"I'd better stop by Rob's. I'm not trying to hide this from him, I just didn't want to have the 'returning your truck—it's fine, keep it,' discussion. This way, it's a done deal."

"Okay, good luck."

He was home by the time I got to his place, just climbing out of his truck. Usually he'd showered by the time I arrived, so I sucked in a sharp breath at the sight of him sweaty and dirty after a hard day's work. His hair was a little shaggy, grown out for the winter. Rob was the kind of guy who got, like, three haircuts a year, two of them during the warmer months. At the moment, he had the beginnings of a beard, and I was inclined to encourage him to grow it.

I swung out of my car. "Hey, you."

"Hey, yourself." His gaze went to the Civic. "Can I figure Tessa's back in the garage?"

I nodded and told him where to find the keys. "Thanks for letting me borrow it."

"Not a problem." Maybe he was too tired to argue; that could be good for me. "You want to come in?"

Huh. That was a decidedly cooler greeting than I usually got from him. By now he'd ordinarily have grabbed me and kissed me, said something adorable, sweet or both. *Before, you said I didn't need to call before stopping by.*

"Not if you're busy." Pain splintered outward, starting with a weird, awful tightness in my chest.

"It's fine, come on." He headed for the door, unlocked it and wiped his boots on the mat outside. Before stepping onto the polished hardwood, he pulled them off and left them outside.

My shoes weren't as filthy, but I took them off and left them on the rug just inside. *Holy shit.* The living room was done, completely finished, painted and furnished. Rob's taste ran to simplicity, but he had phenomenal style. A soft ecru rug centered the room, allowing the floors to shine in darker contrast. He'd added a chocolate-and-caramel-striped sofa and a plain brown love seat. Clearly he'd made the coffee table himself, and it was a gorgeous piece with flat surfaces above and below for magazines and remotes, then drawers below, likely for hiding stuff, like afghans or snacks. I'd picked out the paint for the walls, but I couldn't have imagined how nice it would look all pulled together. No pictures yet, but the whole downstairs was done.

"I can't believe you didn't tell me. The place looks fantastic."

He folded his arms, unresponsive to my praise. "We're just *full* of not telling each other things, huh?"

"Is this about the car?" I tensed, gearing up for our first real argument.

Before now, I never stuck around long enough to have these awkward moments, where we stepped on each other's feelings and then had to figure out how to make it right. My instincts told me to run. *Huh. So maybe it's not just guys who bail.* Somehow I kept the awful swirling in my stomach from driving me out of the front door.

"You're the smart one. Figure it out."

That pissed me off for, like, ten reasons. "Maybe I should let you cool off."

He let out a sigh. "No, we have to settle this. It's been a long, crappy day, and it's harder than I expected at work without my dad. And then I come home to…this. You want the truth? This hurts, Lauren. I mean, you didn't talk to me or ask me to inspect the car before you bought it. That's the *one* thing I know about—fixing things. I can't do a lot for you as a boyfriend, and it makes me feel like a worthless sack of shit when you cut me out. It's not that I don't want you to have a car, I just want to feel like my opinion matters."

I never thought about it that way; I only saw it as asserting my independence, taking care of myself so Rob didn't have to. The ache in my chest intensified. It would be better if he were mad, but the look—a raw mixture of pain and sadness—in his eyes said I'd made him feel *just* like everyone else, as if he wasn't smart enough for me to solicit his input.

"So…you just wish I'd taken you with me to look, is that right?"

"Yeah," he said quietly.

"But…you said it was a waste of money. I didn't want to argue."

"You think we're never going to butt heads? That's not how this works. If you've made up your mind, it doesn't matter what I think. It's your money and your call."

"I'm sorry. In hindsight, I should've asked you. But…that seems like a super couple-y thing to do, and…I didn't know you were my boyfriend."

He actually flinched like I'd smacked him in the face. *Oh, shit. You made it worse.* "What the fuck do you think we've been doing? I went to your work, remember, and set your boss straight, made it really clear that you're off-limits."

The last thing I ever wanted to do was hurt Rob. Tears threatened, and I hadn't cried in front of anyone besides Nadia in years. I chewed on my lip, trying to control the melt-down. This time, though, it wasn't panic. I'd thought an anxiety attack provided the worst feeling in the world, but nope. Knowing I'd trampled all over his feelings like a thoughtless asshole—that was the pit of hell.

"I thought that was just…you doing me a favor, getting Davies off my back."

"No." He spoke the word flatly. "Look, when women hit on me, I tell them I'm taken. Is that wrong?"

I pushed out a shaky breath, fighting the tightness of my throat. "It's not. I just didn't know, when did you clarify? I'm *really* sorry I hurt your feelings about the car, but you can't expect me to guess where we stand. I wasn't in any hurry to pin a label on it. Hell, I like being with you, even when you're mad at me."

Before he could respond, I went on, gathering steam. "And dammit, Rob, you need to get it right out of your fucking head that you have to *do* anything to be with me. It's not a contest. I'm not ranking your performance. This will never, ever work if you don't accept the fact that you're enough for me, exactly as you are. In fact, right now, you're kind of being an ass, and the best part is finding out you're not this endlessly patient, perfect person, because *I* am so incredibly screwed up, yet you still seem to see something good in me."

"You are *all* the good," he said softly.

Hot tears trickled down my cheeks, alerting me to the fact that I'd lost control, but it didn't shut me up. I didn't even wipe them away. "And okay, this is how crazy I am. Deep down, this mess makes me happy because it means you trust me enough to show how you feel, because I know damn well you never let people know they've hurt you. So by fighting with me, you just inducted me into a VIP club with a membership of me."

With rough hands, he tipped up my chin and kissed away my tears. Then he wrapped his arms around me. Another girl might've protested the dirt and sweat, but it was so good to be close to him. I settled in, winding my arms around his waist and listened to his heart for a few moments in silence, wondering if he thought I was completely nuts.

"You scare me to death," he whispered.

"Why?"

"Because of how you've cracked me open, how well you see me."

"It's mutual, you know. I've never fought with anybody before. Not like this."

"Nadia?"

"It's not the same. When we hurt each other, we don't fight. We stop talking, and when we're tired of it, one of us offers sweets as an apology and then we skate past it."

He kissed the tip of my nose. "I never felt sorry for my sister before."

"Huh?"

"She's missing out on you."

"Are we okay?" My knees literally felt shaky. I had no idea how people withstood tumultuous relationships full of moments like this.

"Yeah. Congrats on the car. I'm sure you did a great job finding a reliable one. You're right, I was kind of being an ass about it. Like you need me to help you do that."

"Need and want, remember, Rob? We had this talk. It's not weakness to let an expert offer guidance. I should've realized that."

"*Expert* might be the wrong word."

"Quiet, you."

"Yes, ma'am." Still holding me, he eased back enough to gaze into my face. His eyes were like twilight, dark and full of shadows. "What you said about just wanting to be with me… I'll work on that. I can't promise to change my head overnight, but…I've always had to earn everything. So it's hard not to look at you and see this amazing girl I have to bust my ass for."

"It's just the opposite. In fact, why don't you go take a shower, and I'll make dinner. I've been dying to get in your sexy new kitchen."

"So it's my appliances you're after?"

"Definitely."

Teasingly, I smacked him on the ass as he walked away, and he shot me a look so smoky that I almost followed him up the stairs. *Down, girl. You promised.* I was a better baker than cook, but during my mom's breakdown, I'd learned by necessity to fix a few things. Rummaging in his pantry and fridge convinced me that chicken and rice would be easiest, if not the fastest dish. I thawed the chicken in the microwave, then layered it with rice, mushroom soup, water and cheese. He also had the makings for salad, so I threw that together.

I was on the couch when Rob came back down. "Where's my food, woman?"

"In the oven. Can you last another forty-five minutes? If not, we can have salad now."

"No, I'll be fine. But you're really far away."

Smiling, I moved down the couch and snuggled against his side. I hadn't been here since he finished the living room, so we'd never done this before. Cuddling in bed inevitably led to sex, so there was a quiet beauty to these moments: his arm around my shoulder, Rob flicking through channels on the remote. Maybe it was wishful thinking, but it seemed like there was a new layer of intimacy and understanding between us.

"Keep next Saturday free, by the way. We're going to an engagement party."

He grinned. "You'd tell me if it was ours, right? Unlike the car."

"Don't even joke."

"Who, then?"

"My mom and Stuart. She didn't confirm it, but I can't imagine any other reason they'd be throwing a fancy party at the Grove."

"Good guess," he agreed. "Are you okay with it? With your dad and everything—"

After thinking for a few, I nodded. "I like Stuart—he makes my mom happy. And it's not like I'm a kid who'll be stuck with him trying to parent me."

He seemed to accept that. "So I'll need a suit?"

"Probably. I can't wait. I might wear that red dress you remember so fondly." Provided I could still wriggle into it. Drinking wasn't a sport that left you fit and trim.

"Evil."

We watched half an hour of TV before the timer went off and I went to check on dinner. I opened the oven, pleased to find everything had come together in the simple, one-dish meal I remembered. While Rob relaxed, I set the table. In the back of my head, it seemed like we were playing house, though why I didn't feel that way when he cooked for me, I had no clue.

"It's ready."

After dinner, we snuggled on the couch for a couple of hours. I could tell he was too tired for sex, and oddly, that was okay by me. In fact, I had the urge to take care of him. When he rolled his shoulders and winced, I tested his muscles with a questing hand.

He groaned. "I'll be fine in a few days."

"I can make it better tonight." Without waiting for him to move, I crawled behind him and perched on the arm of the couch. At first it was like massaging a block of wood, but as I worked out the knots, he relaxed into my hands. I did his neck, back and shoulders, kneading until my hands hurt. *Worth it to see his face look like this.*

"I now believe in Santa Claus," Rob murmured.

"Why's that?" I kissed the top of his head with a tenderness that scared me.

"Because I've been asking him for you for years, and you're finally here."

CHAPTER NINETEEN

Thanks to a week of eating salad and protein bars, I did wriggle into the red dress. Back when I bought it, I thought it was the prettiest thing I'd ever seen. Even five years later, it didn't seem dated, mostly because it was a retro design; I still loved the sweetheart neckline, the slim straps so I didn't have to worry about a special bra and the beaded silver band that cinched in my waist. Made of sexy red satin, the gown suited me, and the cocktail length showed off my cute red shoes with the dainty crisscross around my ankles.

I twirled, checking out my hair and makeup in the mirror on the back of my bedroom door. I'd put my hair up and pinned the curls in place with silver and crystal hairpins, adorned with lacquered red roses. Since this was basically everything I'd worn to the party that night, I hoped that I lived up to Rob's memory. Certainly I had higher expectations of him than the date whose name I barely knew even then. When he rang the bell, I trotted carefully down the stairs to let him in.

"Wow," Rob said.

"I'll take that as a compliment. Let me get my wrap." One of my casual, puffy jackets wouldn't suit this outfit at all, so I had a silver pashmina. Fortunately, it was deep enough into spring that the nights weren't bitter cold.

I couldn't remember seeing him so dressed up before, but he looked incredible in the stark tones he'd chosen: black suit, white shirt, red tie. "You're so handsome."

"Thanks. Ready?"

"Yeah, let's go."

He set a hand on the small of my back to guide me to the truck, then he opened the door and lifted me in. For a few seconds, he stared at my mouth. "Am I allowed to kiss you?"

"Absolutely." I lifted my silver evening bag. "I can redo my lipstick, if the package lied and it smears."

Smiling, he bent down and kissed me lightly. "I won't risk it. Where's your mom?"

"Stuart picked her up earlier. They're finalizing a few arrangements at the Grove."

Rob closed the door, went around the truck and got in. "Do you know how many people will be there?"

"People from his work, hers, friends and family. I don't think the private facilities will hold more than fifty guests, so it can't be too big a party."

That was the only thing keeping me calm. I didn't have to worry about meeting new people; I just had to look happy for my mom—easy enough, even with my issues. Yet since I was facing the occasion sober, it was hard not to be a little nervous. Rob distracted me by speculating what kinds of tiny food would be on the menu, so I didn't fret as much on the way there. Tonight, there was valet parking at the Grove, so he swapped his keys for a ticket and escorted me inside. A host in formal attire guided us from the front door to the back parlor; the doors were closed and a gilt framed sign proclaimed BARRETT-LEE ENGAGEMENT PARTY.

"Told you," I whispered to Rob.

The guy opened the door for us, and my mom waved in excitement when she caught sight of me. "So glad you're here. How does everything look?"

I took in the old-fashioned elegance of the patterned carpet, tables covered in white linen. A heavy crystal chandelier shone overhead, reflecting off the small dance floor. From the white roses to the flutes of champagne, the whole room was gorgeous and romantic. Even Stuart had risen to the occasion in a black tux, and he looked every bit as happy as my mom.

"It's gorgeous, complete perfection," I assured her.

"Thank God. There was a small snafu with the florist, but the roses look good, right?"

I nodded. Before I could say more, the other guests started arriving. Like Rob and me, people had certainly glammed up for the occasion, but in my admittedly biased opinion, we were the hottest couple here. For dinner, we sat with Stuart and his family; his dad stared at me until I could practically hear him thinking, *Look, it's bathrobe girl,* but Rob took my hand, distracting me from what could've been a bad moment.

From then on, I focused on him, letting my mom chat with our soon-to-be relatives for both of us. The menu card in front of me promised green salad with vinaigrette, mushroom soup, roast chicken with rosemary potatoes and crème brûlée for dessert. We ate an hour after arrival, then the speeches started. A woman from my mom's work was apparently her maid of honor, so she told some funny stories about Mom and Stuart, then his best man took over, warming up the crowd further with more jokes.

Once he finished, he glanced at Stuart's brother, a guy I'd

just met. "Time for the families to weigh in. You're up, Randall."

He pushed his chair out and strode to the mic, much more confident in his body language than Stuart. "When I found out my bro was getting married, I said, 'Seriously?' Because we'd all given up on the idea that he could find anyone to put up with him."

Everyone laughed but I didn't think it was too funny. From Stuart's expression, he wasn't superamused, either. His smile was stiff and frozen, and I wondered if he was like Rob—used to seeing himself as a disappointment. From what I recalled, he'd grown up in Illinois, so his family must be visiting for the party. Given how extravagant it was, they must've been planning it for months, maybe even before I came home. Pondering that, I stopped listening to Stuart's brother.

So I was completely flummoxed when Randall said, "Now I'll turn the floor over to Lauren, Miriam's lovely daughter."

Shit. You didn't tell me I have to talk, Mom. I shot her a daggered look as I pushed back from the table. Rob shot to his feet as I stood, a gesture that prompted an approving smile from Stuart's mother. I skirted the tables, heart hammering too fast. *You can do this for her. You can. You're the only family she has.* Taking the mic, I felt sick to my stomach until I found Rob in the crowd. *I'll talk to him. Everyone else is invisible.* My other hand curled into a fist, nails biting into my palms.

"I'm a little unprepared," I said softly, trying to avoid feedback. "But it's easy to see why my mom chose Stuart to share her life. She told me she practically fell in love the minute she heard him sing, and I can confirm that he's really talented. He's also kind, intelligent and hardworking. He's such a sweet guy, and I'm glad to welcome him into our family."

There, that's long enough, right? Rob gave me a thumbs-up as if he could read my mind. I finally broke eye contact with him and glanced at Stuart, who was smiling much brighter now. "So does this mean I can borrow the car...Dad?"

Everyone laughed, as I intended, but it wasn't the kind of humor that made him the butt. He grinned at me and called, "Maybe," as I put the mic back and worked my way back to my place at the table.

Rob hugged me to hide the fact that I was shaking. He held me until I had a grip on the nerves I'd hidden the best I could. "You did great," he whispered.

Afterward, they piped in slow, romantic music. The party room was compact, not big enough for a DJ or a band, but the speakers were good. As others coupled up, Rob led me onto the floor, a surprise since I didn't peg him as the dancing type. Yet he was graceful, light on his feet as we moved together; he was big enough to make me feel delicate and dainty in his arms.

"I could kill my mom," I mumbled.

She was dancing on the other side of the room, trying to catch my eye. *Sorry,* she mouthed. A tap on Stuart's shoulder, and they circled toward us until we were close enough to talk. I considered ignoring her, but that would be childish.

"Evelyn and Chris came up with the idea for speeches," she whispered.

"And Randall added himself to the program," Stuart put in.

Yeah, given the impression he made, I could picture that. No point in ruining their big night. I got through it. So I smiled at them. "It's fine. I was just a little nervous."

Understatement.

Mom flashed me a knowing look as Stuart said, "I appreciate everything you said about me. We don't know each other very well, but I'm looking forward to changing that."

"Me, too," I said.

"You'll have the chance in September," Mom said. "Stuart just listed his house."

"When is he moving in?"

"We're getting married in September, so definitely then, if not before."

It felt a little weird that she was telling me this instead of talking it over with me, but she had lived by herself for two years before I'd come back. I couldn't expect her to consult me, like I'd be sticking around forever. Still, I didn't know how I felt about living with Stuart. They were both watching me, a touch anxious, so I dug for a bright smile.

"I hope you don't have any trouble selling your place," I murmured. "And congratulations again."

Only Rob spoke fluent enough Lauren to sense I needed to get away from them. He spun me into an ambitious maneuver in time to the upswing of the music, twirling me out and back in, and the movement separated us from the other two. My mom didn't try to follow; she only rested her head on Stuart's shoulder with a dreamy half smile.

"How do you feel about that?" Rob asked.

"Don't know yet. I need some time to process."

"Understandable. I can't imagine my mom with anyone but my dad. Not that our situations are the same."

"I know what you mean. But she's definitely happy with him, and it's not like I planned to live at home forever. I'd be an asshole if I pitched a fit over her finally having a life."

He put his mouth close to my ear. "Doesn't mean you want a close-up of newlywed bliss?"

Picturing that, I couldn't help but grimace. "You make a sound point."

"You could move in with me."

Startled, I almost jerked out of his hold. "I could what now?"

"I'm serious. There's plenty of room and I don't need help with house payments."

"I can't mooch off you, Rob. I'd feel like a kept woman."

He grinned. "Problem?"

"For my self-esteem, yeah. But if you let me buy groceries and pay utilities while you cover the mortgage, I might be okay with that." Saying that, I waited for the panic to kick in, but for once, my brain was quiet. "Can I think about it? We don't have to decide tonight."

"Of course, beautiful. For you, there's no limit on how long I'd wait."

Stretching up, I kissed him. "Sweetness like that will get you underneath this red dress."

He shifted his hand a touch lower, more on my hip than my waist. "I'm counting on it."

That night, I made his secret, dirty fantasy come true.

A few weeks later, my phone rang in the middle of the night. I was at home because Rob had spent the evening with his parents; they'd wanted to talk about his dad's condition, which I wasn't supposed to know about. I groped for my cell, dropped it on the floor. "What?"

"It's time. I need you to meet me at the hospital, Lauren." Oh, shit. "Krista?"

She moaned, breathing fast before she could reply. "You know someone else who's having a baby?"

"I'll be right there."

Before heading out, I texted Rob, letting him know I'd be at the hospital with Krista for who knew how long. He didn't reply, unsurprisingly; he was probably asleep.

I was a shambles when I ran into the emergency room. Krista and her mom were already there filling out paperwork. Red-faced and sweaty, Krista was hunched over in a wheelchair, looking like she might pass out. I ran over to her, kneeling beside her. Her hand clamped onto mine, and she nearly broke all my fingers.

"Contraction?"

Note to self: adopt. Or get a dog. Anything else.

Before long, they had us in a birthing room, which didn't look a whole lot different from a regular one. I expected a whole lot more action, but after they checked her dilation, the nurse said, "Get her some ice chips. It could be a while."

"But it really fucking hurts," Krista snarled.

Her mom stroked the hair off her head, and she smacked her hand away. Krista snapped, "I don't want you in here seeing this, Mom. Any viewing of my vagina is off-limits to close family relations."

"Fine. Send Lauren if you need me later." Janet seemed sad when she left, but it was unwise to agitate a woman in labor.

I didn't know what else to do, so I got the ice. When I got back, the nurses were doing things to Krista. To the best of my recollection, nobody ever told me how slow babies came into the world. On TV, it was always done in half an hour, but I sat there sympathizing with Krista for *ten* hours before things progressed. They gave her some kind of medicine to speed up the process and made her walk around, and then the party finally got started. Four hours later, her daughter was born. At that point, I'd never been so exhausted in my life, and all I did was hold her hand, let her yell at me and feed her ice chips.

"Isn't she amazing?" Krista murmured, as the nurse set the baby in her arms.

"Did you decide on a name?"

"The last time I Skyped with Kenji, he said he likes the name Naomi."

"That's pretty."

Tiredly, she nodded, tracing the baby's tiny features with

a fingertip. "Would you mind calling my mom in? She's still here, right?"

Since I hadn't been out of the room in five hours, I couldn't be sure. "Be right back."

Janet was asleep in the waiting room down the hall, so I woke her up with a gentle hand on the shoulder. "Your granddaughter's finally here. Ready to meet her?"

"Oh, Jesus, finally." Her spine popped as she staggered to her feet.

I steadied her and followed her back down the hall. Krista was sweaty and tired, but she beamed when she spotted her mom. "I did it. No epidural, no episiotomy."

"Oh, honey, it would've hurt a lot less with pain meds."

"If there's a next time, I'll try it that way. I just wanted to know if I could, that's all."

"You're braver than me," I said around a jaw-cracking yawn.

"You must be dying for some food and a nap," Janet said. "I've had a whole pot of coffee on my own, so I can take it from here, if—"

"Thanks for everything," Krista cut in.

"If you're sure, I could use some sleep. I'll come back tomorrow during visiting hours." Luckily it was Sunday, so maybe I could get enough sleep so I wouldn't be a wreck for work on Monday morning.

"Does Naomi need anything particular?" Krista hadn't wanted a shower because she thought it was better to wait until the baby was born. That way she could be sure she didn't end up with a ton of pink stuff for a surprise boy on the off-chance the ultrasound was wrong.

"We'll have the baby shower when I get home," she said with a grin. "I know, I do everything backward. Baby before wedding, shower after childbirth."

Shrugging, I dismissed the idea that there was a right way

to live. "I'm so happy for you. I bet you can't wait to see Kenji and show him her little face."

She sighed softly. "I can't wait for him to come home."

"How much longer?"

"Ten months or so. Give or take."

Bending down, I kissed her cheek and touched the top of baby Naomi's pink hat. Then Janet hugged me and I stumbled out of the room. Though I couldn't put my finger on it, that experience changed me. Maybe it would sound stupid if I said it out loud—and shit, Krista would laugh at me—but what I'd just seen was...inspiring. Krista was now essentially a single mom, but she wasn't panicking, even though the guy she loved was across the world. It made my problems seem small by comparison.

More to the point, her faith resonated in me, making me want to be stronger, *better*—and to believe in happy endings, even if I'd never really seen any. If my mom could take another crack at one, maybe I could stop seeing the world as such a dark place. Wearily, I climbed into my Civic and looked at the time.

Not quite five.

My eyes burned, and I had a headache clamping around my temples, a combination of exhaustion and lack of caffeine. The obvious solution to both those problems? Crawl into bed; don't get up until tomorrow. Instead, I drove to Rob's. At some point—and without my realizing it—he'd become my home, not the house I grew up in. And right now, for reasons I couldn't articulate, I really needed to see him. There was a tightness in my chest like something terrible had happened, only it wasn't that way at all. Could be the fatigue, but I felt like crying for no reason, and I didn't want to do it alone.

I texted, Krista had her baby. Be there in ten minutes.

Rob: im here.

As the dusk pooled in purple shadows between the trees, Rob opened the door as I pulled into the drive. He was waiting in a pool of golden light, arms opening to pull me in before I even realized how bad I needed it. *I love you, Rob. I love you* so *fucking much*. Throat clotted with too much emotion, I turned my cheek against his chest, eyes closing.

"How's Krista? Is the baby okay?"

"Yeah, they're both fine. She had a little girl, and I think they're naming her Naomi." Seeming relieved, he cupped the back of my head in his big hands and went to work on the knots at the base of my skull. I nearly melted into a puddle. "Thanks."

"And how are you? You look beat."

"I am. But I wanted you more than sleep."

His smile was like sunrise over the ocean, banishing all shadows and bathing me in a gorgeous shimmer of blue and gold. "I'm glad you came."

Taking a second look, he seemed exhausted, too. "What's up?"

He hesitated before admitting, "My folks talked to Nadia this week. About Dad."

That must be why his parents wanted him to come over.

"How did she take it?" God, I was turning into such a shitty long-distance friend, like out of sight meant out of mind. I'd lost contact with Krista when she moved, too. Though we'd been emailing regularly, Nadia and I needed some face-to-face time soon.

"Well enough, I hear. I guess, based on how they started the Serious Talk, she thought he was dying of cancer, so Parkinson's didn't seem as bad."

"I'll call her."

"Okay," he said. "Come on, I'll make something to eat."

I shook my head, arms tightening on his waist. "Can we stay like this for a bit longer?"

"As long as you want," he promised. "I'm not going anywhere."

And like an idiot, I believed him.

CHAPTER TWENTY

In early June, I started my online classes.

The lack of classroom attendance made it much easier for me to focus, and as I'd hoped, the day job didn't offer enough stress for me to worry about work when I wasn't at the car lot. I got a sympathy bouquet from one of the office ladies, and when I gazed at her blankly, she dropped her eyes. I had no idea what this was about, until she touched me gently on the arm.

"I'm friends with Avery Jacobs's mother," she whispered. "I know. Avery mentioned it to Margaret, and she knows I work with you…I'm so sorry for your loss."

Oh.

I felt even worse, but since I made up that story and Rob came in, Davies had been the most professional butthead in the world. "These are beautiful. But if it's all right, I'd rather not talk about it."

For so many reasons.

"I'll let the other girls know."

"Thanks." Feeling like a jackass, I got back to work, greeting customers and answering phones.

June melded into July in a flurry of work, school and Rob. That night I did some programming for the first time in ages, other than what I did on a regular basis on Rob's site or promoting his channel online. It was crazy how popular "At Home with Rob" had become. Obviously people got famous on YouTube, but usually it wasn't a guy talking about building tables or refinishing a floor.

Yeah, but look at Rob.

At this point, I could hardly stand to read his comments. He laughed at the sexual propositions and girls who were like, *Rob, I think I love you.* But the subscriptions kept ticking up, though he didn't get more orders than he could handle, despite the impressive number of women who liked watching him build things. The longer we dated, the less I liked imagining countless women gawking at my boyfriend. *But fuck it, I'm happy he's got a following. Maybe we can parlay it into sponsorship money somehow.*

Too bad more people weren't willing to spend money on his beautiful furniture, and I had no idea how to rectify it. He was still doing construction full-time, making tables and things on nights and weekends. Between that extra work and my classes, we didn't spend as much time together as I wanted. At the end of June, Stuart's house hadn't sold, and I was three months away from living with him and my mom, still considering Rob's suggestion about moving in together.

Sunday morning, I got up and checked my email. There were some bullshit "jokes" from a guy in one of my classes. He was always sending me stuff like, "God, this assignment was a bitch. I wish I had boobs so I could get an A too, right? LOL."

My classes were a mix of people my own age and guys coming back to school after being downsized or whatever. So

I faced two different brands of discrimination: the usual internet kind from immature dudes who hadn't learned better yet, and graven-in-stone prejudice from fifty-something men with a sincere belief that I was an intellectually inferior being.

Most of my professors were okay, but there was one weirdo who was constantly digressing to tell Vegas stories, most of which included strippers: his favorite anecdote involved a woman wearing nothing but Saran wrap. I could only wonder if the other two women in class with me were the same level of revolted. Another thing that pissed me off—group projects. Because the guys I was partnered with treated me like a personal assistant, demanding I handle PowerPoint presentations and the graphic portion while they did the "hard" stuff. I'd noticed, too, that the faculty didn't seem to take me quite as seriously. They tried to steer me toward graphic design, like I was an artist who knew some HTML, not a real programmer.

But I ignored that crap and pushed on, coding as assigned. It was exhausting to fight about it, and since I had nothing to prove, I usually went with the flow. *I'm not here to impress you idiots.* Sighing, I checked forums and the cloud for my next project. *Moving on.*

It had been forever since I checked any of my favorite web comics or humor sites, so I took my laptop downstairs to surf while I ate my cereal. As usual, my mom wasn't around. These days, she spent most days at Stuart's, helping him improve the curb appeal of his house. I suspected that wasn't all, but that was the last thing I wanted to think about.

Scrolling through my feed made my eyes glazed over. I'd missed all kinds of cuteness: baby owls, meerkats, regular cats, a dog that could dance…then a headline caught my eye from MaryJane, a site similar to Jezebel, only with more traffic and shares. At Home with Rob: His or Mine? For a few seconds, I just stared. *No way.* I clicked through, just in case it wasn't a coincidence. Nope, *my* Rob was featured on the main page, his latest vlog embedded. My stomach churned as I read the "article":

For pure handyman hotness, we're crowning him the king of delts and lats. Ladies, he definitely knows what to do with his tools, and he can fix anything. We're calling him the best thing on the internet this week. The best part is, you have weeks and weeks of delicious to glom. It might even be helpful to those who need actual help with home improvement. I can't speak to that because every time he picks up a hammer, my ovaries melt. There's just something about a guy with a tool belt...

It got worse from there, devolving to a complete dissection of his features, like he wasn't a person. In comments, they approved of his shoulders and chest, claimed his ass needed work and that he had an odd brow ridge, but his eyes were just too sexy for words. I skimmed through, so mad I was practically shaking. Over a hundred already, some threaded so deep you couldn't even read them. HotThing998 wrote: *Oh, shit, yeah, I need some of that. I'll just duct tape his mouth so he can't bore me by talking.* I pretty much wanted to burn down the whole internet; Rob would die if he saw this. But the post already had over 500 shares. When I checked his channel, the number of subscribers had quadrupled, and his views were through the roof.

As I stared at the screen, my phone rang. Rob. "Hey, you."

"So it seems like I'm internet famous." His voice was quiet. "If the guys on the crew see this, I will never live it down."

"It might help your business," I said faintly.

"Maybe."

"Are you mad?"

"Not at you. At the world, a little. No matter what I try to do, it always comes back to one thing, huh?" He sounded so tired.

"Want me to come over?"

"I'm spending the day with my parents. My mom and dad are stressed, getting ready for Nadia's visit later this week."

"Right, she's bringing Mr. Hot Ginger to meet the family."

Happiness sparked through me when Rob laughed. "Is that what you call him?"

"Yeah. You'll understand when you meet him."

"The ginger part, maybe. You think he's hot?"

He can't possibly be jealous, given that the whole fucking interwebz would like to bang him wearing nothing but a tool belt and work boots. I'd read *so many* handyman porn scenarios while skimming the comments on both the MaryJane site and his YouTube channel. It appeared modern womanhood, as a collective, had a secret fetish for guys who worked with their hands.

"He's good for Nadia," I said, skirting the question.

"You'll pay for that dodge, next time I see you."

"And when will that be?" It was as close as I ever came in my life to begging a guy to spend some time with me.

Not that I suspected Rob of avoiding me. We both just had a lot of stuff going on this summer. He'd have more time when the weather cooled off again.

"July Fourth? You have the day off, right? I promised to show up for the family picnic, but I'd be a lot happier about it if you came with me."

"Done. If you want, I could come over the night before, spend the night. I'm actually counting the weeks until the ground freezes again."

His voice deepened. "I miss you, too, beautiful. But my parents need some help with the house. My mom wants to rearrange furniture, like the queen's coming."

"I'm sure Nadia will appreciate it. She'd *better*…since you're busting ass for her instead of seeing your girlfriend." Saying it out loud always gave me a secret thrill.

"This is more about making my mom happy," he said. "Anyway, I have to go. I'll see you later, okay?"

"Counting on it."

I spent the rest of the day studying and working on a project that was due in two weeks. I'd never be able to talk about my work with Rob, but that was fine. I didn't need that from him; there were plenty of people online who could hold that conversation with me. Nobody else could make me feel like he did. Safe. Precious. Important.

Later, I sat in front of my computer, wondering if I should buzz Nadia for a Skype chat. Part of me wanted to tell her about Rob and me before she got here, but the other half thought I should do it in person since I'd already waited this long. In the end, I shut my laptop and decided to be brave. After the holiday, I'd do a group chat with her and Angus, maybe Max, too, unless he preferred to pass. I'd understand, if so.

The dealership was busy with the pre-Fourth of July sale they were running, so work went fast. Soon, I was speeding over to Rob's place. He pounced on me, not even letting me hop out before he kissed me so hard that I almost fainted like a damsel in a silent movie. Suddenly I didn't care so much what they were saying about him on the internet. All of those women might think he was the hottest thing ever, but they didn't get this.

"I have some bad news," he said.

"Crap. What?" If he was canceling on me, I might cry.

"My mom wants me to come to dinner tonight. Apparently they'll be back from the airport in an hour or so. She wants me there waiting, fuck if I know why."

That sounded like Rob's mom. She was always trying to foster a closer relationship between her kids, not realizing that her pushing only aggravated Rob and made Nadia feel awkward. "You're not planning to ditch me?"

"Hell, no, I'm taking you with me. They know we're together, the whole town does. Have you talked to Nadia about us?"

I shook my head. "It's too deep for Skype, and we have other stuff to clear up, too. Plus, it feels weird to break the news that I'm doing her brother online."

He groaned. "I wish you were doing me. How long's it been? Ten years?"

"A week and a half." I suppressed a smile.

"That's ten years in no-sex time. Do you mind driving? I'd need to put gas in the truck, and my mom will bitch if we're not there to give Nadia a big welcome when she rolls up."

"No worries, I'll save you from maternal scolding. Just let me change real quick. I still have jeans here, right?"

"Upstairs, bottom drawer of my dresser. You have two T-shirts and a hoodie, too."

I tossed him my keys as I climbed out of the car. "Back in five."

Rob was already in the car with the motor running. The flats I'd worn to work didn't look bad with jeans, and I'd probably kick them off as soon as we got inside anyway. I was close enough to part of the Conrad clan that nobody would think it was weird for me go barefoot. He raced across town, and we pulled up to find we'd beaten them back.

"All clear." He unlocked the door and let us in.

I could see evidence of Rob's hard work in the changes to the living room—it was prettier and more inviting. He sighed in relief, gave me back my keys and collapsed on the sofa. A wicked urge whispered in my ear, and it was beyond me to resist.

"How much time do you think we have?" I asked.

"Hard to say. My mom's driving, and she tends to be cautious."

"So…we could fool around?" I licked my lips teasingly and put my hand on his thigh. His muscles jumped beneath my hand.

"You're the devil in woman skin. Don't tease me."

"I'm not. Text your parents, ask how far away they are."

For a few seconds, he stared at me, then he did. We watched his phone for two minutes in silence until his mom pinged back, Thirty miles, so a little over half an hour. See you soon!

"Get a towel," I suggested.

Though I expected him to argue, he practically ran to the linen closet. Apparently Rob had a little bit of naughty in him. Once I had the old beach towel, I spread it out on the couch and then reached for the button on his jeans. Before I popped it, I cupped him, found him hard as hell. His breath hissed through parted lips.

"This will be fun." Getting out my phone, I set the alarm for twenty minutes, allowing for cleanup time afterward.

Rob shook his head, watching me. I unfastened his jeans and shucked them down to his knees. As his cock jutted free, he sighed in relief. "Can't believe we're doing this."

"Come on, don't tell me you never thought about me sucking you off right here."

"Once or twice," he admitted on a groan.

"Sit back and enjoy it. But if we're both getting off without getting caught, we have to be fast. No trying to control yourself, okay?"

"I couldn't if I tried," he mumbled, tugging my head down.

No time for teasing, so I got into position, stretching out

perpendicular on the couch, then I licked him up and down to get his shaft good and wet. His fingers tightened in my hair; I sucked his cock into my mouth. Rob bucked upward, lunging into motion. There was no finesse about the way he took my mouth, just urgency.

That's it. Go. Go for it.

His breathing escalated faster than I'd ever heard it. "Fucking shit, that's good. Harder, Lauren. Teeth, just a little…"

In answer, I scraped lightly downward. Most guys didn't like it, but I'd already figured out that Rob enjoyed a whisper of pain. With one hand, I raked my nails over his balls and he jerked, snarling out a sound I'd never heard from him. So I did it again. Then I licked a fingertip and touched him lower, lower. He shuddered and pushed all the way into my throat, thrusting until I could hardly handle him. I couldn't ask if he liked it, but he moved his hips against my fingertip, silently encouraging me. The second I pressed inward, he came, flooding my mouth in hot, convulsive pumps.

He fixed his clothes with shaking hands and then he was completely purposeful about stripping my jeans down, as I'd done to him. "Spread," he rasped.

My knees pretty much melted, dumping me on the towel. Rob dropped to a penitent position and eased his mouth onto me, gradual enough that I didn't tense up, but once he was there, he went at it, licking until I couldn't stop screaming. Then he added a couple of fingers, working me from the inside while he sipped at my clit. The idea that we could be caught actually turned me on more. I imagined people walking in, seeing us like this, and I lifted my hands, humping against his face. The pleasure spiked fast since I was already worked up from sucking him, and he knew just how to touch me.

"Come on, beautiful. No thinking." His words, growled

against my slick flesh, bumped it up a notch. "Just feel this, feel me."

He hooked his fingers, pressing upward, and I arched up, astonished by the orgasm slamming through me. Rob licked until the shivers stopped, then we stumbled to the bathroom to wash up. We'd just hidden the towel in the bottom of the hamper, sprayed a little Febreze and settled on the couch when his family pulled into the driveway. I picked up my phone to make sure I'd turned the alarm off; that might be hard to explain.

"That was insane," he whispered. "I don't think I have the strength to stand up."

"So they'll think you're tired from work." I settled next to him, feeling just about as wrung-out. Maybe that was just as well, or I might be nervous about seeing Nadia, given the significant secret I was keeping from her.

The elder Conrads came in first, with Rob's mom steadying Ned. Nadia and Mr. Hot Ginger followed. I had to admit, he was attractive, all aquiline nose and sharp, ascetic features. He was leaner than Rob and more austere, though his eyes were a warm brown, topped by the copper hair. Trailing behind, Ty's son looked just like him, plus overexcited from the trip, so that should make for a fun night. I smiled at all of them, but I didn't get up. Instead, I waited for Nadia to get settled. Seeing her again evoked a complex wash of emotions: nostalgia, vague anxiety, regret that I hadn't been 100 percent honest with her before I left Michigan. Mostly, though, it was *so* good to see her, even if I was a little worried about how she'd react to finding out that I was now Rob's girlfriend.

Eventually Nadia plopped down beside me while Mr. Hot Ginger showed his son around upstairs. I gave her a hug and she made small-talk noises.

"You're in summer school?" she asked.

"Yep. Most of my credits transferred. I'm basically a sopho-more, but I'm happier in computers. I can do something use-ful, something concrete. There are still problems, of course. I'm the only girl in a lot of my online classes and you wouldn't believe how much crap I get."

"And you dish it right back."

I smiled. "Hells, yeah, I do. So tell me, is Courtney your new best friend?"

When I moved home, Courtney had taken over my half of the room I'd shared with Nadia; she'd bought my furniture, too. I hadn't known her well, but I hoped she was dependable and didn't argue with any of them. It was weird to imagine her wandering around the apartment in my place. *Does she snug-gle with Angus, play video games with Max and bake cookies when somebody's down?* A pang went through me; though it wasn't the life I'd chosen, I missed everyone a lot.

"Friend," Nadia said. "Not best. That'll always be you."

Soon after, her mom asked if they were hungry. I noticed she didn't ask about Rob and me, though we'd both skipped dinner to get here on time, coming straight from work. He just got up and put the leaf in the table without being asked, quietly taking care of things like he always did. *You absolutely do not get enough credit around here.* The distance between Nadia and me had been building for a while, but thinking about it hurt. I couldn't blame her for all of it, either. Like the fight I had with Rob, when I told him he couldn't expect me to know things without being told? Nadia was in the same situ-ation with me, mostly because I couldn't stand to admit how fucked up I was.

I'll talk to her, I promised myself. We'd been friends too long for us to wither and die.

Over soup and sandwiches, Nadia and Mr. Hot Ginger dominated the conversation, but that was understandable. Her parents had known me for years; they were trying to figure out if he was a good guy or not. For the most part, Rob was quiet, but I could tell he was still super relaxed because nothing made any impact on his smile. *Yeah, fooling around was the best idea ever.* After dinner, Rob made an effort with the boyfriend, extending an olive branch about the construction business, though Ty worked on the office management side. Since he seemed to make Nadia happy, I was glad they were back together.

By nine, though, I was so ready to leave. Work, quickie sex, the strain of trying to decide when and how I should tell Nadia about us...damn. That was enough for one day.

I whispered to Rob, "I'm heading out."

Louder, I said goodbye to everyone else and went out to the car to listen to the radio. Five minutes later, he joined me. "That wasn't as horrible as expected."

"Nope. And we have all day tomorrow, too. Can't wait to watch the fireworks with you."

"Don't tell my family about the internet stuff, okay? I don't think they'd get it."

"Whatever you want." I never meant anything more in my life.

CHAPTER TWENTY-ONE

Rob and I met his family at the fairgrounds the next day at three.

Nadia was really distracted by Mr. Hot Ginger and offspring, or I suspected she would've noticed the new vibe between her brother and me sooner than she did. As it was, we ate lunch together, napped in the sun—Rob's head in my lap—played Frisbee and then put away the leftovers as the sun went down without her saying a word. Rob got a blanket out of his truck and we followed everyone else to get comfortable for the fireworks later.

Today, more than usual, I noticed the change in Ned Conrad. He held on to his wife's arm, and I glanced up at Rob, checking his mood. His jaw was set, his eyes blazing with helpless pain. I slipped my hand into his and he squeezed tight, telling me wordlessly that he wanted so bad to fix it, and there was nothing he could do. Nadia and her boyfriend walked ahead, next to her parents, while the kid bolted off, until MHG called him back.

Eventually we found the perfect spot, and Rob spread out

our quilt, then he went to see if his parents needed anything. For some reason. Mr. Hot Ginger went off on his own and when he returned, he radiated sorrow. With peculiar gravitas, he shot off a confetti bottle rocket, but the little dude seemed to think it was awesome. When Rob came back, I shifted to make room for him beside me.

"All good?" I asked.

"Yeah, they're fine. Happy to have us all together."

Glancing over, I saw that Nadia and her guy were nesting like Russian dolls, her in his arms and Sam snuggled up between her knees. That wasn't in the cards for my near future, but she looked so happy that I knew it had to be the right move for *her*. Curling my legs to the side, I rested lightly against Rob. Smiling down at me, he wrapped his arm around my shoulders, drawing me even closer. Another look at Nadia confirmed it; yeah, she'd finally noticed, and she could've done that silent talking thing with her eyebrows, as we'd perfected the *WTF* look ages ago, but she smiled instead. I took it to mean she wasn't mad, so I whispered, "Thank you."

"Hmm?" Rob tilted his head toward me.

"Nothing. But I think Nadia just gave us her blessing."

"That's a relief," he said. "I was losing sleep."

Grinning, I dug my fingers into his side. "Smart-ass."

The fireworks were gorgeous—half an hour of spectacular colors and starbursts brightening the night sky. He held me close the whole time, and I couldn't remember a more magical night. No public speaking, no talking to strangers, no pressure. Just Rob and me, surrounded by people who cared about us, even if they didn't always understand. That was probably the best definition of family anyway.

Afterward, it took forever to get out of the fairgrounds. While we waited to merge onto the main road, he asked, "Do you want to go home or to my parents' place for a while?"

It was late enough that we could call it a day but I should really sit down with Nadia. Since I'd be working the rest of the week, I had no idea if I'd see her before she left. Since I'd claimed to be waiting to talk to her in person, this was my shot.

"Casa Conrad…for a little while anyway."

He nodded. "I'll keep Ty busy while you square things with Nadia."

"You know me so well."

"I'm going for a Ph.D. in Lauren Barrett studies."

I ran a hand gently across the back of his head. "That's a complicated discipline, but I approve of your diligence. There will be extra homework tonight, by the way."

He rolled his shoulders, hinting none too subtly that I should rub his neck. So I did, lengthening the tendons on either side with thumb and forefinger. Rob made a pleased sound; his skin was smooth and warm beneath my fingertips, and I didn't think I'd ever seen him look so relaxed, particularly after a whole day with his family. These days, the comments just rolled right off him. I'd like to believe I had something to do with it.

We waited for his mom to park, then pulled in behind her. It was after ten, and the kid had conked out in the car. As Mr. Hot Ginger carried him inside, I nudged Nadia. "Back porch?"

"I'll get some iced tea and be right out."

In truth, it was more of a deck, beautifully built by Rob and his dad. The Conrads had a fantastic backyard; I'd always loved hanging out back here. I got a box of matches and lit the citronella candles set along the railings. Fireflies signaled to each other, lighting amber here and there, but the mosquitos would eat us up if without some repellent. I sprayed my bare bits, then settled in a glider chair to wait.

Two minutes later, Nadia came out, offered me a frosty glass. "So…you and Rob?"

"Yeah," I said. "I probably should've said something sooner."

"We stopped telling each other everything a while ago," she pointed out.

"I don't know whose fault that is."

"Let's not worry about that. But…I really miss you, Lauren. Your emails are fine, but I can read between the lines. I know when I'm being shut out."

"Not on purpose."

There were just things I couldn't tell her, maybe ever. Shit, I'd confessed to Rob about being pulled over while giving a drunken blow job, and that wasn't even the worst thing that happened when I was in Michigan…because of me, because I was out of control, denying I had a problem. My drinking didn't escalate all the way to alcoholism, but it could have.

I added, "You didn't tell me about Ty, either. Well, not before anyone else."

"Then let's split the blame halfway and decide what to do about it."

"Okay. On my end, no more emails like I'd send a pen pal. I'll tell you what's really going on, and I'll bitch like we used to."

"I'd like that. And I promise I won't keep secrets from you, either. I'll keep you posted on what's up with Ty and me. Plus, I'll try to be more…aware of what's going on with you. I'm *so* sorry that I didn't notice—"

"It's fine. I was doing my best not to let on." And my ability to fake a whole personality, a whole life, was pretty solid.

"Are we okay?" she asked.

Setting my tea down, I got up and hugged her. "We're great."

"I don't want certain details, but…you and Rob? Really?" She sounded so dubious.

"You're his sister, you're not supposed to get it. If you did, it would be *über*-creepy, *Flowers in the Attic* style."

"But you're actually going out."

"Yeah. Okay, secret confession time. I've had a thing for him pretty much forever. There's a reason I spent, like, every weekend at your house in high school."

Nadia laughed. "Dude, I guessed that five years ago. But I thought you got over it."

"Not really."

She hesitated, as if unsure she should ask me this. "Is that why it was a no with Max?"

Max, the roommate I'd confessed to sleeping with, back when I was trying to shock Rob. Not that it worked.

"Partly." But Max was also entangled inextricably with the worst night of my life, the night I realized I could do myself irreparable harm, unchecked. I'd never be able to look at him without remembering.

"I hope he makes you happy. And vice versa."

"So far, so good."

We talked for an hour more, catching each other up with gossip in Michigan and Nebraska. She was amazed to hear about Krista's baby, even more shocked that I'd made friends with Avery. Nadia almost fell to the floor when I told her about the fight at the Stop & Go. In turn, she filled me in about Angus's boyfriend, and how Courtney was working out as a roomie replacement. By the time Rob came out to get me, I felt like we were in a better place than we had been since our freshman year.

"When are you leaving?" I asked.

"Day after tomorrow. You're working?"

"Yeah. I'll try to swing by after my shift ends."

"If you can't, it's okay. You have shit to do, I get it."

"Your mom doesn't," I muttered.

Nadia cocked a brow. "Huh?"

Rob tried to shush me, but I explained, "She made us jump hoops, like you guys are visiting royalty. She had him moving furniture all day Sunday."

Nadia sighed. "Sorry about that. I'll talk to her. It's just because I'm not here that much."

He grinned and messed up her hair. "I didn't do it for you."

"'Night," I called as he wrapped an arm around my shoulders and urged me out.

The next day at work, the whole dealership was in an uproar. I had no idea why until one of the office ladies paused at my desk with a conspiratorial look. "Find a reason to peek into the garage. You won't be sorry."

Puzzled but intrigued, I set my stuff down and went to join the huddle of sales people, peering through the door that led into the maintenance bays. *Holy shit.* I recognized the chief butthead's prized white Lexus, but someone with a major grudge had seriously fucked it up. Red paint was splattered all over it, I assumed in lieu of blood, and the hood was dented like somebody had taken a sledgehammer to it. On the trunk, it read, FUCKING PRICK. On the whole, I couldn't disagree.

I wondered who he'd pissed off, but I went back to work and didn't think any more of it until I heard him shouting into his cell phone, demanding that somebody go pick up that crazy Rob Conrad, who was in here recently, threatening him. *Fuck.* I tried calling Rob, but he didn't pick up. While I greeted customers and manned the phone, I texted a warning. But I still hadn't heard from him when I left the car lot.

He's working. He can't be texting while he's pouring concrete. Or whatever. In all honesty, I had no idea what Rob did on the construction site all day. I imagined sawing wood, hammering things, or maybe using heavy machinery. He and I would never talk about our day jobs the way some couples did.

While I was waiting for him to get home, a sheriff's car drove past twice, which made me think they were taking Davies seriously. The deputy slowed but didn't pull in. I was getting really twitchy when Rob finally rolled up.

"It's nice to find you waiting when I get home," he said as he hopped out of the truck. "But you could've gone inside."

"Where's your phone?" I demanded.

"Inside. I forgot it this morning."

Before I could explain, the squad car drove up. The deputy got out and ambled toward us, one hand hooked in his belt loop. "Robert Conrad?"

"That's me."

"I need to ask you some questions. We can do it here, if you're friendly and let me look around your property. Or I can haul you in, waste your whole night."

Rob frowned. He was visibly hot and sweaty, face streaked with dirt, and his T-shirt was grime-encrusted. Whatever he'd been doing all day, it was messy. So he didn't look like he was in any mood to deal with this shit. I had no idea what to do.

"Questions first, or search?" he finally asked.

I'd ask what the guy wanted with him first, but Rob had nothing to hide. So when the deputy pointed at the detached garage and said, "Let's start there," he just shrugged and opened the doors with the remote.

His workshop space was clean and well-organized with a couple of tables in progress from recent net orders. Tools hung neatly in their places, and the green truck seemed to have been washed recently. I let out a quiet sigh of relief when I spotted no red paint; he only had stains in various hues and the earth tones he'd used in the house.

"You're a carpenter?" the deputy asked, inspecting his tools. Rob did have a sledgehammer, probably used for busting up walls inside, but it didn't seem to have any scrapes of white paint, like, say, from an expensive car.

"Self-taught. I have a furniture business to keep me busy in the winter."

The other guy nodded. "Do you have a basement, storage shed, anything like that?"

"Nope. But you're welcome to poke around the house."

Fifteen minutes later, the deputy apologized for bothering us and left. He never did explain what it was all about, but since I knew, I didn't let Rob press for more info. Once the man left, I babbled the whole story, along with an apology. I concluded, "I have no idea who Davies has pissed off, but I hate that you got dragged into this because of me."

He smiled at me tiredly, then kissed my forehead. "It's not a big deal. I didn't do it."

"Wonder who did."

That question wasn't to be answered anytime soon.

Through the rest of July, I got busy with school programming projects and work kept me occupied, too. Rob's popularity kept increasing, and his furniture orders finally did, too. Not enough for him to quit his job, but enough that he had to start warning people that it might take as long as six weeks to finish and ship their items, not a deal-breaker for most of them, who had their hearts set on owning something Rob made.

Around the first of August, I made up my mind at last. I was excited to tell him, so I let myself in the house after work and cooked dinner. I had food waiting on the table when he got home, along with lit candles and soft music. The house had changed so much since I first saw it last winter. Downstairs, it was mellow, warm and welcoming, evidence of his talent and hard work. That actually gave me an idea for his next vlog; he could give his fangirls a tour while explaining the work he'd done.

"This is a nice surprise," he said. "Do I have time for a shower?"

"Sure. Make it fast if you can. I have some news."

"You've got me curious. I'll be back in five minutes."

By the time he came down, toweling his hair dry, I had steak and potatoes on the table. I sat down across from him, practically wriggling with nerves and excitement. "I've been thinking a lot about what you asked me back in May." By his blank look, I needed to give him more context. "At the engagement party?"

"*Oh*. Right." A smile formed on his beautiful mouth, and his blue eyes brightened. "You've made up your mind?"

"Yeah. If the offer's still open, I want to move in. My original terms still stand, though. I buy the groceries and pay utilities."

"Have you told your mom yet?"

"No, I wanted to talk to you first, make sure you still want me here." I ducked my head, feeling weirdly shy. I'd lived with guys before as roommates, but never like this.

"That's not even a question, is it?" He tipped my chin up and kissed me.

For a few seconds, I just savored the moment, then the nervous babbling started. "Maybe not. Is this weekend too soon? I'm bringing my bed, the one you built for me, and we can put it in one of the other bedrooms for guests once we finish the floor. But otherwise, I don't have much furniture. Just clothes and computer stuff."

"You know, I happen to have a truck. We'll get you moved, beautiful. Can't be soon enough for me. I fucking hate sleeping alone."

"Me, too," I admitted.

After dinner, I jingled my keys suggestively. "Let's go for a ride."

"Where?" Rob was already on the sofa, seeming settled for the night.

"You'll like this surprise. I hope. Come on, I really want to do this with you."

That piqued his interest, so he followed me to the car. I drove out to the humane society, hoping this wouldn't end in an awkward, perplexed silence on his end. I'd already called to make sure they'd be open, so the attendant took us straight back to check out the dogs that were available for adoption. Rob wore an inscrutable expression as she left us to answer the phone.

"Lauren?"

I took a deep breath. "I've always wanted a dog, but my mom's allergic. So I thought…maybe, unless you hate them, we could get one…together."

If it turned out he loved his hardwood floors too much to risk a dog damaging them, I'd be disappointed, but no big deal, right? Not everyone loved dogs. *But they're just so cute with the big eyes and the furry tummies and the cold noses…come on, Rob.* When he was younger, the Conrads had a dog, but after she died of old age, they never replaced her. I seemed to remember him playing with her in the backyard when I was, like, seven. He was quiet, walking along the cages.

"It's okay," I said. "Never mind. Moving in together is a big step, and this is too much, it's a weird idea. Stupid, even. I shouldn't have—"

"Lauren," he cut in.

"What?"

"I'm finding the perfect dog for us. You're very distracting when you act so adorable. So cut it out."

With a smile so broad it almost hurt, I ran to him, and he hugged me. As we stood there, the beagle mix nearby perked up and set her paw against the door. The card on her cage said she was just over a year old, spayed, vaccinated and fully housebroken. I didn't care about any of that. Her soulful eyes said, *Take me home,* and I died when she cocked her head, asking silently why we weren't adopting her already.

"That's the one," I said, just as Rob knelt down.

He nodded. "She's ours. Now we just have to decide what to name her."

"Happy," I said instantly. "Because that's how I feel when I'm with you."

When the attendant came back, she had to clear her throat three times to get us to stop kissing long enough to sign the papers and pay the fees.

As I carried Happy out to the car, I thought, *This is the start of something beautiful.*

CHAPTER TWENTY-TWO

Both Happy and I settled in nicely.

Rob built a fence in the backyard, which was enormous, and installed a dog door in the kitchen; we got a fancy one with a radio collar, so stray cats and random raccoons couldn't come in to ransack the cupboards. Given the woods around the house, the latter seemed more likely. The weekend after I moved in, we finished a second bedroom and set it up as an office, where I could work, though I stashed my twin bed in there, as well.

At first it was a little strange, but I got used to coming home here, just like I had the apartment in Michigan. For the first time in my life, I felt like a functioning adult. No wild drinking, and my anxiety attacks flared less. Routine helped, and life with Rob definitely ran on a pattern. He got home from work later than me, so I usually made dinner. He cleaned up, then we snuggled for a while on the couch.

Around nine, he went to the garage to work on his furniture orders and I went up to my office to write code. Happy usually went with me and curled up on the bed to nap. She was a good dog, not prone to chasing things or barking, though sometimes the squirrels taunted her beyond all bearing. At eleven, Rob met me in the bedroom for sex or sleep, usually the first, then the second. Sometimes I caught myself humming when there was no music, just full of such joy that I couldn't contain it.

Now that I was living with him, though, I made a point of hanging out with Krista, Avery and Jillian on Friday nights. I couldn't be one of those girls who turned her boyfriend into her whole world. Krista was generally glad to get away from adorable Naomi for a few hours, giving her mom a chance to spoil her. The rest of us weren't as enthralled with the endless pictures, but then we instituted another rule for girls' night— no baby pics or talk about dudes. Once we established that, it was a lot more fun.

In September, my mom got married. It was a small service with dinner for friends and family afterward, much less formal than the engagement party. Stuart's family flew in for the big event, and I found Randall just as obnoxious the second time. But he wasn't the best man, so he didn't get to give a toast. Things wrapped up early because the bride and groom were heading to the airport to catch a late flight, stopover in L.A. and then on for two glorious weeks in Hawaii.

"You look beautiful," I said, hugging my mom.

"Thanks. You're doing well with Rob, right? I hope you didn't move because—"

"Is this really the time to check that?" I teased.

My mom had taken it well when I told her I was moving out. She might deny it, but I suspected she was a little relieved that she could start fresh with Stuart without me around cramping their style. I'd asked her why she was so weird about confessing to the engagement and she was quiet for a while.

Finally, she'd said, "I was afraid you'd be upset. You had so many…challenges when you got home. I was worried Stuart would be another stressor for you."

Then I'd realized she was talking about my anxiety issues, something we usually tiptoed around. Well, I could understand, though it hadn't been necessary to walk on eggshells for me. Anyway, I liked Stuart, and it was fine.

I'm happy.

"Sorry," she mumbled.

Aloud, I said, "Things are great. Don't worry, have an amazing honeymoon. Take lots of pictures. Of the *scenery!*" I added at Stuart's look of mock alarm.

Rob came up beside me as the car drove off. "Your mom's all grown up. It's so hard to watch them leave the nest, huh?"

I poked him. "Don't be cute. Oh, wait, you can't help it."

It was late when we got home, and Happy was beside herself with joy. She pranced around our ankles, begging for belly rubs. Out of habit, I checked around for accidents, though she'd gotten the hang of the dog door weeks ago. *Nope, no problems.* Rob sat down at the computer to look at his furniture orders.

"Damn. At this rate, I have enough work to keep me half through the winter."

"In a couple of years, you won't need to work construction at all. I'm so proud of you."

He pulled me onto his lap, encircling my waist with one arm. "You did most of it."

"Bullshit. The internet fell in love with you, not me."

"Not sure that's the right word." But his tone was distracted, so I leaned over to read the message that had him so wide-eyed.

Dear Mr. Conrad,

First, let me say that your house is absolutely fantastic; I especially love the floors, but your furniture designs are impressive and stylish, as well.

I'm with the Hearth & Home Network. If you're unfamiliar with us, we're a cable TV station in Toronto that specializes in home improvement programming. One of your fans saw a posting on our site about an open call for a new host, and she sent us a link to your video channel, along with an enthusiastic endorsement. She made it really clear she'd love to see you on TV, and now that I've perused your videos, I agree. You have the X factor that should appeal to our target demographic. I'd like to set up a meeting to discuss some mutually beneficial opportunities—at our expense, naturally. If you're interested, write back at your earliest convenience, and I'll make the travel arrangements. Please come prepared for a screen test and to brainstorm ideas with our producer. I look forward to hearing from you.

Sincerely,

Annette Caldwell

Rob glanced up at me. "Is this for real?"

Taking the keyboard, I checked a few things in the hidden header data and nodded. "It seems to be. I've heard of them."

"That's crazy. They want to put me on TV?"

"You should email her," I said, though inwardly I was freaking out. "At worst, you get a free trip to Canada."

"Would you go with me, if you can get time off?"

"Sure, if you want me."

"You're the one who started all of this. It wouldn't feel right without you."

With my help, he drafted a professional-sounding reply, explaining that he had time constraints and it might take a little while for him to free up his schedule. If she truly was interested, I guessed that she'd say "no problem." And sure enough, by afternoon the next day, she replied, Just let me know when you can make it, and I'll take it from there. I talked to Da-vies while Rob made arrangements with his foreman. Avery agreed to house-sit with Happy, which was kind of weird.

We both applied on rush for passports, which took about a week. Way faster than I wanted, we were on a plane to To-ronto. Rob paid for my ticket while the network took care of everything for him.

This is exactly the kind of thing that'll give me a panic attack.

A driver with Rob's name on an iPad screen was waiting for us at baggage claim. They shook hands, and he explained the plan as he opened the rear door of the Lincoln Town Car. "I'll wait while you get checked in, and then I'm taking you downtown to meet with Ms. Caldwell."

"Sounds good," Rob said.

The back of the Lincoln was completely lux, all leather and automated everything. It had tiny bottles of water, candy and packs of peanuts. If I wasn't so nervous, I'd sample the fancy European chocolate. But that would probably end in me barfing over the seat, so I sat quietly while Rob talked to the driver, asking questions about Toronto. I'd never noticed it, but away from his family's scrutiny, he did really well with people.

We pulled up outside a posh high-rise hotel, the sort of place I'd never stayed at in my life. I'd only flown four times in total, and the vacations my mom could afford before I left home didn't stretch to penthouse suites. A doorman hurried to escort us out of the car, and looking at his uniform, I felt really underdressed in jeans, boots and a faux-leather jacket. Noth-ing seemed to faze Rob as the valet asked about our luggage.

"Just this," he said, patting his shoulder bag, "but thanks."

At reception, everything was already arranged. The girl didn't even ask for a credit card. She peeked at Rob's ID and gave him a thousand-watt smile. "You're on the eleventh floor, and you've been granted access to the hospitality suite. It will be down the hall and to the right. From here, the elevators are across the lobby and past the bar. Did you have any questions?"

"No, that's fine, thanks." Rob smiled at her, and I swore I heard her heartbeat speed up.

This was…weird. And awful. So much awful. But if I didn't want Rob to be successful, then I was a horrible person, an anchor around his neck. So I swallowed the bad feelings, pretending I didn't feel completely invisible. At check-in, the girl didn't look at me once.

The driver called, "I'll be in the car, come when you're ready. They're waiting for you."

"Have a wonderful time, Mr. Conrad. Do let me know if there's anything at all I can do to make your stay more enjoyable." It wasn't what she said so much as how she said it.

Fighting the urge to hiss, I followed Rob to the elevator bank and up to our room, which was gorgeous, ultramodern but perfectly furnished. He dropped his bag on the bed and crossed to the window to stare out at the city skyline for a few seconds. When he turned to face me, his face was alight with excitement, eyes as bright as I'd ever seen them.

"Can you *believe* this?"

"It's amazing," I said.

I'd never had to hide how I felt from Rob before. There was nothing good about my mood, but it would be worse to dump all over his enthusiasm. Setting my backpack down, I admired the view, though my heart wasn't in it. All of the cars passing below only reminded me how many people were all around me, and I might have to talk to them.

But this isn't about you.

"Bathroom." He ducked inside, and I rested my head against the cold glass, sick to my stomach like I was in Michigan.

Booze would make this better.

Ignoring that idea, I went with Rob down to the lobby.

Outside, the driver bounded out when he caught sight of us. Apparently he had orders to offer full VIP treatment. September in Toronto was beautiful, bright and clear, but my nerves didn't allow me to enjoy the short drive to the station. House Beautiful occupied five floors in a skyscraper a mile and a half away, and Ms. Caldwell came down to greet us in person; she was a beautiful brunette in her late thirties, expensively dressed in a black suit and phenomenal shoes. If I was right about the brand marked by a red sole, they cost more than everything I owned except my car.

"So great to meet you," she said, offering a hand to Rob. "Likewise."

In the elevator, he introduced me and I got a nod. "Right, you said that your girlfriend handled the technical aspects of your web series. Don't worry, we have people for that."

It was hard *not* to take that personally. But I pressed my lips together. *I'm moral support, that's all. I won't screw things up for him by arguing with Annette.* There was a whole team waiting in a conference room with job descriptions I forgot as soon as I heard them. They had a concept ready to run, provided Rob tested well on screen and with various focus groups. I blank-stared through a lot of it, though I tuned back in toward the end.

Annette Caldwell was saying, "We'd like to fold your video series into the show, do a segment called 'At Home with Rob.' That way, you keep the brand you've already built, but we can also work within the framework of *Hot Property* to grow your name recognition."

Seriously? He'll never agree to that. If I knew him at all, it would push all of his buttons in the wrong way.

But Rob was nodding thoughtfully. "The focus of the show is renovations that will increase the resale value of the home?"

"Yes, we'll let you pick projects from a pool of homeowners, all of whom are willing to invest a minimum of ten thousand dollars in their homes in the hopes of turning a profit when they flip it. In return, they'll be featured on the show with you and receive a reduced rate on your renovations. You'll also be in charge of a crew of five assistants, and you can select from the prescreened candidates earmarked by the producer. A number of them sent résumés for the hosting call, but they aren't quite what we're looking for in a show anchor."

You mean they're not hot enough, I thought sourly.

"It's a fun concept," Rob said. "When's the screen test scheduled?"

"In fifteen minutes, provided you're still on board."

I expected him to look at me, as he usually did, but he tapped his fingers for a few seconds, then said, "Let's do it."

Ms. Caldwell turned to me. "Feel free to make yourself comfortable in here or in the waiting room. This shouldn't take long. I mean, given how many videos Rob's made already, it's a formality to satisfy the sponsors and the tech crew." She smiled at me, too many teeth for me to read it as sincere. "I can have the receptionist bring you some coffee or tea. Juice? Water?"

"No, I'm fine. Thanks." I got out my phone because that was what people did to pretend they had something important to do.

By the time they got back, my battery was virtually dead. On the plus side, I didn't have to talk to anyone. Rob was laughing at something Ms. Caldwell said, seeming completely at ease with all of the people surrounding him. Just as well, if this was actually happening, and he'd be crazy to turn them down. Probably some higher-ups would have to approve the budget and give the producers the green light, but it seemed promising, so much that my stomach hurt. And I hated myself because I *liked* our quiet life. I didn't want things to change, but it seemed like the world had finally noticed what I knew all along.

Yeah. Rob's special.

"Everything looks really good," she said, poised in perfect silhouette in the doorway. "Naturally, there will be a number of professional appearances during launch week. Parties, openings, interviews. We want to get you in front of national media as much as possible. Are you familiar with sweeps?"

He shook his head. "Sorry, I'm not much of a TV guy."

That appeared to delight her, maybe because it meant he wouldn't turn into a fame-hungry diva so fast. "I'll explain later. Once we get the go-ahead, I'll email you the contracts to look over. But…we're getting a bit ahead of ourselves." She touched his arm, smiling. "I have a good feeling, though, don't you?"

He smiled back. "You've been really nice."

I stood up, swallowing a sigh, because I had the crazy idea I could walk between them and neither one would even see me.

She added, "Feel free to charge dinner to the room. Normally I'd take you out to celebrate, but I suspect it's been a full enough day already."

"Definitely." Rob was just too handsome for his own good. In plaid flannel, he glowed with a wholesome charm that made women want to eat him up.

By Annette Caldwell's expression, she'd have him for breakfast. "I'll walk you down and make sure the driver's ready for you."

I didn't say much of anything on the trip back. Rob filled me in on everything they'd discussed, and I nodded a lot. His enthusiasm was infectious—or it should've been—but I had nothing but knots tangling my circulatory system, so my heartbeat felt wrong, and I tasted copper in my mouth. Most people associated it with blood but for me, it was dread.

"You're quiet," he noted as we climbed out of the Town Car.

"It's been a long day."

"What do you think?"

"It's an incredible opportunity," I said honestly.

While I didn't love the show's name, it *was* catchy—with a solid premise. Moreover, it was something Rob could do and do well. Back before we got together, he'd told me how he wanted to flip houses for a living instead of work construction. Now he might be offered a shot to do that—on TV. Apparently, it would only be airing in Canada to start, but they had a good track record with American syndication.

"I can't even…" As we got in the elevator, he trailed off, shaking his head. "It's so hard to wrap my head around. Some lady sends an email, Annette clicks a link and…all of this."

I forced a smile. "It's your X factor."

Grinning, he swept me off my feet and into his arms. An older couple was waiting on eleven when the doors opened, but Rob only smiled at them and carried me down the hall to our room. I caught the woman checking him out as he set me on my feet outside the door. *Yeah, he'll play well with a certain demographic.* We ordered a fancy dinner to celebrate this momentous occasion, but for me, it felt like the end of life as I knew it. Rob didn't notice that my smile was frozen as we ate. But he picked up on it as I got ready for bed.

"You sure you're okay?"

Not ruining this for you. I refuse.

So I dredged up a sheepish look. "Would it be weird if I FaceTimed Avery so I can see Happy? I miss her."

His gaze softened. "Not at all. You're adorable, you know that, right? And don't worry, we'll be home by this time tomorrow."

CHAPTER TWENTY-THREE

After we got back from Toronto, it seemed like we were in a holding pattern.

I'd gotten As in my summer classes, and the two I was taking this fall were going well also. On the surface, nothing had changed; we still did everything we had before, but now life seemed to be stamped with a doom clock. Perversely, in my spare time, I promoted Rob's channel even more. At his request, I posted a notice on his website that he was no longer taking orders—he had to catch up on the backlog, and he reported a flood of emails.

"Listen to this one," he said, laughing. "'Dear Rob, I was totally going to order a bedside table, so I could put your picture on it. By the way, I'm the one who contacted Hearth & Home about you. It would mean the world to me if you wrote back. Keep me posted, okay? They won't tell me anything, even though I've emailed at least five times. Your biggest fan, Carina.'"

I managed a smile. "You should start a line of trading cards with various action-man building poses."

He laughed and kissed my temple. "Cute. It's so weird when you say stuff like that. Don't they realize I'm just a normal guy?"

"You're not *just* anything."

That night, when we had sex, for me it had an edge of desperation. I was storing up Rob memories because unlike him, I knew our time was limited. Already it felt like he was somebody different and foreign, not the guy I had been living with. Before going out to his workshop, he spent an hour a night responding to fan mail.

In mid-October, he got the call I had been dreading. It was Thursday, and we'd both just gotten home from work. It must be late in Toronto, but Annette Caldwell must be eager to talk to him. From the astonishment and joy in his expression, it was good news. I left the room, not wanting to overhear the details, and went out to the backyard with Happy to throw the tennis ball for her. It was chilly enough that I needed my jacket, but I didn't have it. Soon my fingers were numb and clumsy as I chucked the ball.

Rob came to the kitchen door. "You're going to freeze. Come in, we need to talk."

Was it *ever* good when somebody said that? I whistled for the dog and went inside to find hot cocoa waiting for me. After giving Happy a cookie, I sat down at the table for two by the window. He smiled as he joined me, apparently not grasping that things were about to fall apart.

"So they offered me the show. They want me to move to Toronto, pretty much as soon as I can." He hesitated. "But I don't think this will work. I mean, with my parents and all, Nadia out of state. If my mom needs my help...I just *can't* go, can I? When we were there, I didn't think it would actually happen. So it was like...a pipe dream or something."

"And now you have an offer." Part of me wanted to agree

with him. *Yeah, Rob, don't be a bad son. How can you even consider leaving your folks? And me.* But I loved him too much to stand in the way of his dreams, even if they couldn't include me. "Don't worry about your parents. I'll help them out if they need it."

He stared like I had pulled a handful of change out of my own nose. "That doesn't even make sense, Lauren. The only way I take this offer is if you go with me."

Fuck. Here we go.

"No," I said quietly. "This is something you have to do on your own. It's a fantastic opportunity for *you*. Not me. I'm not quitting my job and moving to Canada."

And I don't want to. I could picture the kind of life he'd have, chaotic and unsettled, lots of parties and media attention, so many strangers to schmooze. In other words, it would be my definition of hell. The panic attacks would kick in again, twice as hard, and pretty soon I'd be drinking more than ever. I was just starting to get a handle on my issues. Leaving now would drop me down a hole darker than I'd ever been.

I can't do it. Not even for you.

"Then I won't go, either," he said, as if it were settled. "I'll call Annette and say no."

And I was *so tempted* to let him chuck his future for me. I stared across the table at his dear, beautiful face as my throat tightened. Tears filled my eyes, but I didn't let them fall. I willed them away, setting Social Lauren firmly in place. She didn't care about anything; the party girl never cried. I lifted my mug and took a sip.

"That's a mistake." My voice was cool.

"I'm not leaving you. With my parents, it would be an obligation. But you and Happy, you're everything to me."

"Ah. Damn. Then it's time to admit…I don't think this is working out."

His face froze. "What?"

"Us. Whether you leave or stay, I'm moving out. I've been talking to Avery and Jill about getting an apartment together." That was the biggest lie I ever told in my life, and it was a wonder he didn't sense it because Rob was usually so good at seeing through my bullshit.

The naked pain in his eyes almost wrecked my hard facade. "Where's this coming from? I had no idea, I thought we were—"

"Happy? That's the dog, and she's a little less complicated." Yeah. A dog would *never* break somebody's heart this way, but if I didn't take it all the way to the bitter end, he'd never go, and I couldn't be the reason he turned down such an opportunity. Whatever it took, I wouldn't let Rob limit his potential because of my fear.

"This is good timing," I said. "It'll be easier for you to make a fresh start in Toronto."

"I don't want that. I want *you*." He stared at me fiercely, openly, the Rob who never hid anything, not from me.

I wouldn't have it for much longer. As soon as he accepted that I meant it, the bars would come down. "If you're thinking about staying to work things out with me, don't bother. I'm not ready for all of this, it's too much, and I need to focus on school. So go have this amazing life. You deserve it. Prove to everyone how much more you are than they ever imagined."

Of everything I just said, the last thing was the only part I meant. But my poker face was too good for even Rob to penetrate. It almost killed me when he lifted his chin, blinking long lashes against the tears. Mine were frozen into a solid core, nuclear winter in my chest.

"Why are you talking like this? It doesn't even sound like you." Tilting his head, he frowned in perplexity. "Why can't we do long-distance, if you don't want to move?"

Shit. He's not entirely buying it.

"Rob…if I was planning to move out, why would I tie myself to a boyfriend I can't even bang before bed? That's *all* of the limitations of a relationship, none of the fun, and I was already feeling kind of…trapped."

He flinched. "I'm sorry life with me wasn't…fun."

It was so much more; it was perfect.

"I'll start looking for a place," I said, pretending his pain didn't slash me open.

I never wanted to hurt you. Not you. I'm so sorry. But you can't stay and I can't follow.

Wiping his eyes, he reached down to rub Happy's head, and her tail thumped against the floor. "No, you should stay. I want you here, even if…you're not with me."

"No way." I couldn't live here without him. That would just be an endless turning of the knife, and I'd never get over him.

"It would help if I had some rent coming in to cover this house payment. And you're already here. I don't have time to look for a tenant before I leave."

After stomping on his heart, I couldn't say no. "Okay. Are you taking her?"

His hand slowed in rubbing between the dog's ears. "She'll be better off with the yard and all. I'll be in an apartment, and I don't know how much time I'll have to play with her."

"I'll take good care of her. With the dog door, she can run outside as much as she wants, even when I'm at work."

"I have one request."

"What?"

"I want to take the stories you wrote with me. I haven't finished yet. I need to know how it ends."

That opened me up but I couldn't break, not with his whole future depending on my strength. My hands trembled, so I curled them into fists. "Sure, you can take the binders. I don't need them anymore."

He swallowed hard. "I was afraid you'd say that."

"Rob—"

He held up a hand, an invisible wall between us. "Back to business. If it helps, you can ask Avery to move in, split the rent with her." He cleared his throat, his face set in impenetrable lines. "It would help me if you look in on my parents now and then, like you said."

"No problem."

Rob made a fist and slammed it against the table, rattling the mugs, so hot chocolate slopped over the side. A whimper escaped Happy and she jumped away from him to huddle against my knees. I patted her, hurting so bad I couldn't breathe.

"Tell me one thing…you owe me that. Did you ever love me at all?"

I smiled at him wryly. "Not enough."

Too much. More than anyone, ever.

"I never said it because I was waiting for you to tell me how you feel. I thought, any day now, she'll kiss me good-night and whisper it in my ear."

Until this moment, I didn't realize I was holding the words hostage, a last ditch self-defense mechanism. Not telling him didn't keep me from falling hopelessly in love, though. I could only whisper, "I'm sorry I hurt you."

"You've destroyed me," he corrected quietly. "If you just wanted to fuck, you shouldn't have encouraged me to think I matter. I wish you hadn't let me hope."

There was no way this conversation would get better, and if he unleashed any more emotional honesty, I might break. "I should go."

He shook his head, shoving back from the table. "I'll pack my shit and take off."

"Tonight?" I wasn't prepared for that, though maybe I should've been.

"Why not? What's keeping me here?"

"Don't you want to have dinner with your parents or something, share your good news?"

Rob shrugged. "So they can tell me I'm not as smart as Nadia and I'm kidding myself that anyone will take me seriously in Toronto after they listen to me talk for ten minutes? I've had enough of everyone in this town, I'm out."

Finally, I thought. *My work here is done.*

"Be careful. Make sure you rest. It's a long drive." That wasn't even remotely what I wanted to say.

By his expression, I shouldn't have bothered. "Stop. I won't be your friend, I'm not going to pretend you haven't yanked my heart out of my chest, just so you don't feel bad."

"That's fair," I managed.

"I'll send you the rental agreement. Have a nice life, Lauren."

He got up and strode out of the kitchen. Upstairs, I heard him packing. I stared into my cocoa mug, moving the dregs with a spoon, until he went out of the front door. Happy trotted after him, and she whimpered when he shut it quietly in her face. She loved riding in his truck, and she didn't understand that this time, he wasn't going to Safeway or the Stop & Go. This time, he wouldn't be back. I didn't move until I couldn't hear his engine anymore. Rob was gone. *Gone, gone, gone.* I'd accomplished exactly what I set out to, but I'd never felt worse in my life. The dog trotted back in the kitchen to paw my leg, and I slid out of my chair to sit on the floor with her. When she licked my face, I realized I was finally crying.

Leaning forward, I wrapped my arms around her and sobbed into her fur. Surprisingly, she didn't try to get away.

Half an hour later, I staggered to my feet. I needed to eat but I didn't want anything. For fuck's sake, I'd just driven the person I loved most out of my life. The fact that I had to live here without him, Jesus, what kind of cruel and unusual punishment was that? Everything felt bleak and hollow, and all I wanted to do was drink myself unconscious. I shouldn't.

You were doing so well.

For a while, I resisted temptation. I gave Happy her dinner and cuddled with her on the couch while tears came in intermittent bursts. Talking might help, but I couldn't face anyone. So I went to the kitchen and dug out Rob's stash. He liked good whiskey now and then, not enough to worry me. Of the two of us, I was the one with the potential problem. I got a glass and carried the bottle to the couch. I poured some out and stared at the amber liquid, then on a rush of horror, I shook my head and got up. Gathering all of my resolve, I poured the liquor out and then dumped the rest of the bottle down the sink.

Not doing this. Otherwise you might as well have gone with him.

When I went back into the living room, Happy greeted me with a wag of her tail. I sat down beside her and clicked on the TV, currently set on HGTV. *I could be watching Rob on here, this time next year.* It sounded both impossible and sad. Eventually, I'd end up telling people online that I used to date the insanely sexy guy from *Hot Property.*

Nadia. I should call her.

I got my phone, but instead of hitting the contact button, I pulled up Google Maps and input our address along with the studio location in Toronto. *Twenty-three hours.* I wouldn't be able to relax until I knew he got there safely. If he didn't sleep—I swallowed hard.

Then I tapped Nadia's picture without thinking about the time difference. By the time she answered, I realized it must be close to ten in Michigan. "Hey, Lauren. What's up?"

"I broke up with Rob."

"Shit, what happened? What'd he do?" It was sweet that she immediately took my side, but perversely, it also pissed me off. She was *his* sister.

"It's not like that." Quietly I outlined the circumstances, along with the incredible opportunity Rob had considered giving up for me.

"Holy shit, he's getting a home improvement show?" Finally, she sounded impressed. "I can't wait to tell Mom and especially Dad. He'll be so excited."

"When you tell them, make sure they understand he was just swept up in the excitement. He had to rush off to start filming." The last thing Rob needed was an earful of guilt about the way he'd left town, on top of everything else.

"Oh, totally. I understand why you didn't want to chuck everything to follow him," she said after a short silence. "But I don't really get why you felt like you had to cut the cord so completely."

Maybe explaining it would make it easier to bear on my end, too. "The idea of being a public figure horrifies me. Like, more than most people." Taking a breath, I told her about the anxiety attacks and my drinking. "I never let on because…I was ashamed. I know now that I can't help it, and I'm doing better, I really am."

"I wish you'd told me." Nadia sounded choked up, and I could imagine the way she'd be curled up, arms around her knees. She drew in like a turtle when she was hurting.

"I just wanted to be normal," I whispered.

"That's…nobody. It's a myth."

"Maybe you're right. Anyway, I couldn't cope in the life

Rob's heading off to…magazine articles, reporters, interviews, people occasionally taking pictures of us when I least expect it.…" I almost had a panic attack thinking about it. "If I didn't break it off hard, he'd be looking over his shoulder, split between his new life and his old one."

"You wanted to ensure he has the best possible chance to make a go of this, gave him complete freedom to shoot for the moon."

"Yeah," I said in a voice thick with tears.

"Wow. You really love him a lot."

That was all it took to get me crying again. The tears stung my eyes, tickling in my nose and burning my throat. "I have to go. Make it okay with your parents, all right? He's given everything to everybody else for so long, he *deserves* this. And don't worry about them. I promised Rob I'll help out when needed."

"Are you sure? I can come home."

"No, it's fine. I'm here. I've got this." Happy licked the tears from my cheek.

"Then I'll square things with Mom and Dad. If nothing else, years of being the golden child means when I talk, they listen."

"Thanks. You'll never know what this means to me."

She paused, and in the silence, I heard Mr. Hot Ginger say something in the background, but she shushed him. "Just like Rob will never know how much you love him?"

If the admission to heaven was dictated by the degree of sacrifice, it shouldn't matter what I did with the rest of my life. I'd taken a figurative knife to my chest in cutting Rob out. The wound was still fresh, raw meat of the soul.

I swallowed the pain and answered, "It's for the best. In every girl's life, there's always one who got away."

CHAPTER TWENTY-FOUR

Though I resisted the urge to get drunk off my ass, I couldn't face work on Friday. So I called in and my throat was so sore from sobbing that I sounded convincingly hoarse. After texting Avery that I wasn't up for girls' night, I fed Happy and then went back to bed. I just wanted to sleep because when I was unconscious, I couldn't feel.

I woke up to the sound of someone pounding on the front door. Gummy-eyed and dizzy, probably from low blood sugar, I stumbled downstairs and opened it. I was astonished to find Avery standing on the porch, still dressed in work clothes. From the angle of the sun, it was just past five.

"You never cancel," she said, giving me a worried look.

"What're you doing here?"

"Being a friend. I think. Am I doing it right?"

"Go away." I tried to shut the door, but she shouldered it open and pushed past me.

"Where's Rob?"

"Toronto. In case you didn't know, he's internet famous these days, soon to be Canadian famous."

"I have no idea what you're talking about, but you smell. Go take a shower or I'll scrub you myself." Apparently Avery believed in tough love.

Since I was afraid she meant it, I crawled up the stairs and stood in a stream of hot water until I could muster the energy to wash. When I came back down, she'd made sandwiches and fed the dog. Happy seemed to like her, though her favor might spring from the fact that Avery had opened the expensive cans. I sank into the chair, watching her move around the kitchen with a sense of unreality.

She put a plate in front of me. "How long has he been gone?"

"Since last night."

"And you already look this bad? I don't know if I'm impressed or disappointed."

"You're not funny," I mumbled.

As Happy licked her dish around the kitchen floor, I nibbled on the sandwich: turkey on wheat, Swiss cheese, no mayo. It was kind of dry, so I washed it down with the water she'd poured for me. Her cooking might not be very good, but Avery was here, more than I could say about anyone else. Deep down I knew that wasn't fair; I'd told Nadia not to come home and my mom had no idea how fucked up my life had become. I hated the idea of bringing her down, though, because things were going so great with her and Stuart.

"At least I don't have to worry about Rob getting arrested anymore."

That caught my attention. "Huh?"

"I heard they questioned him about what happened to Davies's car."

For some reason, her tone set me on high alert. "What do you know about that?"

"Simple. *I* did it."

"What the hell…why?" I put down my water glass, arrested by the glaring truth that Avery was troubled with capital *T*.

"Men like him, they have all the authority. I just wanted one of them to pay for once. They get away with *everything*, always. Nothing we do matters, nothing we say, either."

"This clearly isn't about my boss," I said quietly. "You want to talk?"

"Not really. I'm supposed to be helping you, not the other way around." But her eyes were so sad that it made my problems seem small by comparison.

"Maybe we can do both. It would help me to focus on you, I think."

"I am *not* okay," she said shakily.

"I get that." Standing up, I put my hand on her shoulder and guided her into the living room. "I'm not, either. But we can be broken together, right? If you don't want to talk, we don't have to. But if you're flipping out and demolishing cars, I think maybe you need to. If not to me, then someone else."

She bent her head so red hair spilled into her face. "There's nobody else."

"What about Jillian?"

"She follows the friend code I set down long ago. Don't ask, don't tell."

Happy bounded between us, seeming to understand that we needed her equally. I put my hand on her head, rubbed the back of her neck just as she liked, and she closed her eyes in doggy bliss. Avery stroked her back. The silence seemed laden with unspoken, awful things.

Maybe it'll be easier for her if I go first.

"I'm about to tell you something nobody else knows. Well, except the three guys involved, and I pray to God two of them were too drunk to remember. One was definitely sober, and if I never see him again, that would be okay. Which kind of sucks, because he and I, we were friends, before that night."

"Lauren, you don't have to—"

"No, it's okay. I want to tell you. Not that many people know this about me, but…" As I had with Nadia, I laid out my issues, and this time, there was no accompanying burn of embarrassment, as if talking about it made it less shameful each time. The fact was, I shouldn't feel so bad about emotions I couldn't help or control. "So to cope with this shit, I started drinking at school. Not the usual college partying but an escape hatch, so I didn't have to be me at all."

"I stole my mom's Valium for years," Avery said softly. "And sometimes I thought about taking the whole bottle."

"I'm glad you didn't."

A tilt of her head, as if I'd said something funny. "You're probably the only one."

"I'm sure that's not true." But from her expression, I shouldn't take the think-of-the-people-who-love-you path through the woods, so I went back to my own story. "Anyway, there was this guy who was kind of into me, and he hated watching me self-destruct. Before I even knew how he felt, he tried to talk to me about it. I laughed him off. In fact, I got drunk and banged him, just to prove no matter what he said, he was just like everyone else."

Her face didn't express what she thought about that, thankfully. "How did it work out?"

"Not well. I spiraled further out of control. Until one night, we were both at a party, Max and me. I got so drunk, I had *no idea* what I was doing. Ended up in a bedroom with two guys. Max stormed in and got me out but the assholes jumped him, and there was this huge fight. I'm not saying there's anything wrong with a threesome under the right circumstances, but it wasn't a decision I made or something I wanted. And Max got hurt…because of me. It was a frat party, and they piled on, pounded the shit out of him. If not for him, I'd have ended up a cautionary tale—'look how she was dressed, how much she drank, she was asking for it—'"

"Stop it." Avery had both hands clenched into fists, tears standing in her eyes. "It's not your fault. It's not mine, either."

"What isn't?" I held my breath, wondering if she'd tell me.

"My uncle. I was eleven when it started."

That's why she pulled away from Nadia. My stomach clenched, and I fought down a wave of nausea, knowing I had to be strong for Avery just like I had been for Rob. "You told your parents?"

"It went on for years before I worked up the nerve. My uncle said he'd deny it. 'Who do you think they'll believe?' But…my senior year, I got proof. I thought it would finally be over when I showed my dad."

I wanted to hug her or maybe put my hands over hers, but something told me that would be a bad idea right now. "What happened?"

"He slapped me. Said there was something wrong with me for recording it. Then he smashed my phone and said nobody would ever know my shame."

"I'm going to kill him."

She managed a sharp, painful smile. "I thought about it. Before, when you said you were glad I didn't eat a bottle of pills? That's the thing. I did."

"You were out for two weeks," I said, remembering.

"Yeah. I went to a clinic in Omaha. My family said they'd leave me there if I didn't come home and settle down, stop being dramatic. I was seventeen, I didn't know what else to do. But it's hell because I still see the bastard at family parties. He acts like *nothing* happened."

"I'm surprised you didn't run as soon as you turned eighteen." But I'd never been in her shoes; I had no idea what it was like.

"I have a trust fund," she said quietly. "My father controls it until I get married or turn twenty-five. I knew I wasn't stable enough to handle campus life without melting down."

"Like I did." That much, I understood. Sometimes the devil you knew was best.

"Not what I was getting at, I wasn't sniping, but…basically. So I got a job at the bank and played good daughter, marking time."

"You thought Rob might offer you sanctuary and financial independence?"

"I hoped so. I want out of that house so bad, you have *no* idea. But I have to be careful or my dad has the power to cut me off."

"Is there any reason for him to object to you moving in with a friend?" I asked.

"Who? Jill still lives at home, and there aren't any decent apartments in Sharon. If I suggest moving out, he'll demand to inspect the place and then say, 'No daughter of mine will shame me by living in filth and squalor.'"

"I hate your dad," I muttered.

"Me, too."

"Move in here. Rob already suggested it, and now that I know your situation, I want you out of there yesterday. Does your mom know?"

"She pretends not to and takes lots of antidepressants. I've considered dumping them, so she'll have to deal with the ugliness like anyone else, but she'd just get a refill."

"Spend the night, then I'll go with you tomorrow. If your father says anything, I'll play the excited, ditzy blonde while strangling the urge to kick him so hard in the balls that he'd have to pull them out of his nose."

Avery took a startled breath and then laughed. "I'd pay to see that. But…are you sure this a good idea? We're both pretty messed up. I snapped and went after your boss, for God's sake. Though I'm sure if they'd traced the crime back to me, my dad would've gotten me off the hook and then shipped me off to punish me for humiliating him."

"No more of that," I said firmly. "You make enough at the bank to live on and rooming with me is no reason for him to do anything with your trust fund. A few more years and you're home-free. You can travel, invest the money or apply to the college of your choice. Like I told you before, you don't need a guy to save you, not even Rob. You've come this far on your own, and you're going to be okay."

"You think so?" She sounded so dubious.

I nodded, putting my hand over hers. "And in the meantime, I've got your back. I'm *not* letting your horrendous family hurt you anymore."

"How in the hell are you the best friend I've ever had?" she demanded in a choked voice. "I fucking slapped you in the Stop & Go."

"So? I smacked you back and threw nachos at your head. One moment doesn't define us, Avery. We can be whoever we choose to be. *I* choose to be your friend."

Happy raised her head and glanced between us with sleepy eyes, apparently troubled by the intensity of our tones, but she decided we weren't upset with her and went back to sleep. That prompted a watery smile from me. Avery reached over the dog and hugged me. I held on to her, and neither of us cried. We'd done enough of that.

That night, we watched TV until we fell asleep on the couch. I woke up to a text from Nadia. Rob's safe in Toronto. Thought you'd want to know. Jesus, based on my look at the map, I guessed he'd driven straight through. *He must feel like shit. Well, it's mutual.*

Thanks, I sent back.

You okay?

Been better. Been worse. The night Max saved me from myself, for instance.

Avery stirred on the other end of the sofa. "What time is it?"

"Not quite nine. How're you doing?"

"I feel like crap, and I have to pee."

"Go ahead. Then let me brush my hair and we'll get you moved."

A frisson of fear flickered behind her green eyes, but she only nodded as she went upstairs. By the time she came out, I was ready to go. First, I fed the dog and patted her on the head. She had to be so confused with Rob leaving, and soon Avery's presence would bewilder her more. *It'll be fine, dogs are adaptable, right? As long as I'm here to love her.*

"I'm ready," she said, squaring her shoulders.

It was amazing how put-together she could look after crashing on a couch. Before, I'd thought she must spend hours on her appearance, but now that I knew her, I understood her lacquered finish came from attitude as much as anything; it was the way Avery carried herself, chin tilted against the world as if daring it to take her on.

Since we'd been hanging out, I had dropped her off at her house more than once. I'd always thought the place had a creepy vibe, and now I knew why. I didn't imagine I was psychic or anything but it wouldn't surprise me if Avery's misery had imprinted on the bricks. I parked the car and got out; I'd driven so they couldn't try to keep her here. Her car was at the house, and I wasn't leaving without her. I'd prefer for it to go easy, but I'd fight these assholes if I had to. Somehow I didn't think her dad would let it get that ugly.

The neighbors might be watching, you fuckwit.

I followed Avery inside and up a curving staircase. When we were kids, I never visited because she was Nadia's friend and I was kind of jealous and threatened by the whole thing, so back then, I always greeted Avery with a sneer and a lip curl. When they stopped talking, Nadia thought it was because her family didn't have enough money. As it turned out, she couldn't have been more wrong.

A maid came out of one of the bedrooms. I didn't realize it was Avery's until she went in. "I'll only take what'll fit in the car, my clothes and personal things."

I nodded. "We don't need furniture. You can sleep in the room I'm using as an office."

The maid dropped something with a clatter and then hurried away. I tilted my head to glance into the hall. When I turned, Avery was already packing.

"We need to be fast. She's reporting to my dad."

"That is *so* fucking Victorian."

But that was no exaggeration. Five minutes later, an older man with carefully dyed dark hair appeared in the doorway, wearing a smile that chilled my blood. "What's going on, dearest? You should have told me you were bringing home a guest."

"It's my fault," I said brightly. "I'm just so superexcited that Avery agreed to room with me. My housemate bailed on me, *Thursday night,* if you can believe it, and otherwise, I just don't know how I'd make rent, and it's such a great house, plus my mom just got married, and I'd die if I had to move home. Your daughter is just *the absolute best!*" Extrovert Lauren barely paused for breath, and I gave that performance maximum ditz, beaming up at him with such dim friendliness that he actually stepped back.

He cast a wary look at Avery. "So you're doing your friend a favor?"

"It's a lovely house," she said calmly. "And I suppose it's time. It will be a good test of my maturity, won't it?"

I recognized the moment when Mr. Jacobs realized he was trapped. He couldn't protest without it coming off strange, even to the goofy blonde. I mean, it wasn't like she was proposing to move to Alaska with a drunken lumberjack. Rooming with a female friend in your hometown? Not the stuff scandals were made of.

"It's just the two of you?" he asked.

"I have a dog. She's *so* sweet but very protective. Don't worry, we'll be safe."

"There's also an alarm," Avery said, smiling. I'd say she was enjoying this, finally taking back a little of her power.

"Your mother will be upset," he finally said. "It's such short notice."

I blinked at him, pretending confusion. "But I told you, my housemate only left on Thursday. There's no way to plan an emergency, sir."

"I suppose that's true. Well…good luck in your new place." By his icy look, that wasn't at all what he wanted to say, but I wouldn't budge.

"That's so sweet! Should I help you with the rest of your clothes?" I acted like I was oblivious to the tension, and that seemed to reassure her dad.

Yeah, she's a good girl, she's keeping your shitty secret. Not.

In under half an hour, we had all of her things packed up—well, the stuff she intended to take—and her father had the maid help us carry the suitcases down. They filled up the backseat and the trunk with some judicious Tetris-style packing.

As I pulled away from that horrible house, Avery broke down, crying into her hands. "I can't believe that worked. I can't believe I'm free."

"We'll be all right," I promised.

Not now, but one day we would be. Hope opened like the first blooms of spring. While leaves might be dying all around us, falling off the trees, winter never lasted forever.

CHAPTER TWENTY-FIVE

For the first month after Rob left, I stalked him online. I set up Google Alerts and I kept track of him long-distance. Nadia also sent updates because she knew I was still crazy in love with him, even if I was pretending otherwise. I drove his parents to the doctor a few times, and work was still fine because Davies didn't know Rob was gone, and I saw no reason to inform him. Avery and I did pretty well together. Half the time, we hosted girls' night at the house. She didn't talk about her issues and I said nothing about Rob.

But in early December, I suggested the idea that had been chewing at me since she moved in. "You think we should see someone?"

"Like a psychic?" She was pretending not to get it.

"No, more like a therapist. I don't want to medicate, but I need to get a handle on this, and I can't live my whole life avoiding the things that freak me out."

"And I clearly have some…feelings to process."

I nodded. "We could talk to the same person, if it wouldn't be weird, share rides, and then get dinner afterward. I don't know about you, but it makes it seem less…drastic, if you're in it with me."

"That sounds like a good idea."

After dinner, we got online and searched. Avery read over my shoulder while I eliminated people based on crappy websites. She added, "Nobody local. You know how word gets around in this town. There might be a confidentiality agreement but someone will see us go in the office, and my dad will mobilize."

"Agreed. We can drive to Edison or Whitney." I hesitated, unsure if I should ask this. "Have you thought about pressing charges?"

She didn't ask who I meant. "Constantly. I even looked up the statute of limitations."

"Shit. Has it been too long?"

Avery shook her head. "But the timing is awful, comically appalling. If the abuse happens when you're a minor, there's no limit to when you can file. But once you turn twenty-one, if you don't report it in four years—"

"Then the bastard gets off scot-free. So if you wait for your trust fund like your dad wants, you also let the clock run out on prosecuting your uncle. You keep quiet and take the hush money or you blow the lid off and take your chances in court."

A nod, as she pushed her food around her plate. "I weigh it constantly. I might be able to challenge my dad as executor of the trust, but if the criminal trial goes against me, it's likely that any civil challenge won't go well, either. I might end up dragged through the mud, lose my future financial security and come out with nothing."

"While your uncle gets away with what he did."

"That's why I flipped out on your boss. They *always* seem to. I don't have the power my dad does. You're the only person I've ever told who believed me."

I hesitated. "I can't tell you what to do. You're the one who will have to tell the story, over and over. But regardless, I think we both need some outside help."

"How about this one?" She tapped the screen to bring up the website.

The design was nothing for me to complain about, simple and functional. I read the woman's qualifications, along with her welcome message.

In our sessions, we'll concentrate on you as a person, and I'll help untangle the emotional knots so you can enjoy life again. Right now, that may seem impossible, but it's not. Together, we'll identify challenges, discover solutions and collaborate to make you feel whole. I have twenty years of clinical experience (background in psychoanalytic therapy), but I now prefer a more personal approach. Don't fight this battle alone. Call my office to make an appointment today.

I glanced up at Avery. "What do you think?"

"That I'll be scared, no matter who we call. She looks like she'd be easy to talk to."

Clicking on the woman's picture to enlarge it, I studied her face. She was in her late forties with glasses, long salt-and-pepper hair caught back in a careless braid. Then I nodded.

"Let's do this."

Two weeks later, we had our first appointments. Some people might think it was weird to do it back-to-back, but I needed the moral support. It was harder than I expected to walk into the office and dump my crazy on a stranger's desk. But she was supportive, warm and kind.

"So, Lauren, before we get started, what are your goals? And what would you say is your biggest challenge right now?"

Online advice had suggested I prepare a summary of my biggest issue, so I just read that to her, and Dr. Reid nodded. "Social anxiety is a common problem. We'll work on it. Today, I'd like to get to know you, so why don't you tell me about yourself?"

"Like what?"

She smiled. "Anything you like."

By the time I left, I didn't feel like such a mess. This time, there had been no invasive questions, though Dr. Reid did direct me occasionally or ask for clarification. Avery went in after me, and I read on my phone while I waited for her. She was shaking when she came out, but she mustered up a real smile as we paid.

"It's...it was good," she said, as we went out to my car.

"Do you think every two weeks is too often?"

"In my case, it might not be often enough. But I can't afford more."

"Me, either." We were both doing private pay. So I couldn't manage tuition, living expenses and therapy on a weekly basis. "Did she offer you a prescription?"

"Nope. You?"

I shook my head. "If she had, I'd be looking for someone else. That's not what I want out of this collaboration, as Dr. Reid puts it."

"That's how I feel, too. I've got a lot of anger stashed away."

"For obvious reasons. Are you hungry?"

"I didn't think I would be, but yeah. Do you want to text Krista and Jillian, ask them to meet us at Patty's in an hour?"

"Sure. Do you plan to tell them...?" I didn't know how I felt about that.

She shook her head. "Jill's starting to feel left out because she can tell that you and I have gotten close. The other day, she asked why I moved in with you so suddenly, why I didn't talk to her first if I was thinking about getting a place. And what can I say? I'm not *ready* to tell anyone else. It was hard enough to dump it on Dr. Reid, and that's her job. If I decide to press charges, then I'll start with telling Jillian. When I think of how long she's stood by me, even when I was horrible to her, I feel like such a bitch for not wanting to open up."

"Wow. I had that same situation going with Nadia."

"Does she know you're in therapy?"

I shook my head. "I suck. The worse it got at Mount Albion, the less I told her. I got so busy pretending to be happy that I forgot how to be a friend."

"I know how that is." Avery was obviously talking about Jillian.

"I think she'd just want you to feel better." From what I'd seen, Jill was a hell of a good friend, loyal to a fault. Which was why she'd been like a pit bull after me when she thought I was cheating with Rob.

"I hope so. I hurt her feelings, and that sucks so hard. But I don't know what to do."

"So you're buying her pancakes?" I grinned as I merged onto the highway.

"Hey, she loves them."

"Who doesn't?"

In a few minutes, we got affirmative texts from Jillian and Krista, though she warned us her mom was busy, so she'd be bringing Naomi. I hadn't seen the baby often since the seemingly endless night of her birth. Counting back, I realized she had to be seven months old or something like that. *Holy crap.*

"Something wrong?"

"I was just realizing how long I've been home."

Avery nodded. "Almost a year."

"Wow. I'd say something like, 'Time flies,' except then I'd

have to beat my head repeatedly against the steering wheel for being such a verbal cliché."

"Then we'd spin out of control and end up in a snowbank."

"Don't worry, we'll live to eat pancakes for dinner."

The weather made that tough, however, as halfway to Sharon, the light snow turned into serious weather. It reminded me of driving back to Michigan with Nadia, last year after Thanksgiving. I hadn't wanted to leave at all, but at that point, I wasn't ready to admit how bad things had gotten. It took a serious fuckup for me to take stock and admit I had to change everything, or I might self-destruct. This trip didn't end in a crappy motel, though. I got us safely to Patty's Pancake House, where Jillian and Krista were already waiting; they had a booth with Naomi in a high chair at the end.

"This is crazy," Avery said, bending to kiss her on the head. "How can you be this big?"

I wouldn't have pegged her for a baby person, but she talked to Naomi more than the rest of us, even Krista. Jillian had lost a little weight but I didn't say anything because it always pissed me off when people commented on it with me, like being skinny was my chief goal in life.

"So what brought on the midweek pancake craving?" Krista asked.

Avery shrugged. "I just wanted to hang out with you guys."

"This isn't an official girls' night," Jillian pointed out. "Does this mean we can talk about guys?"

"Sure, if you want." I had nothing to say on that topic, but I was happy to listen, especially if someone had good news.

Krista handed Naomi a cracker, just before the baby lost patience with our blather. "I'll start. I just found out that Kenji will be stateside in March."

That was only three months away. No wonder she was so excited. "Oh, my God, that's amazing news. For leave or…?"

"Nope. He's earned enough for college, and he's coming home."

In her shoes, I'd be having panic attacks over him finishing his tour. If he were my fiancé, he'd explode in my head, over and over, only days before he boarded the plane, and he'd die, never having seen his baby daughter. That kind of shit burrowed deep into my brain, until I couldn't think about anything else. Thanks to Dr. Reid, I had some idea how to stop the mind worm, or at least keep it from ruining my life. Not that I was fixed after one visit. There was a long road ahead, but I had the stamina to survive it.

"Congrats, that's fantastic. Will he let you keep coming to girls' night?" Jillian asked.

"*Let* me, ha. You don't seem to understand our relationship. I do what I want, and he loves me." She grinned as she ate the rest of her bacon.

That sounds…perfect. Worse, it sounded like how it was with Rob. Pain throbbed through me, a reminder that I'd pushed for a clean break. *And I got one.* Now the only news I had about him came through Nadia or the internet. Now and then I dug up articles about *Hot Property,* a few pictures circulating on TV blogs. Like an obsessed fangirl, I'd downloaded a professional one, where he was posed in front of a woodsy backdrop, smiling for the camera. He looked impossibly polished and handsome. Now it was the screensaver on my laptop, though I'd die before admitting that to anyone.

"Me next." Jillian rapped on the table to pull our attention away from the awesomely romantic soldier's homecoming.

"Go for it," I said.

"So I've been dating this guy, off and on. He travels a lot… he's not even from here, but this weekend, he asked me to be his girlfriend."

Krista grabbed for Jill's phone. "Pics or it didn't happen."

Shoving her away, Jillian flipped through her gallery until she found the right shot. "Here, it's a selfie but you can see more of Ben's face than mine."

Avery leaned over to check him out. "Wow, he's hot."

He was blond and tan, what I'd call a surfer guy, but if he traveled for work, and he was wearing a suit, the look must be misleading. Mentally I rated him as cute, but nowhere near Rob's level. Of course, I was biased. I hadn't looked at a guy sexually since we broke up. A few dealership customers had hinted they'd take me out if I gave the go-ahead, but I always shut them down. Mentally *and* emotionally, I was a mess.

"Definitely." But there was just no way I could resist. "So does this mean we get to call you Billian? I don't think I can stop myself, the train has left the smush-name station."

"Whatever." Jillian flipped me off but she was smiling.

"Tell us about him," Avery ordered.

Apparently Ben was a regional salesman of office equipment, not terribly fascinating, but I wasn't the one who'd have to talk about his job with him. As Jill ran out of steam, Naomi decided she had been ignored long enough and pitched a fit. Sighing, Krista took her to the restroom to change her diaper. I so couldn't imagine myself in her situation, and for a moment, I entertained the idea that Nadia might have grabbed the smart end of the stick by coming into a kid's life after he stopped crapping his pants.

Avery paid the check while Jillian and Krista were gone. I narrowed my eyes at her but I didn't argue. It was her way of trying to make it up to Jill, the fact that she was keeping secrets. Maybe pancakes weren't a magical fix, but her heart was in the right place. Krista hurried out first, baby cuddled against her.

"This has been awesome, but I need to go. I try not to disrupt her routine too much. So how much do I owe? Are we splitting four ways?"

I hugged her. "Don't worry about it. Just take Naomi home. Text us when you get there."

"Okay, I'll get it next time. Say bye to Jillian for me!" Krista hurried out into a night that was rapidly getting snowier.

"I guess the party's ending early," Jillian said, coming back in time to see Krista back out of her parking space.

"Babies ruin everything," I mumbled.

Avery smiled with a melancholy air. "That's definitely the message in every teen drama I've ever watched. 'Don't do sex, girls, you'll get pregnant and die.'"

I nodded. "Harsh but true."

"I'm off, too," Jillian said. "Not to interrupt this depressing convo, but y'know."

She didn't offer to pay, which made me wonder if this was how Avery and Jillian operated. Like Nadia and I didn't always talk like we should, but sometimes we made other gestures full of subtext. Maybe friendship didn't have one concrete definition, one certain way to be; maybe it was enough to love somebody however they let you and for the pieces to click in, however felt right.

They hugged as I went on out to the car. Avery caught up with me a few minutes later, seeming to be in a better mood. "All good?"

She nodded. "I think so. Better anyway. Sometimes that's all you can manage."

"With Dr. Reid's help, our scope will improve." I said it like I believed it, not just for her but for me, too.

Maybe I wasn't in a hurry to tell people I was getting help, but I wasn't ashamed of it. On the way home, I drove slowly, avoiding the worst of the billowing gusts. I was a little worried about Happy, but when I parked in our driveway, she was bouncing up and down in front of the door. Thank goodness she had the sense to come in from the cold, if she was playing in the backyard earlier.

Inside, I knelt and hugged her, rubbing my hands over her sides. "Who's a good girl, huh? Who's a good girl?"

"Is it me?" Avery poked the back of my head.

"Obviously. People in Sharon may not agree, about you *or* me, but we're fucking wonderful, better all the time."

"Would it freak you out if I said I love you?" She crouched down on the other side of Happy, smiling at me with such vulnerability that I couldn't joke.

"Not if I'm allowed to say it back. I couldn't go down this road with anyone but you."

She pushed out a breath as I hugged her. "I'm scared, but I want to feel better."

"Me, too." I wanted to be someone who didn't melt down over small things. Deep in my heart, I imagined seeing Rob again, rebuilt like *The Bionic Woman*: stronger, faster, smarter. Well, I'd settle for stronger. To follow where he'd gone—to live in his world—I couldn't spackle over my problems and call it good. Before, I couldn't even imagine doing that. But now that I'd taken the first steps, I wanted Rob back, no matter what it took. First I had to ID my triggers and learn how to defuse the fear. Dr. Reid could get me there in time. With her history, Avery might have more work to do, but I wouldn't let her quit before she healed.

Our future might not be assured, but like a true video game geek, I was ready to buckle on my armor, take up my +5 vorpal sword, and do battle.

Too bad the dragon I have to slay lives inside my head.

CHAPTER TWENTY-SIX

The holidays completely sucked without Rob. I missed him more with every passing day. But I had a nice Christmas with Stuart and Mom, who cooked a full-on feast for the first time in years. I sang carols and drank eggnog, opened presents and pretended I didn't have a hole where my heart should be. When classes started in January, I didn't even care about the rampant sexism anymore. I just quietly turned in projects and ignored everything else.

Over time, my sessions with Dr. Reid helped.

Every two weeks, I shared a little more and she responded with constructive techniques to help manage my emotions. Breathing helped; so did relabeling my responses—like instead of thinking, *Crap, I'm freaking out,* I substituted, *Wow, I'm really excited about this.* She also reminded me that anxiety was natural, and that I wasn't abnormal for feeling this way. Dr. Reid also pointed out that I needed to make realistic corrections to my expectations and stop creating exaggerated mental failure scenarios.

The thing she said that made the most difference, however,

was when she told me, "Understand that there's nothing wrong with you, and that it isn't your fault."

Before I heard that, there'd been a sharp sliver at the heart of me, constant pain and shame, because I just couldn't be normal. I wasn't trying for that anymore; I just wanted to be happy.

When my mom asked me to go with her to a work thing because Stuart was at a conference in Lincoln, I said no problem. I didn't know many of her coworkers and I could remember a time, not too long ago, when I'd be hunched over in a bathroom, horrified by the idea of meeting so many people, making small talk, dealing with their looks and wondering if they could tell there was something wrong with me. Tonight, I wasn't looking forward to it, but I was okay, stronger, like I'd hoped.

"Thanks for coming along last minute. I know you prefer to have some mental prep time for stuff like this." Mom looked beautiful in a fitted blue dress, wearing a lapis lazuli necklace Stuart had bought for her in Hawaii.

"It's fine. I'm doing better." Before, I never would've said that, never would've admitted to her that there was a problem. I'd have deflected with a joke and changed the subject. To me, it felt like progress. "If you don't mind my asking, how did *you* snap out of it?"

"The depression?" She fumbled the keys for a few seconds.

"Yeah."

We never really talked about things like this. Like Avery and Jillian, we had more of a don't-ask, don't-tell policy. So I thought maybe she wouldn't answer because she got in the car and after a few seconds, I did the same.

But as she put it into Reverse, she said, "I got help. It's not something I enjoy admitting, the fact that I didn't have the energy to do *anything*. Or that I was thinking maybe the world would be better off without me. But I couldn't go on like I was. It took me a while before I didn't feel like there must be something seriously wrong with me because I couldn't pull myself up by my bootstraps and snap out of it. Some people can. I wasn't one of them."

"I'm seeing someone, too."

"I thought you might be. But it would be hypocritical of me to make you talk when I don't. So we muddle along."

I thought about that as she drove to the retirement dinner. A senior staffer was retiring after forty years of service, so the company was throwing a party to honor him. For me, it was such a welcome change not to have the whispers in the back of my head about everything that could go wrong. That wasn't to say they were gone for good, but I knew how to manage them better now.

"Maybe we should try harder…to be honest with each other."

"Maybe. It's hard to know where to start. Possibly with Rob?" She cut me a look as she parked, and I didn't bother to hide my flinch.

His name still had the power to tie me in knots; though I didn't regret sending him off to see what he could do in Toronto, I hated the fact that I'd hurt him, even more when I contemplated how much I still loved him. The pain was still sharp—nothing about it had faded, and matters weren't improved by living in the house we'd restored together. I'd never told my mom the whole story, only that he got a job out of town, and we were done.

So instead of the usual chitchat over dinner, I told her everything, including what I'd done and why. She'd obviously been taking communication lessons from whoever she was talking to professionally because she didn't tell me I was stupid or that I didn't have the right to make that decision for him. Because the thing was, if Rob hadn't wanted to go, deep down, he never would've let me drive him away. I *knew* how stubborn he could be. So I stepped into the villain's shoes and gave him a way to go without feeling bad for leaving me behind. Which sucked for *me,* but I didn't doubt it was right for him, even now.

"Do you miss him?" she asked.

"Every day. At this point, I'm used to it. But…in a way, I was using him as a crutch, hiding from life. Running home was an avoidance tactic, not a coping one, and I was really in *no* shape to sustain a relationship."

"I'm glad *you* said it." She offered a half smile and raised her wineglass. "But you're into your third semester here, making excellent grades, still working at the dealership, no problems living on your own. That's fantastic."

I sighed. "I don't need you to pat me on the head, Mom. Verbally or otherwise."

"Then why are we having this serious talk?"

Leaning over, I whispered, "Because the people at our table are boring?"

She glanced around and conceded with a shrug. Before I could say anything else, the guest of honor appeared onstage and gave a rambling speech of thanks, wherein he reminisced about the old days and asked four times for someone named Connie. Then they gave him a gold watch and helped him down the steps.

"Huh. And to think Stuart missed all of this," I muttered.

Dinner was decent, though, and we were out of the hall by nine. Mom dropped me off at the house—with Rob gone, I still didn't think of it as home. Avery was still up, watching TV with Happy.

"Have you finished carousing already?"

"I haven't decided yet. Is there rabble to rouse?"

"Not much, even on Saturday night. You grew up here, you know the drill."

Nodding, I collapsed on the couch and kicked off my heels. "I did okay. No flares, no sweating, no nervous vomiting or heart palpitations. You?"

"No urges to trash cars or punch men who ogle me." We fist-bumped, and then I got up.

"I'm making hot chocolate. Want some?"

"Sure." Avery had gained a little weight since we started living together, maybe ten pounds. Before, she didn't eat as a silent protest to her father, but since he'd rather have a compliant, starving daughter, he didn't care about her food issues. She was working on that with Dr. Reid, too.

To celebrate another good day, I put marshmallows in the cocoa. We toasted and I sipped at it, watching the last of whatever movie this was, something violent, my definite preference. To look at me, you'd think I loved girlie films, but give me action or sci-fi any day. Once it ended, I stood up and stretched.

"Has Happy gone out recently?"

She considered, then shook her head. "Not since five or so."

"I'm on it."

"Thanks. I'll do the dishes in the morning."

Calling the dog, I jogged to the kitchen and went out the back door, luring her with a treat since it was pretty brisk out. I wished I'd jammed my feet in some shoes as I hopped back and forth, waiting for Happy to do her business. Afterward, I fed her the biscuit and rushed back in.

"Okay, I'm off to kill stuff for an hour or so before bed."

She raised a brow. "With anyone else, those words would alarm me. 'Night, Lauren."

I flicked a hand at her as I went up the stairs. Happy followed me. Though she liked Avery, she was still *my* dog. She cocked her head at me as I hesitated in the threshold of the bedroom I'd shared with Rob. Months later, and it still hit me every time, like a punch in the sternum, that he was gone and not coming back, that *I'd* made it happen.

"I miss him," I whispered to her as I closed the door behind us. "What about you?"

She sighed at me like that was a dumb question. A non-dog-lover would question how I anthropomorphized her, but I swore she understood me. Happy leaped up on Rob's side and turned around three times before settling down. The sheets had been changed and washed a hundred times, more maybe, but I wished I had the luxury of crawling into bed and breathing him in. I'd never admit how long I waited before swapping the linens after he left; now there was only Happy and me scenting the bed covers, along with touches of detergent and fabric softener.

I put on my pajamas and sat down at my computer. There were always class projects, code to write, barbs to respond to from buttheads in my data structures class. But I backslid a little and checked for Rob Conrad Google Alerts before deciding what game to play or doing something more productive, like finishing a paper for IT ethics.

There wasn't a ton about him; he wasn't an A-list celebrity, but I found a new photo posted to a Toronto-centric site. Headline: Internet Sensation Rob Conrad Enjoys Time Off with a Lucky Lady. Is There Romance Behind the Scenes at *Hot Property?*

My chest ached as I read a short blurb about the show, then scrolled down to see him waving to the press with Annette Caldwell beside him. The picture was dated two days ago, and the caption offered the usual crap about him being really sweet to his fans. I had noticed that they were shooting promos for the show and posting them to Rob's channel, professional quality unlike the vids we made, but these were still called *At Home with Rob.* His idea, not mine. I touched the screen lightly, closing the browser tab, but it felt like goodbye, as well.

For an hour or so, I stabbed monsters online, but my heart wasn't in it, so I brushed my teeth and went to bed. Some nights it was hard to fall asleep for thinking about Rob, wondering what he was doing, if he was happy. I'd really like the answer to the last question, but I couldn't become the lame girl obsessively grilling Nadia for updates. She told me what she knew as she learned it, and it would have to be enough.

The following Monday, I found a package waiting when I got home from work, left by the UPS man. I took it inside and set it down, pausing to pet the dog, who was so excited to see me. Then I got a knife and cut the box open. Inside, I discovered my three binders, fantasies I'd written about Rob when he was like a prince from a story to me, not a real person at all. Now I knew better; I knew what he liked the best in bed and how to hurt him the most. Though I searched, there was no note.

That's the message right there.

Tears trickled down my cheeks as I hugged the binders. I'd lied when I said I had no use for these, so I was glad to have them back, even if it meant Rob didn't want them—that he skimmed the stupidity, laughed and put it aside, moved on to more important things. There would always be room in my heart for dreams of him, wrapped around the memories that chased me in and out of each day like weary ghosts, reminding me of how sweet life was before. Yet even with the pain, I couldn't regret my decision.

It had been a while since I'd wept over Rob, but today I couldn't help it. Happy eyed me and then nudged against my legs, so I knelt down to hug her. Then I took the past upstairs and tucked it on the bookshelves Rob had built. Everything in this room had his imprint all over it, and if I had the right, I'd ship him the furniture, start fresh. I couldn't live here forever; I knew that, but I couldn't bring myself to discuss looking for a new place with Avery because it would mean contacting Rob, other than the check I mailed once a month. Damn, even the utilities were still in his name… Trusting of him. If I were an asshole, I could stop paying the bills and ruin his credit. Which I'd *never* do—and maybe deep down, he knew that. Regardless, I had to make a move; things couldn't continue like this.

I just couldn't decide what to do.

But there was one step I could take immediately. I got on my laptop and pinged Nadia, stifling a burst of glee when she answered right away. "Hey! Sorry we couldn't make it for Christmas. I miss you. Everything okay?"

"Yeah. No. Well, gainfully employed anyway." *Still paying Rob's mortgage, with Avery's help.* That seemed so strange and backward.

"Have you talked to Rob?"

"Nope. How's Mr. Hot Ginger?"

"I'm right here, I can hear you," a male voice called.

A high-pitched question: "Why does she call you that?"

"Crap, did I call at a bad time?"

"We're trying to get Sam ready for bed. Can I get back to you?"

"Sure, no problem."

Even if she was busy, at least I'd made the effort. I could feel good about that. This felt like closing the circle, trying to be a good friend again. In that same vein, I tried Angus next, but he didn't show online. I left a text message on his Skype account, then stared at Max's icon. Despite the awkwardness between us, I hadn't deleted him.

And he's signed on.

Taking a deep breath, I requested a chat, then I bit my lip, wondering if he even wanted to break the long silence. After thirty interminable seconds, the video connection went live, revealing a dark-haired guy with eyes so dark you could hardly see the pupils. He was lean and handsome in a scruffy sort of way. Just now, he had on sweats and a T-shirt, shaggy hair tumbling into his eyes.

"Long time, no talk," he said.

"Yeah." I took a breath. "I know it's been a long time, and maybe you don't think about it anymore, but…really, I just want to say sorry."

"About what?" Cool, almost icy. I couldn't tell if he'd really forgotten.

"That night. Everything, actually. I just want you to know that it *really* was me, not you. I was kind of…broken."

"Are you better now?" he asked.

"Getting there."

"That's all I need to know, then."

We talked a little more, mostly about Nadia and Angus. When he said he had to go, I felt okay. At least Max wasn't one of my regrets anymore.

The second week in March, Krista called us over to meet her man. Since Kenji had come home, she'd skipped the last couple of girls' nights. They had a lot of lost time to make up for. For the moment, they were all living with her mom, but I didn't see that situation lasting long. Krista and Kenji had to be eager for some privacy—well, as much as Naomi allowed.

She had dinner ready when Avery and I got there. Jill was the last to arrive. Kenji was a good-looking guy with nice hair, a little on the short side, and he obviously adored Krista and Naomi. The whole time we were at the house, he never put his daughter down, not when she had to be changed, when she spit up on him, or when she smacked him in the nose. His smile never faltered.

"So what's your secret?" I asked, once the table had been cleared and Naomi was napping in Kenji's arms.

"To what?" Krista sat against her fiancé's side, one hand possessive on his thigh.

"Making it work. Everyone I've ever talked to who tried long-distance said it was horrible and things fell apart pretty fast."

Jillian perked up. She was still seeing Ben, who wasn't around nearly as much as she'd like. Traveling to sell office equipment wasn't remotely the same as deployment, but I could tell she was interested in the answer. "I could use some tips for sure."

Thoughtful, Krista tipped her head for a few seconds, glancing at Kenji, who leaned over to kiss her forehead. Then she answered, "It was awful when I'd hear reports of artillery or IEDs near his posting. And there's no question that sometimes I got so lonely, I'd wonder if this could possibly be worth it. Then I'd imagine life without him and the answer was always yes."

"That's it?" Jillian asked.

Krista raised a brow. "It's not enough?"

"For me, it helped to envision the ending," Kenji explained. "No matter how dark it got over there, I knew she was waiting. There were a few times I might not have made it out if not for her. I wouldn't have had reason to move so fast or push so hard."

Avery tapped Jillian on the arm. "So the real question is, do you love Ben enough to wait however long it takes before you guys can be together, enough to fight if things get tough?"

My breath caught, because she might as well be asking

me that question. *How much do I love Rob? That much? Or not enough.* Like I said that terrible day.

Jillian seemed frozen, indecision playing across her round face. "I'm not sure. We have fun together, but...I don't feel like we have what you and Kenji do." She cursed softly. "I think I have to break up with him."

Kenji tilted his head against the couch. "Are your friends *always* this depressing, baby?"

I smirked. "Sometimes we do body shots off each other and try to see how many phone numbers we can get in a night. You'd be surprised at how many guys were into Krista's midriff."

"Lauren! God, don't tell him that."

He aimed a teasing smile her way. "Why, because it's true? From the pictures I've seen, you were pretty hot with that baby belly."

"That's our cue to leave," Avery said, standing up.

Jillian nodded. "Thanks for the advice. I'll let you know how it goes. Nice meeting you, Kenji. We've all heard so much about you that it seems like we know you already."

"All good?" he asked.

"Definitely. Dinner was delicious. See you soon, guys."

Avery was driving tonight, so I got in her Bug, waving to Jillian as we drove off. Evidently rooming together had given her some kind of Lauren-dar, however, because before we were halfway home, she said, "Spill it."

"What?"

"You got this deer-in-headlights look when Kenji and Krista were being adorable."

"I was just thinking, that's all."

"About what?"

"Rob," I admitted.

"Alert the media."

"You asked. Do you want to hear this or not?" The car was quiet for too long. "Hey!"

She teased, "I'm thinking. Fine, tell me your deep thoughts."

"Basically, just that I'm sure. I love Rob that much. My life will always be better with him in it. He's worth waiting for, worth fighting for. I had to…I dunno, fix myself a bit before I could be a real partner, but I'm closer now. I'm better."

"Are you trying to convince me?" Avery asked.

"No, I mean it. I think he needed to take this shot on his own, see how well he did without me backing him up. Not sure if you noticed when you were together, but he's not the most confident guy."

"I did," she said softly. "I took advantage of it. And I should apologize."

"You and me both. But the thing is, maybe he's done. He sent back some things that belonged to me. It might've been a sign, letting me know that it's definitely over." Or maybe it meant something else entirely, though for the life of me, I had no idea what.

"Do you care? You already said you'll fight for him. So go, kick ass and take names. Hold your head high, give him hell. Don't stop 'til you get enough."

"Are you just quoting random song lyrics at me now?"

"Maybe. I'm bad at this encouragement stuff, huh?"

I shook my head. "In fact, it's just the boot in the ass I need to go get my man."

CHAPTER TWENTY-SEVEN

First thing the next morning, I called Nadia. For once, the time difference served me well, so I didn't wake her up. She answered on the second ring. At this hour, she was probably at the day care center. "Everything okay? You never call me when I'm at work."

"Your parents are fine. I'm about to ask you a favor, and I'll understand if you say no. But if you do, I'll find another way—"

"Tell me what you need, LB." When she cut into my babble, she sounded amused.

"Rob's address."

"That's easy. I'm forwarding his contact info to your phone."

"Wow." I'd geared up to really beg her in case she didn't want to get in the middle of our drama. "Thank you."

"I'm glad you're finally calling him. The two of you are driving me nuts."

"Huh?"

"You think I haven't noticed the way you perk up when I mention him? And Rob's the same. I talked to him a week ago, and he was all supercasual. 'So how's Lauren doing? Who's she dating these days?' I told him I didn't know because I figured you'd kill me if I said you're still as hung up on him now as you were six months ago. I *still* don't get it, by the way. But I hope you can patch things up."

My phone pinged with Rob's new cell number and his home address. His email was the same. But I only needed to know where he lived because this wasn't the kind of conversation we could have online or even on the phone. I had to talk to him, face-to-face, and find out if there was any hope of fixing the broken between us.

"Me, too."

"Good luck," she said. "I have to go before these hooligans duct tape my assistant to something."

When I hung up and turned around, I spotted Avery perched at the foot of the stairs. "When are you leaving?"

I liked that she didn't secretly expect me to chicken out. "I have to put in for vacation days. I'm not calling in sick. I have to do it right."

"Well, for what it's worth, I hope he forgives you."

"Me, too."

After taking care of Happy, I got ready and went to work a bit early. The office staff was already on site, so I asked for the paperwork and filled it out during my lunch hour. According to the documentation, all such requests required a week to process, so I wouldn't be getting my three-day weekend this pay period. But they approved it for the following Friday. Afterward, I was so wound up that I probably scared the prospective customers with my too-wide smile.

Finally, five o'clock rolled around, and I zipped home. Happy was glad to see me; I fed her and opened a can of soup, then I went upstairs to make travel arrangements. Flying alone was the kind of thing that could send me straight into a panic attack before, but as I bought the tickets, I breathed through it. *Why are you so scared? Is it really the flying?* When I analyzed the tightness in my chest, the fear came from the prospect of facing Rob. It wasn't that I was afraid to grovel, more that despite what Nadia said, he wouldn't care how I felt or what I had to say.

Unpacking the emotions gave them less power over me, though. I worked through the feelings as Dr. Reid had taught me, and then stowed them in their proper place. For the next week, I kept busy. I worked extra hard on my data structures project and I turned in my ethics paper early. By Thursday night, I was packed and ready.

I didn't bother to rent a hotel room. If things went badly with Rob, I'd just change my return and hang out at the airport until I could go home. That possibility filled my stomach with lead as I drove two hours to the airport, where I left my car in long-term parking and then caught the shuttle to my terminal. This was so different from the time I'd come to Toronto with Rob. I didn't realize how well he managed things until I had to get in lines on my own.

Somehow I survived the waiting and the flight. At the Toronto airport, I stopped in the restroom to check my hair and makeup. Refreshing my lipstick made me feel better, then I went down to the taxi stand, got one and gave the guy Rob's address. I'd looked up the location on Google Maps the night before, but it wasn't the same as seeing the city open up all around me. The cabbie seemed to sense I wasn't in the mood to chat, so he made no small talk as I clutched my backpack and stared out the window at the passing cityscape.

Maybe I should've called.

Normally I'd be sweating and hyperventilating by now, so this was a great field test for the coping strategies I had been practicing. Wryly I thought, *I'm definitely stronger.* Too soon or maybe not soon enough, the taxi stopped outside a white stone building. It didn't have a lot of personality, nothing to separate it from the ones on either side. With a mental shrug, I paid the driver and got out. He pulled away as I stood at the curb, staring up. The place wasn't fancy enough to have a doorman, but there were intercoms. I hadn't considered that I wouldn't just be able to go knock on his door. *Crap, defeated by small-town mentality.*

But I'd come too far to stop now. So I marched over and pressed the button for his apartment. Nothing. It was just past one in the afternoon, so maybe I'd timed it wrong. He could be shooting for the show or doing an appearance. *Dammit. What now?* Disheartened, I walked a couple of blocks until I found a coffee place and bought a latte, then I went back to his apartment and pushed the button again, like I could will him to answer. It didn't work.

Then I'll wait.

Sitting on a bench wasn't how I envisioned this reunion. Like the last time I was in Toronto, I got out my phone and read while keeping an eye on passersby. The last thing I wanted was to miss Rob and end up spending the night here. Getting arrested for vagrancy wasn't part of the plan. It was chilly enough that the cold bench numbed my butt, but if I went back to the café, I might miss him. Two hours passed, and I'd long since finished my drink when a familiar figure strode down the sidewalk toward me.

He was a little leaner, probably because he wasn't doing hard labor on construction sites anymore. His face seemed more chiseled, eyes brighter in contrast to his dark hair. He was wearing jeans, a black shirt and a fleece-lined jacket, the perfect amount of rugged. I could easily imagine TV viewers all over Canada falling in love with him when the first show aired. The sight of Rob after so many months apart hit me harder than I expected; I froze, unable to speak as he drew closer, and he almost passed me. Then his gaze sharpened, his steps slowed, then stopped altogether, no more than five feet away.

"Lauren," he said.

That was all. That one word gave me no clue how he felt. I hadn't talked to him since that awful night. I met his gaze, wondering if I had the courage for this. Then I remembered what Krista said about imagining life without the one you love. *I'll swing for the fences.* What was it people said about moments like this, *Go big or go home?*

"Hey. Do you have a minute to talk?"

"Just one?"

"Possibly more. We can go to the coffee shop if you don't want to invite me up."

"No, it's fine. Come on." He beckoned me toward the building, and my legs were so stiff that I could hardly toddle. "Jesus. How long have you been sitting here?"

"Dunno. Two or three hours."

"Are you crazy?"

I smiled. "Less than I have been, actually."

Rob unlocked the lobby doors and headed for the elevator. Apparently he lived on the sixth floor, near the top by my calculations, considering how long I'd been staring at the building and counting things. The ride up was quiet, but it wasn't like I could just launch into my speech right here, and I'd forgotten most of what I intended to say in the waiting. He let us into his apartment, which was open and modern— hardwood floors, stainless steel. It didn't have any of the charm of the place we'd restored together.

"I'll make some coffee," he said.

I waited politely in the living room, unable to breathe for the tightness in my chest. *What did you think, that he'd be over-*

come with lust the minute he spotted you, sweep you into his arms and you'd have make-up sex without talking first? Maybe. It would've been easier; that was for sure.

When he finally brought two cups, mine fixed just as I liked it, I glanced up from my lap. I caught…something in his eyes, a familiar look, just before he shuttered it, and it gave me the courage to speak. "You're probably wondering why I'm here."

"Well, yeah. You made things pretty clear before."

"I need to apologize to you."

"For dumping me?" He folded his arms, propping a hip against the edge of his chair.

With him towering over me, I had a hard time finding the words. But I pushed on. "No, for *lying.* I knew you'd never leave if you understood how much I love you. And you needed to go, every bit as much as I needed to get my head together."

"Love?" he asked quietly.

"I never stopped. I don't know if I ever will. And it's okay if you can't forgive me. I know I hurt you, and I'm so sorry. But I couldn't go with you, not then, and I was afraid you'd be too focused on a long-distance thing with me to give this—" I gestured vaguely at the apartment "—your best shot."

"It would help if you told me why."

"Why I couldn't come with you?"

Rob knew about my anxiety, but I hadn't been honest with him. So I took a deep breath and told him about the extent of my drinking, the night with Max, just how bad things had gotten at their worst and how much damage control there was to do before I could be with him as a real partner.

"Jesus," he said softly.

It was impossible to meet his gaze. "I was a mess. And though I didn't realize it at the time, I was using you as glue to hold myself together. I really am better now, though, or I wouldn't be here. You should know, saying those things to you, it was like cutting out my own heart. After you left, I cried until I couldn't see. But…I understand if this is too little, too late."

"Say it again." He tilted my chin up.

"Huh?" I blinked at him, bewildered.

"That you love me."

"I love you, Rob. I always have. I was in love with you before you kissed me. Until you, I never even remotely believed in the possibility of a happy ending."

"So what happens now?" He was being so cagey, so guarded with his reaction, that I had no idea how he felt about me, no matter what Nadia thought.

"That's up to you. This is what I came to say. I could grovel more, but the core message will be the same—that I'm sorry and I love you, and that I'll do anything you want, anything it takes for us to be together. If it's not enough, then—"

Rob plucked the untouched coffee from my hands and pulled me out of my chair. At first, I half thought he was showing me the door, but then, for the first time in so long, I was in his arms. He put his cheek against my hair and breathed me in; I was doing the same to him through a rush of tears.

"Do you have *any idea* how much I missed you? God, Lauren, you weren't just my girlfriend, you were my best friend, my family…everything."

"I'm sorry," I whispered.

"No…you were right about one thing. If I'd been looking back to Sharon, I don't think I'd have done as well at this. Because I came here angry and with something to prove. But the longer we were apart, the more I realized that whole night was weird."

I lifted my face, puzzled. "It was?"

"If I *really* had faith in us—in you—I wouldn't have bailed so fast. I'd have argued with you. That's because, deep down,

I never thought I could be enough for you. So when you confirmed I wasn't, all my worst fears came true, and I had to get out."

"I told you before, you don't have to do anything to be with me. I'm not a prize to be won like a stuffed bear at a carnival."

"You said it, but I didn't believe it. Not really. I needed to get out of Sharon and find out what I could do on my own."

"Is the show going well?"

He nodded. "I've picked the assistants for the team, and we start filming in a few weeks."

"I'm happy for you."

Rob ran his hands through my hair, stroked my back. "Nadia is a pain in the ass, you know that? She wouldn't tell me anything."

I smiled, rubbing my cheek against his chest. "Don't be too mad at her, she gave me your address. To update you, I'm still working at the dealership, still in school, still in love with you. And no, not dating anyone else."

"I notice you're not asking."

"It's not important." Okay, that was a huge lie. It would kill me if he'd been with someone else, but I loved him too much for it to be a deal-breaker.

"For the record, I love you. And that means I'm not interested in anyone else. There have been some photo ops, but I've slept alone since the night I left."

"Not me." I paused long enough for his eyes to narrow, then added, "I've got Happy."

"Damn, Lauren, that's not funny."

"Sorry, I tend to joke when I'm nervous. So what're we going to do about this? Us?"

"I want you back. I want you with me." The firmness of his tone sent a shiver of pleasure through me.

If it was even possible, I loved Rob more. A lot of guys

would've made this difficult, pretended not to feel anything. Some of them would've refused to forgive me, but he was pure goodness, down to the bone. In all likelihood, he was better than I deserved.

"Would it be okay if we skipped to the make-up sex? We'll talk about all of the important stuff afterward, I promise."

"I could be convinced." Rob swept me into his arms and carried me to the bedroom.

He had a huge bed and I was naked in it before I could do more than glance around. In seconds, he had me in his arms again, but instead of kissing me, he buried his face between my neck and shoulder. I held him, knowing exactly how he felt.

"Love you so much," I whispered into his hair. "I was so afraid you'd meet somebody else while I—"

"Stop. I met all kinds of women but…there's no replacing you. They only want the nicely wrapped package, they don't care about what's inside. Before I made anything of myself, you believed in me. You always thought I was somebody."

"You were. You are."

"Shit, Lauren, not even my own family saw anything in me. Without you, I'm empty. And no matter how far I climb, it'll always feel hollow if you're not with me."

I kissed him then; I couldn't help it. His mouth was rough satin, hungry, as I remembered. Running my hands down his back, I felt it when he shivered. Rob took over with greedy surges of tongue, nibbling my lower lip and tasting me so deeply that I almost forgot how to breathe. As we kissed, I rubbed against him, savoring the feel of his big body after so long. His cock was so hard against my belly that it must have ached. I reached between us, and he jerked, pumping into my hand with a pained look. But he didn't try to stop me and his eyes locked on mine as I worked my fingers up and down his shaft.

"Are you trying to make me come?"

"Would it work?"

He thrust again, eyes heavy-lidded. "Keep doing that and find out."

Though I desperately needed to be close to him, I also wanted to watch Rob lose control. It must be something he wanted, too, because he didn't stop me as I stroked up and down, encouraging him to fuck my fingers, coming up against the softness of my stomach on each downward motion. His breath quickened as I watched his face. Heat built in his cheeks, a sure sign he was getting closer. When he started biting his lip, I'd know he was almost there.

"Why are you letting me do this?"

The way he growled out the answer sent a shiver through me. "You're mine. I want to come on you."

"*Fuck,* Rob."

"In a minute." Teasing answer, last thing he said before the pleasure got away from him.

I moved with him, as much as the position allowed, and I felt like he was staking a claim—my hand, his cock, my belly, now slick with his pre-come. Everything narrowed to his face above mine, and then he sank his teeth into his lower lip to muffle the sound. I wanted his moans, too, so I reached up to kiss him, and as his tongue touched mine, he throbbed in my fist, coming all over me in hot spurts. Groaning into my mouth, he kissed me fierce and deep as the last pulses shivered through him.

My skin was sticky as we pulled apart. "Marking your territory?"

"Something like that. Is that weird?"

"It's hot." I squirmed, needing to come, but I didn't want to self-service when I had Rob right here.

Before I could point out the fact that I was still horny, he got a washcloth and wiped off my belly and hands. Surprised, I noticed his cock was still hard, an impressive display considering what we'd just done. I thought I'd get lips or fingers until he recovered.

He caught me staring and offered a sheepish smile. "Clearly you have no idea how much I want you, and…it's been a long fucking time."

CHAPTER TWENTY-EIGHT

"Round two?" I suggested with a cheeky grin.

Before I could say another word, he had me on his lap. I sank down on his cock with a muffled whimper, already so slick and sensitive that this felt incredible. I didn't know if I had the self-control to move without humping wildly, but he didn't leave it up to me. Rob cradled my hips in his hands and worked me up and down, watching my face as I had his.

So sexy. God, I love you.

"Love you, too, beautiful." I didn't realize I'd said it out loud, until he replied and rewarded me by nuzzling my breasts.

His mouth on my nipple sent sheer pleasure sparking through my body, amping up the hot, sweet friction. I took the lead, no longer letting him move me on him; I worked my hips in tight circles, then up and down, until I found the perfect rhythm. Riding him was one of my favorite things because his hands and mouth were everywhere while I set the pace, building to orgasm at exactly the right speed. It was up to me how fast and hard I came. Right now, I wanted it quick and dirty, so I reached down and stroked my clit. Rob grabbed my hand and pulled it back, teasing me. I gasped when his fingers replaced mine.

"Harder? Softer?"

"Harder," I managed. "Longer."

"Like that?"

My hands came to his shoulders, holding on as the orgasm rolled closer. Tension tightened my thighs and belly. "Need you… So close. Lean back." My voice sounded thick and demanding, but Rob complied, and I followed.

Much better, pressure on my clit. Faster and faster, I pushed down on him, and he cupped my ass, working my cheeks open, so I felt embarrassingly exposed. Yet that only increased my pleasure; Rob could do anything to me, and I wouldn't stop him. *Anything, yes. Yes.* I came in a hard, clenching rush, trembling in his arms.

"Mmm. You feel incredible. But we're not done." He rolled me under him and took over.

At first, I just laid there panting, stroking his back, but the longer he thrust, the more I perked up. Soon I wrapped my legs around his hips and worked with him, digging my nails into his shoulders. The spark of pain spurred him on, so I bit his chest lightly, over and over.

He snarled a little. "Driving me crazy. No matter how much I have you, it's not enough."

"I'm here, I'm right here. And I'm yours."

He shuddered in my arms and let go, his whole body arching with the force of it. His intensity flickered me to a quiet, second peak, nowhere near as powerful as the first. But it was warm and sweet with him on top of me. I traced along his nose to his mouth, and then he lay down on me entirely, completely relaxed.

"Don't ever leave me again."

"Technically, you left, not me."

Rob cracked one eye open to give me a look. "Really?"

"Sorry. I promise I won't. I'll fight to make it work." It was a little hard to get my breath with him on top, but there was no way I'd complain.

He knew; he always did. Rolling to the side, he cuddled me against his chest. Before long, his hands tangled in my hair. Playing with it had been one of his favorite things, and I was glad I hadn't gotten it hacked off in a fit of grief.

"So now to the important stuff?" he asked.

"Yeah. This might be presumptuous but I didn't book a room for tonight."

Rob's eyes widened. "What did you plan to do if I passed on getting back together?"

"Go back to the airport. If you don't want me here, there's no reason to stick around."

"I do. But…can you?"

I knew what he was asking. "New situations—and change—don't freak me out as much as they did. Because…I've been seeing someone. Professionally. If I move, I'll ask for a referral so I don't backslide."

I was a little afraid that he'd think less of me for therapy, like it was self-indulgent, so the silence was awkward until his troubled look deepened into a frown. "If?"

That was when I realized he was focused on the uncertainty, not my mental issues. "Well, I can't just *assume* you want to move in together again. Maybe you have reservations—"

"Fuck that," Rob said. "I want you in my life and in my bed, full-time. I want my damn dog back. So let's figure out how to get this done."

"Wow."

"What?"

"I was afraid this would be…harder."

"Why would I be a pain in the ass over something I want so bad?"

He made a compelling point. Lying in his arms, I thought about the logistics. "School isn't a problem. As long as I turn in my work, they won't know if I move. Any hard-copy correspondence, my mom can scan and email to me." That bothered me a little, though. "I guess it's a little unethical to pay the in-state tuition rate after I leave—"

"It takes a while to establish residency," Rob cut in. "So don't worry about that."

"What about the house? I'm living with Avery now. Are you thinking of selling it?"

He kissed the tip of my nose. "I missed the way you think about things."

"What does that even mean?"

"You're such a planner. It's awesome to watch you work."

"Yeah?" It felt a little odd to be complimented for my overactive brain, but Rob gave every impression of sincerity.

"Definitely. And no, I won't sell it. That house is where I've been the happiest. I haven't given up the idea that we'll live there together again someday."

Love swelled in my chest, so sweet and immense that my body could hardly contain it. "Who knows? We'll probably be here for a while." Once I couldn't have coped with a big city, but I was stronger now. Anywhere Rob was, that was where I needed to be.

"Probably," he agreed.

"Once you make your fortune, you can fund your furniture business properly. How are you handling that, by the way?"

"The studio hooked me up with a local carpenter. He let me use his workspace in return for some screen time on my channel, and I finished up the last of my orders a while back. Now the store's closed while I see how *Hot Property* does."

"I'm glad you're not flipping the house," I admitted.

"Maybe Avery would like to find a roommate and stay put? Cost of living is higher here, so it'll be tough to swing an apartment and the mortgage, too."

"But you're a big-time TV star," I teased. "Don't they pay you the big bucks?"

He laughed. "It's more than I made in construction, but for us to find a decent place that allows pets, our rent will be at least fifteen hundred, plus we have two cars to park, and that's more expensive than you'd expect."

"Wow." Until I graduated, I'd probably have a hard time finding a job that let me easily cover half of that.

"Stop scowling. Like before, I'll cover rent if you get utilities and food."

"Okay. But you don't want to stay here?"

"Hell, no. I just didn't care enough to look for anything else before. This is a furnished unit, and I'm on a month-to-month plan, because when I first got here, I didn't know if things would work out. But now that you're here, we'll find an apartment together."

"Feels kind of like you were waiting for me."

He smiled, his eyes warm and bright as a summer sky. "I was."

"You know I'm only here for the weekend, right? I have to wrap things up, I can't just take off with two pairs of panties for an international move."

"Your practicality is killing my dreams." But he was obviously joking. "Of course I do. You have to give notice, talk to Avery, get Happy. Lots to organize, so you should enjoy it."

"I'm already happy," I said.

"Funny. But I'm still glad to hear it. I'm not making you feel trapped?"

Ouch. I wished I hadn't said so much of that shit, but maybe we'd still be clinging to each other in codependent dysfunction if I hadn't. "You never did. As I already told you, I was *lying*. Should I apologize again? I'll do a knee-grovel if you want."

"When I get you on your knees, it won't be to talk about how sorry you are."

Damn. Even though we just had amazing sex, I was…interested. "So how much have I disrupted your weekend? Do you have appearances or interviews, anything that—"

"There's nothing going on. I work out, sometimes I have lunch with Annette. That's about it. So far, they've kept me too busy to meet a ton of people."

Annette.

"She's married," he added, probably in response to my look. "And her husband thinks the stories about us are hilarious."

"Oh. I wasn't worried or anything. You're in bed naked with *me*."

He produced a mock-astonished expression. "How did that happen?"

A stray thought occurred to me then, and I had to know, though it was kind of a non sequitur. "I was wondering… why did you send the binders? Without a note or anything."

"Sad, you're supposed to be the clever one. Obviously, it was Lauren bait."

"You expected me to call or something? Ask about them?"

"I was hoping. But you went one better. Look how well it worked." Rob seemed really smug as he kissed my temple.

After that, the weekend was a sex blur. I ate a few things, but mostly I rolled around naked with Rob. Sunday morning when he took me back to the airport, I cried. Though I said he didn't have to, he parked his truck and walked me all the way to the security gate.

"I'll be back soon," I promised.

"How long?"

At this point, I couldn't be sure. "A month? Two at the most."

He kissed me, hard. "If you're not back in six weeks, I'm coming to get you."

"Deal. Let's see how I perform under pressure."

We did a long, extravagant airport kiss—to the point that people around us were staring when I finally pulled back. It was so hard to walk away from him and go through the security line; I turned and turned, until Rob was out of sight, and I was on the other side of the walls.

Oh, my God, so dramatic, it's a few weeks, not forever.

Since I didn't have an international plan, I'd shut my phone off before landing in Toronto and when I switched it on as I landed, I had messages from Nadia and Avery, demanding to know how it went. As we taxied, I sent back to Avery, Rob, and an emoticon heart. She could take it however she wanted; I'd be home in a few hours. To Nadia, I wrote a proper response since she'd helped me find him.

Nadia: OMG, so happy for you both. Sisters forever??

I laughed, startling the old man next to me, then tapped out, We're back together, not getting married. But who knows?

Once I retrieved my car from the lot, I drove back to Sharon, which seemed better and brighter than I remembered. It was late afternoon, and I had so much to do that I had no idea where to start. *Mom,* I thought. So I swung by the house to tell her my news in person.

She and Stuart were watching *Antiques Roadshow* when I knocked. I hugged both of them and said, "I hope I didn't come at a bad time."

"Of course not. What's up?" That was Stuart.

Mom made a pot of coffee as I explained that I was moving to Toronto to be with Rob. "But…what about school?" she asked, clearly worried.

"I have a plan." Understandable that she'd be concerned, given my history of running off whenever things got bad.

Crap, I'm more like my dad than I'd care to admit. But it's not like that this time.

I outlined my idea about continuing with school in Canada. Since they were online classes, it shouldn't prove to be a problem, provided she was willing to let me keep using their Nebraska address. "If not, it's okay. I'll pay the out-of-state tuition rates once I—"

"No, that part's fine." She seemed bemused, focused on the mug in her hands.

"What's wrong?"

"You've thought it through. So this isn't a wild hair— And you're really going. I will miss you *so* much, Lauren."

"Me, too," Stuart added.

I stayed a little longer, after I was sure I had their blessing, but soon, I headed off to talk to Avery. In a way, this conversation would be harder than the one with my mom. She had Stuart now and a happy life that didn't revolve around me. Part of me felt like I was abandoning my friend when she needed me most.

Happy greeted me at the front door, shivering with excitement. She didn't like it when I was gone, maybe worried that I'd vanish like Rob. Imagining the dog's reaction when I reunited them put a smile on my face. I knelt to rub her belly, whispering, "It won't be long now, honey."

Avery was in the kitchen, making a grilled cheese when I got home. "From your cryptic text, I take it things went well?"

"You could say that." I took a deep breath, bracing. "I'm relocating, probably in the next month or so." When she didn't reply, I went on, "You can ask Jill to move in. I know she'd love that, and you were talking about how you'd like to be closer—"

"I filed."

"What?" At first I didn't even know what she meant.

"After you left on Friday, I couldn't stop thinking about how I told you to go for it—to be fearless. Yet I'm letting a pervert get away with what he did, because I don't want people to talk about me? Or because I might lose some money? Bullshit. Half the town already hates me, so what does it matter? I'm not selling my soul for that trust fund. Fuck my dad and fuck my family. I went to the sheriff's office and told them everything. It took hours. I repeated the story to, like, four people, and it got easier every single time. I was eleven years old and I didn't seduce him. It wasn't because I was so pretty he couldn't help it. I didn't do this, and I shouldn't be paying for it all by myself."

"Oh, my God, Avery. I had no idea. Why didn't you tell me? I'd have gone with you."

"This was something I had to do on my own. You've helped me so much, but you couldn't carry me all the way where I needed to be."

"Can I hug you?"

"You have two arms," she said in that snarky tone that made everyone think she was a bitch, but really meant she was hurting.

She *had* been for so long. Dropping my backpack, I hurried into the kitchen and squeezed her close. "Are you all right?"

"Closer to it than I have been in a long time. I have no plans to stop seeing Dr. Reid, and it doesn't matter if my family never talks to me again."

"They don't deserve you," I snapped.

She pulled away, turning back to the stove. "Agreed. I'm way too good for those assholes. Want a grilled cheese?"

"Sure. Airport food is overpriced."

At the kitchen table, we hammered out a plan, confirmed

with a quick call. Jillian would be moving in at the end of the month, after I completed my notice, and just before I left for Toronto. I had a brainstorm as I devoured the last of my sandwich, now cold and gluey.

"We should have one last girls' night, invite Krista to sleep over. Jillian, too, obviously."

"What do you mean, last? Do you think you're irreplaceable? The three of us will continue to rock out, long after you're gone."

"I'm glad. You're amazing, and I want so much for you to be happy."

"Shut up. Stop making me feel things."

I hugged her, determined to make the most of the time we had left. Exciting as my new life promised to be, I'd miss aspects of the old one. We watched movies until late, and the next day, I went to work to hand in my notice. The office ladies didn't say much, just processed the paperwork. In the evenings, I busted ass on assignments and Skyped with Rob, sometimes at the same time. At the end of my two weeks, Davies called me into his office for an exit interview. From the tone of his questions, he was wondering if his behavior had something to do with my departure. I answered noncommittally, amusing myself by making him sweat. On my last day, they threw a party for me with cupcakes and Kool-Aid.

That only left girls' night to be ticked off my to-do list. Krista left Naomi with Kenji and since she'd just stopped breast-feeding, she came prepared to party hard. I had *never* seen her get so drunk, and by the time she passed out, she was wearing a plastic mixing bowl on her head and pretending to sword fight with a spatula. Avery tipped her over on the couch, snickering softly.

"And it's only eleven," I mumbled.

The rest of us drank slower, telling stories about high school.

I'd forgotten a lot of them, but Jillian had a keen memory. I wondered if she knew about Avery, who caught my eye and nodded. That felt like she was telling me, *Don't worry, you can stand down. There's somebody else in my corner now.* Offering me the freedom to leave with a clear conscience was the best gift in the world.

We said goodbye two days later, before she left for work. Before taking off, I made sure Happy's vaccination records were in order and loaded up my car. I'd boxed everything up the night before. Now I was following in Rob's footsteps on the long drive to Toronto. Unlike him, I planned to do it in shifts, not straight through. Happy was confused but excited as we pulled away from the old house. As expected, the drive took forever, twenty hours and counting. Even after putting up at a motel that allowed pets, I was still stiff and sore when I hit the bridge for border crossing near Fort Erie-Buffalo. The official checked my passport and Happy's medical records, then he waved us through. Three more hours, and I parked outside Rob's place.

For a few seconds, I just sat in the car, staring up at his apartment window. He had been sending are-you-close? messages for, like, an hour. Since I was driving, I didn't reply. Now I picked up my phone and sent, I'm home. I was still clipping Happy's leash in place when Rob burst through the front doors, coming at a run. He opened my car door and his expression was so alight with joy that I misted over.

"Took you long enough," he said, kissing me and ruffling the dog's fur in turn.

"Worth waiting for?"

"Always. As long as you love me…and I know you're coming back to me."

Our life together might not be easy. I'd never lived in a big city before, never dated a guy who might be famous in a few

ANN AGUIRRE

years. But those were problems I'd face when the time came, not before. I was done borrowing trouble, done refusing to be happy. In that regard I could take a lesson from the dog, who was wriggling in Rob's arms. Once he finished petting her, he set her down and handed me her leash.

Then he literally swept me off my feet, carrying me toward the front door. "What in the world are you doing?" I demanded.

"This is how the story ends, right?" His eyes were so very blue. "King Rob carries the sorceress off in his arms because he finally realizes he loves her and can't live without her, even if she's not of royal blood."

"That's how I wrote it," I managed, conscious of the looks we were drawing with his extravagant gesture and the dog trotting along behind him.

"I have to say, I'm a lot smarter than book Rob."

"Oh, yeah?" I held on to him as he juggled me in getting the lobby door open.

"Yep. Because *I* knew that all along."

Oh, Rob. You are, and always have been, so much more than anyone knew. Even you.

There was no way he could've made me feel more at home than by proving that he'd finished the story, even after I stopped believing. He'd completely rekindled my faith in the potential goodness of others; with Rob, I could envision such a beautiful life. In the future, there would be a car to unload, a dog to feed, application for a work visa, and then I needed to find a job. *So many details…*

But as he strode with me to the elevators, I let go of the worries and tumbled into my happily ever after, as I had fallen for Rob, endlessly and forever.

BONUS SCENE:
THE END IS THE BEGINNING (ROB)

The Toronto skyline is beautiful just after dark. But I can only see manmade lights from other buildings. No stars. I can't hear any street noises with the balcony door closed, and everything looks brand-new, so shiny-modern that the whole apartment feels like somebody else's shoes. They might be the right size, but they're not broken to my feet.

I never pictured myself here without Lauren. Really, I never imagined anything without her. She was like a tiny boat pushing the barge from behind, the barge being me. I've always been afraid to dream. When you come up with your parents acting like you'll be lucky to get a job hauling garbage, it's hard to expect more. Ever since I could remember, I wanted somebody to believe in me—to see below the surface. But I was afraid of that, too, because maybe there was nothing good to find. Secretly I've wondered if maybe I'm a faulty puzzle and if somebody wasted her time putting together all the pieces, she'd just find out that I'm incomplete.

And I guess she did.

Or I wouldn't be alone.

The apartment's so quiet. I miss my dog.

During the day, it's not so bad because I have stuff to do at the studio. But when I'm done, the nights are a thousand years long. Lately, my life's like running on a treadmill; sure, it looks good but no matter how many miles I put behind me, I end up in the same place. I have too much time to think, to wonder if there was a way I could've made things turn out right.

My cell phone rings. Every time, every damn time, my heart leaps. I want it to be Lauren, but it never is. This time, it's Nadia, checking in.

"Are you busy?" she asks, like I have this crazy social life.

"I can talk." As always, I have this bizarre push-pull reaction when I talk to Nadia.

Part of me wants to be a dick and cut her off because when I hear her voice, I also get a thousand echoes of our folks saying things to her that I'll *never* hear, no matter what I do. But it's not her fault—it never was—and I remember how she used to tag along after me, convinced there was nothing I couldn't do. She figured that for bullshit soon enough, but when she was eight, I was a god in her eyes; I pulled her out of trees and put Band-Aids on her knees.

"How are things?"

"I'm fine. Busy with work." The first thing was a lie.

I'm anything but. I'm gutted. I'm a shell. But I can't say that to my sister, Lauren's best friend. There's no way it doesn't get back to her, and if I ever hear from her again, I don't want it to be out of pity. There's a pitiful flicker in me; maybe it's hope, that this isn't the end—that instead, we're waiting, figuring things out. I don't know what to do, other than let her miss me. I'm so afraid it won't be enough. But she's seen everything I've got to offer.

And I'm alone.

"You're filming now, right? Is that weird?"

"Pretty much. I bet you never saw *this* coming."

"You've got celebrity looks, bro."

"I guess." I try for a casual tone. "So how's Lauren doing? Is she seeing anyone?"

Nadia pauses. "She seems okay. I don't know about her social life, but she's still working at the dealership, hanging out, working on her degree. You ever think about calling her?"

Only every day.

I mumble something. "Have you talked to Mom and Dad?"

"Yeah, a few days ago. They seem to be okay. Lauren's filling in when Mom needs a hand. I should send a present."

It sucks because I can't even hear her name in casual conversation without an iron vise tightening around my ribs. "Let me know. I'll chip in. Ty and Sam doing all right?"

"Yeah. In fact, it's bath time. I have to go. I'll talk to you next week."

In the background, I hear her laughing and the sound of Sam giggling. Nadia hangs up before I can answer. I can't wrap my head around the fact that my baby sister is *parenting* right now. I mean, what the hell? But Ty seems like a decent guy, so there's no need for me to step on his neck and terrorize him.

There's no need for me to do anything, except work out and talk about home remodeling projects on camera. This should be the best thing that ever happened to me. And…it's cool, no question. More than I expected to achieve on my own. But really, I didn't. Lauren was with me the whole way, mapping the route; I just followed the trail she marked, something any monkey could manage.

I can't bring myself to look at any of the paperwork Annette has emailed me. No point, as I'll have my lawyer check it before I sign. I remember my grandma sighing once when she didn't know I could hear. *Poor Rob,* she'd said. *He's just smart enough to know he's dumb.* That pretty much sums it up. So I won't pretend I understand this party of the first part, second part, with respect to whatever. Ignoring the fan mail, I shut down my laptop and head into the bedroom.

The binders I took from Lauren have been piled up on my bedside table for months. The pages are faintly yellowed, crinkled, and she's doodled pictures of me in the margin. While she might be a decent writer, her art is awful. But I run my fingers over the smudged ink, seeing myself through her eyes. A king. A hero. I'm none of those things, but it kills me that she saw me that way, even for a minute.

I'm a slow reader, and even at thirteen, Lauren knew all kinds of good words. So I have a pocket dictionary, too. Which is embarrassing. Even if it takes ten hours, I'll finish the last book tonight. Since I'm not a book guy, I can't say if these stories are any good, but when I imagine her spending so much time on them, I can't help but love them.

Just like her.

Settling back against the headboard, I flick the light on and open to the final quarter of the third volume. When I left off, the sorceress and the young king had been separated by two armies. He was leading one, and she'd been captured by his enemies. I flip until I find the exact sentence where I stopped before. I hate the idea that Laurenara is locked up while King Robert is too far away to help her, but I should've known it's not that kind of story. Twenty pages later, the sorceress rescues *herself* and then rushes off to help her guy kick some ass. Book Robert is kind of dense, though. He doesn't seem to realize that she's crazy in love with him, and that's why she's always around, why she'll do anything for him.

I settle in. Read one page. Another. It's past midnight when I turn to the last page. My eyes feel grainy; I'm not used to focusing this hard, and I have a headache tapping at my skull. But I keep reading.

"This woman has been by my side for years," King Robert decreed, taking Laurenara's dainty, slender hand. "And I have come to value her more than my own life. Let any man who would keep us apart face my sword."

The court was silent, not even a whisper from the lush velvet skirts worn by the ladies in waiting who had eyed the young noble from behind their fancy lacquered fans. Then a courtier broke from the crowd to stride toward the king.

"You object?" Robert's sparkling cerulean eyes narrowed dangerously.

"There is no precedent," the man lisped, as was the court custom.

"I have waged one war for her already," King Robert said coldly. "Shall we have another?"

"N-no, sire."

The king fixed a hard gaze on his court. "I care nothing for her lineage. Know this, she has a pure heart, a lion's courage, and she will be my queen."

I close the binder. *So they got a happy ending.* I'm glad of that, but the real Lauren seems really far away right now. So much that it hurts. I only feel whole when she's looking at me, and without her, I might disappear.

But something's bugging me. If King Robert's dumb for not realizing that Laurenara does everything because she loves him…I wonder. Digging isn't my specialty, and I'm really scared of being wrong. Maybe I'm reaching because I want this to be true. But…maybe Lauren sent me off alone *because* she loves me. I'm not really sure why; in the story, though,

ANN AGUIRRE

the sorceress lies because she doesn't want the king finding out the truth and getting hurt.

This is all I have; I'll hang on until she tells me I'm wrong. I'll believe that the end is a beginning waiting to happen.

So I go into the living room and find some paper. I write six different drafts, but I can't find the words. I sound like an idiot, no matter what I say or how I put it. Eventually, I just head out to a twenty-four-hour parcel store with the binders. If I think too long about this, I'll chicken out. The lights are too bright in here, and the guy behind the counter looks tired and bored. While he's typing in my information and getting a box big enough to hold what's left of my hope, I hug the binders, hard. *Hope he didn't see that.* The corners bite into my arms, a good, sharp pain, better than being numb.

Call me. Call me, beautiful.

She's everything to me. And I'll wait for her forever.

★ ★ ★ ★ ★

#

PLAYLIST FOR
AS LONG AS YOU LOVE ME

"Looking for Shelter" —Good Old War
"Across the Ocean" —Azure Ray
"Hard Out Here" —Lily Allen
"A Moment Changes Everything" —David Gray
"May It Be" —Enya
"It's Time" —Imagine Dragons
"If I Had a Heart" —Fever Ray
"This Isn't Everything You Are" —Snow Patrol
"Wrecking Ball" —Miley Cyrus
"In Your Arms Again" —Josh Ritter
"Unpretty" —TLC
"Ho Hey" —The Lumineers
"Hey Ya" —Obadiah Parker
"Come & Find Me" —Josh Ritter

Thank you!

I'm so glad you read *As Long As You Love Me*. I hope you enjoyed it.

Would you like to know when my next book will be available or keep up with my news? Visit my website at *www.annaguirre.com/contact* and sign up for my newsletter. You can also follow me on Twitter at *twitter.com/msannaguirre*, or "like" my Facebook fan page at *www.facebook.com/ann.aguirre* for excerpts and contests.

Reviews help other readers, so please consider writing one. I appreciate your time and your support.

As Long As You Love Me is the second book in my new adult romance series. The first was *I Want It That Way* and the last is *The Shape of My Heart*.

Again, thanks for your readership; it means the world to me.

ACKNOWLEDGMENTS

Thanks to Margo Lipschultz for being incredible. We've both worked so hard, and the books reflect our effort. The whole Harlequin team has been phenomenal, practically achieving feats of wizardry on my behalf, and I appreciate their tremendous support more than I can say.

Thanks to Laura Bradford for being my chief ally and biggest fan, always.

So much appreciation for Bree Bridges, who shared her experiences with earning a computer science degree when you possess two X chromosomes. Any mistakes or liberties are my own.

I must also acknowledge the contributions of women who have shared stories with me over the years. Please know that your voices were heard and that I remember. I did my best to speak…because the world silenced you.

All gratitude, respect and admiration to Donna J. Herren, Lauren Dane, Megan Hart, HelenKay Dimon, Tessa Dare, Courtney Milan, and Yasmine Galenorn for the unconditional friendship and sisterhood.

Karen Alderman and Majda Čolak have been my beta readers for years. At this point, I have no idea how I'd write books without their input. Ladies, don't ever leave me.

Thanks to anyone who offered me a kind word when I needed one. And thanks to those who never kick me when I'm down. Thanks to the people who help restore my faith in the fundamental goodness of others.

Which leaves my family. I'm *so* proud. The fact that you believe in me is the only reason I've come this far, and I adore you all. Thank you for your patience.

Readers, you're always on my mind. I hope my words make you laugh a lot, cry a little—feel all the things—and that you close the book a little happier than you were. Thanks for supporting me, and as always, read on.

Read on for a sneak peek of Max's book,
THE SHAPE OF MY HEART,
coming soon from
Ann Aguirre
and Harlequin HQN!

CHAPTER ONE

If my life was a romantic comedy, I wouldn't be the star.

I'd be the witty, wise-cracking friend, telling the Reese Witherspoon character to follow her heart, and I'd be played by America Ferrera, Hollywood's idea of an ugly duckling. But not conforming to societal beauty standards didn't cause me any angst; I wasn't harboring a secret desire to take off my glasses and flip my hair, so my secret love interest would realize I was beautiful all along. In my view, my looks supplied simplicity. Anyone who got with me wanted the *real* me, no question. Romance ranked dead last on my to-do list at the moment, however.

"You're too picky," Max said.

He was curled up on my bedroom floor, skimming emails on his tablet. With her boyfriend's help, our soon-to-be-ex-roommate, Nadia, was currently carting the last of her belongings downstairs, and the other half of my room was conspicuously empty. I scowled and threw a common cold plushie at his head. He batted it away with impressive reflexes, still scrolling. Since he'd posted flyers around campus, along with his email, Max was handling first contact on the apartment.

"Swap with me. You and Angus can share the master bedroom and then you can put whoever you want next door."

As expected, he passed with an *as-if* gesture. "We'll keep looking. How about this one? 'Hey, my name is Kara. I'm a physical education major, I work part-time at Kelvin's and I'm a sophomore. I saw your flyer, and I'd love to meet you guys. My apartment fell through when the landlord sold the place out from under us and now I'm scrambling.' She seems fine. All the words are even spelled correctly."

I pretended to mull it over. "Basic language skills *are* important to me. Put her on the call-back list."

"You make it sound like we're casting a movie."

"This is way more critical," I reminded him. "This person will be living in my room, potentially watching me sleep."

"I wish you'd let me help," Nadia said, coming in to grab the last of her boxes.

Ty, her tall, ginger boyfriend, plucked a carton from her arms. His four-year-old son was running around the living room, bothering Angus, who didn't seem to mind. I waved at both of them but didn't get up. Truthfully, I was more than a little *verklempt* over her leaving, even if she was only going downstairs. In the six months since I'd moved in, we'd become good friends. When I moved in, I'd taken over Lauren's half of the room; she had been Nadia's best friend from high school, so it wouldn't have been surprising if Nadia had resented me. Instead, she did her best to make me feel at home. And it wasn't like she hadn't given us notice that she'd be moving in with Ty. I just didn't act on it because I secretly hoped their cohabitation wouldn't pan out, like maybe she'd realize what a huge step it was to take on someone else's kid.

"It's fine," I said. "I'm the one who procrastinated."

Max nodded. "If I hadn't made flyers, Kaufman here would still be waiting for the perfect roommate to drop out of the sky."

"It could work. A skydiving roomie would be pretty sweet." Ty grinned. "I'd be worried about the rent."

"The man makes a good point." Max waved as they left, taking the rest of Nadia's worldly belongings. "Here's another possible. 'Saw your ad. About me: Carmen, drama major, junior. I have no annoying habits and an aversion to being homeless. Email me back!'"

"How am I supposed to choose—"

"She attached a picture." Max handed me the tablet. "I'm inclined to say yes."

When I saw it, I knew why. Carmen had long silky black hair, golden skin, big brown eyes, and an amazing body. While I'd definitely bang her, I didn't want her living in my room. The possibility for problems boggled the mind.

Shaking my head, I passed the iPad back. "No way."

"Why not? She's perfect!"

"She sent a wet T-shirt contest photo, dude. To random strangers. Does that speak highly of her common sense?"

He sighed. "Not really."

"I don't want to come home to someone shooting amateur porn in my room."

"Are you sure? I'm positive that would look great on a résumé."

"You're such a weirdo."

"Guilty." Max glanced toward the doorway, where Angus had propped himself like a fashion model.

In different ways, my two roommates were both hot as hell. Blond-haired, green-eyed Angus radiated the moneyed, *GQ* vibe; he was always put together, clean-shaven, well-dressed and delicious smelling. Max, on the other hand, was a dimpled and scruffy, tattooed, motorcycle-riding hooligan. Right then I had the bad boy *and* the dream boy in my bedroom, pretty much winning the whole hot guy lottery, but neither was interested in me. Angus had a boyfriend, and Max always had women blowing up his cell phone. Still, for pure eye candy, it didn't suck to be me.

"House meeting," Angus said, sauntering over to flop across the foot of my bed. "Any progress on the roommate issue?"

Hunching my shoulders, I wrapped my arms around another plushie microbe, an adorable ovum this time. "I'm working on it."

"It's true. She's rejected four possibles since I came in."

I cut Max a look. "You're not helping."

"But I've been reading emails to you for the last ten minutes."

Ignoring that, I nudged Angus's thigh with my foot. "Do you know anyone who's looking? Preferably not a random stranger."

"Actually, that's part of the reason why I'm in here."

When I bounced, his head jogged on my mattress. "Spill it."

"I've been in premed with Kia since freshman year. She mentioned she wants to break up with her boyfriend, but she's been putting it off because it'll mean moving out. I didn't say anything because I wanted to talk to you guys first. But—"

"Is she nice?" I cut in at the same time Max asked, "Is she hot?"

Angus smirked. "Yes and yes. I think she'd make you both happy."

Then he got out his phone, flipping through the gallery until he found a selfie of him with a pretty African-American girl. She had a great smile, bright and friendly, dark skin and short, natural hair. Sometimes the faces people made in photos gave me a vibe about them, and she seemed like she'd be fun.

I took his cell, brought up her contact info and said, "Call her."

"You mean I made flyers for nothing?" Max grumbled, but I could tell he was glad to have it settled. Maybe.

He got off the floor and wormed his way between Angus and me. Three people on a twin, probably not what the manufacturer intended. "If you break my bed—"

"Shh. It's ringing." Angus frowned at us like we were delinquent children. "Kia? It's me. Do you have a minute?" That sounded like code for, *can you talk freely?*

The volume was loud enough for me to hear her reply. "Yeah, I can email you the notes."

"I get it. Call me back when you can."

"Whoa," Max said. "Sounds like he's a controlling asshole."

Angus nodded. "I've been telling her to get out for three months."

"Is he abusive?" The answer wouldn't change my mind about rooming with her, but we might need to amp up security around here.

"Depends on your definition. In my view, he's overly invested in where she goes and who she talks to. And he disapproves of me. A lot."

"Homophobe?" I asked.

"Young Republican, so…probably? He wears a lot of sweater vests, comes from a conservative political family in the Bible Belt."

"Ah. He's lousy with privilege," Max guessed.

Angus's phone buzzed then, and he grabbed it on the first ring, putting it on speaker. "Kia?"

"What's up?"

"Is Duncan giving you a hard time today?"

"Always." She sounded tired.

No wonder. Between the last year of premed and a demanding boyfriend, she must be sick of the drama. But we needed to speak up before she said something she'd hate revealing to strangers. "Hey, this is Courtney, one of Angus's roommates."

"And I'm Max, the other one."

"Are we on a conference call?" She sounded amused more than annoyed, so that was a decent start.

"I talked to them and if you really want to dump the d-bag, you can move in here. Courtney would be sharing with you. Want to come over, see if it's a good fit?"

"Yes, please." Her response was heartfelt.

An hour later, Kia was on our couch, after a quick tour of the apartment and my half-empty room. She was taller than me, thinner, too, no surprise there, but nowhere near as imposing as Nadia. From listening to her conversation with Angus, I already knew I wanted this to happen. If it didn't work out and we had to call in Physical Education Kelly, I'd be bummed.

"I feel like I need to be up-front about this," I said.

Max elbowed me. He thought I was going to tell her that I was bi, but there was no reason to lead with that. Frowning at him, I went on, "I'm a touch OC and I might alphabetize your books and/or CDs if you decide to move in."

She laughed. "Girl, have at it. That's not my thing. I don't have time to obsess. But it won't bother me if you organize. Just don't move stuff so I can't find it."

"Don't worry, you won't come home to find all your makeup sorted by brand."

"Hey, I'd much rather be sharing with somebody who cleans. My boyfriend doesn't."

"You mean your ex?" Angus asked hopefully.

"Give me a few days. Is next weekend soon enough?" Kia pushed to her feet with an inquiring look.

"Yep, it's great." I fought the urge to hug her, mostly because it was settled.

"Let's swap numbers." Angus forwarded her info before she finished speaking, and I sent a test text. Her phone pinged again, suggesting Max had done the same.

Kia grinned. "I guess I don't have to worry about being welcome. Wish me luck."

"Dump him." That was my best encouraging tone.

Max walked her to the door. "Agree. Dump the crap out of him."

Once the door closed behind her, I grabbed Angus's hands and whirled him around in a circle. "She's perfect. Seriously, thank you. You don't know how relieved I am."

"Save the victory dance until she moves in. You never know, Duncan could talk her into giving him a second chance. She's been on the verge of leaving him for, like, a year."

I sighed as the satisfaction drained away. "Now you tell me."

"You worry too much. If need be, we'll split the rent three ways until we find the right person. I can manage a month of that, and I know Angus can." Max slung an arm over my shoulder and hauled me to the sofa. "Come on, let's shoot stuff."

Angus ruffled my hair and I pretended to swat him. "Hey. Hands off the purple."

"Can't help it, it's all adorable and spiky."

My mother called my current look a "punk" phase, and she expressed a devout wish for me to get over it every time I saw her. She hoped I'd trade Doc Martens and cargo pants for dresses that sparkled, grow my hair out, and get a nose job. That would never, ever happen. Which bummed my mother out; she'd rather I marry a nice Jewish doctor than become one. Of course, that wasn't on the table, either. Since I didn't know exactly what I wanted to do, I was studying business, though friends who'd already graduated were telling me I needed to specialize or there was no way in hell I'd find a job.

But the idea of wiping my originality like a dry-erase board for a corporate gig bummed me out. I liked my piercings—at last count I had eight: eyebrow, nose, three in my left ear, two in my right, plus the belly button ring; I couldn't remember if my mother had ever seen the latter. Maybe I'd use the money my granddad left me to start my own company, though at this point, I had no idea what product or service I'd offer.

Max bumped me with his shoulder. "Are you playing or not?"

"I'm in." Picking up the controller, I joined him onscreen, though it pissed me off that in most of these shooters, I always had to play a dude.

"Have fun. I'm out with Del tonight." The brightness in Angus's voice told me things were going well, so I just waved as he left, focused on not shooting Max in the back.

We played for an hour before I got hungry. I pushed pause on the controller and ambled to the kitchen. Max came up behind me, resting his head on my shoulder as I peered into the fridge. Max was exceptionally hands-on with his friends; maybe he didn't get hugged enough as a kid or something. When I'd first moved in, I thought he was hitting on me, but he thumped and patted Angus about as much, so I went with it.

"Cook something," he pleaded.

I jabbed him in the gut with my elbow. "Get off me and maybe I will. How do patty melts sound?"

"Like manna from heaven. I speak for all starving college students everywhere when I say, words cannot do justice to your munificence."

Snickering, I put the ground beef in the microwave. "Calm down, I already agreed to make the food. No need for sweet talk."

"But it's fun. Your nose wrinkles when you laugh at me."

I fought the urge to cover said nose. Some girls could do adorable bunny wriggles, but mine was too long, beakish, according to an ex who'd had enough of my shit. As personal problems went, however, it wasn't exactly original. There were tons of other Jewish girls in the same situation; I wasn't special. In fact, I probably wasn't even the only princess rebelling with piercings and alt-hair. So I made a face instead of revealing that he'd made me feel self-conscious for a few seconds. On two occasions, Max and I had made out. Both times, we were messed up emotionally and it was good that we'd confined the rebound sex to kissing. Otherwise it might be tough to fry meat while he talked about the work he was doing on his motorcycle.

"Wait, I thought you were done?"

He sighed at me. "The mechanical overhaul is done, but now I'm working on cosmetic restoration. I can't stop until it's finished."

"The fate of the world hangs in the balance?" I teased, shaping the thawed meat into patties. Next I sliced up some onions to caramelize.

"I promised somebody, that's all." His expression was strange and serious, unlike the guy I'd known for three years.

But Max was…odd. Like, he gave the impression he was all jokes, all about the party, but then he flipped a switch and revealed a glimpse of the real person underneath. In all honesty, I was much more interested in that guy—the serious, smart, intense one. Most people had no idea he was a mechanical engineering major, which required knowledge of physics, thermodynamics, kinematics, structural analysis and electricity. And hell, I only knew that because I looked it up on Wikipedia after finding out what he was studying.

"That sounds like a story," I said quietly.

He held my gaze for two beats, then looked away. "I guess it is."

Message received.

I finished our food, and we ate in front of the TV, then went back to killing things in the game. But by nine, I was bored. I put down the controller, stretching my stiff muscles in an exaggerated arch of my back. "Okay, I'm done."

"Don't go," he said.

"Huh?" Startled, I swung back toward the couch, catching a bleak, sad look in his dark, dark eyes.

It was like realizing a friend had been hiding raw slashes under their sleeves all this time. His thick lashes swept down, covering the expression, but it was too late. *I can't unsee it.* My chest felt tight with indecision. If I made a joke, he'd take his cue from me, and it would be like this never happened. Maybe that would be for the best.

"I don't want to play anymore," I answered.

"We could go for a ride."

To me, it seemed like Max didn't want to be alone tonight. He rode his bike when he was running from something, but he'd never invited me along. There was no excuse to refuse since classes hadn't started up again. I made a snap decision.

"Okay, let me get a jacket." My pants and concert T-shirt were fine, so I added boots and a hoodie with a skull on the back.

"That was fast." He jingled his keys with one hand and grabbed me with the other, yanking me out of the apartment and down the stairs. As we approached his bike, he asked, "Have you ever ridden one of these before?"

"What do you think?" I was curious what he'd say.

"Probably...yes."

"You are correct, sir. Don't worry, it's not my first time."

"If you knew how happy it makes me to hear that." He

flashed a flirty grin over one shoulder, but I identified it as bullshit.

The wounded eyes? That was real. Not this. So I put on the helmet and wrapped my arms around his waist, content to be the warm body on the back of his bike. I didn't need to be beautiful to be a friend when he needed one.

Just for a few seconds, he set his hands over mine, where they rested on his abs. "Hold on tight. I'm about to show you something amazing."